PROPRIETY AND PASSION

Tryg Peerson—strong, tough-minded, self-
made, making his own living from the age
of twelve, going through law school against
all odds, climbing the political arena to wreak
vengeance for past wrongs to his family, taking
as his wife a woman who once had seemed
so far above him, and taking as his mistress a
woman of fiery sensuality who would stop
at nothing to possess him.

Sarah—the wife who yielded to Tryg's ambition
and desire, became part of his fiercely loyal
family, but could not resist the virile, magnetic
man in her past who had taken her innocence
in a moment of unforgettable ecstasy and
now came back into her life to awaken the fire
that smoldered within her.

**A man, a woman, a family—bound together in a
spellbinding saga as powerful and passionate as the
dreams and realities that made America. . . .**

SEATTLE

Lives in the Current of History

SEATTLE

by
Charlotte Paul

A BERNARD GEIS ASSOCIATES BOOK

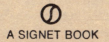

A SIGNET BOOK

NEW AMERICAN LIBRARY

PUBLISHER'S NOTE

This novel is a work of fiction. Names, characters, places, and incidents either are the product of the author's imagination or are used fictitiously, and any resemblance to actual persons, living or dead, events, or locales is entirely coincidental.

Copyright © 1986 by Charlotte Paul

SIGNET TRADEMARK REG. U.S. PAT. OFF. AND FOREIGN COUNTRIES
REGISTERED TRADEMARK—MARCA REGISTRADA
HECHO EN CHICAGO. U.S.A.

SIGNET, SIGNET CLASSIC, MENTOR, ONYX, PLUME, MERIDIAN and
NAL BOOKS are published by New American Library,
1633 Broadway, New York, New York 10019

First Printing, January, 1987

3   4   5   6   7   8   9

PRINTED IN THE UNITED STATES OF AMERICA

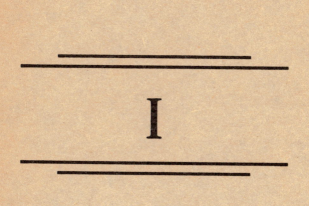

I

1

1897

Young Einar Trygve Peersen IV, known by his middle name, or "Tryg" for short, was pumping air into the reed organ at the Ballard First Lutheran Church of America. At the front of the organ, Miss Amy Hutton was tromping valiantly on the pedals.

Although she was a vigorous musician, Amy Hutton did not have the stamina to keep the bellows full for an hour and a half. So at the back of the organ, hidden from her critical eye, twelve-year-old Trygve augmented her efforts by pumping a wooden bar up and down. He was paid twenty-five cents for Saturday practice, twenty-five cents for Sunday service, and fifteen cents for choir practice—fair wages, considering grown men were getting ten cents an hour in the logging camps for greasing skids.

Like most of his contemporaries in the tidewater village of Ballard, Trygve had been working at some sort of spare-time job ever since his ninth birthday. Hard labor paid the most, and here Trygve had an advantage over boys his own age; he was stronger and taller than any of them. When the village needed a man to haul rock for road gangs, Trygve got the job, and he was the only laborer under the age of eighteen to be hired for loading freight wagons.

Physically Trygve was a perfect replica of the finest of the Peersens from Trondheim—wavy wheat-colored hair, a firm chin, deep blue eyes that expressed his frequent changes of mood. Just as simple but hearty Norwegian cooking had built a body of great strength, faith in hard work as the primary source of a man's honor had nourished his mind. In a word, he was exuberantly healthy, both mentally and physically. He had been born into a poor but happy world, where honor came from working and honest work bestowed pride.

Trygve had two sisters. Mina, the firstborn, was small and dark-eyed like her mother. Anna was tall, unusually strong for a girl, but nevertheless graceful. She had the pale gold hair, the blue-blue eyes, and the blooming complexion of the pure Norwegian stock.

While they were still in school, both girls had worked part-time filleting cod and gutting salmon in the fish cannery and doing laundry for Ballard's two boardinghouses. Anna, the more imaginative of the girls, began what proved to be a small but profitable catering service when she was only twelve. With the help of her sister she packed lunch boxes for the fishermen who didn't have someone at home to do it for them.

The three young Peersens had always turned their wages over to their parents. Their father, too, put all his earnings into the same community treasury. So much was counted out for trolley fare, so much for the next mortgage payment on their sturdy clapboard house, so much for household expenses. Always, even if the salmon run was so poor it hardly paid their father to put the *Konge* into the water, the children received a portion of their earnings to be spent in any way they chose. Sometimes the extra money was pathetically skimpy, but it was never withheld. Even when the fledgling state of Washington was suffering through the panic that gripped the country in 1893, there were coins for the children's private use, allotted every week when family finances were reckoned before they all left for Sunday service.

In the Peersens' world education beyond the first eight grades was not nearly as important as finding a steady job. Both girls had gone to work instead of going on to high school. Anna was now a full-time live-in housemaid for a family on Seattle's prestigious Capitol Hill. Mina began work as a housemaid when she was fourteen years old. Now she was married to a young Irishman named Tim O'Donnell and living for the day she would bear her first child.

Trygve, the only son Einar and Emma Peersen had been blessed with, was expected to take his place, at the end of the next school year, in the long line of Peersens who lived off the sea. Yet Einar and Emma sensed a restlessness in Trygve and feared it instinctively, as they did his tendency to daydream. Trygve's father warned him occasionally about the dangers of putting his head in the clouds, and because Trygve loved and admired his father, he knew he was wrong when he let that happen. But his mind never wandered when he was in school. Nor did he daydream while he was loading wagons or shoveling coal, for there were plenty of work-toughened men to take over if he couldn't keep up.

Pumping air into a church organ was another thing altogether. The job was too easy. By the end of his first practice he had learned everything there was to know about the design and mechanism of reed organs. Again and again Trygve forgot to work the wooden bar and the volume of sacred sound dropped from a roar to a breathy whisper. Miss Hutton's displeasure at those times was loud enough to rattle the windowpanes.

On this particular sunlit morning in July, Miss Hutton was practicing a hymn called "Oh Be Joyful!" Crouched on his stool, pumping halfheartedly, Trygve felt as if joy was something he would never feel again. Today it wasn't a daydream that took his attention away from honest labor, it was the unhappy memory of a conversation he had had with his father the day before.

Very little in the world outside the village of Ballard could hold Trygve in awe for longer than a few minutes. The Territorial University founded in 1861 in downtown Seattle was one of the rare exceptions.

It stood alone, visible from Seattle's business district, but in Trygve's eyes far above it. It was a splendid structure with four classical columns two stories high, an elaborately carved balustrade, and at the top, like a queen's bejeweled crown, a fluted six-sided cupola. As a child he had simply stared at it, sensing that mysteries behind its magnificent carved oak doors were not meant to be revealed to the son of a Ballard fisherman. Then one day when he had an hour to himself before he and his father were to meet and walk back home, he strode up the steps, through the wide entrance, and into a world he recognized immediately as the place that was meant for him.

The halls were crowded with young men strolling from one classroom to another, with books tucked casually under their arms and with an air of easy familiarity. Most were wearing suits like the blue serge he wore on Sunday. The fact that *they* wore their blue serge suits during the week impressed him more than anything else.

A bell clanged, the halls emptied. He was alone, knowing that the privilege of entering did not extend behind those classroom doors. But he didn't feel like an intruder. A college education was *not* beyond his reach, even if, as he knew, only seven boys from Ballard had ever attended the downtown university.

The dream born the day he first went inside the Territorial University had been taking shape slowly and secretly over the past two years. Yet until now Trygve had not even dared to ask his parents to let him attend high school. That in itself was a bold request. The stronger the hope, the surer he was that it would hurt, maybe even anger his father. So he had kept it secret, even from his sisters, who would probably tease him and call him silly in the head.

He hadn't planned to reveal the secret yet, but when he saw the new University of Washington campus for the first time, he couldn't help himself. The new building had arisen on a slope above the lake, as splendid and remote as the old downtown building it had replaced. While his friends jeered, Trygve had stared at the wonder of Denny Hall, and something like first love took possession of him. At that moment he made up his mind that the vision of himself as a college student was going to be more than a dream.

Yesterday he had gone fishing with his father. There was always a special intimacy when the two of them were alone, and Trygve could not contain his secret any longer. His dream-wish, like a grail shining through the mists of the future, was that he, Einar Trygve Peersen IV, son of a fisherman—grandson, great- and great-great-grandson of fishermen—was not going to become the fourth Einar Peersen, and perhaps the hundredth Peersen, to live off the sea.

It all came out in a rush, the heretical words tumbling over each other.

His father listened and puffed on his pipe until finally it was all said. Tryg straightened his shoulders, looked directly into his father's sea-blue eyes, and awaited judgment.

His father spoke slowly. "It will be two years before you are ready for high school."

"No, Father. Miss Funk says that with my grades she'll let me try to do the seventh and eighth grades at the same time."

His father looked studiously into the bowl of his pipe. "You have already talked to Miss Funk about this." It was a statement more than a question.

"Yes, Father."

"Before you talked to me."

"Yes, Father."

"Mmmm . . ." The elder Peersen knocked his pipe against his boot heel and refilled it before he spoke again. "I was fishing alone, with my own boat, when I was only three years older than you are."

"Yes, sir."

"By the time I married your mother, I had saved up enough so I could build her a house. Now you are already standing six feet tall. You are big for your age and stronger than most grown men. If you start fishing next year, in eight years you will be able to do what I did. You will have your own boat. You will have money saved up so you can build a house for Christina Franzen."

From somewhere below his chin Tryg felt heat rise and spread across his face. How did his father know that he secretly thought of Christina as the girl he would marry? She was Swedish. The Franzens went to the Evangelical Church on West Sixty-first Street. And yet his father was talking as if they weren't different from the Peersens.

The older man paused, waiting for his message to be absorbed. "Seven years from now, what do you want to be? A man well started on his life, or a boy just starting to be a man? It is to your credit that you will be allowed to do the seventh and eighth grades in only one year, but still, that is one more year of school. After two years in high school, four more years in college—and then what are you to be? To what use can you put those long years? College will not make you a better fisherman. Will it make you *better* than a fisherman?''

"Oh no, Father. Not better. I don't feel that way about it."

Once again his father seemed to be looking for words in the bowl of his pipe. "You are a dreamer," he said, and there was both acceptance and sadness in his voice. "Remember your Uncle Gunnar?"

Tryg did indeed remember him. Gunnar Frodesen, his mother's older brother, had attended the university. When the family spoke of him, they always called him "poor Gunnar."

"Gunnar was also a dreamer," his father said. "He almost killed himself with work so that he could finish high school. And after that, the university. All those years, every penny he earned was spent to pay his way. At the age of twenty-two he was a pauper and thin as a skeleton. He had to borrow my suit to wear at his graduation. And then he became a missionary, or what they call a lay preacher. After eighteen years of that, up north in Whatcom County, he was still walking his circuit because he had never been paid enough money to buy a horse. He loved a girl all his life, but he never asked her to marry him because he couldn't expect any woman to suffer that kind of life. He died of pneumonia, half-starved and without a warm coat. He did God's work as he believed he was born to do. But, Tryg, my only son, I want a better life than that for you. Now we have talked enough. It's time to mind the nets."

"Trygve Peersen!"

Miss Hutton's indignant screech had the melodic quality of a Protestant hymn played with both elbows. Tryg gripped the wooden bar and began pumping furiously.

Miss Hutton had more to say. "For the fifth and last time, will you please put your mind on what you're doing? Don't you sleep at night?"

Tryg murmured, "Yes, Miss Hutton."

"Is the work too hard for you? Do you want me to find someone else?"

"No, Miss Hutton."

". . . someone who can stay awake between six and eight o'clock on a Saturday morning? Someone who . . ."

Silence descended. In the sudden quiet Tryg heard the hollow sound of leather boots marching purposefully down the aisle. And then Miss Hutton's voice, sweet as warm taffy, "Well, good *morning*, Mr. Peersen."

"Good morning. I'm sorry to interrupt, but I want my son to come with me."

"Well, I . . . we haven't finished practicing, Mr. Peersen."

"Some things can't wait."

His father almost always spoke softly, even when he was angry or giving an order. The voice on the other side of the organ, indisputably his father's, boomed like a foghorn as it ordered Miss Hutton to stop the practice although there was still an hour to go. Tryg listened in astonishment.

"The steamship *Portland* will be docking in an hour and Trygve and I are going to be right there on the pier when those sixty-eight prospectors walk down the gangplank carrying all that Klondike gold."

Einar Peersen was not the powerful man his son was on the way to becoming; there was a grimness around his mouth that concealed a basic resemblance to Trygve, but the deep blue eyes were the same, and today there was an expression in them Trygve had never seen before. They were usually as open and clear as a summer sky. They could twinkle with repressed mirth, shine with a gentle humor, or become dreamy and inward-looking when he recalled the days of his youth. But now they gleamed strangely when he exclaimed, "Gold, son! Gold!"

"Coming, Father," Trygve said, but he felt uneasy, as if he had been told to leave home with a stranger.

2

The steamship *Portland* wasn't due for an hour, but all streets within a four-block radius of the Schwabacher pier were already choked by the waiting crowd. Newsboys in knee breeches, blouses, long stockings, and high button shoes were still crying, "A ton of gold! A ton of gold . . .!" though they had nothing left to sell; the entire early-morning edition of the Seattle *Daily Tribune* had been sold out fifteen minutes after it was on the street.

Here and there a hansom cab, hired by someone who could afford to be driven to the foot of Union Street, was trapped like a ship locked in a frozen sea: horse, driver, and passenger immobilized by a throng deaf to the neighing horses and exasperated shouts of the driver.

On the far edge of the crowd, the streetcar conductor was clanging the big brass bell in a valiant effort to keep his car in motion. The car was so crammed that heads and arms protruded through the windows. Three boys in knickerbockers were perched on the roof. Narrow wooden ledges running the length of both sides of the trolley provided a precarious foothold to a few more, including Einar Peersen and his son, Trygve.

The trolley's progress grew more and more uncertain; finally, four blocks from the pier, it came to a dead halt. The bell rang furiously, the motorman bawled, "Out of the way!" but no one stepped aside.

"Son!" Einar called over the tumult. "This is where we start walking."

He jumped down and Trygve followed. As if their defection

15

had given the signal, the boys scrambled down from the roof, the running boards cleared, and the passengers inside the car spilled onto the street.

Einar paused at the front of the deserted car. The motorman wore an expression of total bewilderment.

"It's no use, Jack," Einar said. "Don't try to drive a streetcar through three thousand people."

"You're damn right." The motorman stepped off the trolley. "The hell with the job," he said cheerfully. "I quit."

"For today?"

Jack shrugged. "Who knows? Maybe for always."

Trygve's gaze swiveled from the motorman to his father and back to the motorman. He had seen his father become excited, but he had never *looked* as excited as he did now. He and Jack Nelson were grinning at each other as if they shared a secret. Trygve's thrifty parents had taught him to revere work and to hold fast to a paying job. It seemed to him that the man had gone crazy. "You're quitting, Mr. Nelson? What are you going to do if you don't run a streetcar?"

Nelson grinned. "I'm going to hustle myself down to North American Trading's ticket office and buy passage on the *Portland*'s return trip. And I bet your father will be right behind me."

Einar chuckled. "Neither of us is going to buy a berth on the *Portland*'s return trip. A man next to me on the trolley said the last ticket was sold two hours ago."

"Well, there are other boats. Let's you and me go shopping, and do it fast."

Einar shook his head. "Maybe you're going to race to the nearest ticket office. Not me. I'm an old-fashioned squarehead fisherman. When I put out to sea, it's in the *Konge*. The only prospecting I do is for salmon. And it always pays off. I never come back empty-handed, and I get home in time for supper every night."

"From what I read in the *Tribune* this morning, a man can take out a thousand dollars a day from an average drift claim. You really believe peddling fish at five cents a pound is better than bringing home fifty, sixty thousand dollars' worth of nuggets, like those men coming in on the *Portland*?"

"Maybe not. But the Peersens are fishermen. Fishing is

my life, and it'll be Trygve's too in a couple of years. You go north, Jack, and I'll pray for your safe return. For myself, you'll never find me lining up to buy a ticket to the Klondike.''

"You're sure?" Jack said quietly.

"I'm sure."

The finality of his father's reply seemed to close the subject, but there was something in his face that didn't fit the serenity and common sense of what he had just said. It was in the eyes, the same brightness that was there when he burst into the church and brought Miss Hutton's practice session to an end. Something had been locked up inside his father, something strange. Without knowing why, Trygve felt afraid.

Shoulder to shoulder, Einar and Trygve squeezed through gaps in the nearly solid human mass. When they reached the wharf where the *Portland* was to dock, they hit a crosscurrent of people who were being pushed off the dock toward the street. The planks and pilings creaked dangerously under the weight of the mob. Police officers in helmets and long-tailed coats were forcing several hundred spectators back to the railroad tracks running north and south in front of the piers. Their indignant voices were raised in complaint, growing louder and more discordant with every foot lost to the police.

"Up there," Einar said quietly, pointing at the roof of the thirty-foot-high wooden structure that ran the length of the pier. "This way!"

Einar turned around, and Trygve, though puzzled, followed suit. Now they were facing the street, as if they were moving with the crowd in obedience to the police officers' loud commands to "Back up! For your own safety, back up!"

Einar grabbed Trygve's hand, keeping his boots firmly planted on the shaky planking. For a few moments they forced the crowd to divide and flow around them. Then, with another expressive gesture, Einar showed Trygve what they would now try to do.

Still facing the street, seemingly part of the retreating mob, they began to back up unobtrusively, a step at a time as they moved to and fro at a right angle to the forward movement of the crowd. Soon they reached the corner of the dock building without attracting attention. A ladder near the corner was Einar's goal. He jerked his thumb over his shoulder. Casually, without pushing, they came abreast of the ladder. They were climbing it when someone in the crowd yelled, "Hey! Look at them!"

A lone police officer heard the shout and started for the foot of the ladder. He had just finished retrieving two overjoyful gentlemen from the cold water of Elliott Bay, and he wasn't much of a swimmer. He was still too wet and cold to feel like much of a climber, either. Weighing the merit of pursuing two men up a shaky ladder against keeping his feet firmly placed on the wooden planking, the officer shrugged. He grinned, waved at Einar and Trygve, and walked away.

Einar and Trygve crawled along the roof until they reached a spot directly above the area where the *Portland* would tie up. Below them were laborers in rough clothes, loggers in stagged-off pants and calked boots, gentlemen in high collars and derbies, women in dresses with mutton-leg sleeves and high button shoes. The human swarm was packed so solidly that from their vantage point it looked like a sea of hats—a becalmed sea, where the somber browns and blacks of men's bowlers, caps, and fedoras floated among bright ribbons and flowers.

Trygve's eyes were fixed on the far side of Elliott Bay. Maybe he would be the first to spot the gold ship, the first to shout, "There she is!" One hand clutched the precious extra edition of the *Tribune*. He had read the story about the *Portland* three or four times, but it still didn't sound like something that had really happened. "The paper says the prospectors are millionaires," he said to his father. "I don't think I've ever seen a millionaire."

Einar smiled. "Do you see that man with the cane, the tall one right below us?" He pointed to a man advancing along the pier as if he were leading a cavalry charge. When he came up to the group of policemen standing shoulder to shoulder to hold back the crowd, the cordon opened up and he walked through without saying a word or even slowing his pace. He was dressed in a morning coat, striped trousers, and a dark green vest, as if to defy the summer heat. There was defiance in the way he continued to move through the crowd, his shiny black cane swinging in rhythm to his long strides. He didn't go around the clusters of people; he went through them, and when he came to a halt at the most advantageous spot from which to watch the incoming steamer, he stood alone in a magic circle of empty space.

Trygve whispered, "Yes, I see him. Is he a millionaire?"

"Maybe twice over. Nobody knows. That's Judge Dorsett."

In Trygve's mind a judge was a heroic figure, yet his father spit out the name as if the words had a bad taste. "Do you know him?" he asked, amazed that his father could keep something so important to himself.

Einar shook his head. "People like me don't even get close to people like him, unless they're in trouble. I recognize him because there were so many pictures of him in the *Chronicle* last year when he was running for judge. The truth is, the *Chronicle* won the election for him."

"Was that wrong?"

Einar smiled at the simplicity of his son's approach to politics. "Judge Dorsett wouldn't think so. If there was something dishonest about his campaign, nobody's dared say so in public and nobody's come up with proof. What bothers me, Tryg, isn't as easy to explain as the difference between right and wrong. I worry because a rich newspaper publisher was able to put a close friend into a position of great power, and I ask myself: What must our new judge have promised to do in return?" Einar paused, eyes resting thoughtfully on the imperious figure. "That's a man used to getting what he wants. Men like him aren't always particular about the way they get it."

At last a dark shape appeared at the entrance to Elliott Bay. Trygve's voice rang out from the top of the roof like a muezzin calling the faithful. "The ship! The ship's here!" The *Portland* was little more than a smudge on the horizon, but an excited murmur rippled across the crowded pier. As the ship's outline became more distinct, the medley of voices grew louder.

Chains rattled, bells clanged, and people cheered until they were hoarse as the *Portland* staggered into port. She was twelve years old, and only a hundred and ninety feet from stem to stern. She would lose a race against the commonest tugboat, provided the tug had nothing in tow. Although not the most impressive vessel on Puget Sound, there was a certain grace in the way the *Portland's* single stack sloped back at the same angle as her fore and aft spars. Today she approached with whistles pluming. Rival ships might be newer and finer, but which of them was sailing into port with a million dollars' worth of gold?

All sixty-eight miners on board were at the rail when the *Portland* made fast. Even the least of them was a man worth seeing close up, as far as the spectators were concerned. The gap between the pier and the ship was no wider than eight feet and the deck was only a few feet higher than the pier. Miners and spectators were almost at eye level—so close to each other they had to either stare or look away.

The miners were far from embarrassed by the frank curiosity of the crowd on the pier. They were four deep along the railing, vying with each other for the best spots to see and be seen. Peering across the narrow gap, the spectators saw that men with more money in their satchels than they themselves were likely to earn in a lifetime were wearing ragged work pants, jackets with elbows out, and frayed cuffs, broad-brimmed black felt hats, and muddy boots. Their faces were grimy and unshaven. Whatever skin showed around their beards was as creased as old leather.

Einar and Trygve watched in thoughtful silence until Einar, pointing, exclaimed, "Good Lord! It's Svien!"

For the second time that morning Trygve was astonished by his father's capacity to keep things to himself. First a millionaire judge. Now a millionaire prospector. That his own father might know or even recognize someone on the *Portland* had never occurred to him. "Father?" he asked incredulously. "Do you know one of those men?"

"That man standing next to the five-gallon milk can. Svien Frodesen, your mother's cousin. You've met him, but you were a small child and wouldn't remember."

"Why has he got that big milk can?"

"Look carefully. You don't see any fancy suitcases, do you? Even the biggest and strongest men on deck will have a hard time just lifting their luggage. Gold is heavy, and Svien is a small man. I guess he put his gold in something he won't have to carry. See what he's doing? He isn't trying to pick up the milk can. He's rolling it.''

Tryg's head brimmed with questions, but something in his father's manner warned him not to ask anything more. It was confusing. His father had never been reluctant to talk about that other Frodesen, the "poor Gunnar" who wasted his youth on a college education and starved to death preaching in the wilds of Whatcom County. Why, then, did he sound almost angry at this cousin who could not be called "Poor Svien"? Tryg decided to risk one more question. "Father, don't you like Svien Frodesen?"

Einar smiled in his usual open and affectionate way, giving Tryg's arm a reassuring pat. "I like him very much."

Deeply relieved, Tryg blurted out, "You didn't sound like it."

"Didn't I? Well, I suppose I was thinking about the last time I saw him. That was a year ago, when I went down to San Francisco to buy the *Konge*. Svien had put together his grubstake and he was about to leave for Alaska. So here he is, back home and a wealthy man."

"And a lucky one."

Einar nodded. "Yes. He was lucky, all right. Or maybe it was more a matter of being smart enough to know when a man should risk a lot in order to get a lot." A moment later he added quietly, "You see, Tryg, Svien was set on my going with him. He tried his best to convince me, and the money I had to put down for the *Konge* would have paid for my passage and bought me my outfit. It was head for the Klondike or buy a boat. I chose the boat. I turned him down."

Einar and Tryg descended the ladder just as the *Portland*'s gangplank went down and an eager mob of spectators surged forward and began to climb aboard.

A command rang out from the bridge, and a shout from the pier: "Stand aside!" The crowd pulled back from the gangplank and parted like the waters of the Red Sea. With rifle barrels glinting in the sunlight, a contingent of Wells Fargo guards marched through to form two lines at the foot of the gangplank.

"Attention!" their leader bawled above the murmurs of the spectators and the groans of the *Portland*'s mooring hawsers. "Prospectors will please debark in single file! We will escort you and your baggage to the Wells Fargo office! Stand back, everybody. Stand back!"

One by one the miners descended. Some of them dragged their boxes or suitcases. Many who had managed to shoulder their burdens were staggering under the weight. One dumped a bedroll at the foot of the gangplank, threw an appraising glance over the crowd, and hired two of the biggest men to carry his gold. The last to leave the ship was Svien Frodesen, still rolling his five-gallon milk can.

Einar and Trygve were just outside the cordon of guards. Einar called out, *"En hjertelig velkommen, Svien!"*

"Tusen takk, Einar!"

"The boy and I will help you."

The guard nodded approval and stepped aside to let Einar and Trygve pass. The two men greeted each other warmly. "I am happy to see you, Svien. And surprised. Congratulations, cousin. How is it to be a millionaire?"

Svien was small, moved like a cricket, and talked fast. "I'm a long way from knowing. You better look for someone with *two* milk cans." He turned to Trygve, whose chin was even with the top of Svien's head. "Your son, Einar?"

Einar nodded. "We use his middle name. Two Einars in one house sounds like an echo. He is called Tryg."

Svien squinted impishly at Trygve. "And how old is this little boy of yours, Einar?"

"Twelve."

"What do you feed him, Einar?"

Einar laughed. "He and I eat at the same table, but you wouldn't know it, would you? For the rest of my life I'll have to look up at my own son."

"Ha!" Svien snorted. "My whole life, I've had to look up at everybody." He dipped into his coat pocket and pulled out a long, slim chamois sack. "This here's my whiskey money," he explained as he loosened the drawstring, probed the interior of the poke, and produced a lump of dull yellow ore about the size of a pea. "This is for you, Trygve. If your father had listened to me a year ago, he'd have his pockets full of these." He held up the piece for Einar's inspection. "Take a close look, Einar. See how the edges are jagged? That means it wasn't washed far from the mother lode. When I go back, that's what I'm going to look for. The vein this nugget broke off from."

A command sounded from the head of the line. The guards closed ranks and the slow procession from the pier to the Wells Fargo office began. In the crowd at the foot of Union Street, Trygve saw his sister Anna. Anna was never hard to spot, for she was nearly six feet tall and could look over the heads of almost everyone around her. If Anna had been a boy, she would have been another Trygve. She had the same loosely curled gold-blond hair, the same straight high-bridged nose and determined chin. People noticed Anna, as they were doing right now—she was waving and hallooing over the shoulders of spectators who were plainly opposed to her moving up to the front. A little farther along, she broke through, her long full skirt flapping against her boots as she ran to catch up. She was holding her straw sailor hat flat on her head with one hand, while pulling along a little red-headed girl with the other. The girl was laughing delightedly as her feet skimmed the surface of the cobbled street. When they caught up, the ruffles on Anna's shirtwaist were trembling with every breath and her straw sailor hat had settled at an angle over her left eye. "Father! I thought I would see you here."

For the next block Anna and the girl walked beside the column. There were hasty introductions. "Svien, this is my daughter Anna. You haven't seen her since she was a baby. . . . Anna, this is your mother's cousin, Svien Frodesen. . . ." And from Anna, "Oh, Father! Cousin Svien! This is Sarah Whiting. I keep house for Sarah and her father."

Trygve didn't speak, and for the few minutes before Anna turned back and waved good-bye, the conversation eddied around him but didn't include him. He was grateful. Sarah didn't say anything either. She just danced along beside him, so close he felt like telling her to get out of the way. Once he turned his head to look at her, and was met by the boldest and brightest eyes he'd ever seen in a girl. They were sea-colored, green mixed with blue, like when the sun's rays make the water shine. They looked up at him, and kept looking, and didn't once blink. Well, he had something that would make those eyes open even wider. He pulled the nugget Svien had given him out of his pants pocket. "See this? It's a real gold nugget."

Sarah's eyes dismissed the treasure with the briefest of glances. "You should see what *I* have at *my* house. It's a penny, and it's thirty-two years old. When my father was a little boy he saw President Lincoln's hearse go by and he threw a brand-new penny out in the street. The hearse ran over it, so it's scrunched."

"A *penny*?" Trygve countered. "My nugget is worth a lot of money."

"Our penny is more important than money. It's an heirloom."

Trygve was disconcerted by this girl half his size who used a word he read in books but had never known how to pronounce. But he rallied. "*Our* penny. So it doesn't even belong to you. This nugget is *mine*."

There was no retort from Sarah, but she continued to hop along at his side. Trygve was reluctant to get into another match with her, so after that he looked straight ahead and concentrated on ignoring her. But he felt her presence, and it lingered with him long after she and Anna had gone. He wondered why Anna was so fond of a girl like Sarah. Probably because Anna was the kind of person who never seemed to dislike anybody. All the way to the Wells Fargo office Tryg was comparing Sarah with Christine Franzen, the girl who had promised to sit with him at the church box social the next night. In all respects the comparison was unfavorable. Christina was pretty, soft-looking, and shy. Sarah Whiting was going to have to change a whole lot, or she'd end up an old maid.

Judge Timothy Dorsett was involved in a number of enterprises with no clear connection to his career as judge of the King County Superior Court. He always conducted such non-judicial business in chambers, or *in camera*, as he preferred to call it when dealing with someone who couldn't possibly know what that meant. Being summoned to the courthouse had a different effect on a business associate than meeting in a saloon, where all men were equal as long as they could pay a nickel for a glass of beer. To the sanctity of the building itself was added the somber interior of his private office—his name engraved in gold letters on the frosted-glass door, his tiers of lawbooks, and his massive mahogany desk. The judge's appearance was intimidating, too; his eyes were critical, his thin lips were frequently pursed in disapproval—all his features united in an expression of icy superiority. No matter what the negotiation that bound Timothy Dorsett to his visitor, the visitor started as the lesser man.

Today the judge had summoned Jake Lund. Dorsett was a good deal more eager to talk to him than he wanted Lund to know. Lund was believed to own a small shipyard. The yard did not build ships. Repair and salvage was Lund's real business, and he was something of a salvage job himself. He was a drunk, a sea gypsy, an extraordinary shipwright when sober, but overall a man with more talents than virtues. He was the owner of Lund Shipbuilding courtesy of Judge Dorsett, who had plucked him out of the county jail and financed the rebirth of an abandoned shipyard, all for reasons of his own.

The judge had found that Lund was not always as easy to direct, nor as drunk, as he had expected. The success of the plan he would present to Lund today depended on how quickly it could be put into operation. Dorsett was anxious to get the discussion under way; he was deeply relieved when there was a rap on the door and his bailiff said, "Your Honor, Mr. Lund is here to see you."

Lund had the shoulders of a man half again his height and the legs of a bowlegged child. In waterfront taverns he was known as the Little Giant. When he sat across from Judge Dorsett, he looked like a large man, though his feet were inches from touching the floor. "Good morning, Judge."

The judge nodded, lit a cigar for himself, and closed the box. "You read the paper. You know about the *Portland*."

"Christ! A ton of gold!"

The judge frowned. "You know I don't tolerate such

language. Now, let's consider what the immediate effect the arrival of the *Portland* is going to have.''

Lund chuckled. ''Half the men in Seattle are going to head for the Klondike. I would myself if I had legs. I'd like to see what if feels like to be rich.''

''Maybe you will. But not prospecting. Right here in Seattle.''

''How am I going to do that?'' Lund grinned. ''From what I've seen of life, getting rich and staying honest are hard to do at the same time.''

The judge waved the humor aside. ''There aren't enough ships on Puget Sound to carry all the men, and probably women, too, who will want transportation to the Yukon. They'll be willing to pay five times more than the usual price for passage north. We've got a ship in the yard that could carry more passengers than the *Portland*, if she's fitted right.''

''You mean the *Gypsy Queen*?''

Judge Dorsett answered with a dignified nod. ''Exactly.''

''Goddammit!'' Ignoring the judge's obvious disapproval, Lund leaned forward and thumped the desk with a clenched fist. ''She's way past being salvaged. She spent a couple years on the bottom of San Francisco Bay. The reason we haven't repaired her is that there's nothing solid you can nail a board to. She's all rust and rotting planks. The barnacles are all that's holding her together.''

''You're exaggerating. You've been drinking.''

Lund shook his head. ''Maybe I have, maybe I haven't. Either way, I know what I'm talking about and I think you do too. The *Gypsy Queen* is jinxed.''

''That's what they used to say about the *Portland*.''

''Huh! But the *Gypsy Queen*'s been wrecked twice already, even when she was in good repair. Fifty people have already been lost at sea because of her. She's a devil ship.''

The judge's tone was haughty. ''Don't be dramatic, Lund. She's afloat. Her boilers are in fair condition. She needs a little patching, but if you hire extra crews and work them in shifts, you can have her ready to sail in a week.''

''And sit here in Seattle, safe as a possum in its mother's pouch? With other people's money in our pockets, while a bunch of poor gold-hungry saps put out to sea in a ship you and I know goddamned well couldn't sail across Lake Union on a summer afternoon?'' He paused, shook his head several times, and then carefully slid off his chair.

Their heads were on the same level—the respected judge seated on his throne and the vagrant artisan who was willing to steal anything except other people's lives. They confronted each other in silence, dwarf and giant taking the other's measure.

At length Lund spoke. "I suppose you'll fire me.''

"Not necessarily. There will be plenty of work in the yard. Of course I will have to put someone else in charge.''

"Will you now! Someone who won't object to fitting out the *Gypsy Queen*?''

"I've got to be practical,'' the judge replied in the manner of a patient father explaining why he must give his son a whipping. "A shipyard is a business. In this case, a business that can double or triple its profits. The *Queen* isn't the only vessel on Puget Sound that can be put into service with a little work. She's just the first we'll get floating.''

"You'll never get a government inspector to clear her.''

Judge Dorsett's tone was cheerful as he retorted, "I already have.''

"I don't believe it. Something's funny.'' Lund threw back his shoulders. Standing as tall as he could, he said, "I'm saying thanks for taking me off Skid Road, and I'm saying good-bye. But—now hear this—if you launch the *Gypsy Queen*, I'm going to the Coast Guard, the mayor, the port commissioner, and the police.''

The judge shook his head. "I'm sorry to hear you say that. Really, Lund. You know something about ships, but you know nothing about the law. It's not illegal to launch a ship. What are you going to tell them? That you *think* the *Queen* might go down? And if such a disaster took place, how do you think you could prove what caused it? You'd never be able to, Lund. Never.''

With a wise, cagey look, Lund said, "Don't you see, Judge? Don't you get it? I won't *have* to prove anything. The rumors I start will ruin your reputation. The kind of rumors you can't afford. So, I'm telling you right now—I'm going to do what I have to do.''

"Of course you will, Lund. And so will I." The judge watched the crooked figure limp to the door. He already knew what he was going to have to do.

3

It was only twenty-four hours after the *Portland*'s triumphant arrival, but Seattle was already gripped by madness; even its most prudent citizens were not entirely immune. The mayor was visiting in San Francisco, but sent a telegram to the Seattle City Council with his resignation. Sixteen police officers pooled their savings, had enough to grubstake three prospectors, and then selected the lucky three by drawing straws. An enterprising *Tribune* reporter had managed to board the *Portland* while she was waiting for customs clearance, in the Strait of Juan de Fuca off Port Townsend. He had three hours on the ship before she docked on Elliott Bay, and he used this time not only to achieve the most spectacular news report in Seattle's history but also to buy a ticket for her return trip to the North. While others scrambled for passage, he spent Sunday shopping for a dozen carrier pigeons. His masterful plan was to use them to send dispatches from the Klondike.

Simple arithmetic should have discredited the notion that when sixty-eight men return with $700,000 worth of raw gold, they're all millionaires. But in manic Seattle, that's what they were called. One weather-beaten bearded "millionaire" did a lot to spread the myth.

He stumbled out of a saloon, spotted the red-white-and-blue pole of a nearby barber shop, and decided to get a bath and a shave, his first in ten months. He was thwarted by a locked door and a sign saying "Closed on Sundays." A cluster of amused bystanders watched him beat on the door with his fists until the barber, who lived above his shop, could no longer ignore the racket and came down to admit him. That in itself was a good show, but the climax was better. Scrubbed, shaved, and somewhat more sober than when he went in, the miner pulled a moose-hide poke out of his pants pocket, loosened the strings, selected a nugget the size of a pullet's egg, flipped it to the startled barber, and strode out without asking for change.

Few trolleys were running because a number of conductors had quit their jobs within an hour or two of the *Portland*'s arrival. Cars still in service couldn't get within three blocks of the waterfront because yesterday's crowd was back today, fighting for position in the half-crazed mob outside every steamship ticket office.

One man had purchased a ticket the week before. Waving it over his head like a flag, he eased his way into the human jungle. Ten minutes later he sold it for fifteen hundred dollars, ten times what he had paid for it.

The excitement sweeping over the city was like an exotic scent no one could keep from inhaling. It was strongest wherever men were competing for passage. By midafternoon on Sunday, all Alaska-bound ships with regular schedules were booked to capacity for their next three sailings. The word "capacity" had taken on a new meaning.

One man suspected that his ticket would get him to Skagway but not necessarily in comfort. He challenged the ticket office, where the clerk admitted he had been assigning ten men to every cabin with three bunks. With a pleasant smile he invited all dissatisfied purchasers to return their tickets and get their money back. There were grumblings, but no one asked for a refund.

The stampede didn't end when the last established ticket office closed its doors. Overnight a curious flotilla of discards was launched and passage was bought out in less time than it took to print tickets. Every shipyard on Puget Sound got into the race, repairing vessels whose rotting hulls had been beached for so long that only a dedicated waterfront historian could recall where they had come from or what they had originally been used for.

There were safety standards and government inspectors to enforce them. Both were ignored; the shipbuilders knew that boats launched in such haste were not fit for ocean tides and storms, let alone for the tricky Inside Passage to Alaska. But some people were so intent on going north that they refused to recognize the chance they were taking. Einar Peersen, Trygve's father, was one of these.

For the Peersen family the evening meal on Thursday was a respected ritual. Ordinarily only Einar, Emma, and Trygve ate at the long table in the kitchen. But on Thursday evening, the traditional maid's night out—and therefore Anna's free night—all six Peersens gathered in celebration of their continued good health, good fortune, and trust in one another.

They were handsome, these sons and daughters of the old country. Anna and Trygve were Peersens in every detail—in their erect carriage, their height, their blondness, and the bold stare of their deep blue eyes. But the firstborn, Mina, was a Frodesen like her mother. They were both short and small-boned, with brown hair and eyes so dark they were almost black. The Frodesens came from the stony Lofoten Islands, where three hundred years before Spaniards had come to work in the cod trade, and many had stayed. "An octopus eater," Einar liked to call his gentle wife, for the strangers from the south had passed on to the native Lofotens a liking for common Mediterranean food. Emma's voice was soft; the children had never heard it raised in anger or despair. Mina had her mother's generous mouth and thoughtful dark eyes, and was just as quiet.

There was no pomp or glitter to these weekly reunions. The Peersen home was too small for the luxury of a separate dining room, and fishermen like Einar had no money for the kind of store-bought delicacies Anna reported seeing on the dinner table of the people she worked for. However, frugal as she was forced to be, Emma added touches that changed a simple dinner into a ceremony. The worn oilcloth on the dining table was covered with a tablecloth she had crocheted when she was fifteen years old and beginning to fill her hope chest. He modest set of "good dishes" came out of the china closet, as did the slender stemmed glasses for Einar's apple wine. There was always a bouquet on the table: flowers from her garden or, in winter, a centerpiece of fragrant cedar boughs.

Einar belonged to the first generation of Peersens born in this country; his Old World sense of tradition was strong. From the start, aspects of the Thursday ritual were firmly established. Even the smallest deviation was not tolerated. Yet Einar wanted his children to respect the old ways out of understanding, not obedience, so he never failed to explain the roots of the customs he asked them to observe.

He told them that their positions at the table were determined by the role each played in relationship to other members of the family. Father's chair was at the head of the table, mother's at the other end facing father. Trygve, first son, sat at his father's right, a closeness that symbolized his eventual succession to his father's chair. Mina sat at her mother's right, because the eldest daughter shared responsibility for the proper rearing of the younger children. Her husband Tim's place was in the honored chair to the right of his wife, because after she married, the wife's first loyalty was to her husband. Anna was seated opposite her sister.

For other evening meals when only Trygve and his parents were present, the food was placed in the center of the table and they served themselves. On Thursday, the serving dishes were placed in front of Einar, and he filled each plate as if it were his duty to see that the food was divided equally.

On most nights Einar spoke a few simple words of grace as they stood at their places. On Thursdays he recited the Lord's Prayer in Norwegian, and everyone except Mina's Irish husband was expected to join in.

That Thursday, Trygve, who was much closer to Einar than his sisters and more sensitive to his moods, heard something in his father's voice that made him uneasy. He told himself nothing was wrong, and almost believed it until his father did something he had never done at Thursday dinner.

After the prayer, when they were all seated, Einar remained standing as if he had an important announcement to make. They all waited expectantly for him to speak, but for what seemed to Trygve a very long time he didn't say a word. His gaze moved around the table, resting thoughtfully on each member of his family before going on to the next.

His daughters were smiling the way they had as children, when they loved surprises so much that they insisted on putting off the unveiling so they could play the guess-what game. But as the silence lengthened, their smiles faded and their eyes, fixed on their father's face, were brimming with anxiety. No one dared speak, for to do so would be disrespectful.

Trygve searched his mother's face for a clue to the riddle of their father's strange behavior. The pain in her eyes and her almost total lack of facial expression told him she knew what they were about to hear. Whatever it was, they would never learn how she felt about it. She was a loyal partner to any decisions her husband made, but they were his to make. If she ever disagreed with him, she kept it from her children.

At last Einar's silent inspection of the family ended. His stern face softened in the humorous half-smile that was so characteristic as he told them, "I've come to a decision that affects us all."

With that he sat down and began ladling barley broth into wide, shallow soup bowls. "I have already told your mother that I'm going to go north."

He paused, waiting patiently for their reaction because it was courteous, not because he was asking for their approval. Anna and Mina were too startled to speak. Trygve had the curious feeling that he had heard his father's declaration before. "Gold fever" was what everyone called it. The fever had been in his father's eyes the day the *Portland* arrived. Since then Trygve had been watching his father anxiously, sensing his restlessness, knowing but pretending not to know why he came to dinner every evening with a new collection of reports and rumors about the Klondike. He repeated every tall tale with a kind of innocence that wasn't like him at all. Trygve had always looked up to his father as the symbol of enduring family life. But tonight the man at the head of the table had been swept into the dangerous current of the stampede. To go north was a wonderful adventure when others did it. But his own father? Trygve was confused and fearful.

Mina was the first to get her voice back. "Father! What a surprise! How exciting!" Humor twinkled in her eyes for a moment as she added, "I think I should go with you, in case you bring back more gold than one person can carry."

Like Mina, Anna had a fine sense of humor. Both were also practical to the bone, but in Anna the practical side was usually the first to express itself. With a worried frown she asked, "What will happen to the *Konge*?"

It was more than a question about their father's boat. The *Konge* provided their food, their clothing, the kerosene for their lamps. It was the breadwinner, to be respected and cherished as a member of the family.

With a nod of understanding Einar answered. "I will see to it that the *Konge* is properly cared for. She must be used. A boat left idle begins to die."

"But who will use her?" Anna insisted. She was looking at Trygve and her slight emphasis on the word "who" was plainly meant for him.

"I hope it will be Carl Franzen." Glancing at Trygve, he added, "That would keep the *Konge* in the family."

The Franzens were close friends. Carl Franzen supported his family by peddling the fish Einar and other independent gill-netters brought in. Keeping the *Konge* "in the family" was a reference to pretty little Christina Franzen.

Such gentle teasing did not embarrass Trygve. Christina was his girl, and he didn't mind that everyone knew it. Sometimes he thought about kissing her, but he had never tried. It was difficult enough to decide whether he should hold her hand.

Trygve said solemnly, "Father, I can fish the *Konge*. I know how."

"Yes. You do." Einar was equally solemn, for among the Peersens of Trondheim, Norway, sending a twelve-year-old boy out to sea was not something to joke about. "You have made me proud. You keep your mind on your work. And you are almost as strong as I. But, son, you're not ready. In another year you will be. In the meantime you are not to go out alone."

The soup bowls were empty. Anna carried them to the sink and returned with a large platter, which she set down in front of her father. Einar looked with appreciation at his favorite dish. An entire salmon was steamed, skinned, swimming in a lemon sauce, and surrounded by Norwegian potatoes, which were small, oval, pale yellow, and sweeter than ordinary white potatoes. Einar's hands were scarred and workworn, the tools of his trade for almost twenty-five years. But they were deft as he spooned a generous portion onto each plate. No one spoke while he was serving, and the silence continued as they began to eat. But they were all bursting with curiosity. Trygve was so choked with questions he was unable to eat.

Einar put his fork down and said quietly, "I see in your faces many different feelings. You are worried when there is no need to be. I'll be gone for just three months, no more, because it would be foolhardy to spend the winter in the Yukon. I will come back before the ice forms and the ships cannot break through."

He paused, sipped a little apple wine, and smiled warmly at Anna. "Don't fret. The *Konge* remains in the family. When she is no longer seaworthy, she will leave us with dignity. We will pull her out of the water and burn her on the beach. That is the proper way. But that won't happen for many years. When the time comes, there will be another Peersen boat, another *Konge*. Nothing important has changed. Now, don't let your food get cold. Your mother prepared a fine dinner and she meant it to be eaten hot." He took another bite of fish and watched with approval as Trygve did the same. "Peersen men do not have nervous stomachs. Peersen women do not waste food. So while you eat, I'll talk about my plans.

"You're wondering: Why am I going prospecting? The answer is plain. I think I can find gold. Others have. Even before the big strike, men were coming back with enough money to buy a business. And when we got off the *Portland*, your mother's cousin Svien Frodesen was carrying his gold in a five-gallon milk can.

"You might be thinking your father's a fisherman, not a miner. He doesn't know anything about hunting for gold. But we all read in the newspaper that some of the *Portland*'s passengers who had never prospected before brought back so much gold they had to hire others to help lift it." His eyes twinkled with humor as he added, "It's too much to hope that I'll need that sort of help. But, Trygve, just in case, you must be there on the dock when I come back."

After a brief pause and another sip of wine, Einar continued, "Another question. When do I leave? We've seen hundreds of men pushing and shoving each other in the rush to get on the first boat for Alaska. I'm lucky that I didn't have to do that. I heard about a steamer that is up on the ways but will soon be ready for launching. I have a ticket right here in my pocket." He patted the pocket. "I was one of the lucky ones—" He broke off, looking down the table at Emma. Her eyes met his, as level and as thoughtful as his. When at last he spoke again, it sounded to Trygve as if he were speaking only to his mother. "I hope my decision to go north is the right one. But I cannot know that it is so. I can only do what seems right."

In the morning Einar went in search of Carl Franzen. Trygve, the soon-to-be temporary head of the household, went with him. They found Franzen on the pier where the *Konge* was moored. Carl Franzen was close to the Peersens because he shared many of Einar's traditions, but he was humorless, conservative, and nervous in any unfamiliar situation. His reaction to Einar's news was typical. He stared at Einar, his voice hoarse as he tried to reason with the stranger Einar had become. "But what if you don't find gold?" he pleaded. "Trying to find some, you'll miss the whole fishing season. This is going to be a wonderful year, friend."

Einar nodded. "Yes, Carl, I will miss a summer season, but the *Konge* won't. That's what I'm here to talk about."

Trygve listened intently while the conversation veered from Carl's gloomy remarks to Einar's buoyant enthusiasm, and back again. In the end they came up with a plan the dour Carl could accept. He even began to show a degree of enthusiasm about the role he was to play.

The *Konge* was not to be sold. While Einar was in the North, the *Konge* would, in a sense, be rented to Franzen. Franzen agreed to pay Emma a share of his catch in return for the use of the boat. This would give him an opportunity to make a lot more than he had been earning by selling other people's catches. If it worked out as Einar expected, Franzen would be able to save enough by the end of the season for a down payment on a boat of his own.

That agreed, there were no other major problems to be solved. Most of Einar's modest savings had gone to buy his passage.

Carl Franzen said, his face sober, "You didn't tell me yet, what boat are you taking?"

"The *Gypsy Queen*."

"*Gypsy Queen*? I don't know any ship by that name."

"I didn't either until I got talking with a man who works at the shipyard where she's been dry-docked for a couple of years. She's been repaired and refitted. She'll be ready for launching sometime next week."

Carl's worried frown deepened into a scowl. "A boat that's been in the junk heap? They can make her safe in a week and a half?"

"I've seen her. She's not new, but she didn't come out of a junkyard. She was in good condition when they took her off the run. They did it so they could pretty her up inside, make her into one of those new fancy passenger ships. But they changed their minds and bought a new steamer instead."

Carl was still skeptical. "I wish I knew the people who've been telling you all this."

Einar and Trygve said good-bye and started back toward town, Carl watching them as long as they were in sight. Then he turned and looked at the *Konge*, and the flame of excitement he felt about being her skipper flickered weakly and went out. He got aboard the *Konge* and with slow deliberate strokes begin to scrub out the inside of the fishbox.

The *Gypsy Queen* was to sail at noon. As a matter of courtesy, the Peersen women arranged their own farewells so that father and son could have their last talk in privacy. Emma and the two sisters remained at home while Trygve went to the pier with his father.

The hysteria of the first few days after the arrival of the *Portland* had waned somewhat, but the atmosphere along the waterfront was still turbulent.

A crowd had been collecting on the pier alongside the *Gypsy Queen* ever since the homely little freighter belched out her first cloud of sticky black smoke. Envious eyes followed Einar and Trygve as they approached the *Queen*. Two robust seamen were stationed at the foot of the gangplank; to leave it unguarded was to sail with at least one stowaway. Einar showed his ticket, and got permission for Trygve to come aboard until departure at noon.

Some good-natured joking was heard when Einar and Trygve continued up the gangplank. One voice, blurred by the keg beer served at the saloon across the street, called out, "Hey, Doc! I'll buy that ticket of yours."

Another voice shouted, "Don't listen to him. Sell it to me and I'll give you double what you paid for it. I'll buy your gear, too."

Einar shook his head and waved to the sea of upturned faces. "See you in Dyea!" Then with Trygve at his heels, he walked along the deck to a spot in the bow that was out of sight of the boisterous roughnecks on the pier.

"Those men were serious," Trygve said. "I think they really would buy your ticket."

"I'm sure they would. They envy me because I'm luckier than they are. And they're right. It was luck, hearing about this boat while there was still a berth left. But, Tryg, luck makes no promises." Suddenly his attention went to their physical surroundings. He saw rusty funnels, splintered, deeply scarred decking, freight stacked one crate on top of another from port to starboard. When Einar had boarded the *Queen* the day before to bring his gear, the old boat's flaws hadn't been as noticeable. Today, with only thirty minutes before she took out to sea with no turning back, the rot and the rust came into focus.

Trygve was puzzled by the abrupt change in his father's expression. "Father?" he asked. "What are you thinking? What's wrong?"

"Nothing to worry about. I was thinking that if I had a choice, this wouldn't be the boat I'd pick for a trip to Alaska. But it's a little late for that, and all I want is to get to Dyea. I didn't expect to travel there in style."

Einar began to go over his instructions about Trygve's responsibilities during his absence. In a few minutes it became obvious that he didn't need to repeat himself because

Trygve had already memorized them all. Just before sailing, he said, "My dear son, I can't leave without saying something about our conversation the last time you and I went out on the *Konge*—when you told me you wanted to stay in school and make something different of yourself."

Trygve remembered the conversation with painful clarity. "We don't have to talk about it now. And anyway, it was just a dream."

"*Just* a dream? Yes, that's the way I treated it that day, but I was wrong, because I was saying that the way to your future should be found in my past."

The whistle blew, a deckhand shouted. Einar threw his arms around his son, hugging him fiercely. Trygve had never doubted that his father loved him, but in this last desperate embrace his father seemed to be saying that the love was so deep he didn't know how to express it any other way.

Einar reached into his pocket and pulled out his old-fashioned watch in its silver casing that his father had carried when he left Norway as a poor immigrant fisherman. Pressing it into Trygve's hand he said, "Keep this for me. And remember—I'm not a gold-hungry fool, though you might think so. You see, Tryg, it's going to take a lot of money to pay for your education. What I want more than anything else is to help you pay for it. But I can't do that in a fishing boat. I'm hoping I can do it in the Klondike. Now, son, good-bye."

Einar turned Trygve around and gave him a gentle shove in the direction of the gangplank. Trygve stood on the pier while the *Queen* slowly gathered the power to back up. Leaning over the railing, his father smiled down at him and shouted, "Just remember this! A good fisherman is better than a bad lawyer!"

Trygve didn't move until the *Queen* was out in Elliott Bay, heading for the open sea. Then he turned his back to the ship and started for Ballard, clutching the watch as if it were a promise that his father would come safely home.

4

The rivalry between Seattle's daily newspapers had been bitter from the start. The *Tribune*'s roots were in the past; it was the descendant of a weekly newspaper founded in 1853, the year a vast wilderness north of the Columbia River was severed from the Oregon Territory to create a new territory in the nation's far corner. The *Tribune* was a scrappy paper with an unsophisticated editorial policy that never deterred its reporters from blasting the upper classes and even sometimes encouraged them to do so.

After several years of suffering the *Tribune*'s libelous attacks on the establishment, a triumvirate of wealthy businessmen financed the birth of the *Chronicle*. Its reason for being was simple and direct. It was born of hate and dedicated to fighting the "uneducated, misguided, flamboyant" journalists who published vicious lies about people in high places. The rivalry between the papers was a classic struggle of liberal versus conservative, labor against the powerful conglomerate that plotted its exploitation over lunch at the Cascade Club.

When sharp noses in the *Tribune* city room detected a cover-up in a *Chronicle* story, the troops were sent into the field to sniff out the reason for it. The manner in which the sinking of the *Gypsy Queen* was reported was true to each newspaper's policy. The *Chronicle* protected those responsible for the tragedy. The *Tribune* tried to find out who they were.

The *Chronicle* article was terse. After hitting an uncharted rock, the ship went down. A disaster that caused the death of twenty-eight people was covered in less than a paragraph and appeared in an unobtrusive spot on the fifth page.

The *Tribune*'s sleuths spent hours trying to track down the facts that they surmised the *Chronicle*'s version of the sinking had blatantly ignored. Their effort was a failure. The best they could do was to quote a veteran sea captain who claimed that if the *Queen* had indeed hit a rock in those waters, it was because the goddamned skipper didn't have an up-to-date chart, or more likely, didn't know the first thing about how to read it.

But no proof. Not a single reliable eyewitness, for not one of the twelve survivors knew enough about charts to understand what had happened.

When the *Tribune*'s best investigative reporter found that a government inspector had checked the *Queen* the day before she was launched and had officially approved her as safe and seaworthy for the Alaska run, the editor-in-chief called in his staff. "I don't like this," he said. "I don't like it at all. But we've gone as far as we can go. The truth went down with that ship."

When Pastor Luchesen came to see her, Emma was grieving so deeply she couldn't cry. She listened patiently to his monotonous recital of her husband's Christian virtues, thinking that it was kind of the minister to try to comfort her but that she had never known the man he was talking about. Einar's planned church service was to be like every funeral she had ever attended. Like the "deceased" the minister kept referring to, his whole pious litany had nothing to do with Einar himself.

The physical Einar lay somewhere in the frigid depths of the North Pacific. Though Pastor Luchesen intended to preach that the soul of the man is his true and everlasting self, and the body has nothing to do with his salvation, he kept referring to the absence of a body as if he, the director of the last act, was going to be deprived of his best dramatic material. The open casket. The solemn men and tearful women passing by single file, each one pausing to look down and then move on. The pallbearers, lifting and carrying the burden of their friend. The graveside blessing, the symbolic shovel of earth dropped into the grave. None of this would happen, and Pastor Luchesen seemed to be saying: What's left?

With an effort Emma interrupted him. "Pastor Luchesen, I don't want to offend you, by my husband's funeral will be different from the usual service."

"Yes. What a pity. How hard it must be on you. No remains . . . But he will be with us in spirit."

"I wish to make two changes in the memorial service you've been describing."

"Yes?" The minister was plainly unsettled by such a bold statement from a female parishioner. "What changes, Mrs. Peersen?"

"For one, I wish it to be on Thursday."

"But I've already announced it will be on Tuesday. Is there some special significance to your preference for Thursday?"

"Yes, there is," Emma said firmly. "When the girls first left home, we began to have dinner for all the family once a week. We chose Thursday because that was a day off for Anna. We haven't missed a Thursday since."

"A fine thought, Mrs. Peersen. I understand."

"You see, Pastor Luchesen, the family dinner was my husband's idea. I want his funeral to be a personal, family affair. Perhaps you can't understand this, but holding the service on Thursday makes it his much more than it would be on another day."

The minister nodded. "And the other change?"

"Can you say the Lord's Prayer in Norwegian?"

"My grandfather taught me to recite it when I was four or five years old. We say it at home now and then, but I haven't in church out of consideration for members of the congregation who are not of Norwegian descent."

"I would like the service to end with the prayer. After we hear Einar's grace, spoken in Einar's tongue, there is nothing left to be said."

Throughout the service the Peersens scarcely moved. As Emma had asked, it ended with the Lord's Prayer in Norwegian, and the minister's voice became eloquent as it hadn't been before, as if it were a conduit for Einar's unseen presence.

Fader Var
du som er i himmelen!
Helliget vorde ditt navn;
Komme ditt rike;
Skje din vilje som i himmelen
Sa og pa jorden . . .

Her face ravaged by weeping, Mina clung to her husband like a frightened child. Trygve had hardly spoken since his father's death; now he sat with his head bowed and his eyes closed. The feelings they held in had so immobilized them that, except for Mina, they were beyond the point of knowing how to release them.

At the end, even through the recitation of the Lord's Prayer in Norwegian, there was still no crack in their self-control. Dry-eyed, their handsome Viking figures as erect as a color guard, they left their pew and walked down the aisle, followed by the Franzen family. In the churchyard they stood close together while everyone who had attended the service, many of them crying openly, walked past, nodded, or smiled in sympathy and respected their right to be alone.

At length the ordeal was over. It was time to go home. Emma began to walk away and the others followed. In a few minutes the silent procession reached a turn in the road. A few more steps toward home, and the church would be hidden behind a stand of timber. There Anna stopped suddenly and turned to look back. The others faltered, and then they too stopped, not for a last glimpse of the church but to do what they could to help Anna. Anna's mask of courage had deserted her. She was sobbing uncontrollably, tears coursing down her cheeks, fists clenched, her grief riddled by anger at whatever man, or men, had caused such a senseless death.

To Emma and her daughters, Einar's death was an act of God, and if the act seemed cruel to them, they were guilty of losing faith and must seek His forgiveness. But they were not passive people. God had his reasons, Pastor Luchesen had said, but that wasn't enough. A good man had been struck down when half his life was ahead of him. What could be

God's reasons for that? They knew that many fishermen were lost at sea. In every generation at least one of the hardy young Peersens of Trondheim had lost his life in the fishing grounds off the northern coast of Norway. If Einar had died that way, they could have accepted it, for a man who fishes alone in a simple wooden dory knows, and his family knows, that every minute in the open sea is a gamble.

But to die as Einar had, on a steamship so large it carried forty passengers as well as freight? To die because a ship broke up mysteriously and sank on a cloudless summer day? The three women sat together like mutes, the pain of their loss hidden behind dry eyes and stoic silence. Even Mina had exhausted her ability to cry.

Trygve sat alone at the long oak table, reading and rereading the *Tribune*'s account of the sinking. His mother and sisters weren't talking, yet they seemed to be communicating without saying a word. He watched them helplessly, separated from them and weighted down with a terrible truth that no one else knew. He alone knew it was his fault that his father had died.

The silent group across the room believed his father had gone to Alaska simply because he thought he might be as lucky as others had been and find gold. That was true as far as it went, but the rest of the truth was Trygve's private burden. No one else had heard his father explain he was going prospecting in the hope of finding money to put Trygve through the university. That's why, in spite of all his knowledge of ships, Einar hadn't let himself see the rust and splintered decking and rotten hawsers. That's why he was aboard the *Gypsy Queen*. That's why he died.

Trygve was to blame for his father's death, and nothing could excuse him from his Christian duty to tell his mother and sisters. It didn't occur to him that there was any other course to take but confession, and the thought of it terrified him. How to tell them? When to tell them? How to say it?

These questions had been eating into him all day. His guilt hurt most when he looked at his mother and sisters. Suddenly it was too much for him. He left the table, ran up the stairs to his bedroom, and closed the door.

When his mother came into his room, Trygve was sitting in

a chair by an open window, looking out into darkness so thick there was nothing to see. He stood up and faced her, knowing that now, right now, the dreaded moment had finally come.

He hadn't lighted the kerosene lamp, so her face was hidden in the shadows. In a small way that made it easier. He plunged through his confession, the words tumbling over each other in their haste to be said.

When he finished, his mother sat down by the window. "Please, pull up that other chair. I want to sit with you for a while."

Her voice was soft, so soft at times that he missed a few words. There was sorrow in it, but no anger. "I always knew the real reason your father wanted to go prospecting. Oh, he was excited about searching for gold, just like everybody else, but I wouldn't respect him if getting rich were his only reason. You must understand, Tryg. Your father made the decisions, but never without asking my opinion. The honest truth is that he wouldn't have gone to Alaska if I hadn't agreed that it was the right thing to do. You see, dear son, your father was a wonderful man. He was able to let you decide your future for yourself, able to respect you even when you were turning away from all the traditions that were sacred to him."

She paused. Trygve had never seen his mother cry. If she was crying now, what should he do? He felt helpless, and was ashamed of it. But she continued, her voice steady. "You say you are to blame for your father's death. What you see is that your father wouldn't have gone to Alaska if you hadn't told him your feelings about college. *I* am seeing that he wouldn't have gone if I hadn't agreed to it. Which of us should carry the blame?"

With a deep sigh she said, "I know where the blame should be laid, not only for your father's death but for all the passengers and the crew that went down with the *Gypsy Queen.* I cannot believe that no one—not one seaman, not one shipyard worker—knew the ship was not fit to go to sea. The newspaper report said a government inspector went through the ship and approved her for sailing. Can that be true? I wonder, too, about the owner. A boat is never launched without permission of its owner. But now no one seems to know who owns the *Queen*. Whoever he is, he must have known . . ."

Her voice broke off. She stood up. "Please remember, you are not responsible, Trygve. I am not responsible either. Now it's time for us to sleep."

Trygve had rarely encountered anyone he couldn't trust. The idea that there was a person—perhaps several persons— who had deliberately sold passage on a boat known to be dangerously unfit for the open sea was so awful that it was beyond comprehension. What kind of people could be capable of such terrible wrongdoing? "Mother," he said hoarsely. "Mother, it's the same as murder." The word for the greatest of all sins exploded in his mind. "Murder! And nobody knows who did it! Someday I'll find out—"

His mother placed a forefinger against his lips. "Don't think such thoughts. They won't bring your father back to us. Trygve, my dear son, you're too young to talk about revenge."

"But those people, whoever they are . . ."

"Please." She kissed his cheek and slipped out of the room as noiselessly as she had entered. Trygve got into bed and tried to sleep, but the sentence she hadn't let him finish had to be said. He could say it now, privately, a promise to his father. "Someday I'll find out who owned the *Queen*, and he will be punished, I swear it."

5

Emma Peersen was going through the motions of living as if the slightest departure from the daily routine of her life with Einar would destroy the only remaining bond between them. She awakened promptly at five. Fifteen minutes later she was moving briskly about the kitchen, her glossy dark hair braided, coiled, and neatly pinned on the top of her head, her face shiny pink from the energetic scrubbing she had given it with her own lavender-scented homemade soap. As always, she put a fresh apron on every day, a garment so heavily starched that it crackled with every step.

The first ritual of the day was to boil coffee as her mother, grandmother, and a long line of Frodesen women before them had done. The last was to drink a final cup of coffee and read a chapter of the Bible. The day began, the day ended. Emma slept, she awakened; the relentless cycle began again. Baking, mending, putting mutton chops into brine, churning butter, making cheese, cutting and stitching scraps of cloth for a quilt—these chores had always been the fabric of her existence. She continued to perform them exactly as she had always done because, in her grief-stricken state, she knew how to live as Einar's wife but nothing about how to live as his widow.

Stumbling along the uncharted course of life without a father, Trygve was confused and a little frightened by his mother's preoccupation with keeping things just as they had been. He stood by helplessly, at a loss to find some way to communicate with her. Though what she did was as familiar as the fragrance of lavender and the snap of her apron, she did everything at a furious speed, seldom speaking unless he asked a question. He knew that what looked right and familiar was only a brittle surface covering emotions that were tearing his mother apart.

After a week of trying to cope with his mother's strange behavior, Trygve decided to speak with Anna. She was the member of the family everyone turned to when hope was needed to believe that tomorrow was going to be a better day. As a child Anna had suffered all the ills connected with the risky business of surviving the first twelve years of life— measles, broken bones, a fall through the ice while skating, pneumonia. Yet she had grown into an optimist who could lift almost anyone's drooping spirits with her good-natured banter and lively sense of humor.

Anna had remained at home for a day or two after the funeral, but now she was back working for Professor Whiting and his daughter, Sarah. Trygve arrived at the Whitings' back door when Anna was kneading bread. She greeted him, as always, with a spontaneous smile that told him that just looking at him made her happy.

Her smile faded quickly as she studied his flushed face, with drops of perspiration on his forehead, and his eyes, clearly filled with pain. "Did you have to run all the way?" One hand sticky with bread dough, she gestured toward the sink. "Throw some cold water on your face. There's a clean towel in the drawer." The other hand pointed at the icebox. "Take out the pitcher of lemonade. The glasses are on the shelf over there."

Anna rapped out the orders like a good-natured sergeant. The very sameness of the way she looked and sounded did a lot to put Trygve's world back where it belonged. When she had covered the dough with a clean towel and scrubbed her hands at the sink, she sat down at the kitchen table and filled their glasses with cold lemonade.

She drank with gusto, putting the glass down with a sigh of pleasure. "Ah! How good that is. Now, Litt Bror . . ." That, too, was Anna as usual: the big sister who started calling him Little Brother when he was barely old enough to understand the words and had never thought of calling him anything else, even when he stood an inch taller than she did.

"You're troubled," she said quietly. "It's Mama, isn't it?"

Trygve nodded dumbly. "She doesn't act like herself. I mean, she acts all right, but the way she does everything. . . ."

"It's natural for her to be sad. She'll never really be the same. It's too soon to expect her to smile."

"I know that."

"But that's not why you came here."

"No." Trygve swallowed hard, clinging stubbornly to his vow that no one would see him cry, not even Anna. "She hardly ever talks. Sometimes she looks at me as if she doesn't know who I am. She works all day long. She never *stops* working. It's like she's afraid . . ." He finished the sentence in a whisper. "Like she's afraid she won't get everything done before Father comes home."

Anna reached across the table and gently patted his hand. "It's a hard time, Litt Bror, hard for all of us. Hardest of all for Mama. People have different ways of getting used to their losses. Mama's way is what you said—work, work, work. But that will change."

Anna was interrupted by the sound of the swinging door between the kitchen and the dining room. The little girl Trygve had met the morning the *Portland* docked came into the kitchen. She was wearing a ruffled pinafore that matched the sea-green color of her eyes. Her hair, shining like copper in the sunlight, was tied with a wide green ribbon.

As she approached, Trygve jumped to his feet. He had thought about her many times since their meeting on the pier, mostly because she had made him so uncomfortable. It hadn't been like talking to a girl. With Sarah talking had been a contest—her rapid-fire questions against his commonsense answers, her dancelike kind of walk contrasting with his long and deliberate strides. Now he had no idea what she expected him to say, or what she would ask; with the prescience of the doomed he knew that whatever it was, he'd end up second best.

Sarah planted herself next to him and looked up into his face without a trace of embarrassment. Though her green-blue eyes were bold and her smile as impish as he remembered, her expression was one of frank, uninhibited adoration.

"You remember Sarah," Anna said, pouring a third glass of lemonade. "Professor Whiting's daughter." She handed the brimming glass to Sarah. Sarah accepted it and drank without taking her eyes off Trygve's face.

In Trygve's code, blushing in the presence of a girl was even more unmanly than crying in front of your sister. To his dismay he felt the traitorous heat flood his face.

Anna's blue eyes twinkled. "I see you *do* remember Sarah, Tryg."

At least she hadn't called him Little Brother, Trygve thought gratefully. "Hello, Sarah," he squeaked as his changing voice selected this particular moment to rise an octave. "Pleased to meet you." This was wrong, too! He *had* met her, and now felt more foolish than ever.

Sarah's unblinking eyes were still fixed on his face. She didn't seem to notice his awkwardness, nor his flushed cheeks, nor his voice's sudden switch from baritone to alto. "What grade are you in?" she asked.

"Seventh and eighth. I'm doing them together."

"You don't go to my school."

"No," Trygve murmured. "I go to Ballard."

"Where's that?"

Trygve tried to appeal to Anna, and got the same mischievous smile. "Ballard? Well, Ballard's . . . it's right on the water. On the sound."

"That must be nice. I'll come to see you."

"Oh, no! You can't do that! It's way the other side of the city. It's miles and miles from here. You'd get lost."

"I would not."

"You would." For a moment Trygve savored the taste of victory, minute as it was, when Sarah didn't challenge him with another "I would not."

The feeling was short-lived. Sarah had conceded that she would get lost, but the issue of whether she could come to visit him was by no means settled. "Anna will bring me." She turned to Anna. "Won't you?"

"Of course, Sari."

"See?" This was directed at Trygve, but there was no

gloating in it, only her spontaneous delight in going to a far place called Ballard. Facing Anna, Sarah offered two proposals. "I could go home with you tomorrow. Or I could go home with Trygve tonight. He won't let me get lost."

Anna shook her head. "Not tonight, Sari. And not tomorrow either. We are all too sad to have company. We have to be by ourselves for a little while. But I promise you truly, I will take you to Ballard. My mother and my sister will be very happy to meet you, because I've talked about you a lot."

Sarah's mood changed abruptly as Anna's words reminded her of the terrible thing that had happened to their father. The happiness drained from her face as she looked at Anna, then at Trygve. Her wide green-blue eyes filling with tears, she turned and bolted through the swinging door. The door swung shut and the sound of her running footsteps became fainter and fainter as she ran across the dining room and up the stairs.

"What happened?" Trygve asked. "Did I make her cry?"

"No, Litt Bror, no. It was what I said." Anna sighed and shook her head. The sadness seemed to be all around them, whatever way they turned. "She's a shameless little girl when it comes to asking questions. But she's also sensitive. What I said reminded her that you and I have just lost our father. It's only a year since her mother died, so I brought back the memory of losing her mother. Right now she's in her bedroom weeping for her mother. But Sari is a proud little girl, so I'm not going to follow her, though that's what I long to do. Poor lonely, brave child. She needs a mother badly."

Anna finished her glass of lemonade and went back to kneading dough. "You'd best go home now, Litt Bror. Watch after Mama. After dinner tonight, I'll come home and talk with her."

"Will Professor Whiting let you, when it isn't Thursday? He's kind of strict, isn't he?"

Anna said, "Oh, yes, he certainly is. He makes the rules for all the students in his classes at the university. He makes the rules for Sari and her brother, Benjamin. When I came to work here, I agreed to the rules he made for me. But he's not a monster. You tell Mama I'll be over tonight."

Philomen Whiting had been a gentle woman with large sad eyes and a sweet smile. Her children adored her. She was their refuge from their father's stern Puritan definition of acceptable behavior for the tenth generation of Whitings to be born in this country. She remained silent during her husband's lectures to the children; more often than not these ended with a reminder that the abundance of successful authors, distinguished doctors, ministers, professors, and attorneys in the Whiting line was due to the fact that they neither drank nor smoked and faithfully attended the Congregational Church. But Philomen didn't share the merciless conscience that the East Anglian dissenters had passed down from generation to generation, along with the Whiting nose—slender, perfectly shaped, patrician—and high forehead.

Benjamin never defied his father. He would drop the issue as soon as he saw it was something he and Professor Whiting would never agree on. Sarah was cut from different cloth. She clung stubbornly to her side of an argument no matter what the punishment, nor how obvious it should have been that such a tactic would never "settle" anything. At five she had refused to recite her father's favorite maxim: "When duty calls, or danger, be never wanting there." She hadn't been spanked because Professor Whiting was opposed to violence. He had taught his only daughter to read when she was barely four years old, so the usual penalty for one of her short-lived insurrections was to read the Sermon on the Mount— once to herself, once out loud to her father.

Philomen knew how to take the sting out of his decrees without the slightest hint that he might, on occasion, be less than the judicious patriarch. Her death, when Sarah was eight and Benjamin ten, was a shattering blow.

At first the loss was so numbing that Sarah couldn't cry. When she finally broke down in the privacy of her bedroom, the hurt began to heal and gradually her spontaneous enjoyment of almost everything began to return. But some memories still had the power to invoke the pain. One was the fragrance of dried rose petals, for it brought back the many times she had been held in her mother's arms, her face pressed into the soft valley between her mother's breasts, where a sachet of rose petals was pinned inside her camisole. The fragrance of water lilies also opened the wound.

When Philomen Whiting had come home from the hospital, the nurse told Sarah and Benjamin, "She will get well much faster if she is comfortable in her own bed." Soon they both knew it was a lie. But the day their mother came home was the first day of summer, when the water lilies were in bloom and so abundant they blanketed the surface of the lake. Sarah waded out far enough to pick some for her mother. When they faded, she walked through the woods to the lake and brought fresh lilies to float in the cut-glass bowl on the commode beside her mother's bed.

For three weeks Sarah stayed with her mother as often and as long as the nurse would allow it. Every day of that vigil the scent of lilies mingled with the little girl's helpless anger. Her mother was dying and no one knew how to stop it.

Friends sent wreaths and bouquets for the funeral, but the flowers on the casket were the water lilies Sarah wove into a blanket so long and wide that no one could see the box where they had put her mother.

Sarah didn't cry then, nor for several days afterward. Then one day, walking to her piano lesson, she took the path that skirted the lake, and the odor of water lilies brought her grief out of hiding. She sat down at the edge of the lake, sobbing and clutching her satchel of sheet music as she would have the hand of a friend. Gradually the spasms grew weaker, and at last she was through weeping. Her eyes were red and swollen and her pinafore was so tear-soaked it felt cold against her skin, but the voices of Puritans past reminded her that a Whiting always does what she has to do. She got to her feet, picked up her satchel, and proceeded to her piano lesson.

Professor Whiting's library was a shrine dedicated to the Whiting heritage. Photographs and daguerreotypes of Whitings past kept silent watch over the living with expressions of undisguised disapproval. There was an extraordinarily close family resemblance in most of the portraits. The several Jeremiah Whitings in their ornate gilt frames were men with the professor's elegant profile, inquiring eyes, strong chin, and thin-lipped mouth.

In a way the library was also a museum. The oak roll-top desk had belonged to Professor Whiting's grandfather. The hand-knotted Oriental rug was a trophy of a much earlier Jeremiah Whiting's thirty years as a missionary in China. It had served so many generations that the coarse warp and weft showed through its once glossy silken pile. Whitings prosperous enough to travel had always favored the Middle East and the Mediterranean, so here and there were pottery scarabs from Egypt, an elaborately carved teakwood chest from Persia, and ancient Roman coins discovered by a Whiting who supervised an archaeological dig on the ancient site of Caesarea Philippi.

To the Philistine eye the room probably looked more like a warehouse than a study where a scholarly gentleman prepared lectures for biology students at the University of Washington. What Professor Whiting saw was his family, and the room was such a private place that even his children did not dare enter without first asking approval, like junior officers requesting the captain's permission to come aboard.

When Anna came to speak with him, the professor was writing at his desk. She stopped just outside the door, waiting for his invitation to enter. For several minutes he continued to write. Only after he had completed the paragraph to his satisfaction did he look up and say, "Yes, Miss Peersen?" He didn't smile. This was not a social call and would not be treated as such.

"My brother just came here to see me because he is worried about our mother. She has been having a hard time trying to get used to my father's death."

Professor Whiting nodded. "I understand."

"I knew you would." Anna's smile was warm, but tinged with sadness. She had been in the house when Philomen Whiting died; she knew better than anyone how deeply he had been affected. "I might be able to help my mother. This isn't my day off, but I would like to go see her after I've finished the supper dishes."

"If you leave after dinner, it will be late when you get

there. I believe you told me that the last trolley back leaves Ballard at ten o'clock. I think it wiser to go this afternoon.''

"But I wouldn't be here to cook dinner.''

His nod was solemn but there was an unmistakable glint of amusement in his eyes. "Miss Peersen, for the past two years you have been leaving at noon on Thursday and returning for breakfast on Friday morning. I can assure you, I have not fasted during your absence.''

"Thank you very much.'' She curtsied as she had been taught to do, holding the starched ruffle of her apron between thumb and forefinger, bowing her head ever so slightly as her right foot moved behind her left and she bent her knees.

"You will also have your Thursday off,'' the professor said, "as usual.''

"That's generous of you, sir, but then I won't be here to cook your dinner tomorrow, either.''

"I suggest you give me a hearty lunch.'' With that he swung his chair around and went back to his lecture.

She had been dismissed, but not unkindly. It was funny the way his eyes could betray a twinkle when the rest of his face was serious. It's something little Sari never sees, Anna thought, yet it must be there for her, too. Yet she's too young to understand it. How terrible it must be for a child to grow up in fear of her father.

When Anna arrived, her mother was in the woodshed splitting kindling for the black iron range in the kitchen. It was an unusually hot day. Her face was flushed with both the heat and the exertion, and a strand of shiny black hair had fallen across her forehead.

Anna said, "Hello, Mama,'' and took the hatchet out of her hand. "That's enough. We're going inside.''

She put an arm around her mother and guided her into the kitchen. Emma looked around the room, frowning a little as if she were undecided as to what the next chore should be. So far she hadn't spoken.

"No, Mama. You're not going to wash clothes, or polish the stove, or scrub the floor. You're going to sit right here with me.'' She led her mother to the oak rocking chair, where a knitting basket overflowing with brightly colored yarn was on one side and a basket of mending on the other. Emma sat down, obedient to the pressure of her daughter's hands. Resting her head against the antimacassar, she closed her eyes and sighed. It was the first sound she had made.

"Mama, did you eat lunch?"

Emma shook her head.

"You've got to eat. If you don't keep up your strength, you won't be able to help us, and we all need you very much."

Emma opened her eyes and looked up at this Viking princess who was her daughter. Her eyes moved from Anna's thick gold braids to her deep blue eyes, to the full lips that were so often curved in a smile. Emma seemed to be refreshing her memory. When the inventory was finished, she smiled and said softly, "Anna, do you know you are beautiful?"

"Am I really?" Now that her mother had been drawn out of her unnatural silence, the trick was to keep her talking. "Everyone says you're beautiful, Mama."

"Is that so?" Emma retorted with a hint of the playful spark that had always brightened conversations with her children. "Well, I know someone who thinks you're beautiful, but he never said the same thing to me."

"Oh, poof."

"Poof indeed!" Emma retorted. "You know whom you're poofing about?"

"I'd be lying if I said I didn't." Anna had been seeing a young man, Ivar Hilsen, for the past year. They were planning to be married as soon as Ivar returned from his last voyage on the freighter *Modig* in July. But Anna was not here to talk about herself. She went out to the root cellar, a cave dug out of a slope at the back of the house. She returned with a cool bottle of her father's homemade wine. As she was filling their glasses, Emma exclaimed, "My goodness, Anna! This is only Wednesday! Why are you here?"

"Because tomorrow is Thursday. I wanted to tell you that we will all be here tomorrow evening, for our Thursday dinner and family meeting."

"No!" Emma protested. "I can't get ready in time. There's the baking. And the bedroom curtains have to be washed. Besides—"

Anna's calm voice broke in. "Yes, you do have a lot of

work to do. However, everyone will be here for dinner. Mina, and Tim, and I. Trygve—"

"What will I cook? How can I make a meal?"

"Mama!" Anna raised a hand to stop the recital. "Mama, it's all decided. You're going to fix *dyresteg* and mashed rutabagas. Have you forgotten how to cook them? Would you like to borrow a cookbook from somebody?"

Emma shook her head and then broke into laughter. "You win, Anna—as usual."

6

For twenty years Emma Peersen had been content to live in her husband's shadow. In the eyes of their children, Einar was the leader, Emma the follower. She was cheerful, intelligent, with approval in her eyes and a loving smile for her children, but always a quiet woman who, as far as they knew, had never taken the initiative in matters of importance to the family.

In truth, the parental roles were assigned by Norwegian tradition, and both Emma and Einar had been content with them. Their separate areas of authority and responsibility were clearly defined. Emma accepted hers without feeling that it was less important than her husband's. It made for a comfortable marriage—the definition of a woman's "proper place" and what constitutes a "good husband" were clearly spelled out.

Anna's visit jolted Emma loose from the lethargy that had numbed her from the moment she had learned that Einar was gone. For the first time she began to look ahead. Now that her protector, mediator, and judge had been taken away, there were serious problems that could be solved only if she dealt with them herself. But did she have the strength to sit in Einar's chair?

Reluctant but determined, Emma took stock of the situation. The *Konge* had been the breadwinner when Einar was alive, so the first decision she had to make was what part the boat would play in their lives—for Carl Franzen as well as for the Peersens.

Before he left on the *Queen*, Einar had added a codicil to

his oral contract with Carl. Einar was to remain in the Klondike for exactly three months. If he came back earlier, he would not reclaim his boat until the stated period of Franzen's temporary ownership came to an end. Franzen had been guaranteed a full season during the time of year when the catch was heaviest. It was his first chance to put together a grubstake for a boat of his own.

Emma decided the agreement must continue as it would have if Einar were alive, although it was already plain that Carl Franzen was not the fisherman Einar had been. He had come to the house a few days after the funeral and conscientiously counted out her share of the sum he received for his first catch. Distraught as she was, Emma stared at it blankly, unable to connect the pitiful offering of pennies and dimes with his reason for bringing it to her. She refused it too quickly, and the hurt pride she saw in his face cleared her mind. "Thank you, Carl. You are always as good as your word. But I do not need money just yet."

Franzen looked at the coins he held in the palm of his hand. "I think I figured this right."

"Of course you did," Emma said quickly. "Don't be disappointed, Carl. There are days when Einar brings home less." Hearing herself speak of Einar as if he were still alive, somewhere out in the Sound pulling his net, she choked and couldn't say more. Franzen left, still clutching the coins. The next day Emma went to the Franzen home and told Carl's wife, Marta, who was pregnant with her sixth child, that Carl was not to share his catch until the big chinook began to run and he was netting a full boatload every day he went out.

It was fortunate that she did not need to provide for her daughters. Mina was married, and her husband, Tim, who worked in the big sawmill, was a good provider. Anna would be married as soon as Ivar Hilsen returned; she not only lived on the five dollars a week she received as a housemaid, but she had opened a savings account the day she went to work for the Whitings. Since that time Anna had never once failed to deposit one dollar every Thursday afternoon. Einar had said of her, "Anna takes care of everybody. But do not worry, Emmerle. When she has to, Anna will find a way to take care of herself as well."

*   *   *

For Emma, trying to find the solution for herself and Trygve was a search without clues. She had an urgent need for a plan, and yet time and again she was overwhelmed by her feeling of inadequacy. Who would pay wages to a woman of forty-two, a woman who hadn't even completed the sixth grade? She had left school in order to help her widowed mother. Now another twelve-year-old, her only son, was ordained by tradition to inherit the responsibility of a missing parent. In order to respect Einar's pledge to Carl Franzen, Trygve could not ask that the *Konge* be returned until three months had passed. Meanwhile, there were the sawmill, the logging camp, and several other places where a boy who learned quickly might find work. To support himself and his mother, Trygve would have to work full-time, winter and summer. He would have to give up his schooling, as Emma herself had done.

But was that right for Trygve? "A dreamer," Einar had called him, and yet finally Einar had accepted the dream and was determined to do whatever he could to help his son go to college.

Thursday morning Emma was in the kitchen lingering over her coffee, the first cup of the day. Anna was forcing her to bring back the family dinner, a ritual that was so completely Einar's creation that she hadn't wanted to think about it. To make matters worse, Anna had told her that *dyresteg,* roast venison, was to be the main dish. Surely Anna remembered that was the meal Einar had insisted would be his first when he returned from Alaska.

All at once she understood what Anna was trying to do. She realized she had been dealing with the disaster of Einar's death by closing her eyes. Because she couldn't bear to sleep in the bed where, as a new bride, she had lain with Einar and learned how tender an act of passion could be, she moved into the spare bedroom. Since seeing Einar's clothes distressed her, she had closed the old walnut armoire the day he died and hadn't opened it since. Anna was telling her: Dearest Mama, it's time to open your eyes.

The workshop Einar had built for himself inside the shed

was the cruelest reminder of all. It was his sanctum. He was everywhere, in his tools, his wood-carving chisels, his fishing gear. So when she needed something there, she asked Trygve to fetch it. Avoiding Einar's workshop was a way of forgetting him, but was that what she really wanted to do?

Emma put down her cup, wrapped herself in a pale blue shawl, and walked purposefully to the shed. At the door she froze. Her heart was hammering and her legs were so weak she was afraid she would fall. The spasm lasted for several seconds, and then she turned the doorknob and went inside.

The shop was alive with Einar's presence. She circled the room slowly, studying each object carefully and with great affection. When she walked back to the kitchen she was smiling and eager to start cooking *dyresteg*. And sauerkraut flavored with caraway.

Everything was as Einar would have had it. Grandmother Frodesen's stemmed wineglasses, the tablecloth that Emma at fifteen had crocheted for her hope chest, the seating arrangement at the long oak table; this Thursday dinner scene was perfect in every detail, except for the vacant chair at the end of the table.

Einar had encouraged family banter and took part in it with genuine pleasure, but tonight it was a quiet meal, with long silences and many glances at Einar's chair. At length the table was cleared and the coffee cups refilled. An expectant hush settled over the table. Their weekly family meeting, if there was to be one, should begin now. For all of them this was the moment when the heartbreaking emptiness of the chair at the head of the table struck full force.

Anna's head was high, but her eyes were sad. Mina, always the helpless victim of her emotions, was weeping silently. Trygve looked stern, but his trembling lips betrayed him.

This was her first test as a leader, not a follower. Emma wondered how she could ever have thought she would be brave enough to live up to it. Last night's resolve was challenged now by an all-consuming sense of her inadequacy. Her children's eyes were bright with sympathy. They would excuse her for retreating. But that was not what she wanted—

she must find her voice and speak with assurance. Suddenly it came to her that there was a better way to announce her new role. Without a word she pushed back her chair, rose to her feet, and walked resolutely to the head of the table. She sat down in Einar's chair.

There was a moment of absolute silence, and then Anna's voice. "Good, Mother! Good."

Emma bowed her head in acknowledgment. "It isn't easy to take your father's chair, but I think nothing will come easily for a long time, perhaps never. I have prayed for the strength to do what I have to do . . ." Her voice faltered.

Anna said, "We will all help."

Emma nodded. "I know that. That's why I'm sitting here."

Anna added, "We know you're worried about money. But Mama, please, you don't need to. We've got enough to take care of you. Professor Whiting says that starting next week he'll pay me seven dollars a week."

Though Mina was the eldest, she made no effort to join in. She had stopped crying and had withdrawn into the protection of silence.

"Mrs. Peersen, may I say something?" Tim O'Donnell's voice was soft. "You are a brave woman! Please, do not worry for the future. I am not a rich man, but I will help in any way I can."

"You're a generous man. But truly, I can't accept anything from you and Mina. There are many years ahead of me, so I must learn to take care of myself."

Trygve had remained silent, but Emma had seen impatience building up in him. "I think you have something to say, Trygve. Please speak up."

Trygve's big news came bursting out. "I got a job! A full-time job! Six days a week, thirty-five dollars a month, just like the men!"

"Where is your job, Trygve?"

"In the cannery. I talked to Mr. Roberts and he said I could start tomorrow."

"Am I right, son, that the cannery has a short season? Three months, maybe?"

"Yes, Mama. But then I will work someplace else. The

best would be to work as a longshoreman. The strike is over now and they're getting over forty cents an hour.''

"I see." Emma smiled at her man-sized son. His deep blue eyes were so like his father's. ''And what about the *Konge*? Will you fish our boat when Mr. Franzen's time is up?''

Trygve's answer was hesitant. "I *could* fish the *Konge*. But if Mr. Franzen keeps fishing it, he will be able to pay you your share. That way you'll have money from him besides the money I'll be earning on a job, and that,'' he added with conviction, ''will bring in twice as much money.''

Tim nodded his approval. ''That's a smart man speaking. Keep it up, Trygve!''

They all had spoken. Now was the time for the new Emma Peersen to take charge. ''I thank you from my heart. You are generous and you are loyal, all of you. I've been thinking seriously about the ways you are offering to help me. I agree that your plan would give me everything I need. But I am asking myself: Is it the *best* plan?''

The ring of authority was faint but unmistakable. ''First, about you, Tim and Mina. When the baby comes, there will be many needs for everything you earn, Tim. The room you want to add on, the clothes, and the midwife. I cannot let you sacrifice even a little in order to take care of me. So with my deepest thanks, I tell you that I cannot accept your offer.''

Emma paused while Anna refilled her mother's coffee cup. They all waited in respectful silence while she picked up a cube of sugar, tucked it inside her lower lip, and with a sigh of pleasure strained sips of coffee through the sugar. Putting down her cup, she began again, in a tone that became more assertive with each word.

''Dear Anna, it is good news that Professor Whiting has promised you seven dollars a week. But you must save extra dollars for your home, for your life with Ivar. When he finally comes back from his last long voyage, his head will be full of the plans he has made for both of you. He has built you a beautiful little house. I know you want to surprise him with the things you have put into it. And when you are married I most certainly will not come to live with you. Ivar will have a wife to support. He doesn't need to take care of a mother-in-law as well.''

Anna shook her head. "That is the old way, Mama, the proper way. You have told me yourself that in the Lofoten Islands, the old people are cared for by their families. It is a disgrace not to make an old person the honored head of the house."

Emma smiled. "Anna dear, I am not that old. Wait a little. I'll be sitting by your hearth soon enough. Anyway, it has always made me unhappy to have you work as a housemaid, cleaning someone else's house, cooking in someone else's kitchen. Some people consider these simple tasks. I do not. I think there is dignity in such work when a woman does it in her own home, for her own family. Housework should never be done for money in the house of strangers."

"Mama!" Anna exclaimed. "You never said such things before."

Emma nodded. "Because once your father had decided that the Whitings were decent people, he gave you his permission. So I kept my feelings to myself."

Anna said quietly, "I guess not altogether, Mama. I remember the day you and I were on a trolley to Green Lake, and two women sitting in front of us began talking about hiring a maid. They were rich—their clothes told us that—but I think being rich was new to them. They sounded like they were pretending to each other that they had never scrubbed a pot or pushed a carpet sweeper. One was complaining." Anna's voice rose in imitation of the woman's snobbish whine, "She said, 'It's so hard to get good help these days!' And the other woman said, 'My dear, look around Ballard the way I did. Those young Swedes and Norwegians are ignorant, but they make good housemaids.' Mama, I saw your face when they said that."

"I was not as clever as I thought. But I wonder—you heard what they said just as I did. How did it make you feel?"

"I thought: It's a shame stupid people have all the money. But I know what you're asking me. Does it hurt me to be the ignorant Norwegian who works for Professor Whiting? Believe me, if that's the way the professor treated me, I'd be right behind Tryg asking for work at the cannery. But I'm not treated that way. Sometimes the professor is so strict you'd think he was a Swede—he doesn't know a thing about how to handle his little daughter. Still, he shows me respect, and he listens when I talk. And Sarah . . .'' Sadness came into her eyes at the thought of the child. ''Mama, that poor little girl! She needs a mother so badly, and I think that's what I've become for her.''

''So you cannot leave her?''

Anna shook her head. ''No, Mama, I can't.''

''I understand. Now, please try to understand what I have to say. I cannot accept wages you are paid for work I would refuse to do myself.''

Emma turned to address her son. ''And you, Tryg. Do you think your mother has forgotten that before your father left he told you he wanted you to go through high school? And after that, to the university?''

''Mama, things are different now.''

''Oh, yes. But your father wanted you to stay in school. He was proud to have a son who would go to college. *That* hasn't changed.'' Emma rested a hand on Trygve's shoulder and said gently, ''We won't talk anymore about the fish cannery or the logging camp. Because we will not disappoint your father.''

Emma took a deep breath, exhaled slowly, and plunged into the proposal that had kept her awake for most of the night. ''Now I have a question for all of you. Do you like my pastries? *Mor Monsen's kaker*, which we had tonight. *Lefser*, and *brudlaupskling, spritsar*?''

They all nodded energetically. ''No one makes them as good as you,'' Anna said. ''I took some *mazarintarta* to the Whitings. There were only six people at the dinner table but they didn't leave a crumb.''

''That is good to hear. Did you tell Professor Whiting who made the mazarin cake?''

''Well, no,'' Anna admitted. ''He didn't ask. Maybe he thought I made it.''

''The next time you put some of my baking on the Whitings' table, do not wait to be asked. This is the heart of my plan: to sell home-baked Norwegian cakes, pastries, and breads to families that have the money to buy baked goods from a store. We have the advantage over bakery stores in two ways. One is that big bakeries don't want to spend the money for thick cream and fresh butter and the freshest nuts, the way I can. The other is that our salesmen—you, Anna—is right there in the kitchen where she can introduce the good things I bake here at home.

"Our first steady customers will be the Whitings. We will shower the professor with my baking. He must have many wealthy friends, and most women like to boast about the wonderful this or that they have just discovered. Through them we will find more customers."

Anna's blue eyes gleamed. "I have at least eight friends right here in Ballard who work in those big houses on Capitol Hill. They'll be glad to introduce our products. So that makes eight more customers for our fine Norwegian pastries. *Brune kagerm*, and *fyllda strutar*, and—"

"My dear Anna," Emma said gently, "the first of those is Danish, and the second is Swedish."

"Oh," Anna said with a shrug. "*I* know that. But they won't."

Emma didn't speak for several minutes, suddenly feeling as if she had lost her sense of direction in the maze of detail involved in opening and operating a bakery. Finally she said, "There is so much more to talk about. Too much, I think, for tonight. We know how to reach nine families—nine customers—but that will hardly make a paying business. How do we reach the next ten, or dozen, or a hundred? I am the baker. Anna is salesman. Trygve is our delivery boy. How will we manage all this? But my poor old brain is already tired. Think about these things, all of you. We'll talk again soon."

The family left her sitting in Einar's easy chair with her bedtime cup of coffee and her Bible on the table beside her. Trygve had gone to bed. At last the longest day of Emma's life was coming to a close.

7

The outbreak of gold fever that struck Seattle when the *Portland* docked in July spread rapidly across the country, in the wake of the depression following the panic of 1893. Correspondents from Eastern newspapers, as well as impecunious free-lance writers, did their part to feed the fever. And sometimes the most preposterous sounding reports turned out to be perfectly valid.

"Wooden barks are selling for five thousand dollars each. Their lucky buyers will sail for the North in tow of Puget Sound tugboats." True.

"A Seattle schoolteacher went to Alaska on her vacation and returned in one month with eighty thousand dollars' worth of gold." True.

"Tickets are now being sold for rides on passenger balloons from Seattle direct to the Klondike." True.

If some of the tales that found their way into the pages of Eastern publications were based on news gleaned in Seattle's proliferating saloons—one saloon for every citizen, according to a pious gentleman's letter to *The New York Times*—the reporters can be forgiven for passing them along as true. What was actually happening in the brawling, booming streets of Seattle was often more lunatic than anything even the most imaginative writer could dream up.

The reaction to all this was a massive migration, typified by the man in New York City who advertised for companions who could put up five hundred to two thousand dollars to go north with him. He had more than twelve hundred applicants in forty-eight hours. On a street corner an enterprising local was able to hawk a team of goats with the slogan "Better sled dogs than the best dog you can buy."

Frustrated by the newspapers' refusal to carry her advertising, the reigning queen of sin rented the finest teams and open carriages in the city. Every day the girls dressed in the simple elegance only the affluent could afford, rode up and down the busiest streets in the city, nodding and waving to a multitude of appreciative acquaintances. A petition signed by a hundred outraged women demanded that this daily promenade be forbidden. The petition reached the mayor's desk, where, because of some unexplained mishap, it got lost. To writers the burgeoning city was like the widow's cruse. No matter how much they wrote, the vessel magically refilled itself.

In this heady atmosphere Emma Peersen, housewife and mother, with less than six years of schooling and no experience whatever in the business world, was attempting to make a living for herself and her son by selling the products of her kitchen.

Six weeks before, Mother Peersen's Home Bakery had been launched. Thanks to the perseverance of a dozen housemaids whom Anna had recruited, Emma's delicacies were appearing regularly in the dining rooms of some of Seattle's most affluent citizens, the people Einar had once described as "the get-rich-quick who ride in broughams and live in three-story houses with carriage ports."

With her partners seated around the old oak table on Thursday evening, Emma outlined her plan for expansion. "So far we have had great success. More than I dared hope for. Five weeks ago we had one customer, the Whitings. Today we have twenty-three."

Emma discussed her plans for the future step by step. The house-to-house trade was indeed flourishing. But it had limitations. First, by the very nature of this kind of business, each order was small. Second, as the number of customers increased, so too did the miles Trygve had to cover, mostly on foot, to homes scattered all over the city. Emma touched her son's powerful hand as if to protect it. "It sounds strange to say it, but the way we are selling out baked goods now means that every time we add a customer, our work becomes harder."

"They are all good customers, Mama."

"Oh, yes! I don't mean we should lose interest in selling to private homes. Indeed no. That would be a foolish mistake because we need every one of them now, but we should find some way to sell to a larger market."

"A larger market?" Trygve's eyes brightened with understanding. "A bakery downtown?"

"Someday."

"A store downtown?" Anna exclaimed. "What put such stars in your eyes?"

"Not stars, darling. Common sense. It seems to me that if we're to be in a business, it would be foolish to be in one that won't grow. If my coffee cake tastes so good that one person wants to buy it, is it a mistake to believe that hundreds of people would like it just as much?" Emma sighed. "But it's too soon to talk about a bakery downtown. What we must do right now is try to get some downtown customers who buy larger quantities than a private home—the hotels and restaurants."

"How are you going to manage that?" Mina said.

"The same way we got families on First Hill and Queen Anne to buy from us. We put something on their tables that they couldn't buy in a grocery store."

Anna smiled. "Once you eat Mrs. Peersen's *mor Monsen kaker*, you won't eat anyone else's. But how can we do that in someplace like the Seattle Hotel?"

"The same way," was Emma's solution. "Make them eat it."

"Are you two planning to go to some hotel and tell the manager, 'Hey, mister, close your eyes and open your mouth, I've got a surprise for you'?" Trygve said.

"Not me," Anna retorted. "*You're* going to do that, Litt Bror. You're taller than I am and you've got more muscles. So you just march into the hotel, you ask to see the manager, and then you grab him by the shoulders, and if he won't open his mouth—"

"Enough!" Emma raised a hand in a gesture very like the one Einar often used to bring his children's chaotic exchanges of ideas to a halt. "Your sister's joking, but she is almost saying what I planned to say. It's an experiment. To start, I'll make up three boxes."

"Sample boxes," Tim interjected.

"Yes. Each box will contain all six varieties that we've been selling to private homes. Then you, Trygve, will go to three hotels—the biggest, the most expensive—and ask for the manager."

"The manager!" Trygve shrugged his shoulders. "All right. I ask for the manager. That's easy. I give him one of the boxes. Then what?"

Anna said, giggling, "You grab him by the shoulders—"

Mina had been listening apathetically. "Hush, Anna. You always laugh so loud. You make me nervous."

Emma and Anna exchanged a meaningful glance. For some weeks Mina had been peevish without reason, given to crying when, as far as they knew, there wasn't anything to cry about. They guessed the cause. Mina was pregnant for the fourth time, and obsessed by the fear that the baby would be stillborn, as the others had been.

Tim's arm went around Mina as he said, "She's been feeling kind of peaked." To Mina he whispered, "It's all right. We'll go home." They stood up, and with his arm still sheltering Mina as if to protect and support her, Tim led his wife to the kitchen door. Pausing there, he added, "Whatever you decide is fine with me and Mina. Both of us, we'll help any way we can."

There was a murmur of good nights from around the table as they watched Tim open the door. The two walked out, Tim's face troubled, Mina's awash with sudden tears.

Emma began work in the morning when it was still so dark outside that the kitchen lamplight cast yellow streaks across the yard. Einar had claimed that he didn't need a calendar to know the days of the week. When he came home to a kitchen so steamy the windows fogged over, it could be no other day than Monday, when Emma boiled the week's laundry in a big copper washtub at the back of the stove. And when scents of baking filled every corner of the house, it was Tuesday. But there was no such "calendar" now, Emma mused as she opened the oven door and pulled out her third baking of the day. From now on, every day would be Tuesday.

At six o'clock Emma sat down for the first time in three

hours. When Trygve appeared for breakfast, she filled a large bowl of oatmeal for him and a smaller one for herself, ladled thick raised cream into a pitcher, and put it on the table beside a bowl of honey from a wild-bee tree that Trygve had discovered when he was hunting. Once they had eaten, she packed three cartons—her "sample boxes," as Tim had dubbed them—and gave them to Trygve with a reminder of the names of the hotels to whose managers they were to be delivered. "And only to the manager. I don't want my pastry eaten up by people who aren't in a position to place an order." She took two nickels from a worn leather coin purse she kept in her apron pocket—trolley fare to and from Seattle.

Trygve shook his head. "Venn wants to go with me. They don't let dogs ride on streetcars."

Emma looked up at her son, who in the past two months had lost so much of his boyishness, though he was still too young to know his strength or how to put it to use. That she could have carried, and birthed without pain, a child who at twelve years of age had to lean down to be kissed on the cheek was a fact of such wonder that it frightened her. "I don't know what I'd do without you. You are my pride. Come home safe."

Stricken by the sadness in his mother's eyes even as she smiled up at him, Trygve said, "Yes, Little Mother." And with his dog Venn at his side and three boxes in his arms, he set out to walk the six miles to downtown Seattle.

8

All the way to Seattle, along the shore, across the bridge that swayed when a team of horses went over it, along the bicycle path overhung with green foliage and redolent of the fragrance of cedar, Trygve Peersen composed his presentation. Venn applauded by joyfully wagging his tail.

On the threshold of the first of the three hotels, Trygve suddenly felt like what he was—a twelve-year-old kid who was better suited to pumping the bellows for the organ in the Ballard Lutheran church. The moment passed quickly, however, and he strode across the lobby to the front desk.

The gray-haired clerk, whose face appeared to have hardened into a permanent scowl, watched his approach with haughty eyes.

Trygve began boldly, "Sir, would you please tell me—"

"Is that your dog?"

Startled, Trygve wheeled around too quickly for the precious load he was carrying. One sample box slid out of his arms and dropped to the floor, wrong-side-up. And there was Venn, right behind him, wagging his feathery tail, clearly pleased with his first exposure to life in a fine hotel.

Tryge retrieved the fallen box, righted it, and turned to face the desk clerk's disapproving frown. "Yes, he is mine."

"Haven't you heard about the leash law? Do you think we want mongrels running around this hotel? Get him out of here before the manager sees him, or you'll be in trouble. Go on, get!"

"But I want to see the manager. That's why I came."

The clerk seemed to notice the boxes for the first time.

This bold ruffian in ditchdigger's clothes had committed still another offense to the dignity of the hotel and to his status as its clerk. "Do you indeed," he said with a thin smile. "You should know that deliveries are not accepted in the lobby. Take your boxes, whatever they are, around to the back of the building, to the door marked 'Service Entrance.' "

"Service entrance?" Trygve echoed.

"Yes, yes! *Service* entrance. S-e-r-v-i-c-e! If you can read, you'll find it. And take your dog with you."

Trygve was embarrassed but far from defeated as he left the lobby and walked around to the back of the building. With some difficulty he kept a firm hold on his boxes and at the same time got through the door quickly enough to leave Venn on the other side.

He was in the hotel kitchen. Facing him was the fattest woman he had ever seen.

She was sitting on a massive three-legged stool peeling potatoes and plopping them into a bucket of water on the floor. Her dress covered her decently, if not stylishly—it had been designed to conceal the exaggerations of her overample flesh.

The woman looked up and in a friendly voice asked, "What's in them boxes?"

"My mother's pastry. These are samples. I want to talk to the manager, please."

The woman showed no interest in directing Trygve to a higher authority. "Open one up."

Reluctantly Trygve obeyed, realizing too late that he was presenting her the one that had landed upside-down on the lobby's hard floor.

The woman lifted the lid, pulled back the white cloth, and sniffed as if to inhale the richness of the pastry. "What did you do with this box? Sit on it?"

"Well, I . . ." For the first time, Trygve had a premonition of defeat, but he went on doggedly. "It was an accident. I dropped it out in the lobby. But that doesn't change the way it tastes."

"No, it don't," she said. "But it don't do a lot for the way it looks." For a moment she gave the mangled delicacies a thorough examination, her eyes fixed lovingly on the forbidden fruit. Then, just as studiously, she picked up one after another of the six different varieties, taking a large bite out of each.

Her verdict was a sigh of indescribable pleasure. "You told the truth, all right. What your mother makes puts the stuff we peddle here to shame."

Confidence restored, Trygve was eager for the next step. "Would you please tell me where to go so I can show them to the manager?"

"You came here to make a sale, didn't you? You think the manager will be impressed with all this scrambled together and some half-eaten?"

"I guess I could show him one of the other boxes. Only, if I do that . . ."

With a nod so vigorous her several chins bobbed up and down, she said, "Only if you do that, you won't have anything to show the third place you go."

"Yes. I mean, no, I won't."

"Well, don't fret. Leave this box with me. We'll buy from your mother. To start with, one dozen of each kind. When can you deliver?"

"Day after tomorrow." Trygve hesitated, but decided his question had to be asked. "Don't I have to talk to the manager?"

"If you really want to see the manager, you go right ahead. But he'll send you back to me, because I run the kitchen. I decide what to buy and what to serve. He don't, and believe me, he don't even step into this kitchen without having a real good reason. Now, just leave me that busted-up box of yours, and see if you can get to the next hotel without bouncing those cakes off the floor. Where are you going next? The Gateway Hotel?"

"Yes, ma'am."

Tilting her head to look up at him, she said, "My name's Mrs. Colter. What's yours?"

"Trygve Peersen."

"Norski."

"Are you Norwegian too?"

"No, son, but I'd like to be. I know a lot of blockheads

like you, and they're pretty good people. How old are you, Trygve?"

"Twelve."

"Twelve!" She blinked, half-doubting the truth of his answer. "Well, I hope to stay around Seattle to see how tall you get when you're full-grown." With a sigh she picked up her paring knife.

He thanked her and was on his way to the door when she said, "Hey! Dump the pastry on that table over there and take the box with you. That'll save your mother getting a new box."

Trygve hesitated. "She didn't tell me to bring the boxes home."

"She shouldn't have to. You should of thought of it yourself."

At the Gateway Hotel the manager was polite but noncommittal. He listened to the description of Mother Peersen's specialties and accepted the sample box with the same tolerance he might have shown to kids setting up a lemonade stand on top of an apple box.

At the third and last hotel the man was curt, but as Trygve was leaving, he responded to the boy's obvious disappointment. "Look here. I'm sorry I can't give you an order today."

"That's all right," Trygve said bravely. "If you put my mother's baked goods in your coffee shop, you'll have a big order waiting for me when I come back day after tomorrow."

"Is that so?" His tone was a blend of amusement and admiration. "You know something? I hope you're right. I really hope you're right."

His work done, Trygve set out for home. He hadn't gone more than a few blocks when his attention was diverted by a noisy crowd pushed so tightly along both sides of the street that at first he couldn't see what they were cheering for. He ran ahead, Venn panting happily at his side.

He didn't have to push his way through the mob because he was tall enough to look over most of the heads in front of him. And there it was, the wonder of wonders he had seen only in pictures, the real thing in all its glory. A horseless carriage. He completely forgot about getting home in time for supper.

A man in a long dust coat and goggles was seated high above the slender front wheels, his marvelous vehicle completely hemmed in by its admirers. "The only one of them things on the whole Pacific coast," said the man standing beside Trygve. "He bought it with the gold he hit in the Klondike. They say it'll go up to fifteen, twenty miles an hour. Scares horses half to death with the noise it makes, but at least it don't dirty up the streets the way horses do."

"Make way!" the man enthroned on the carriage called. "I'm going to start her up."

The crowd in front of him parted hastily. The driver reached under the seat and pressed a button. As an electric spark ignited the gasoline, the engine came to life with a noise like that of a railroad locomotive starting, though more subdued. With great ceremony he released the brake and the carriage rolled ahead, gaining speed as it moved down the block. The cheers of the crowd followed him as he reached the corner, turned the carriage sharply and prettily in a complete circle, and reversing his course, chugged through the center of the mob again and continued on his way.

The crowd began to disperse. For Trygve, too, it was high time to start for home. He turned to go, but Venn wasn't there.

Had he just wandered away? No, Venn would never willingly leave his master. He must have been stolen. Too late, Trygve saw what a terrible mistake he had made by bringing his dog downtown at a time when any creature who could be passed off as a "sled dog" could be sold for a hundred dollars, and double that if he was put on the market in the Yukon. Trygve whistled and called, "Venn? Venn?" Then he began a methodical search, along busy streets, up and down side roads, from dock to dock along the waterfront, where a stolen dog might be hidden in a warehouse or shed. His pursuit became more frantic with every step, and his anger kept pace. Again and again he stopped strangers on the street. "Have you seen a big brown dog with a long tail and floppy ears?" Some looked at him sympathetically and shook their heads. Two men replied that if he had obeyed the leash law, this wouldn't have happened.

On a narrow dirt road near the old Yesler sawmill, Trygve caught up with Venn and his captor. The dog's jaws were locked inside a leather muzzle so that he could neither bite nor open his mouth. Both front and hind legs were bound together with leather thongs so that he couldn't move. There was a heavy rope around Venn's neck. A man in rough workclothes was using it to drag Venn along the street, pitted with pools of mud from yesterday's rain.

Trygve's anger exploded. Without taking stock for even a second of what sort of man he was attacking, he dropped his boxes and leapt at the thief, hurling him to the ground.

Physically the man was superior to Trygve in every respect—heavier, stronger, quicker to spot openings in another man's way of fighting. He went down because he had been taken by surprise. But he knew everything about street fighting and Trygve knew nothing. He was back on his feet and still in control of the rope around Venn's neck before Trygve had time to take advantage of that first successful blow.

With his free hand he swung a brutal punch that landed over Trygve's heart. A split second later he brought his knee up in a vicious blow aimed at Trygve's testicles. The knee missed its target, but Trygve was staggering from almost simultaneous blows to the most vulnerable parts of his body.

"You stupid son of a bitch," the man spat out. "You think you're big enough to take me on? You looking to die young?" He came at Trygve like a snarling animal, his lip pulled back to expose the pitted and yellow remnants of his upper teeth. Trygve jumped away, too startled to think about defending himself. His mind was consumed by one thought—to attack the ugly thief, to hit him, shove him, kick him, until he could get the rope away from him. Trygve went about it blindly, unaware of the dozen or more human wharf rats attracted by a real curiosity in the lexicon of street brawls—a boy, a tall one, but nevertheless a boy, being methodically mauled by a man with only one hand free to do battle.

"Poor mama's baby," the man taunted, grinning for the benefit of his audience. "Mama's little boy want his doggie? Well, come on! Why don't you just take him away from me?'' To enhance the effect, he dropped his fist. Standing directly in front of Trygve, he extended the hand that was holding the rope. This bit of theatrics had the intended effect on the ring of spectators. Some were grinning, some were tense, all were excited by the last act they were about to see—the blow that would knock the kid out for keeps.

It made a good show. The older man was giving the kid a wide open chance, or so it seemed, to punch his unprotected chin. But instead the boy threw himself against the hand gripping the rope, jerking it free. Now Trygve was at a greater disadvantage than ever. Tied up as he was, the dog couldn't get away, and the man had two hands to fight with.

All at once Trygve's head cleared. He dropped the rope and began pummeling the man with both fists. Trygve took more blows than he gave, but he was scarcely aware of being hit. After four or five furious minutes he realized that the man was becoming desperately winded, his punches seeming less and less punishing as Trygve redoubled his own efforts. Now Trygve glimpsed the first appearance of fear on the man's face, and he kept going, caught up in a relentless rhythm of punching, ducking, coming in with another jab. He didn't stop until someone stepped out of the circle of spectators and grabbed his shoulder.

A shabby little man looked up at Trygve with watery blue eyes and the vacuous grin of a friendly alcoholic. ''He's out, kid. He's out. Yeah, I know he's standing up, but he's out. You don't want to kill him, do you?''

Trygve shook his head. ''All I want is my dog.''

''Sure. We all seen that. He's right over there, kid. One of the boys untied him and took off the muzzle. The two of you better go on home before it gets dark.''

Muddy, bruised, one eye peering through the slit between its swollen eyelids, left cheekbone a blazing red where the skin had been scraped off, upper lip puffy and split in a dozen places—that was the Trygve his mother and sisters saw when he burst through the kitchen door, supremely happy at having won his first street fight.

Emma Peersen gasped. ''Who did that to you?''

Anna looked at her brother's battered face and said with a smile, "You won, didn't you?"

"Yes! Yes, I really did win." Having proclaimed his victory, Trygve had to be honest. He added quickly, "I didn't win at first, though."

Emma nodded. Her consternation over the damage to her male child began to ease as she saw how proud he was. "Not right at first, son, I can see that."

"Well?" Anna demanded. "What happened?"

"There was a horseless carriage on First Avenue. The only one on the whole Pacific coast, a man told me. I stopped and watched it. When there was a lot of shouting, and everybody was looking at the car, a man took Venn. I hunted all over, maybe for an hour. When I found the man, he had Venn all tied up and he was dragging him along the street, right through mud puddles. I got awfully mad."

Emma looked at him thoughtfully. "You fought because you were angry."

"Sure." The question puzzled him. How could his mother think he would have started a fight otherwise?

"Fighting isn't something I want to teach you, even if I could. But it is important that you know how . . . not how to start a fight, but how to defend yourself. Your father would have . . ." A flicker of pain crossed her face, but when she continued, her voice was steady. "I can't teach you what your father would have, but I can tell you something I heard him say many times. He said angry men don't win fights, because when anger takes hold, it keeps your mind from working for you. The winner is the one whose fists are controlled by his brain. The winner *thinks*."

Throughout the conversation Mina hadn't spoken. After the excitement of reporting his victory began to ebb, Trygve noticed for the first time that everyone sounded subdued. Whenever his mother glanced at Mina, there was sadness in her eyes.

"Mina?" he asked. "Aren't you feeling well?"

Mina didn't seem to hear the question. Anna answered for her. "She started another baby. But this afternoon she lost it."

That was all Trygve needed to be told to understand his

sister's silence. He had never been excluded from the discussions between his mother and Anna about Mina's problems. Above all else, Mina wanted children. She had gone into marriage with an image of her first baby that was so real she made a list of names, numbering each of them in order of their succession. Einar would be the firstborn boy, Ilsa the first girl. Thomas for the second boy, Colleen the second girl. She had announced her first pregnancy with such pride that it became the most important event in the lives of every member of the family.

And then came the first heartbreaking miscarriage after Mina had carried the baby almost to term. Then a second pregnancy, before she had fully recovered from shock. Months later, a second stillborn infant. Last year a third baby, stillborn. Mina's despair was deeper and more visible with every loss.

Though frail, she had always been as lively and fun-loving as her younger sister. The family stood by helplessly as they watched her become more and more despondent with each failure to bear a living child.

Trygve had witnessed many of his sister's hysterical outbursts. Her reaction tonight was new and strange. Instead of venting her grief in fits of tears and bitter words, her feelings seemed locked inside. She was ominously quiet. He wished Tim were here; sometimes he was able to bring Mina out of her moods.

Without any warning Mina jumped up and ran out of the kitchen, without even closing the door behind her. For a moment the family sat in stunned silence. Then Emma murmured, "Dear Lord. Help my unhappy child."

At the door Trygve said, "Don't worry, Mama. I'll bring her back."

Fog drifting off Puget Sound had concealed every tree, shed, and cottage from which Trygve could take his bearings. He raced after Mina, stopping often to listen for a sound that would tell him whether she was near. He heard only the soft slap of an incoming wave rolling toward shore, and then a quiet hissing as the water pulled back and pebbles rolled over and over with the tide. Here and there he caught the muffled creaking of a fishing boat moored to a pier and tugging at its line as the receding water tried to take it out to sea.

The only light penetrating the darkness was the pale glow of parlor lamps in the windows of houses scattered along the narrow dirt road. In one such pool of light he saw Mina clearly, and knew she had seen him. But when he caught up to the spot where she had been standing, she was gone. Then he knew for certain that she was trying to elude him.

He pursued her doggedly, guided by the occasional glimpses he caught of her in places where lamplight spilled from a window into the fog. She was taking a zigzag course, darting between sheds and barns, appearing briefly, then vanishing again like a frightened fawn. Crazy as the path of her flight might seem, every change of direction was taking her closer to the water.

Trygve ran south along the beach until something at the edge of the water caught his eye. There in the wet sand was one of Mina's shoes, rolling over and over with the movement of the tide. Seconds later, he found Mina.

She was on her knees, making a sand castle as they had done when they were small children. He said, "Mina, I came to get you."

She looked at her castle, then at her hands, and wiped them carefully on her skirt. She didn't speak, but neither did she resist when Trygve pulled her to her feet. He took her hand, and she walked with him like an obedient but voiceless child. When they came to the shoe she had lost Trygve picked it up. Mina looked at it curiously and said, "I think that's my shoe."

"It is," Trygve replied. "Now let's go home."

The next day Mina's husband, Tim, received a telephone call in his office at the shingle mill. It was from the manager of Seattle's largest department store.

"I'm sorry I have to call you with this kind of news," a deep male voice told him. "I have a lady here who says you are her husband."

"Mina?" Tim exclaimed. "What's my wife doing there?"

Lowering his voice, the man said, "I'm afraid Mrs.

O'Donnell has been shoplifting. However, if you will come and take her home, we won't file a complaint. She doesn't seem to be . . . that is, has she been ill?''

When Tim walked into the store's business office, Mina smiled in recognition but did not speak. Tim hurried across the room, bent to kiss her, and said, "Mina, what did you take?"

Mina pointed mutely to an object on the manager's desk. A life-size baby doll, dressed in real baby clothes of fine white lace with embroidery around the neck. Tim reached into the pocket of his workpants and pulled out a worn leather wallet. "I'll buy it."

"Mr. O'Donnell, you are under no obligation to. That is, we have possession of the doll and all the baby clothes. I regret that—"

"Sir, I want to buy it," Tim said quietly. "How much is it?"

With a troubled frown the manager examined the price tag. "Twelve dollars."

Tim counted out twelve one-dollar bills, his wages for the entire week.

"I'll have someone wrap it for you."

But Mina had picked up the doll and was holding it to her breasts. "No, thank you," Tim said.

With Mina cradling the doll, Tim guided her out of the store and down the street to the trolley line that went to Ballard. On the long ride home, Mina spoke only to the doll. She didn't seem to know that Tim was beside her, though his arm was around her, holding her close.

9

Making deliveries for Mother Peersen's Home Bakery gave
Trygve his first exposure to the habits of people who lived
and worked in the city. In the beginning he studied the scene
like a traveler in a foreign land, whose interest in native
customs is limited to identifying the ways they are unlike his
own. But Trygve had a nimble mind and a fertile imagination. It did not take him long to dream that he would one day
live in a house like those he visited on his route and have his
own office in one of the largest buildings in downtown
Seattle. At the same time, he was as practical as any Peersen.
He knew it would take time to achieve these things. Nine
years, maybe ten. But he could start getting ready for it right
away.

Trygve's bakery route brought him to Seattle at least four
times a week. In the hour or so that he could squeeze in
between his last business call and the trolley ride to Ballard,
he explored the city. But the steady increase in sales of
Mother Peersen's Nordic specialties was creating a problem:
with each addition to his route, he lost some of his precious
leftover time. He was determined not to give it up, and
reasoned that if he worked out a more economical use of his
time, he wouldn't have to.

To that end he drew a detailed map of the city, marking the
location of each new customer and fitting it into his route
schedule so as to keep the time and distance covered to an
absolute minimum. There could be no more lingering. In
spite of his growing affection for the mountainous Mrs. Colter, he no longer paused there for coffee and conversation,

nor in other hotel kitchens, as he had been doing. With his long legs and powerful arms and shoulders, he came close to covering his route on a dead run. Even then, the growing demand for his mother's delicacies defeated him. There simply wasn't time for sightseeing in the land of his future. He allowed himself one exception—the county courthouse.

It was a handsome example of late-Victorian splendor—three or four architectural periods boldly assembled with little regard for authenticity and less for aesthetics. It looked down on the business district from the Olympian heights of Profanity Hill, so named by perspiring attorneys who had to walk six blocks up a street that seemed only a few degrees away from being perpendicular. It was the finest building Trygve had ever seen, but he didn't wander through it starry-eyed. He was there to study its functions, its departments, the judges and attorneys and clerks who walked its corridors with such impressive familiarity. He evaluated the people at work there soberly, as if at any moment he would have to choose which of them he wanted to become. No, he would not give up these excursions to Profanity Hill. Even when school started, he would somehow manage to make his deliveries and still prowl around the courthouse, if only for fifteen minutes at a time.

He soon made friends with a middle-aged telephone operator. Several clerks grew so used to seeing him that they smiled and nodded. On a truly wonderful day, he had his first talk with a judge.

He was lingering at the entrance to a courtroom, not sure whether he dared open the heavy oak door, when a voice at his back said, "Go ahead, son. Nothing in there's going to hurt you."

Trygve swiveled and met the amused eyes of a tall slender man with a handsome mane of coal-black hair, pink cheeks, and a pinker nose, the aroma of whiskey clinging to him as if it were his shadow. He had an amiable smile. "Want to watch a trial? Or someone you know in the courtroom?"

"No, sir. I was just curious."

"Nothing wrong with that. Your name, son?"

"Trygve. Trygve Peersen. I live in Ballard."

"I'm Judge Thomas. I live in the biggest and ugliest house on the sacrosanct slopes of Capitol Hill."

A *judge,* Trygve stared in wonder, unable to assimilate the fact that he was talking to a man who was not only a judge but also a resident of Capitol Hill. "I go to Capitol Hill a lot. My mother makes pastry and cakes and cookies, and I deliver them. I guess I've seen most of those big houses, and they're really beautiful."

"Oh, they are!" the judge said solemnly.

The salesman in Trygve suddenly came to the fore. "If you tell me where you live, I'll bring you some of my mother's baking."

"Three-hundred-fifteen Ponderosa. The red brick house at the corner of Ponderosa and West Beach." The notebook and pencil in Trygve's shirt pocket caught his eye. "I see you're a student."

His manner was serious, free of the condescension Trygve had come to expect from so many of his elders. He responded by entrusting the judge with the most secret of all his hopes. "Yes, sir. I mean, I go to school. I'm in the eighth grade. But this notebook doesn't have anything to do with that. I'm studying to be a judge. I come here as often as I can, mostly to listen and watch the people who work here. I use this notebook to write down the words I don't understand. The next day I look them up in the big dictionary they have at the high school."

"A judge?" Judge Thomas shook his head. "And will you be an honest judge or the usual kind?"

"Oh, an honest judge."

"We could use a few more. By the way, I'm a federal judge and do not inhabit these county precincts except to keep tabs on former colleagues. My courtroom is on the corner of Fourth and Marion. Come see me. I'd like to help with your notebook. Meanwhile, go forth, young Diogenes! Hold your lantern high!" With that the judge walked away, leaving Trygve to struggle with the problem of how to look up the word "Diogenes" when he hadn't the least idea of how to spell it.

The conversation with Judge Thomas spurred Trygve on to further study of courthouse activities. The judge had been slightly intoxicated, but his reference to honesty left a persistent aftertaste, fitting perfectly into the conversation with his father when the two of them were perched on the roof of a waterfront warehouse waiting for the *Portland* to arrive. Until today he'd forgotten the figure they saw that morning, dressed in a morning coat, striped trousers, and dark green vest—a man so impressed with his own importance that he obviously set himself apart from the common throng. We could use more honest judges, Judge Thomas had said. Was he talking about *that* man?

"That man," his father had said, "is a judge, elected by the people. I voted for him myself. But lately there have been ugly rumors. They say he has gotten too rich too quickly. That he breaks the law but is never caught because he has friends in high places. Nothing has been proved. Some think he's mixed up with ships and shipbuilders, but no one has any proof of that, either." If it was true that the man in the black bowler had secret dealings with shipyards, was he somehow connected with the yard that launched the *Gypsy Queen*?

From that day on, Trygve's interest in the courthouse narrowed down to a specific search. First, for the name of the judge in the black bowler hat, because he had forgotten it. Second, to uncover the link, if there was one, between the judge and the *Gypsy Queen*. Because, in Trygve's mind, the owner of the *Gypsy Queen* had killed his father.

A few days later Trygve slipped into a courtroom when a trial was in progress and there on the bench was the judge he had been trying to identify. He left the courtroom hastily and found the name he had forgotten on a bulletin board just outside the door. The Honorable Timothy W. Dorsett.

He bolted out of the courthouse, raced down the hill to the waterfront, and on to the shipyard that had sent the rotting *Queen* out to sea. He was out of breath when he charged through the door of the yard's dingy little office and demanded to know the name of the owner.

A rough-cut laborer was seated at the only desk, his boots resting on top of it and his plump arms hugging his belly. He looked up at Trygve with sleepy eyes. "The owner? Well, you can't see him because he ain't here."

"When will he come back?"

With a tired sigh, the man lowered his feet to the floor and walked to the counter. "He won't. He's dead."

"Dead! You mean . . ."

"I mean he got himself killed."

Trygve blinked, too startled to know what to say next. Killed! And the man made it sound as if the owner of the yard was down the street getting a shave. Now he was grinning, obviously pleased with the effect of his words. "Yeah. You heard it right. Killed. Dead. Stabbed to death."

More shocked by the brutal manner in which this tough old wharf rat referred to the death of another man than he was by the brutality of the deed itself, Trygve asked, "When did it happen?"

"Back a couple of months. July, maybe." He picked up the newspaper on top of his desk and slapped it onto the counter in front of Trygve. "It's all right here in the paper. Read for yourself."

It was a short piece. At nine A.M. in the county courthouse there was to be a coroner's inquest into the death of Jake Lund, owner of Lund Shipping, whose body was found July 28 in back of the Eastern Star Saloon. The inquest had been delayed because of certain technicalities . . .

Trygve folded the newspaper and handed it to the man behind the counter. "Thank you very much."

"It was his own goddamned fault," the man said. "Messing around in Jap Town is buying trouble. Jake should of known better. What happened to him happens down there all the time."

So Trygve's search for the owner of the *Gypsy Queen* had come to an abrupt end. The man responsible for launching the boat was lying in the county morgue. Trying to find a link between Judge Dorsett and his father's drowning was a fool's errand. Or was it? If digging for the truth proved that Dorsett had no interest in Lund Shipyard, wasn't that just as important to Trygve's search as proving that he did? A new thought began to form. "Have you worked here for a long time?"

"Long enough."

"Then you were here when they fitted out the *Gypsy Queen*?"

The man's eyes narrowed. "That old tub? Not me. I was around some, but I never worked on the *Queen*. I'm not a shipwright. I do cleanup, lifting and hauling, heavy work."

"But you were in the yard the day she put to sea?"

"That day? Hell, I don't remember where I was, but I wasn't here. I was probably getting drunk at Mack's. I do that a lot. What do you want to know all this for?"

Trying to make his manner casual, Trygve replied, "My English teacher gave us an assignment to write about one of the ships that go to Alaska. Any ship. And I picked the *Gypsy Queen*."

"Well, there's only one man could help you with that story, kid, and someone in Jap Town shut him up for good. I guess you'll just have to write about some other ship."

"Sure. I guess I will. Unless maybe . . ."

The man said irritably, "Unless maybe what? I tell you, you're talking to the wrong man."

"But isn't there someone else, someone besides Mr. Lund, who could help me write about the *Queen*?"

"If there is, I don't know him. And, say, tell me something about that English teacher of yours. I got a boy in school, and it don't start for another two weeks. How come you're back at school already?"

"I guess some schools start earlier than others," Trygve said as he went through the door, closing it carefully behind him.

So far the definition of a coroner's inquest had not made its way into Trygve's notebook. But he was there at nine o'clock, a lone spectator at the back of the courtroom. Yesterday at the shipyard he had found what he was looking for—the identity of the person who had caused his father's death: Jake Lund. What more was there to find out? But he listened, he watched, and occasionally wrote a few words in his notebook. He was studying to be a judge, after all, and this was one of the lessons.

There were three witnesses. The landlady of the boardinghouse where Lund had lived for the past three months. The police officer who had been sent to the scene of the crime. And the man who had discovered Lund's body.

The last was a slender young Japanese. To Trygve's immense surprise, he answered the examiner's questions in meticulous English.

"Your name?"

"Katamari Tamesa."

"Age?"

"I am twenty-two years old."

"Place of birth?"

"Yokohama, the Kanagawa prefecture, Japan."

"Present occupation?"

"I am a student at the University of Washington."

"Will you please tell us what you know about Jacob Lund, whose body . . ."

Up until then it had been a dull lesson, this hearing. Monotonous questions and mumbled answers about a man who, in Trygve's mind, was as guilty of murder as the person who in turn murdered him. When Trygve was confronted with a young man lucky enough to be a student at the University of Washington, his interest was suddenly revived, even though all that Tamesa could contribute to the hearing was the simple fact that he had been the first to find the body. After the hearing, in violation of everything he had learned about the rudeness of asking personal questions, Trygve was waiting in the corridor when the Japanese came out. Hurrying after him, he called, "Mr. Tamesa!"

The young man stopped and turned around. "Yes?"

Trygve had seen many Orientals, but they were laborers working on a railroad, or in a logging camp, or as seasonal field hands in the vegetable farms south of the city. The man he was now facing was a gentleman. His tailored business suit said so, and so did the way he waited courteously for Trygve to speak.

"Please excuse me, Mr. Tamesa. I was in the courtroom, and I heard you say you go to the university."

Tamesa acknowledged that he did with a slight nod of the head, as formal as a ceremonial bow. "I do."

Trygve said proudly, "That's what I'm going to do too. I thought maybe I could talk to you about it."

"I am on my way to my hotel. Would you like to walk along?"

"Oh, yes! Thanks."

Tamesa said quietly, "Have you ever been in Nihon Machi, Japan Town?"

"No. I heard about it some."

"Ah, yes. You know then that it is not a nice place."

Trygve nodded. "Well, I didn't hear much. Just that . . ." He broke off. "That's where you live?" It was more of an exclamation than a question. What he knew about Japan Town was that people smoked pipes filled with opium there and street girls sold themselves for pennies. It was unthinkable that a university student, even a Japanese, would make that shameful corner of the city his home.

"Yes, that is where I live. Are you sure you want to walk there with me?"

"I'm sure," Trygve said stoutly.

Nihon Machi, the district, was a network of narrow alleys on a slope above the waterfront. The roofs of warehouses and the tall masts of sailing vessels could be seen to the west. A pall of smoke hung over the railroad yards to the south. It was a cheerless place by daylight, dimly lit by paper lanterns at night, reeking at all times of sweat and alcohol and horse manure. Low wooden buildings and crude outdoor stalls squatted on both sides of the street. Saloons, grocery stores, gambling dens, cafés, tobacco and dry-goods shops, and pool halls occupied the ground floor. In their damp, cold basements were living quarters consisting of large rooms, each furnished with sixty to seventy wooden bunks. The liveliest trade prospered on their second floors—the brothels.

Those with a sign on the door stating "Whites Only" entertained white men exclusively, although no such restriction applied to the entertainers. The second category was the "Pink Hotel," where most patrons were Japanese but blacks and whites were equally welcome. The girl waving and calling from any second-floor window might be a Japanese *hakujinche*, white man's bird, and most probably an illegal alien from a rural Japanese prefecture. Or she might be a veteran white professional who had gotten a little old for San Francisco and in a few more years would head north for Dawson City.

As they walked, it became harder and harder for the boy to believe that Katamari Tamesa was living in an area no decent person would think of entering. Tamesa told Trygve that his father was a prominent businessman, the moving force behind Nippon Yusen Kaisha's [Japan Mail Steamship Company Ltd.] decision to strengthen ties between Japan and the United States by opening a shipping route between Yokohama and Seattle. Katamari was his eldest son. With his father's permission, he was studying economics at the University of Washington. He was to remain no longer than a year before returning home to step into his predestined role as an executive in international shipping.

When they crossed First Avenue and turned left onto Jackson Street, the boundary of Japan Town, Katamari said, "Now we have arrived. We will say good-bye."

"Do we have to? I mean, can't we talk for a little while?"

"Certainly, if you wish to. But at another place."

"But you live here."

"Yes."

"Well, then, it can't be such a bad place. I mean, there are all kinds of apartments and hotels nearer than this to the university, but you're staying here."

Such boyish innocence brought a smile to Tamesa's face. "I know. When I arrived in April, I had a list of good hotels provided by the steamship office in Yokohama. So I left my trunks on the pier and walked around the city. My intention was to choose one of the hotels on my list to be my home for a year. I was so excited and so curious, it was quite some time before I began to notice the way people on the street stared at me. Then I heard someone yell *'sukebi!'* It means 'dirty man.' I was not wanted in that part of the city. So I turned back and came to the only place where I am allowed to rent a room, no matter how much money I have to pay for it. I have never known such humiliation. I have not told my father, for such treatment of his eldest son would be an even greater humiliation to him than it is to me. You see, Trygve, my father has never been in America. He believes I am living in a hotel like the one in Tokyo where he and I have often been together. No man may enter that hotel unless he is wearing a silk top hat." He paused, and then added, "There is a proverb I have heard from the lips of many Japanese living here in Seattle about trying to mingle with whites. The proverb is that the nail which sticks up will be hit."

Trygve's indignation had been rising like a sudden fever. "That's no way to treat a . . . I mean, those people who stared and yelled at you have no right to act like that."

"It isn't a matter of right. It is a fear, the fear people have of someone very different from themselves."

"Well, I'm not afraid," Trygve said stoutly.

"And you wish to come with me, to walk through Japan Town."

"Yes, I do. You don't have to worry about me, Mr. Tamesa."

Only five blocks away the sidewalks were crowded with women in silk and bombazine dresses and merchants in high white collars and neatly trimmed beards. The cobbled streets resounded with the metallic clatter of horse-drawn freight wagons and an occasional brougham from First Hill. Trygve found he was walking through filth and bad odors and shrill noises. His well of questions had gone dry by the time they reached the Dawson House, Tamesa's hotel.

It was a two-story building wedged between a freight company's horse barn and a Japanese bathhouse. In a community of sad and sooty structures, it was noticeably more pathetic than its neighbors. Tamesa hesitated at the door. With a sympathetic glance at Trygve's face, he said, "Please come inside so that we may drink tea together."

Trygve had never seen such a place. The Dawson House was a long narrow room. An elaborately carved mahogany bar ran the length of the wall to his left. A huge mirror covered the wall behind the bar, so that customers perched on stools could stare at themselves as they drank. The opposite wall was a showplace for a dozen life size paintings of nude women. White women, all of them, whose fleshy contours, pale nipples, and abundant pubic hair cast mirror images that the men on bar stools could enjoy without turning around.

Small wooden tables and upright chairs were arranged at random in the center of the saloon. Tamesa stopped at one of these and waited politely for Trygve to sit down before he took the other chair.

A Japanese girl in kimono and cotton shoe-stockings glided across the floor. "You like some sake?"

"Tea, if you please."

Trygve's eyes followed the girl as she left to prepare their tea. She was tiny, smaller than children in the third and fourth grade in Ballard. "How old is she?"

"I think eleven."

"That's too young to be working in a place like this!" Trygve blurted it out and realized as soon as he'd spoken how discourteous it was to refer to Tamesa's home that way. "Please excuse me."

"There is no reason to apologize. You are right. This is not the place for her, and not the place for me. We are both here because of things we cannot change—the color of our skin, the shape of our eyes, our strange sing song voices."

"Why doesn't somebody *do* something?"

"You are young now," Tamesa said quietly. "I hope your indignation will not lessen as you grow older."

The solution popped into Trygve's mind as if it had been waiting impatiently for him to acknowledge its presence. "Where is your room?"

"My room?" Tamesa repeated with a smile. "It is in the basement."

"Aren't there any hotel rooms upstairs?"

"They are used by the girls. In the basement there are nine rooms, and in each of those nine rooms there are fifty beds. For one of them I pay seventy-five cents a day, and also receive my meals. I am more fortunate than many. At the Hashimotoya Hotel, there is one room for seventy beds."

"Mr. Tamesa," Trygve announced, "from now on you're going to live at my house. You will have a clean room and my mother will cook your meals. I'm going to take you home right now."

Trygve's impulsive acts had seldom been foolish. "It's not that he's rash," Einar had once said. "It's that he gets more ideas than the rest of us, and does good things before we've had time to think about them." On a recent afternoon, he had come home leading a milk cow and had startled Emma with the news that it belonged to him. As always when

Trygve got one of his impulses, his plan made good sense once he explained it.

Milk was a necessary ingredient in almost all of Mother Peersen's products. Emma had been buying it from Farmer Dahlgren—more and more of it as her need for butter and whipping cream kept pace with the steadily increasing sale of her pastries. Dahlgren suffered from rheumatism, the poor farmer's common complaint. His hands were now so crippled that milking a herd of Guernseys was a daily ordeal. Loading five-gallon milk cans onto the wagon was even more painful. He had no sons to help him, and his wife wasn't strong enough to do more than the cleaning and scalding of the milk cans.

The placid creature Trygve had in tow was the farmer's best milker. He announced with pride that she was producing two gallons a day of creamy milk that was almost as rich as a Jersey's. The cow was his by act of barter—in exchange for milking Dahlgren's herd and loading up the wagon. There would be no expense in feeding her, he assured his mother. Emma had not realized until that moment that her son's treasury of information included so much about the care and feeding of dairy cows.

"You see, Mama," Trygve said, "east of the mountains where it's dry, a farmer figures he needs four acres of pasture for every cow. Here the rain makes a difference. Everything grows fast and keeps green, so it's the other way around. Four cows to one acre. Between our place and Tim and Mina's, we've got around three acres. You don't have to buy milk anymore."

"That's wonderful. But, Tryg, how can you work on Dahlgren's farm and make your deliveries in Seattle? It's hard enough for you as it is, and it will be much harder when school starts."

"Don't worry, Mama."

Emma, with a bemused smile, gave up and said, "I'll try not to."

When Trygve appeared at the back door with Katamari Tamesa, it struck Emma that the young Japanese was as much a hostage as Farmer Dahlgren's cow. When Trygve stated that henceforth Mr. Tamesa was going to live with them, Tamesa protested that he couldn't consider such an imposition.

Emma had developed a certain amount of tolerance toward her son's extemporaneous arrangements, but this sudden addition to her household caught her off guard. She was embarrassed because it was plain that the young Japanese was embarrassed too. So the more earnestly Tamesa insisted that of course he could not live in her home, the more energetically Emma insisted that he must. Trygve didn't seem to share their problem or even to know they had one. He was busy describing the squalor of the places he had seen that afternoon and the crimes committed by uptown white hotelkeepers who refused to let a Japanese have a room.

After several minutes, Emma's sense of tradition took over. There was a stranger in her house and she had not offered him food or drink. She went about correcting the error with such authority that, in Tamesa's code, refusing to sit down in the kitchen's only comfortable chair or to accept the glass of plum wine she put into his hand would have been extremely disrespectful.

"I admire your beautiful English," Emma said. "And you've only been here since April! What a talent you have for languages, to learn so much in only six months' time."

Katamari spoke quietly, spacing his words so that his simplest statement had a ceremonial tone. "I thank you for your compliment, Mrs. Peersen, but the credit goes to my father, not to me. I am the eldest son. It is my destiny to sit one day in my father's office. In order to prepare me for that position and the close commercial ties between our two countries, he hired an American to tutor me."

Trygve already knew that Katamari had learned English from a tutor, but the purpose of the tutoring was new to him. "You mean that after just a few more months, you're going to leave the university and go back to Japan to work for your father?"

"He expects me to do so," Katamari answered, but not, it seemed to Trygve, as if he were happy about it.

Emma had an uneasy moment when they took their places at the table. For the first time, the thought struck her that the typical Norwegian contents of the big white tureen might be strange food to set before a Japanese. "This is *Bergens fiskesuppe*," she said as she dipped a china ladle into the soup. "That means fish soup, as it is prepared in Bergen. There it would be made with coalfish. Here it is cod, freshly caught this morning, cooked with parsnips and celeriac and carrots, and thickened with sour cream and egg yolks. Those are fish dumplings on the top. I hope it will taste good to you."

"Mama!" Trygve interjected. "Do you know what they give him to eat in the Dawson House? Rice! Just plain rice, soaked in vinegar. And seaweed, and pickles, and that's all!"

"Well, then," Emma said proudly as she filled a bowl and offered it to Tamesa, "this is simple food, but it will give you more strength than rice and pickles."

As the meal progressed, Emma lost her sense of Tamesa's strangeness in her kitchen, and Tamesa's extreme formality began to ease. By the time they had finished, Emma was asking Tamesa questions as naturally as if he were a cousin she hadn't seen for a long time, and Tamesa was answering without the stilted speech he had first used. After dinner, Emma served him the traditional coffee—strong, black, and clarified with egg shells—and then taught him how to drink it through a sugar cube tucked under his lower lip. That night she sent him to sleep in the bedroom that had been Mina's when she lived at home. In the morning she gave him a breakfast of thick oatmeal sweetened with wild honey and enriched by the bounty of Trygve's cow. Then, ignoring Tamesa's diminishing protests, she sent him off to Japan Town with instructions to be back in time for supper with all his clothes and books and whatever possessions he might have in his basement bedroom at the Dawson House.

"I am grateful," Tamesa said, "but you must understand that it would be shameful to me to come into your home without doing my part. If I share your food, you must allow me to share its expense. I am a simple student, ignorant of such things as you and your son are able to do. I do not know how to bake or cook. I do not know how to milk a cow. But I do have money, and that you must be willing to accept from me."

"Fair enough," Emma said thoughtfully. "Yes, I do understand. What have you been paying at the Dawson House?"

"Ah, but Mrs. Peersen! That is not nearly enough. I cannot— "

"Seventy-five cents a day," Trygve put in helpfully. "Meals included."

"Then that's what it will be here," Emma said firmly. "To borrow your own words, it would be shameful to me to accept a penny more. And now, the subject is closed. You will come home for dinner by six o'clock."

10

When Professor Whiting summoned Anna to his library and announced he would have two guests at tea the next day, she knew it was not going to be a casual occasion. While Sarah's mother was alive, there were frequent parties—formal dinners, lawn parties with fringed tents and musicians playing Viennese waltzes, teas for faculty wives, Sunday-evening coffee-and-dessert parties. Since Philomen's death, there had been no parties of any kind. Anna had often wondered if the abrupt end to the laughter and conviviality was one of the reasons sociable little Sarah felt so lost without her mother. Now, incredible as it seemed, Professor Whiting was giving the sort of party he had always ranked as the most unnecessary and futile of all social occasions.

"There will be five," he said, much as he would dictate to a class of first-year college students. "Sarah, Benjamin, and myself. Two guests. A lady and her son, Kurt, who is Benjamin's age. I will leave you to decide what sort of embellishment should be served with the tea."

"Do you think your guests would like my mother's sweets?"

Something like an amused twinkle appeared in the professor's austere gray eyes. "I thought you might make that suggestion. Yes, by all means."

"And besides the pastry, some little *smorebrod*?"

He dismissed the question with a wave of the hand. "My dear Anna, your business is to plan the tea. Mine is to continue work on my lecture notes. Oh, yes, one last detail. I am aware of the fact that tomorrow is Thursday. Unfortunately, it's the best day for my guests. I would be much obliged if this week you could take Friday as your day off.''

Back in the kitchen Anna set about listing the dishes she would prepare and the ingredients she would need to make them. She was happy that Professor Whiting was going to entertain, though two guests for afternoon tea did not seem like much of a party. At the same time there was something about the professor's sudden sociability that made her uneasy.

Why was he including his children? He had always insisted that boys and girls under eighteen years of age had no place in the social life of their elders. To Anna the tea party sounded like trouble for the little girl she had come to love so much.

At noon the next day, there were two Peersens in the Whiting kitchen. Anna and Trygve, because he had brought the tiny cakes his mother baked that morning. Since he had never gone farther inside the mansion than the kitchen, he was trying to make himself useful so he would be allowed to stay, perhaps catching a glimpse of a high-society tea party. His job was twofold: to polish Mrs. Whiting's elaborate silver tea service and to keep out of the way.

Like an art student painting a still life, Anna had designed small open-face sandwiches in the finest tradition of a Danish *smorebrod* Emma Peersen insisted that nothing but genuine Norwegian recipes would ever be permitted to come out of Mother Peersen's ovens. However, when more cakes would be sold if they slipped something typically Danish or typically Swedish into the camp of the typically Norwegian, her daughter was not so uncompromising. Assembled on the kitchen table were sandwich makings as authentic as any in Copenhagen's finest café.

When all was ready Anna set up the tea service on the dining-room table. She would fill the cups and carry them to the living room.

Trygve offered to help by following Anna with the *smorebrod* and pastry. She smiled at his eagerness but shook her head. ''Dressed like a farmhand? No, Litt Bror. Besides, I don't want Sarah to know you're here. If she does, she'll forget about being polite to the company and come running after you. So you keep out of sight. Understand? Out of sight!''

In midafternoon, Anna laid out the fresh pinafore, starched petticoat, and black patent leather Mary Janes that Sarah was to wear. She went up to Sarah's bedroom shortly before the guests were expected and was relieved to see that the child was fully dressed. Sarah had complied with all instructions except that of brushing her hair, a chaotic tangle of soft red curls that hadn't been touched since breakfast.

Anna picked up Sarah's hairbrush and beckoned. Sarah came to her reluctantly. "I hate to have my hair brushed. It hurts. Why do I have to get dressed up anyway? Father never wants me to talk. I don't know who the lady is, but she won't want me to talk, either."

"It won't hurt to be polite," Anna said, tugging energetically on a strand of Sarah's long wavy hair. "You need a little practice at that. I know you don't like tea, but when you have company, you don't make a face and say, 'I don't want to drink that nasty stuff' the way you did once. Oh, yes, you did! I remember. Your father wants me to pour the tea. When I offer you a cup, you take it, Sari. Are you listening? Just take the cup, and when it's cooled a little, sip on it, don't gulp it all down at once as if it's some kind of smelly medicine. And another thing. There are going to be cakes and tarts, and a dozen kinds of sandwiches. You are *not* going to stand over the sandwich tray and pick up one after another and take a bite out of each one and put the rest back on the tray if you don't like it. Oh, yes, I've seen you do that too. With my own eyes, and how glad I was I was the one to see it, not your father. So be a good girl, and when it's over, you come into the kitchen. I'm going to save you some cookies so you won't fade away before supper, and I'll make you some cambric tea.'

"I wish it was over. I hate this. I hate—"

"Sssshh! No more of that. The doorbell just rang. The company is here. Put a smile on your face. You have a pretty smile. Let the lady see it."

Anna gave Sarah a gentle shove toward the wide central staircase and went down to the kitchen by way of the servants' stairs in the back of the house.

While his sister was busy in the dining and living rooms, Trygve got away with more peeking than Anna would have allowed. He decided very quickly that if what he saw and heard was the way rich people enjoyed themselves, he couldn't blame Sarah Whiting for hating tea parties. The only person who seemed at ease was a beautiful woman he judged to be his mother's age. Her dark hair, streaked with silver at the temples, was brushed straight back from her face and wound into a heavy coil at the nape of her neck. He couldn't see the color of her eyes, but they were unusually large and striking in a pale and delicate face. She was dressed in gray silk, the same silvery shade as the sweep of hair at her temples. A gray lady, except for the nosegay of pink silk roses nested on one side of her gray velvet hat. An elegant lady with a soft voice and a warm smile.

But the others! Sarah was sitting on a carved mahogany chair so large that her feet weren't touching the floor. She was watching them intently as she swung them back and forth. She and her Mary Janes could have been alone in the room. The rangy youth in the chair next to her had to be her older brother, Ben. He looked like a serious-minded boy, with a pleasant face and nothing of his sister's irritating snap and sparkle. At the moment Sarah was as silent as Ben, but Trygve had already learned that silence didn't come naturally to her. If Ben wasn't listening intently, at least he was pretending to. Sarah was showing no interest whatever in anything but her shiny patent-leather shoes.

Professor Whiting stood with his back to the fireplace, a teacup in one hand. Trygve had imagined that a university professor would be much older. Though his hair was graying, the professor had no pouches or deep wrinkles in his fine patrician face, no sagging of his lean, erect body. In precise tones he was addressing all conversation to the gray lady, with an occasional polite question for her son, a boy with hostile eyes and petulant mouth whom Trygve disliked on sight.

How different it all was from his own home, where parties were seldom planned, they just happened. There was hearty laughter and hearty food and more party spirit in the small kitchen than the Whitings' richly furnished sitting room had ever seen, if this joyless occasion Trygve saw through a crack in the kitchen door was a fair sample. One day he would have a house as big and as fine as this, but it was going to be a happy place.

The stiff smiles and polite questions continued as Anna refilled the cups and passed the trays of pastry and sandwiches. Then, at a nod from the professor, Anna retired to the kitchen, where she whispered, "I'm not supposed to go back in there unless he rings the bell."

"What's going on?" Trygve asked hoarsely. "Who's the lady?"

"Her name is Mrs. Bauermeister, nosy. I saw you peeking around the corner like an old-maid busybody. Well, if you can peek, so can I. Hush! The professor just started talking to Sarah and Ben. If you keep asking questions, I can't hear what he's saying."

Minutes later, Anna backed away and closed the door. Her face was pale. Turning she said, "He just told the children that he and Mrs. Bauermeister are going to be married. My poor little Sari! He said to her, 'You will soon have a new mother.' Of all the ways he could have explained it, how could he understand her so little that he would choose that way!"

"There's nothing you can do about it." Trygve said. "Maybe, in the long run, it's all for the best."

Anna shook her head. "She's a lovely lady. In fact, she reminds me quite a bit of Sari's own mother. But that isn't going to help. That will just make it worse." Anna poured herself a cup of coffee and sat at the kitchen table.

Trygve resumed his post at the kitchen door. Sarah hadn't moved from her perch on the mammoth mahogany chair, but her pendulum feet had stopped swinging. She was staring mutely at the gray lady while Benjamin got to his feet and said, "Mrs. Bauermeister, we want to say . . . Sarah and I want to say we wish you and our father happiness, and we hope you will like it, living here."

"Thank you, Benjamin. And, dear Sarah, please understand, I will never try to come between you and your memories of your mother, one of the sweetest women I've ever known, because I remember her too, Sarah. She and I were friends many years ago, before Mr. Bauermeister and I moved to his country, Germany."

Sarah slid off her chair and advanced to the middle of the room, where she stood with fists clenched, facing Mrs. Bauermeister. "You don't have any right to live in this house. You are sitting in my mother's chair! That is my mother's place! And that is *my mother's* teacup!"

The professor, white-lipped, broke into the tirade. "Enough!" he said furiously. "You have shamed me and embarrassed Mrs. Bauermeister. Go to your room and remain there until I have given permission for you to leave it."

Looking straight into Mrs. Bauermeister's eyes, Sarah whispered, "You are not my mother. You are not my mother," and then turned and ran out of the room.

Sarah's angry outburst and the professor's order carried into the kitchen. Anna jumped up from the table and hurried up the servants' stairs to Sarah's bedroom. She was still in the rocking chair with Sarah in her arms when the murmur of voices in the hall below and the sound of a closing door told her that Mrs. Bauermeister and her son had left the house.

Moments later, Professor Whiting strode into the room. He was there to dole out punishment and there were no preliminaries. "My daughter," he said stiffly, addressing himself to Anna, "will stay in bed for one week. Not in her usual bed in this room, but in the bed on the sleeping porch, where the fresh air may help to clear her mind and her conscience. She must also be reminded of her duty, and for that reason she is to have no playthings, and nothing to read other than the Bible. Her meals will be brought to her, but you are not to remain there and coddle her, for that encourages her selfishness. At the end of the week, I will come to talk to her. I hope to find her healthier in mind, and then I will discuss the future."

Back in the kitchen, Anna described the scene upstairs. "Nothing to read but the Bible!" she said indignantly. "Sari's only nine years old but she's already reading two books a week. I'm going to sneak some to her. She can hide them under the mattress when she hears someone coming."

Trygve shook his head. "Do you think you ought to go against her father's orders?"

"He is Professor Whiting doing what he thinks is right. I am Anna Peersen and I'm going to do what I think is right. If he catches me, I'll take my medicine. If he doesn't so much the better.''

Trygve was thoughtful. Sarah had been wrong to say such things. She was a hothead, a pesty little kid who didn't act much like a girl and certainly couldn't be favorably compared to Christina Franzen in any way. But he couldn't help feeling sympathy for her, and indignation at her father's harshness.

When he left to go back to Ballard, Trygve slipped around to the back of the house and stood below the open sleeping porch where Sarah was confined. He couldn't see her so he picked up several pebbles and lofted them one at a time to hit the screen enclosing the outdoor bedroom.

Sarah's face appeared immediately, like a little red-haired leprechaun peering around a tree. She smiled in delight, her pug nose pressed against the screen. He waved at her and she waved back, and then he left for home.

Since Anna had given up her free Thursday in order to serve tea, she was home the next day when a uniformed Seattle policeman appeared at the kitchen door with Sarah standing proudly at his side.

"Are you Anna Peersen, miss?"

Anna was too surprised to answer, so Sarah helped. "Yes, that's Anna."

"I think you know this child, do you, miss?"

Somewhat recovered, Anna retorted, "My goodness! Of course I do! Come on in, please. Sit down. I'll set out some coffee. Sari, whatever happened?"

"I found her on Front Street," the policeman explained. "Down near the waterfront. That's no place for a little girl to be alone. So I asked where she wanted to go and she said she was supposed to visit some people in Ballard. She knew your name, but she didn't know your address. Well, being as there's only two phones in the whole of Ballard, the one in the lumber-mill office and the one in the drugstore, I couldn't find you that way. I brought her here on the trolley. The first person I asked told me where you live."

The policeman drank his coffee, refused to accept money for the trolley fares he had paid out of his own pocket, and left with a polite good-bye to Anna and a grin and a wink for Sarah.

"Now, young lady," Anna said, "now that we're alone, I want to hear the whole story. *Not* the one you told the policeman."

Sarah had been alone on the sleeping porch since yesterday's disastrous tea party. Lonely as she was, bored as she was by the Sermon on the Mount and the Psalms and other parts of the Bible she could understand in spite of the funny language, her humiliation was not on display, so for a while she bore it stoically. If her father had permitted her to have a tablet and pencils, she would have kept busy writing stories. But he did not approve of her stories. Imagination is lazy thinking, he told her, an escape from discipline of the mind. So when she got impatient with the begats and doths and saiths of the King James Version, she lay on her back, closed her eyes, and began to make up stories in her head.

She was doing this when someone tapped on the window between her bedroom and the porch. Her eyes flew open. Kurt Bauermeister was at the window, staring at her with his pale blue eyes. She sat bolt upright and yelled, "You go away! Just you go away, Kurt Bauermeister!"

He shook his head and kept on staring. When she yelled again, he laughed. Sarah dropped back and pulled the covers over her head. Silence. . . . After a few minutes she lowered the blanket cautiously. Kurt was still there. When at last he left, she lay in bed trembling. He was gone for now, probably called away, but he would come back. His strange pale eyes would stare at her again. Hiding under the covers wouldn't close out his mocking laugh. She slipped out of bed, dressed quickly, went down the servants' stairs, and was out of the house without being seen.

At first, it was exciting. She didn't have any money to take a trolley, but she found her way downtown by following the trolley tracks. With every eager step she made up stories about a nine-year-old girl running away from home. But it was a long way from Capitol Hill to the city's noisy downtown area. She hadn't had lunch and she was hungry, tired, and beginning to suspect that running away works better if you have someplace to run to. That place, of course, was Ballard.

When the policeman stopped her and asked, "What is your name, little girl? Where do you want to go?" her answer was ready. "I am going to Ballard to visit my friend Anna Peersen."

"Well, now," the officer replied, "I think you took a wrong turn someplace. Best thing to do is to take you home."

"Oh, no!" Sarah said fervently. "You see, that's why I'm going to Ballard. My father is away on a trip, and I'm supposed to stay with Anna until he gets back."

"Why didn't he take you to Ballard himself?"

"Because I always go there by myself. Only this time, I got mixed up."

"You certainly did," the policeman agreed heartily. "It's quite a ways from here to your friend's house. I'll take you there." And so he escorted her to Ballard.

Anna listened patiently while Sarah pleaded her case for staying. It was only for a day, just until Anna went back to work early the next morning. Anna had so much baking to do, it would be good to have someone there to help her—

"Sari, stop a minute," Anna put in quietly. "You aren't thinking about your father. He was angry with you, yes, and he had a right to be. He was harsh, maybe too harsh, but that's his way. But I promise you this, little Sari, you won't feel better for making him suffer."

In the end Anna prevailed and it was agreed they would leave for Capitol Hill as soon as the last batch of spice cookies came out of the oven. Sarah was more reluctant to leave the Peersens' warm little house than she was to face her father. She wasn't afraid of him. She did foolish things, and she was punished for them. It would be that way now. Punishment happened, and then it was over.

When Trygve and Katamari Tamesa walked in, Sarah began to see the situation from a different perspective. Katamari intrigued her.

"Sarah, this is our friend Mr. Tamesa," Anna said. "He studies at the university and he lives here with us."

"How do you do," Katamari said, bowing slightly from the waist. "I have heard Miss Peersen speak of you often."

A Japanese who spoke English without hesitation and dressed like a gentleman was a new experience. And Anna had addressed him as "mister." The white people Sarah knew referred to Japanese merely by their first names. Only the presence of Trygve saved Katamari from Sarah's merciless curiosity. However interesting and different his friend might be, Trygve was the center of her most romantic stories. When she learned that he and Katamari were going to deliver boxes of Mother Peersen's baked goods to ten homes on Capitol Hill, Sarah realized it wouldn't be necessary for Anna to take her home. Ten boxes was a lot for two people to carry, so she would go along and help. After the last box was delivered, Trygve would take her to her father.

Repressing a smile, Anna agreed it was a sensible plan, because she wouldn't have to stop baking cookies. Trygve's objections were written all over his face, but a warning glance from his sister kept them locked inside his mouth.

The three set out together, Trygve and Katamari each carrying four large boxes securely tied into two stacks, and Sarah hugging two small cartons. At the kitchen window, Anna watched and laughed. Katamari was careful to walk at a pace Sarah could keep up with, while her embarrassed Litt Bror strode ahead as if making it hard for Sarah to stay beside him would keep her from asking questions. Sari looked ecstatic. She probably wouldn't even think about the Doomsday waiting in her father's library until the very last moment, when Trygve left her there to meet it alone. It occurred to Anna that Trygve liked the child a little in spite of himself. Katamari's example might shame him into being more patient with her than usual.

11

Friendship between Trygve and Katamari came naturally, despite the difference in their ages—Katamari's twenty-two years to Trygve's twelve. Each was protective of the other. Katamari anticipated that Trygve would be vulnerable to disappointment and hurt by failure; Trygve knew what people said about "those Japs," and wanted to shelter his friend from such insults. Yet they admired each other greatly, for different reasons. Katamari saw Trygve as a free spirit of the Western world, charging into the future without the benefit of wealth, distinguished parentage, or a reserved seat at the top of his country's caste system. By contrast, Trygve's admiration was boyishly simple. Katamari was not only a student at the University of Washington, he was one of the elite twenty-five who would graduate in the spring. He had seen places Trygve had only read about.

Their closest bond was that they were both up against seemingly insurmountable barriers concerning what they wanted to make of their lives. Trygve was penniless and unskilled and uneducated, but had decided he wanted to be a judge. Katamari's future was assured, provided he returned to Yokohama. If he defied his father and failed to go home at the end of the year, eight dollars a week for working in the back of a steamy Japan Town restaurant was all the prosperity he could count on.

Katamari's decision could be postponed until he graduated from the university, but Trygve's problem was immediate. During the summer, Katamari had taken over half of Mother Peersen's delivery route, so Trygve had been able to keep pace with the growing list of customers without neglecting Farmer Dahlgren's dairy herd. Now he was back in school, and it was going to be difficult as he was combining seventh and eighth grades. In only a year he would leap into high school at the age of thirteen, and since Ballard High was a two-year course, he would be fifteen when he presented himself for admission to the university. This was slim preparation. He needed as impressive an academic record as the village high school could provide.

"I know you learn quickly," Katamari said, "but you'll have subjects you haven't studied before. You ask too much of yourself to think you can milk cows twice a day and deliver baked goods, and still find the time you need to study."

"I have to work for Farmer Dahlgren. We haven't finished paying for our cow."

"I will pay for the cow. I have the money."

"But what happens to Mr. Dahlgren? He can't do heavy work, and selling milk is the only way he has to make a living."

"All right, you feel you must help the farmer. That's two hours in the morning, two or three in the late afternoon. But also delivering for your mother?"

Trygve didn't answer immediately. A plan had been forming in his mind for some time, and this morning he had tried it out on one of his schoolmates. "I have an idea," he began. "If it works, I won't make any deliveries, except maybe on Saturdays. A lot of boys at school want to make some money but they can't find anything to do. There's Henrik. He's my age but he's still in the fifth grade. He's not lazy and he's honest. I know at least six others, not slow-minded like Henrik, but they don't study more than they have to. I bet they'd all like to make deliveries for me. I'll pay them by the box, and give them carfare. And I'll have two or three boys as extras, ready to work when we have a really long list of deliveries, or when one of the regular boys gets sick."

The following Saturday morning, Emma Peersen's kitchen was the gathering place for seven boys eager for their first payday. Except for the cookies Emma kept replacing as fast as they disappeared, it was a solemn affair. Cookie crumbs stuck to their lips and chins but their watchful eyes observed Trygve's every move as he counted out the coins.

"Carl Peterson, six boxes. And here's carfare."

"But I didn't take the trolley," the boy said. "I walked."

"You get the carfare anyway. Everybody does. It's yours whether you walk or ride. Henrik? You delivered fourteen boxes. Here . . ."

Henrik, a gangly towhead, stepped out of the ranks and held out his hand. He watched in sheer wonder as Trygve dropped coins into his open palm. "I never got wages before. Next week I'll do more."

"More than fourteen? That's a lot of delivering. What about school?"

Henrik's simple face broke into a broad smile. "I talked to Miss Herter, and she said if I got a job, that was better for me than going to school. Heck, Trygve. I ain't never going to get out of the fifth grade, no matter how hard I try. My granddad says the same thing as my teacher."

Trygve looked thoughtfully at the oldest and strongest of his crew. "You see, Henrik, everyone here wants to make some deliveries. It's only fair to divide up the work. But I might have another job for you. On Dahlgren's farm. You know how to milk cows. Well, this is the way we'll work that out . . ."

Thus Trygve enlarged his role as an employer. In addition to a staff of seven laboring for him on a piecework basis, he had a full-time employee. The world of honest physical labor was Henrik's home. He got things right once they were explained to him, step by careful step. He took over a dozen heavy household chores, relieving Mrs. Peersen's burden as well as Trygve's

The only cloud on Trygve's financial horizon was that paying Henrik and the other boys was going to reduce Mother Peersen's income. As usual he discussed the problem with Katamari.

"Bakery sales are going up all the time," Katamari pointed out. "So sooner or later you would have to hire people to help, even if you weren't going to go to high school. What you need right now is another way to earn money until the business grows big enough to pay for help."

"Enough to put new soles on my boots," Trygve said with a grin. "Besides, I want to save up for a new kitchen stove. Anna will quit being a housemaid when she and Ivar get married next July, and then she's going to help Mother with the baking. Those two are going to need a bigger oven. But that won't happen for another nine months, because Ivar won't come home for good until next July. Right now, what I need is another five or six dollars a week."

"I've told you I have more money than I need."

"You paid for our cow," Trygve insisted. "That's enough. Besides, I'm beginning to think you aren't going to go back to Japan. That means you better hold on to every dollar you can, because starting next June you won't get any more."

Katamari nodded. "Will you allow me to make a suggestion?"

"Sure."

"There's a young man at the university who needs a place to live. If you and I occupied the same bedroom, your mother could rent a room to him. Right now he's living downtown."

"In the dormitory they set up in the old Territorial University building?"

Katamari shook his head. "He's not a student. He's a gardener, one of the crew working on the new campus. But even if he were studying at the university, he wouldn't be allowed to live in the dormitory."

"Why not?" Trygve asked indignantly.

"He's Japanese."

"Oh." Trygve clenched his fist at the invisible body of prejudice. "*That* again. But Ballard is just as far from the campus as downtown is. It won't make it easier for him to get to work."

"That won't matter to him. The only place he can get a room in the city is in Nihon Machi. You remember what my hotel was like. His is worse."

"Tell him to come live here. But tell him three dollars a week. We need five but I'll figure out a way to earn the other two."

Katamari's head bent ever so slightly in the spirit of a formal bow. "He will be happy."

At dinner that evening, Emma Peersen listened with interest to Trygve's proposal that she provide room and board at three dollars a week to a Japanese gardener named Kibun Sakai. She quickly approved of the plan. "You say he is a fine gardener. That is, for planting trees and flowerbeds. Does he know about raising vegetables?"

"Indeed he does, Mrs. Peersen. If you didn't need to use your land to pasture a cow, he would grow you the finest vegetable garden in all Ballard."

"We do need the cow . . ." Emma paused, tapping her upper lip with a forefinger. "Let's see. Tim and Mina have two acres they aren't using. There must be another two or three around the house Ivar built for Anna."

Trygve exclaimed, "That's four acres, maybe five. What a garden! There'd even be room for berries and fruit trees."

Emma smiled in amusement. "In the next breath you'll have us growing so much fruit and vegetables we'll have to open a cannery. Let's go back to our first step. First, the ground must be prepared. Mr. Sakai can do that over the winter. Then in the spring we will buy the seeds. As each crop comes in, there will surely be more than we can use fresh, and more than I have time to can. When that happens, Mr. Sakai will sell what we don't need, and that money will be his. By next fall . . ." She left the sentence unfinished, laughing because she sounded so much like her excitable son. "Next fall,' she said solemnly, "we will have to open a cannery."

12

Seattle *Daily Tribune*
November 3, 1897

Professor Jeremiah Whiting and Mrs.
Angela Bauermeister were united in marriage
November 1 in a quiet ceremony in the
First Congregational Church. The Rev.
Nicholas Paine read the service in the
presence of the couple's three children,
Sarah and Benjamin Whiting and Kurt
Bauermeister, and a small group of friends.

Professor Whiting is a renowned biolo-
gist, currently head of that department
at the University of Washington. Mrs.
Bauermeister is the former Angela Richards,
daughter of a Yakima Valley pioneer
family and a resident of this state until
her marriage to Heinrich Bauermeister, a
noted German lumberman.

The wedding reception was held in the
Whiting home on Capitol Hill.

From her listening post in the kitchen, Anna concluded that
the reception was going well enough. The murmur of sub-

dued voices was a sad thing compared with the boisterous merriment of a Norwegian wedding. But what do you expect? she asked herself. The professor will not have spirits or even beer in his house. Fruit punch! It's no wonder the whole celebration will be over in three hours. If it lasted a minute longer, the guests would start to fall asleep.

Trygve had been recruited to help Anna. Complaining loudly, he had allowed Anna to stuff him into a stiff waiter's jacket so he would be suitably dressed to help her set up the buffet supper. With every foray into the dining room, he made a surreptitious appraisal of the guests.

The bride was the beautiful lady in gray he had seen at the tea party many weeks before. Today she was dressed in a gown of stiff rose-colored silk. A string of pearls was woven into the plaited coronet of her dark hair, and she held her head erect, like a queen wearing a crown. Never far from her side was her son Kurt, home from military school, wearing a dusty-blue uniform with such a high collar that he kept thrusting out his chin as if to keep his head from slipping down out of sight. Trygve liked him no better today than he had the first time he saw him. Pale eyes, a thin-lipped mouth that didn't know how to smile, posture so rigid it was a rebuke to all the males in the room, who seemed, by comparison, to be slouching. He would go back to military school in the morning, and that, Anna confessed, was none too soon for her. "I never felt like a servant," Trygve had heard her tell Emma, "until His Majesty Kurt came into the house. He must favor his father. His mother's as soft and gentle as her name, Angela."

Each time Trygve returned to the kitchen. Anna asked, "How is Sarah doing?"

His reports didn't change. "Fine. Not talking much, but she *looks* polite."

"If she isn't making faces, that's as polite as we can expect her to be."

At last the supper was over and the guests retired to the living room for coffee and mints. Anna and Trygve sat down at the kitchen table. As she filled blue enamel cups from the steaming coffeepot at the back of the stove, Sarah burst through the kitchen door. Though she was dressed in a pink ruffled pinafore and high-top patent-leather shoes with pearl buttons, she looked like David, ready to demolish the first Goliath she ran into. Hands on her hips, head thrown back, green eyes sparkling with indignation, she announced, "Kurt Bauermeister makes me sick!" The statement was for Anna. Trygve, not three feet away from her, might not have been present. "Always bragging about his dumb military school, and how much better Germany is, and he knows all about those countries in Europe because he lived there, and no one in Seattle knows three languages the way he does, and if his father hadn't died—"

"Sssshh, Sari. Sshh!" Anna reached out and pulled the little girl toward her. "When you get excited your voice carries like a mad seagull's. You've been such a good girl. Don't spoil it now."

"Oh!" Sarah exclaimed, noticing Trygve. "I didn't know you were still here."

"Of course you didn't," Anna said, winking at Trygve. "He's kind of hard to see."

Kurt Bauermeister was forgotten as Sarah, now smiling happily, concentrated on her idol. "Have you ever been to Woodland Park?"

"Sure. The trolley to Green Lake goes through it. Whenever I go to the university, I ride—"

"Ben says they have some reindeer there, from Lapland. I've never been to Woodland Park, so you can take me."

"Well, I guess so," Trygve said uneasily. Then he suggested hopefully, "Maybe Ben would take you."

"He's already seen the reindeer."

"He might take you anyway. Why don't you ask him?"

"Oh, fiddle," Sarah said brightly. "He's just my brother."

To Trygve's enormous relief, Sarah's relentless pursuit of the subject broke off as abruptly as it had begun. "I want to show you something. It's in my father's library. Come with me."

Trygve glanced hopefully at Anne. "I've got to help clean up the kitchen."

"No, go ahead," Anna said cheerfully. "I'll get along fine."

"But you see, Sarah . . ." Darn this girl! "You see, I'm

not supposed to leave the kitchen except when I'm serving the guests.''

"Oh, fiddle," Sarah said again. "This is my house. If I want to show you something in my father's library, it's all right for you to come and see it. Because anyway, it's mine. I mean, someday it will be mine."

Trygve decided to surrender and followed her mutely down the hall past the living room and into the *sanctum sanctorum* of Professor Whiting's study.

Sarah went immediately to her father's large roll-top desk. She looked up at Trygve, her fingers resting on the ornate brass pull to the small drawer on the left. "It's in here. My father calls it a talisman. A talisman is a charm."

Didn't she think he knew anything at all? A nine-year-old girl telling a twelve-year-old boy the meaning of a word! "That's superstitious. People just think there is such a thing as a charm."

"I don't just think so, I know so. You know what it is? It's the copper penny I told you about. When my father was a little boy, he lived in Albany. After President Lincoln was shot, there was a funeral procession along the main street and my grandfather took my father to see it. There was a great big black hearse, with Lincoln's body inside, and it was pulled by four big black horses, with black plumes flying from the tops of their heads. When it rolled past the spot where my father and grandfather were standing, my grandfather threw a penny under the wheels, and it got scrunched. Just before my grandfather died, he gave the penny to my father. When my father gets very old, he'll give it to Ben and me. It's inside this little drawer. I'm not allowed to take it out, but I can look at it anytime I want to."

Sarah's bright eyes watched Trygve's face expectantly as she pulled slowly on the brass handle. She saw the terrible truth in his eyes even before she looked herself. The drawer was empty except for a few postage stamps.

"It isn't here!" she cried in a stricken voice. Her fingers searched the meager pile of stamps. "The penny's gone! It's supposed to be here. It's *always* here . . ."

"Maybe your father put it in a different drawer. Like there, on the right." In spite of himself, Trygve felt sympathy for

Sarah. Her distress was so real he could not help sharing it. "Try the drawer on the other side."

"That's not where it belongs," Sarah objected, but she opened the second drawer and groped through it. Not finding the penny there either, she began frantically opening every drawer in the desk. At her back a voice asked, "Is this what you're looking for?"

Kurt Bauermeister was standing just inside the library, one arm extended with a small object pinched between thumb and forefinger. His pale eyes gleamed with malicious amusement as he crossed the room, holding the treasured talisman aloft, until he was so close to Sarah that he was looking down at the top of her head. "Come on, midget. Jump for it."

Trygve said angrily, "Give that back!"

"Ho, ho! You go back to the kitchen. Come on, Sar-*ruh*! You want your stupid penny? Try to get it."

Sarah charged into Kurt's midriff like an infuriated tiger. He gasped and backed up a step, but the penny remained secure, held tantalizingly over her head. "Come on, come on! Try harder! Jump, Sar-ruh, jump."

Sarah rushed again, this time kicking blindly at Kurt's legs. Pale eyes burning angrily, he slapped her hard across the face.

A second later Trygve's left hand smashed into Kurt's jaw and his right fist drove into Kurt's stomach in a blow so sudden and fierce that Kurt grunted and dropped to the floor. "*Verdammte . . .*" A string of ugly Teutonic words spilled out of Kurt's mouth as Trygve leaned down, picked up the penny, and handed it to Sarah.

"Shut up." Trygve's voice shook with anger.

Kurt's furious outpouring rose sharply, then stopped abruptly when Trygve grasped his arm and pulled him to his feet. "I said, that's enough. And don't you touch Sarah again. Never, *never* again."

At the faint rustle of silk, all three turned quickly toward the door. Angela Whiting, a bride for half a day, was watching the three with an expression of infinite sadness in her large brown eyes. She said quietly, "Kurt, your father would be deeply ashamed."

Kurt stared at her defiantly but said nothing. Blood from

the cut in his left cheek was trickling down to his stiff military collar, leaving a dark wet stain. Head high, he walked across the room and past his mother, without a glance or a word of apology.

Angela followed as far as the door, closed it, and turned to face Trygve. "You are Anna's brother, but I'm sorry to say I do not know your name."

"Trygve," Sarah put in proudly. "Trygve Peersen. He didn't start it. Kurt took my talisman, and then he tried to make me jump for it, but I kicked him and then—"

"I know, my dear, I know. I did not see it all, but enough to know what I missed. Trygve, my son owes you an apology. As he grows older, he will learn how to admit mistakes, but he doesn't know how to do it now, and it would be meaningless for me to apologize for him." She turned to Sarah. "Sarah, try to understand why Kurt acted badly. He is clinging to the memory of his father, and now he is hurt and angry because he feels that another man, your own father, has taken his place. He is cruelly wrong to treat you as he has. He's hurt me too, perhaps even more than he's hurt you. Please think about it—about his resentment, his bitterness; surely you must suffer from the same feelings. You want your mother. You don't want me. He wants his father . . ." She paused, silenced by the stubborn lift of Sarah's chin and her unblinking sea-green eyes. After a moment of motionless confrontation, she just barely touched the little girl's cheek. "Someday . . ." she whispered, and then turned and left the room.

13

On a hill in Cuba, a scrappy regiment of American ranchers and cowboys was engaged in heavy fighting against Spanish troops. But the streets of downtown Seattle were decked out with bright crepe-paper streamers, glittering stars, banners, and flags for a joyous celebration of the Fourth of July. Pioneer Place overflowed with spectators in their Sunday best. First there would be a patriotic parade. Later the mayor would unveil a magnificent Alaskan totem pole forty-eight feet high, carved and painted to display the lineage symbols of the Tlingit Indian family from which it had been stolen by Seattle businessmen.

When Trygve came to pick up Christina, he was surprised to find her alone and dressed to go downtown. No matter how innocent Trygve's invitations—a box social, a church picnic, a swim in the bay on a hot summer afternoon—Carl Franzen saw to it that at least one of Christina's several brothers and sisters was never far away.

Today Carl Franzen greeted Trygve with the statement, "I suppose you think you're old enough to take out my daughter without anyone else going along."

It was a question that wasn't a question, and Trygve, feeling as if he had been accused of something, wasn't sure how he was supposed to answer. How could his adored Christina, who was as sweet and pretty as a valentine, have such a sour-face for a father? "I'm thirteen." He meant to add, "and I'm big for my age," but it came out, "I'm old for my age."

"Is that right?" Franzen was three or four inches shorter

than Trygve. He looked up with suspicion at his daughter's suitor. "Exactly where are you figuring to take her?"

"To see the parade. That's first. After that, we'll go to a restaurant."

"Foolish waste of good money. Money isn't easy to come by. You start spending when you're thirteen, you'll end up a pauper. I had Christina pack a lunch. So what after the parade?"

Anticipating Franzen's reaction, Trygve said firmly, "We're going to take a boat to West Seattle."

Franzen's pale eyes blinked. West Seattle wasn't in the city of Seattle at all. As the crow flies it was six miles south of the village of Ballard, but for the earthbound common man it was such an arduous trek along country roads often not passable that to Franzen it seemed like a foreign country. "What will that cost you?" Suddenly he realized that by objecting to Trygve's wasteful spending, he would deprive his favorite child of a treat. "Well, all right. But you be sure to get my daughter back before dark."

Franzen followed this with a series of warnings. "There'll be a big crowd to see the parade. Don't get too close to the street when there's horses going by, and don't get separated. Watch out for strangers who try to strike up a conversation. Don't give nothing to beggars, especially not to one of them Siwash. He'll spend it on whiskey, and when an Indian gets to drinking, he gets mean."

In the past year Trygve had learned more about the city than Carl Franzen would in his lifetime, and had even won his first street fight, but he listened respectfully. Finally he and Christina were allowed to go out on the first day they had ever had completely to themselves. Christina's eyes had never seemed so blue, and Trygve was finding it hard to keep from touching her until they were out of sight of the Franzens' front-parlor window.

On the path to the trolley line, Trygve groped for Christina's hand. "Not here!" she whispered earnestly. "Someone's coming." And not in the trolley, because the car was filled with villagers who knew them. But finally, strolling toward the street where the parade would march, a nameless boy and girl jostled by a crowd of nameless strangers, Trygve reached for Christina's hand. She responded, her fingers curling around his in a way they never had before. Christina was clinging to him as hard as he was clinging to her. That urgent touch was so exciting he couldn't talk, or even dare to look at her.

Trygve's thoughts of Christina were interrupted by a tap on his shoulder. He turned to face the familiar figure of Princess Angeline, daughter of the affable Chief Sealth, for whom the city was named. As usual, she was barefoot. Her squat little body was plumped out by layer upon layer of cast-off garments which she chose to wear all at once, one on top of another. Her bronze-colored face was furrowed by countless wrinkles. Her nearly sightless eyes were half-closed, as if the ancient eyelids were too tired to open wide. That she was one hundred years old was only one of many stories Trygve had heard about her. Another was that she had once saved Seattle's first settlers from massacre by warning them of an attack. If the first story was true, she was born when her father was eleven years old. The second tale had never been recorded, and Chief Sealth was in no position to dispute the facts, having been dead for thirty-two years. Seattle whites didn't care. Angeline lived in a shack on the tide flats near the waterfront and subsisted on the city's generosity. But she was a princess of royal blood, and as the monument of Sealth's memory proclaimed, her father had been a "firm friend of the whites." Trygve felt genuine affection for the old woman.

Christina watched Trygve slip some coins into Angeline's open hand. When the bent figure hobbled away, supported by a sturdy cane, she said, "Papa doesn't let us give money to beggars."

"She's not exactly a beggar. Sometimes she sells clams or apples."

"But she's a Siwash, and Papa says they spend all their money on whiskey."

To have the stingy Carl Franzen's presence evoked not once but twice dimmed the perfection of their privacy. Trygve said testily, "My father never called an Indian a Siwash. There's no such tribe. It's a bad word. To an Indian, it's an insult."

"But she's gone. She didn't hear me."

"I did," Trygve retorted, and was instantly sorry, for Christina's eyes filled with tears. He reclaimed the hand that had slipped out of his and held it tightly. "I'm sorry. Honest, I'm really sorry."

"You scare me when you sound like that."

"Like what?"

"Like . . ." Her unhappy eyes begged for understanding. "Like you're getting ready to fight."

"Fight you?" He grasped both her hands. "I wouldn't, Christi, I couldn't!"

"I don't mean hit me. I mean, fighting with words, and a loud voice."

"Arguing? Christi, I don't want to do that with you, either. I *love* you!" the word was out, spoken for the first time. Until now, Trygve had never said more than "I like you better than any girl I know," and Christina, with a secretive smile, had always answered, "Me too." He had always wanted more of a promise for the future. He had yearned, and ached, and dreamed, but he had never wanted to kiss her passionately as much as he did right now. He was looking at her mouth, wondering what it would feel like, when she pulled her hands free and said, "That girl is staring at us."

"What girl?"

"There, in front of the theater."

And indeed was a girl staring at them, not twenty feet away, the last person Trygve wanted to meet today. His nemesis, Sarah Whiting, with her father, her brother, Ben, and her stepmother Angela. Sarah's eyes were fixed on Christina as if she were memorizing every part of her pretty face. "That's the Whitings," Trygve said uneasily. At the sight of Sarah, still more of his beautiful sense of privacy with Christina was draining away. "We have to stop and say hello."

"The Whitings? Your sister *works* for that man! Are you going to go right up and talk to him?"

"It's too late to turn around or cross the street," Trygve said doggedly, and silently thought: And too late to keep that pesty little girl from spoiling the day.

The introductions went well enough in spite of Sarah's relentless fascination with Christina's soft curly hair and large blue eyes. Professor Whiting was cordial as Christina was introduced, and Ben accepted her with a friendly grin. Sarah appeared to have lost her voice.

Christina, on the other hand, had found hers. Trygve was astonished by how quickly she recovered from her initial shyness and became completely occupied in charming Sarah's father and brother. His timid pretty-as-a-picture Christi was trading pleasantries with strangers and enjoying it. From somewhere she was finding the right things to say. In the face of such sweet innocence, the stern professor had turned soft. Both he and Ben were responding as if Christina had cast a spell.

It was a bad moment for Trygve; he suddenly felt that he understood Sarah better than Christina. In one swift glance Sarah had identified Christina as his sweetheart. She had met the enemy, and every nerve and sinew in her body was tensed for combat. Trygve alone noticed the storm mounting in those wide green-blue eyes. He knew that the pretty blond spellbinder was going to be silenced, and Sarah wouldn't care how she did it.

All at once Sarah's merciless scrutiny of Christina shifted to the theater poster propped on an easel near the box office. "Everybody look!" Her voice rang with excitement as she realized that Julia Linden, "Actress of World Renown," was appearing here in her finest role as Madame Toulouse in *Love's Secret*.

"She's famous all over the world," Sarah continued, ignoring her father, stepmother, and Christina and speaking only to Trygve. "That's what I'm going to be someday. An actress. I'll go to New York, and Chicago, and when I get famous, I'll be on the stage in London too, and Paris. Have you ever been inside this theater, Trygve?"

Trygve shook his head vigorously but she didn't pause. "What does it look like? Is it fancy? Does it have big paintings and velvet seats? I'd like to know because you see I'm not going to go to college. I'm going to study for the theater and learn to act in plays. Plays like *Love's Secret*."

Professor Whiting had had enough. "That will do! No daughter of mine will ever appear on the professional stage! And no daughter of mine will ever view such tawdry dramas as the one showing in this theater. It is a disgrace to the city.''

Sarah was exultant. She had silenced Christina and recaptured the attention of her father and brother. Trygve said hurriedly, ''Good-bye, Professor Whiting. Good-bye, Ben.'' The professor was continuing his lecture on the evils of the theater and scarcely heard him. Ben acknowledged him with an absentminded nod. Trygve signaled to Christina, and the shy sweetheart he knew so well was at his side as they walked away.

They didn't speak for some time. To prevent any physical contact, Christina clutched her reticule with both hands. Finally she said in an accusing tone, ''That girl likes you.''

To his dismay, Trygve felt the heat rise up and spread across his cheeks. ''She's a kid. An ornery little kid.''

''Anyway, she's sweet on you.''

''I guess so,'' Trygve said irritably. ''A little girl with a crush on a boy because he's older than she is. She'll get over it.''

''Call it a crush if you want. But maybe she won't get over it. I've heard of people falling in love who weren't much older than she is.''

Trygve stopped walking and turned to look down into Christina's face. ''Hey! I know better than you do that people can fall in love when they're still real young. Maybe I'm only thirteen but I know I'm never going to love any girl but you.''

''Are you sure?''

''Christi . . . You don't know how sure.''

She smiled softly. ''That makes me very happy.''

''All right, then. I don't want Sarah Whiting to spoil our day. So let's go watch the parade.'' Looking down into Christina's upturned face, he said in a voice husky with feeling, ''Please, Christi, give me your hand.''

''Someone will see us.''

''Let them!'' He broke one resisting hand from its tight grip on the reticule and held it until it relaxed and responded to pressure. It was a true caress. He wanted more, but it would do for now.

*   *   *

It had been Ivar Hilsen's plan to get back to Seattle before the Fourth of July. But the three-masted bark *Modig* out of Stavanger had been becalmed off the coast of Peru. Now, on the night of the Fourth, they were still three days from making port, which to Ivar meant three days until he would come home to Anna Peersen. He had something very special for Anna. A gold locket, his father's gift to his mother the day she accepted his marriage proposal. She had worn it until she was dying, when she put it into Ivar's hand and said, "For your bride." The locket contained tiny photographs of his mother and father in wedding dress. Once he and Anna were married, their pictures would be substituted for those of his parents.

It was Ivar's last long voyage. He had promised Anna that after their wedding he would not go out to sea, except perhaps on one of the new halibut steamers that worked out of Ballard. Standing in the *Modig*'s graceful bow, the bowl of his pipe glowing in the dark, he reviewed their plans for the future.

He had finished building the house, and he had to admit he was proud of it. It was altogether Anna's house, from the spacious kitchen with large windows facing east for the morning sun, to Anna's choice of pale gray for the exterior walls with mustard-yellow trimming on the eaves and window frames—a combination she liked because it was typical of homes along the north coast of Norway. Ivar had told her that for him, building a house for his wife was an act of love. Since he already owned the five acres on a slope above Salmon Bay given to him by his grandfather, she couldn't choose the location of their home; at least she could have what she wanted in the house itself.

"I would like to look across Puget Sound to the Olympics from a great big chair in the sitting room." That was Ivar's only request, and Anna had understood that to him the house was Anna's *hus*. So he had built it, while Anna saved up her housemaid's wages to buy the chair.

Though Ivar was not on watch tonight, he instinctively observed everything along the bark's course. They were in dangerous waters; because of heavy overcast, neither moon nor starlight penetrated the total darkness. Rounding Tatoosh

Island to enter Juan de Fuca Strait, the ship would challenge tides, rocks, and winds that gave the area between Vancouver Island and Washington State a reputation as a ship's graveyard.

Ivar noted that the wind had been coming up for some time. They were approaching Tatoosh, running closer to shore, and he could make out the way the edge of land dropped straight down. Driven by the rising wind, breakers were pounding at the base of precipitous cliffs, foaming up white even in the darkness as they swirled around boulders and rocks, and then with a sucking sound pulled back out to sea. Indians lived in that wilderness. Ivar had seen them many times braving the vicious currents in their long cedar canoes; he had come to believe the claim that their people never die at sea.

The *Modig* was not as vulnerable as a hand-hewn canoe, but tonight her skipper had little help in keeping his vessel off the rocks. He was navigating by dead reckoning, without the aid of stars and with nothing more than a record of courses sailed and the distance on each course. But Ivar wasn't worried. Soon the beacon on Tatoosh would give them their position. By tomorrow morning they would be in peaceful water, and with a fair wind and the Lord's blessing, he would be stepping onto the pier and into Anna's arms the next day.

Like a prayer being answered, the beacon became visible. It cast a trembling light, dimmer and a darker yellow than usual but that only meant there was fog up ahead. The beacon would keep them on a safe course.

Ivar emptied his pipe over the side, reamed it with a nail, and put it away in the pocket of his *sjomann* jacket. Now the *Modig* was veering slightly to starboard, adjusting her course to the direction of the beacon. A time to be below for a cup of coffee, Ivar decided, and then into his bunk. He would sleep soundly, knowing his last voyage was almost over. The beacon was the next-best thing to seeing a light in the sitting-room window of Anna's *hus*.

Ivar was in the galley with three older sailors when the *Modig* smashed into a rock. The impact was so powerful and sudden that he fell to the floor and was lying half-stunned in a welter of broken crockery without knowing how he got there. The sailor nearest him was unconscious, blood pouring from a gash in his forehead. The others were trying to lift his deadweight off the floor, one of them yelling, "You, Ivar! Wake up! We've gone aground!"

Ivar's head cleared. He struggled to his feet, and being younger and stronger than his mates, he picked up the man with the head wound and threw him over his shoulder. The *Modig* was listing badly and the sea was pouring in through her gaping wounds, but Ivar struggled up the hatchway without falling or dropping his burden. He was only a few feet from a lifeboat when the helpless vessel broke in two. With the sailor still on his back Ivar slipped and fell over the side.

The unconscious sailor sank out of sight. All around were men fighting to keep their heads above water. All were trying to swim to shore, though in the confusion and darkness few knew which direction to take. For several numbing minutes Ivar circled the spot where he thought the other sailor had gone down. But his strength was waning, and he gave up and tried to save himself. His last thoughts were: It's a good thing I was carrying the locket when this happened. And then, a few minutes later: How strange! At first the water seemed so cold, yet now it feels so very warm.

Because of his strength, Trygve was allowed to join the rescue party made up of five men from Seattle's Norwegian community. Their only information came from the youngest of three Bjornsen brothers who lived in a cabin on a cliff above the ocean some twelve miles south of the entrance to the Ozette River. He had walked twenty-five miles to the nearest telegraph station, where the news of the *Modig*'s destruction was relayed to Seattle. There were two survivors, the telegram said, but no names were given. Trygve left home with Anna's prayers that one of them might be Ivar.

Led by the owner and captain of a schooner, the party sailed to Neah Bay on the Strait of Juan de Fuca and then proceeded south on foot for thirty miles, crossing rivers and creeks, skirting mountain swales, pushing through dense forest where there were cedars and firs so immense that when all five men stood at the base of a tree with arms outstretched, fingertips touching, they had encircled only half of the trunk. The second night they reached the Bjornsen cabin, where the two survivors of the wreck were recovering. Trygve's desperate hope was put to death. The two who lived were sailor Knudsen and second mate Nestaas. Ivar Hilsen had gone down with the rest.

With the help of Indians, the brothers had dug shallow graves on the beach at the foot of the cliff. For the next three days the Bjornsens, the Seattle party of five, and their Indian guide opened the graves and carried each body up the hill on stretchers they made out of willow saplings and honeysuckle vines. Trygve found Ivar's body, and Trygve alone carried him up the treacherous incline and laid him with the others in the huge common grave they had prepared at the top of the cliff.

The *Modig*'s sails lined the grave, the *Modig*'s planking sealed the tomb. On the fourth day, they gathered for a simple service led by the sea captain. No reference was made to the bitter truth they had heard from second mate Nestaas— that the *Modig*'s skipper had steered his ship onto the rocks because he mistook the lamplight in the window of the Bjornsen cabin for the Tatoosh Island beacon. After the captain's talk, Trygve said the Lord's Prayer in Norwegian, reciting the words with tears in his eyes. He thought of his father as well as Ivar while clutching the gold locket he would take home to Anna.

14

Emma Peersen watched her stricken child suffer and grieved with her. Anna was strong, but Emma had met her own tragedies with the same inarticulate misery she saw in her daughter's pale face and dry eyes. She knew that to be strong is often to be lonely. Just as Emma had after Einar's death —was that really only a year ago?—Anna was living a faithful copy of her normal life. The Whitings urged her to stay home for a week or two and offered to pay her full wages during that time, but she refused.

Encouraging Anna to talk about her feelings seemed to push her even farther away. On Thursday nights she joined the conversation and smiled at the right times, but the clear blue eyes that had always been windows to her thoughts were without expression of any kind. Not anger, not bitterness, not even sorrow.

"I wish she'd let it out!" Trygve said to his mother. "Even if it would mean to curse God."

Though shocked, Emma couldn't scold Trygve for such blasphemy.

The house Ivar had built told Emma just how deep Anna's hurt was. It had been Anna's custom on her Thursday off to spend an hour or so in Anna's *hus*, planting more flowers, washing windows already sparkling clean, counting the embroidered pillowslips and towels and crocheted antimacassars in her overflowing hope chest. Now she refused even to walk along the road that passed the house. To Emma's sympathetic eyes, the pretty silver-gray cottage looked as abandoned as

Anna's hopes. It stood alone and deserted, the emptiness locked inside.

Emma decided that eventually she would have to try to bring Anna out of hiding, and after more than two weeks she felt the time had come.

"Annerle, dear Annerle," she said softly. "You haven't watered your garden or opened the windows to air out the rooms. Ivar built the house for you. You must take care of it."

"I can't, Mama. I just can't. Because Ivar did build it for me, so he's everywhere in it. Just to see it, even from a distance, hurts more than I can stand."

"Would you let me go there, or Trygve?"

"If you want to."

"Then, dear, you must let me have the key."

The housekey, as well as the locket, was hanging on a gold chain around Anna's neck. She slipped it off and silently handed it to her mother.

Inches shorter than her golden-haired Viking daughter Emma reached up and caressed Anna's cheek. "You don't want to go to your house now because everything there reminds you of Ivar. Only a year ago I felt the same about going inside your father's workshop. But the day will come for you, as it did for me, the day when you want to be in the house because it *does* remind you of Ivar."

"Never, Mama. Never."

"Oh, yes, it will, Anna. We can't know exactly when, but yes, it will."

Every now and then, when the house was quiet and she could be alone for an hour or so, Emma filled one of Grandmother Frodesen's stemmed glasses with Einar's wild-plum wine and took stock of herself, her family, and the progress of Mother Peersen's Home Bakery. In mid-July 1898 Emma's world was all hope and sunshine, except for the dark cloud cast by Anna's heartbreak.

"Family" hadn't been an exclusively Peersen affair since Emma began her new life after Einar's death. Mina's husband, Tim, had been considered "family" from the moment they became engaged; now at their regular Thursday dinner conferences, Katamari Tamesa was also seated at the table.

He was not related or connected by marriage, but in a sense, he was an honorary Peersen. Emma's children, her partners in business, her helpful friends—everyone who came to her table Thursdays was doing well, with the exception of Anna.

Katamari had returned to Yokohama briefly to tell his father, face to face, that he had chosen to make a life in the United States. It was a break that hurt and angered the elder Tamesa and left Katamari with a diminishing bank account and no prospect of replenishing it. Though Norwegian to the bone, Emma had an intuitive understanding of her Oriental "son." She knew he had made the right decision. As if to erase any doubts about his plans for the future, Katamari had reinforced his decision by applying for citizenship. He would be far happier earning his future than inheriting it. He had both the cleverness and the courage to succeed in the Western world in spite of prejudice. Newly arrived Germans, Scandinavians, and English were accepted because they came from countries that had provided earlier generations of immigrants and they looked like everybody else. Karamari could not disguise his origins. As he himself had put it, "The nail which sticks up will get hit."

Katamari believed that his future was to be in real estate. For some time he had been inspecting old apartment houses in and near the Oriental community, hoping to find a building so dismally ruined that he could acquire it with the last remnants of his college fund.

"And then?" Emma asked when Katamari told her what he was searching for. "Once you own such a run-down building, what will you do with it?"

"I will clean it, paint it, and repair it. Then I'll rent it at prices the people who live in those miserable holes in Japan Town can afford to pay."

Emma smiled ruefully. "That won't be much."

"No, but it will be filling a need, and I think that is the best foundation for a good business. I'll save as much of the rent money as I can, until I have enough to buy another old building."

"And then clean, and paint, and repair the second building," Emma said, nodding in approval. "And rent that, so you will gradually collect money to buy a third . . ."

"By that time," Katamari responded, "I will be able to finance my plan in an easier way. A Japanese is about to open a bank in Seattle. For the first time, a person of Japanese ancestry will be permitted to apply for a bank loan, which is impossible for us to do now. And I'm fortunate. The man happens to be a friend of my family in Yokohama. He has known me since I was a child."

Emma looked pleased. "I like your plan."

"Unhappily, it will be some time before I can put it into effect. There is a law that states an alien may not own property. When I receive my naturalization papers, it will no longer apply to me. Until that time, I will have to be patient."

Emma considered this for a moment and finally said, "In your situation, patience may not be good business, Katamari. It seems to me that the success of your plan depends on buying cheaply. But thanks to the Klondike, people are coming to Seattle from all over the country, not so much to go prospecting as to buy property and businesses right here. You won't become a citizen for another three years. By that time, everything you want to buy may cost more than you can afford to pay. Which means that you can't afford to wait."

"I have no choice."

"No choice but to get started!" Emma replied with spirit. "I'm a citizen of the United States. You talk to that banker friend of your family. He'll know how you can make me the legal owner, and how I can transfer ownership to you after you get your papers."

Katamari shook his head, his black eyes dancing with admiration. "I can only say that I am deeply grateful. One day I may become as wise in business as you are, but that is a long way off. Meanwhile, I learn from you. But if you plan to help me, you must hear where my ventures might lead you. True, I will start by buying one old building to renovate and rent, but I have already selected two more. In addition, I want to buy up all the vacant lots I can on the tide flats."

"To build on?"

Katamari shook his head. "Even with the help of the new bank, I won't have the money to do that."

Emma smiled. "You already own one building, and you

have your eyes on two more. I'm not a fortune-teller, but I'm sure you'll make a great deal of money during your lifetime."

"I'll tell you in confidence why I must buy land as quickly as possible. Because of a man whom everyone has heard of: Mr. James J. Hill. Jim Hill, the president of the Great Northern railway. Five years ago, his first train left Seattle for the East, and he's still using a flimsy little clapboard building at the foot of Columbia Street for his western terminus. That's not going to be good enough for the great Jim Hill, not for long. And when he decides to build the kind of railroad station he wants, he's going to need more space than he'll be able to find anywhere along the waterfront."

Emma's dark eyes brightened with understanding. "So the space, the location he will need . . . Of course! The tide flats! That's where Mr. Hill's railroad station will be. And he'll have to buy the land from you."

"Only if I can get it before someone else does. And another man is already trying to buy up that land. I know who he is, but I also know he doesn't have much more money than I do. So someone must be backing him, someone who doesn't want to be identified, because I've tried hard and still haven't learned the name of the real buyer."

"Even in the county auditor's office?"

"That's the last place to look for it. You don't uncover things in the courthouse. That's where the cover-up becomes official."

After dinner, Emma sat alone at the table sipping a glass of wine. Her daughters were so unhappy.

For the moment, Anna didn't seem interested in anything but helping Sarah Whiting get used to having a stepmother. All things in their proper time, Emma reminded herself. Anna will learn to face life without Ivar. Poor little Mina will start to be a well and happy person the day she bears a healthy child.

Sipping Einar's wine reminded Emma that only one more bottle of it remained in her root cellar. The wild fruit was theirs for the picking, but who among the hardworking Peersens and semi-Peersens had time to make wine?

She thought first of Henrik, the simple-minded boy Trygve

had added to his staff. Henrik had taken over the milking and farm chores Trygve had been doing for Farmer Dahlgren. He was also the fastest and strongest of Trygve's delivery crew. Last week he had begun to help in still another way.

Nothing seemed to bring Henrik to the kitchen door more quickly than the aroma of baking bread. "I think you can smell it a mile away," Emma commented when, as usual, his happy face appeared at the kitchen door while she was sliding the first trays of cinnamon buns out of the oven. She gave him a bun and then rolled up her sleeves and began to knead a batch of dough for rye bread.

Henrik watched, enraptured. With grains of sugar sticking to the corners of his mouth, he exclaimed, "I sure like to watch you do that!"

"Knead bread dough? Doesn't your mother . . . ?" Emma stopped short. Henrik lived with his grandfather. No one in Ballard knew what had happened to his parents. An idea struck her. Some parts of the baking process had been tiring her more than she liked to admit. Standing up to knead one huge mixing bowl of heavy dough after another, ten to fifteen minutes at least for every batch of it, sometimes made her back ache so painfully she had to stop and rest. Time stolen from a day's work was precious money lost to Mother Peersen's savings toward a larger stove. For months she had been harboring a sinful desire to possess the Acme Sterling Steel Range she had seen in the Sears, Roebuck catalog: nickel-plated, six holes, "oven opening the same size as the oven bottom, thus allowing as large a baking pan to enter as the oven can receive." But it would cost $18.70.

"Henrik?" Emma said. "Do you think you could do what I'm doing?"

"Oh, sure, Mrs. Peersen!"

"Well, go to the sink and wash your hands, and I'll show you how."

Five minutes later, Henrik was punching bread dough with such powerful thrusts that the legs of the old wooden table creaked. His simple face was so ecstatic that Emma had to suppress an impulse to laugh out loud. From that day on, Henrik had been lifting flour sacks, pouring milk out of the heavy galvanized five-gallon cans, and kneading batches of dough three times as large as Emma had the strength to handle.

When she offered to pay Henrik, he refused. "Trygve pays me."

"But that's for delivering. Now you're also a baker's assistant."

If he was teetering on the edge of accepting wages, hearing his title closed the issue once and for all. Emma's protests had no effect at all on Henrik, who had never known what it felt like to be proud of himself for something he could do. In the end she found another way to reward him. Henrik kneaded her bread, and in return she washed and mended Henrik's clothes. She had almost finished knitting him a pair of socks.

Emma knew Henrik could pick plums, but could he learn how to turn them into wine? That might be just complicated enough to confuse him, and when he got confused, he became embarrassed. Let him pick the plums, Emma decided. Kibun Sakai is the one to make the wine.

It was in September of the previous year that Katamari had introduced the shy little gardener, and Kibun became the second Japanese addition to Emma's burgeoning household. It wasn't long before Emma realized that taking him as a boarder was one of the best decisions she had made. Although he worked every day but Sunday on the new University of Washington campus, he had spent every extra daylight hour on the two-acre meadow next to Tim and Mina's house and on the three acres adjoining the house Ivar built for Anna. Over the winter, five acres of weeds and bracken fern and wild blackberry vines had been transformed into five acres of weedless soil so thoroughly tilled that there wasn't a single tree root or lump of clay to mar its powdery texture. He had done all this by hand, equipped with nothing more than simple garden tools and a peasant's fatalistic acceptance of slow, backbreaking labor.

The next step had been to remove the field stone deposited by an Ice Age glacier, a procedure known locally as rock-picking. Kibun went at it the same way, prying out the larger embedded stones with a crowbar and carrying them to the edge of the field three or four at a time. Until Henrik came along to show him a better way.

Henrick knew he wasn't considered bright. "You're a good boy all the same," his grandfather had told him many times, "so just because you don't learn fast in school don't mean you're some kind of an idiot, and if someone calls you that, you got my permission to knock his teeth down his throat, because you're as smart as he is, only in a different way."

Henrik observed how Kibun was going about rock-picking. If Kibun could use a mule to drag a sled like an Indian travois, he could pile rocks onto the sled and clear the field in a fraction of the time. But Kibun didn't have a mule and neither did he, so Henrik made a sled by nailing some wooden boxes to a couple of large curved tree limbs that worked as runners, harnessed himself to the contraption, and was out in the field waiting for Kibun when he got back from working at the university.

When Trygve passed Anna's *hus* on his way home to dinner that evening, he was met by the spectacle of Henrik bent almost double against his improvised tracings, dragging a crude sled while little Kibun darted back and forth loading it with rocks. "That's a great idea," he said to the perspiring, red-faced Henrik. "Did you think it up, making the sled and all?"

"Yeah," Henrik admitted with a proud smile. "Kib was carrying off a couple of rocks at a time, and some of them so big he couldn't take more than one."

Trygve nodded. He had an idea, but he didn't want to demean Henrik's invention. "Too bad we don't have a mule."

Henrik nodded. "That's what I was thinking. Too bad we ain't, so that's how I come to think of doing it this way."

"Maybe we know somebody who's got a workhorse."

"Farmer Dahlgren!" Henrik's eyes widened like an excited child's. "That's what I'll do. Hey, Kib! Don't do no more of this tonight. Tomorrow I'll harness up Bessie and we'll pick this field clean."

As she had promised, Emma bought seeds in the spring, and now Kibun's gardens were patchworks of lacy carrot tops, pale green pea vines, potatoes, beets, cucumbers and broad beans, and cornstalks whose small ears were already beginning to tassel out. Kibun had wanted to plant love apples, which some people called tomatoes, but Emma had heard that they were poisonous and wouldn't allow it. Kibun never seemed to stop working; he was quiet and self-effacing and kept his room as shiny clean as his clothes, which he scrubbed in the backyard washtub two or three times a week. Emma had never known a young man so completely alone, without family and without friends. Yet he was cheerful, and so polite that every Thursday evening he stayed in the garden so as not to intrude on the Peersen weekly dinner and conference. It was time for that to change. Tomorrow, Emma decided, I'll tell Kibun that he belongs at our table when the rest of the family is here.

Now that Professor Whiting was married, Anna had planned to give her notice and come back home to help Emma with Mother Peersen's. But Emma knew her children. Something was bothering Anna.

After Thursday dinner, Emma steered Anna into the parlor. It was understood that this meant the mother and head of the family wanted to have a private talk, and the others remained in the kitchen.

"You're troubled," Emma said. "Is it something I can help you with?"

Anna shook her head. "It's Sarah. She still needs me. The new Mrs. Whiting is a lovely lady, very kind and very patient with that unhappy little girl, but Sari's stubborn. She can't see any further than the fact that a strange woman is sleeping in her father's bed."

"She's only ten!" Emma exclaimed, mildly shocked by Anna's blunt reference to such intimacy.

"Oh, Mama," Anna said wearily. "Don't blush because I actually said the word 'bed' out loud. Sarah resents having a stepmother in her mother's chair in the parlor, in her mother's place at the dining room table, and lying with her father, even if she can't see that part and probably doesn't know much about it. I should stay there for yet a while, so at least the child has someone in the kitchen, someone she doesn't resent because the kitchen was never her mother's place."

"I understand, but I don't agree with you. As I see it, you aren't doing the right thing for Sarah. She's not going to try to get along with her stepmother as long as she has you to run to. From what you tell me, Mrs. Whiting is too wise to force herself on the girl. She's only trying to make friends. You're making it harder for her, and harder for Sarah to discover what a good and loving person her stepmother is.''

Anna shook her head. ''I don't know, Mama, I just . . . Oh, I know you're right!''

Trygve was standing on Ballard's main street when the fire alarm sounded. The station was a little shack where ten official members of the volunteer fire department met two evenings a month. The alarm was a large gong. Someone had spotted a fire and was beating it furiously. In seconds, every able-bodied shopkeeper in the village would race to the stable where the horses and cart were kept.

The sound of the fire gong was ominous; everything in town was made of wood. Fires were a constant menace, doubly dangerous because the gentlest breeze carried sparks from one dwelling or store to the next.

Trygve's instinctive reaction to the gong was to scan the sky over the general location of his own home. No, his house and his mother were safe, but some distance beyond, a cloud of pale wood smoke was dimming the summer sky. It had to be Tim and Mina's house, and Tim was at work in the sawmill. That meant Mina was alone. In her mixed-up frame of mind, she might not know enough to get out of the house.

Trygve began running. Minutes later the wagon and horse cart caught up and passed him; it was drawn by three husky draft horses harnessed three abreast, their hooves thundering on the hard-packed clay road. Twenty buckets tethered to the sides of the wagon clanked wildly as they bumped against one another. The fire hose was useless—it was just barely long enough to stretch three blocks from the village's only hydrant, and even within that area the water often came out of the main in a trickle. Hand-carried buckets of water might save Mina's house, but it was fear for Mina herself that made Trygve run faster than he had ever known he could.

When he neared the house, he saw, to his vast relief, that Mina stood in a small group watching at a safe distance. Several volunteer firemen were already carrying pails of water from the hand pump in the backyard to a wooden ladder leaning against the house. Water splashed out of the buckets as they were handed up the ladder to a fireman who was attempting to soak the blazing roof. The man on the ladder soon retreated. They were fighting impossible odds.

Trygve took over the hand pump from a fireman whose face was red with exertion. While he pumped, he tried to keep an eye on Mina. Surrounded by a cluster of sympathetic women, a docile Mina was watching the destruction of her own home without showing any emotion other than curiosity. Then suddenly her face contorted and a terrified scream burst from her mouth. "My baby's in there! Oh, my God, my baby!" Before anyone could see what she was about to do, she ran to the burning house and through the front door.

A man shouted, "There's a baby in there!" A woman broke into loud sobs. "You take over the pump," Trygve said to a man next to him, and raced toward the house.

It was dark inside, and Mina wondered why, because Tim wasn't home from work yet, so it had to be daytime. The house was full of sounds, like the brittle snapping of cedar kindling in her stove. Voices were calling her name, funny voices from a long way away. But Mina knew how to get to the nursery, the pretty little room on the second floor that Tim had painted pink because her baby was a girl. Neither the strange sounds nor the smoky darkness was going to stop her from reaching that room.

She stumbled once before reaching the stairs to the second floor, but quickly got to her feet. Her throat felt hot and she was coughing, but she grabbed the banister and pulled herself up—left foot onto a step, right foot up beside it, left up a step, right up beside it . . . as she had done when she was little and her legs were too short to take one full step at a time.

At the top she hesitated; something strange had happened. There was a big hole overhead. She looked straight up, and thought: How funny, I can see sky! She looked down and saw that flames were already licking at the edges of the nursery door. They set the house on fire! They want to kill my baby!

They have taken so many babies from me. No, this baby is the only one left, they aren't going to get her now.

Two firemen were restraining Trygve. "It's my sister! Somebody's got to go in there and get her! She doesn't know what she's doing."

"It's too late," one of the men said sympathetically. "Two seconds after she ran through it, the whole doorway collapsed in flames."

A spectator yelled, "Look up there!" and pointed at an open window on the second floor. Mina was draped over the sill, her baby in her extended hands. Two firemen picked up a ladder, rushed to the wall, and propped it up so the top rung almost reached Mina's hands. One of the men climbed up, grabbed the baby, and holding it securely in one arm, scurried back to the ground. Another man ran up the ladder and quickly pulled Mina out. Throwing her over his shoulder, he descended slowly.

Mina stood blinking at the crowd while a woman cried out, "She's got the baby! Thank God, she saved her baby!"

A fireman stared at the infant in his arms. Turning to the next man, he said in an undertone, "Take a look at what she went back for! It's not a live baby. It's not a baby at all. It's a china doll."

15

Emma Peersen was determined that the anniversary of Mother Peersen's would be celebrated in keeping with Norwegian customs. All their relatives and friends would be invited to the party, as well as the half-dozen housemaids who had been their first "salesmen." An entire pig would be properly cured and smoked. Quantities of beer would be brewed; sauerkraut, lamb sausages, and smoked mutton had to be made especially for the celebration. And then, of course, the cakes—to Emma it was absolutely necessary to bake at least six varieties.

"All for one party?" Trygve wanted to know.

"One party" Emma replied. "But three meals."

The Peersens and their Norwegian friends were expected to wear regional costumes, or as many traditional garments as their attics would yield. There were to be three fiddlers. Ballard's Norwegian families provided two of them; the third was an elderly Frodesen cousin who had played for Emma's wedding.

Like Emma's extended Thursday-night family, the guest list was an ethnic melting pot. It began with Katamari Tamesa and Kibun Sakai—both considered family members although by now Katamari had moved out—and included a large group of Norwegians: loggers from camps in the Cascade foothills and fishermen from villages up north in Whatcom County, plus the thirty or forty invited from Ballard and Seattle. There were Henrik and his grandfather, Farmer Dahlgren and his wife, and the Franzen family.

Finally, Anna wanted to invite the Whitings from Capitol Hill.

Emma was hesitant. Anna had described the quiet elegance of Professor Whiting's wedding to Angela Bauermeister, a stately affair as seen from the kitchen. "Do you think people like that would want to come to an old-fashioned Norwegian party?"

"I don't know, but Sarah wants to, and that's important. She's unhappy because I'm leaving. She feels I'm deserting her. If she comes to the party, she'll see we're going to remain friends."

"Then of course we will ask the Whitings," Emma replied. "But you are not to invite them yourself," she added emphatically. "I will send Professor and Mrs. Whiting a written invitation."

Anna laughed. "All right, Mama. I won't say a word.'

"Of course they don't have to accept."

"But they will! Mama, I know you can't forget that the Whitings were in the parlor while your daughter stayed in the kitchen. But they aren't that kind of people. Sarah and Ben will love everything about the party. Mrs. Whiting will be as friendly to Farmer Dahlgren and Henrik and his grandfather and all the Frodesens, and even the Japanese, as she is to the rich ladies she invites to lunch. The professor's eyebrows will go up when he sniffs Mr. Olsen's home brew, but, Mama, he's not a sour old man. He's only forty-one years old. He just sounds old, but believe me, there's plenty of fire underneath. I haven't seen him and Mrs. Whiting together, but I think I know what goes on behind the bedroom door."

"Anna!"

"Oh, Mama, don't be such a *struts*! If father didn't take you to bed, where did we all come from? Making a child is too wonderful to be something we can't talk about, at least when it's between you and me."

"Well, then," Emma said weakly, "let's get back to Professor Whiting. How will he feel about the dancing?"

Anna shrugged. "Don't worry. Everything will go along fine."

Emma insisted on mailing the invitation to the Whitings. Two days later Mrs. Whiting's acceptance came back by the same route.

"You see, Mama?" Anna said. "She thinks like you. You didn't want me to hand her the invitation because you thought that made a servant out of me. She mailed her answer because she didn't want to make a servant out of me either. It seems awfully complicated. I'm a servant only when I feel like a servant. I'll probably be working just as hard for you as I've been working for the Whitings."

Emma shook her head. "But it will be our house and our kitchen."

The weather seemed to have taken its cue from the happy nature of the hostess. The sun shone brightly on Emma's party and meadowlarks sang in fields fragrant with freshly cut clover hay. The celebration began in midafternoon, and the guests quickly filled the Peersen home. Anna noted with relief that Sarah was recovering rapidly from whatever hurt feelings she may have brought to the party. She was already dancing, her long red curls bouncing and arms outstretched like wings, much to the distress of the young Frodesen male. He had been instructed to hold her hand and was trying valiantly to catch it.

Because the Peersen house was small, tables were set up in Emma's flower garden. Five kinds of meat and sausage were accompanied by sauerkraut with caraway seeds, as well as ample bowls of carrots, peas, cauliflower, and green beans from Kibun Sakai's garden. As they ate, one hearty toast followed another. When the feast was completed, the guests formed a procession through the village and on to the Dahlgren farm, where the barn had been cleared and decorated for dancing. At that point Professor Whiting approached Anna. "Mrs. Whiting and I thank you sincerely for allowing us to share this important occasion. We have enjoyed it all. But we won't stay for the dancing. We have a long ride home, and of course the children . . ." Whether he meant Sarah and Ben should not stay up late, or that they shouldn't be exposed to dancing, Anna didn't know. She thanked him for coming, shook hands with Ben, and knelt down to take Sarah into her arms for a last big hug.

"I want to stay," Sarah whispered, but there weren't any

tears. It was a sleepy protest from a child who had been having the time of her life and didn't want to stop.

"It won't be much fun from now on," Anna lied. She knew that a communal punch bowl would be passed around to be filled again and again until the dancing could begin. An hour or so later everyone would sit down to drink coffee and sample all of the cakes. Then more dancing, which, with the help of pea soup, sour-cream porridge, *dravle*, and slices of salt-cured meat, would continue through the night. But this was not for the children, who would fall asleep in the hayloft long before the soup was served. "Really, Sari, you won't miss much. Do what your father says. And then next week you'll come to visit me. I'll send Trygve to get you."

That put the happiness back into Sarah's sea-green eyes. "What day? Monday? Tuesday?"

Ordinarily Anna would have answered, "That's up to your mother." Instead she looked up questioningly at Mrs. Whiting, who responded with a warm smile, "Whatever day you choose, Anna."

Trygve had kept Christina by his side from the moment the dancing began, but now the Franzen family had gone home. While the fiddlers rested and the guests restored themselves with pea soup, he filled a bowl and sat down on a bale of hay next to Katamari.

Trygve had always been allowed a glass of his father's wine or a little home brew at Thursday dinner or on other special occasions. Tonight no one had counted how many times the wooden bowl passed through his hands, and he was feeling light-headed and talkative. "You know something, Kat? You're the best friend I have. I can talk to you about anything. I mean, really *talk*. I'm glad you've got a start in the apartment business, but I sure hate having you move out of the house, way down near Japan Town."

"That doesn't mean I've moved to a foreign country. You're still hanging around the courthouse whenever you have time. My apartment is only three blocks from there."

"Sure. It's not the same, though. You know, not like having those long talks after Mama has gone to bed and we're alone in the kitchen."

Katamari looked thoughtful. "I've wanted to say something to you about our talks. Mostly they have been about your father's death. About who owned the *Gypsy Queen*."

Trygve said grimly, "I won't give up until I find out who it was."

"Listen to me, please. You are only fourteen years old. That is too young to fill your mind with vengeance."

"I don't *want* to think about it. It's just *there*. You know the way my father died. If you were me, wouldn't you want to know who did it?"

"Of course. I'm not deserting you, Trygve. I'll help you. But how can we go about searching? The ship went down more than a year ago. If there was a way to learn who sent her to sea, it's gone now."

"Maybe it isn't," Trygve said stubbornly. "I still keep my notebook about things I see in the courthouse."

"Your notebook is good," Katamari said quickly. "You will learn a lot by watching and keeping a record of what you see. But that isn't vengeance. That's education."

"Maybe it's both," Trygve replied. "I saw an Indian almost beaten unconscious by a police officer. And last election time, there was a man, dressed in good clothes, who took me for older than I am and offered to pay me five dollars if I voted for his candidate. He had a greenback folded up so it was peeking out between two of his fingers for me to see. I listen to trials whenever I can; I saw the son of a rich lumberman get acquitted in a burglary and a couple of days later the same judge sent an old Italian farmer to prison for doing the same thing. I'm trying to learn the rules for the way you have to act in court. I saw the prosecuting attorney break a rule, and the judge didn't do anything about it, but when a defense attorney breaks a rule, he gets fined for contempt of court."

"What does Judge Thomas say when you mention these things?"

"He says, 'Keep looking, keep writing in your notebooks, and someday you'll be old enough and educated enough to do something about it.' "

"He's a judge. Is he doing anything about it?"

Trygve shook his head. "He's judge in the federal court. He probably sees what's going on in the county court, but it's a separate system. Maybe he *can't* do anything."

"Or maybe he's afraid to," Katamari said quietly.

A few days later, Katamari and Trygve met by chance on the courthouse steps. They had said good-bye and were heading in opposite directions when Katamari stopped suddenly, turned back, and grasped Trygve's arm. "Did you see that big Japanese, the man just going in?"

Trygve nodded. "He's got a bad cut on his face. There's a bandage over it, but some blood has soaked through."

"I want to follow him."

They stayed at a distance, but kept the man in sight as he mounted the stairs to the second floor, hurried along the corridor, and went through an unmarked door around the corner from the entrance to a courtroom.

"You know this building well," Katamari said softly.

"Judges' chambers," Trygve replied. "Funny thing is, it's always locked, unless someone on the inside leaves it open on purpose."

"Which judge?"

"It could be one of three. Judge Hackett, Judge Browning, or Judge Dorsett."

"I wish I had seen that man without his shirt . . ." Katamari began. "Trygve, let me explain that foolish remark. An old friend from my prefecture, Tokio Hanada, has just suffered a terrible loss. His daughter was attacked by a labor agent who smuggles Japanese in from Canada. He meant to rape her and force her into prostitution. He carried her to a room in one of those places on Jackson Street, but she fought him. Tokio knows, because it was told to him by a friend of his who happened to be in the next room, and that man heard a man scream out in pain and anger. Then the girl was beaten to death. That, too, was overheard by the man in the next room. He opened his door just enough to peek out, and caught a glimpse of the rapist as he was hurrying down the hall. He was able to tell Tokio a little about the brute who killed his daughter. That he was a big man with long arms. His shirt was torn, so he could see that there was a big tattoo on the man's chest. There was blood on his face, running out of a long cut all the way from his eye across his cheek to his ear. Tokio knew from that description that it was the labor agent who had discovered that he and his wife and daughter had come across the border illegally; with that dangerous knowledge in his possession, he had been bribing Tokio for years. And once, in the bathhouse, he had seen that big tattoo on the labor agent's chest. It's a picture of a ship with many sails.''

Katamari looked thoughtfully at the mute courthouse door. "If the man we followed is that agent, it may be that he is here to demand money for preying on newly arrived Japanese. That would mean there is a link between Japan Town slums and one of the judges who use these chambers. Of course, that's nothing more than a guess. There is no proof.''

"No proof,'' Trygve agreed, but he took out his courthouse notebook, wrote the date, description of the tall Japanese, and the circumstances Katamari had described. Sometime, he thought to himself, perhaps this scrap of information will fit with some other scraps and the whole will add up to an answer. "I remember what you said the night after mother's party, but I haven't given up.''

"I understand,'' Katamari said with a smile. "I don't believe you know how.''

16

On Thursday evening Tim O'Donnell surprised Emma by asking to talk to her privately. Throughout dinner he had been unusually thoughtful. No one expected him to match the high spirits of his in-laws, but he had an easy laugh, a bright twinkle in his eyes, and his own way of commanding silence— usually by raising his wineglass and singing out, "Here's to the lone Irishman!" Tonight, however, he had scarcely spoken, and by the time the girls were clearing the table, Emma had made up her mind to take him into the parlor, where she took all the members of the family when they were troubled and didn't want to talk in the presence of the others.

Tim nodded toward the parlor. "Just for a minute, Mother Peersen."

"You've been too quiet tonight," Emma said when they were alone. "Those nice Irish eyes look sad."

"Mina is pregnant again."

"But that's wonderful news! Why are you worried?"

"Because she says she isn't."

"She says she isn't?" Emma repeated. "Well, then? Surely she knows better than you do."

Tim shook his head. "Mother Peersen, a husband has his own ways of knowing. Mina never lets me touch her when she's having her monthly. We used to joke about it when we were first married. For twenty-five days, we try to start a baby. Then five days rest, when we sleep back to back. It's been two months now. . . ."

"Ah! You mean she hasn't turned her back for two months."

"Almost three, but when I ask her if she's pregnant, she

157

says she would know and why am I imagining such a thing. I've tried to get her to talk sense, but she gets angry. She's already got a baby, she says, and she isn't going to start another one."

"Dear God," Emma murmured, shaking her head. "The doll. To Mina that's still a real baby."

"So real that every Thursday I have to keep her from bringing it here to dinner. I have to tell her the noise and laughing will keep the baby awake. Tonight that almost wasn't good enough. Then I said a doctor told me night air is bad for babies, so she put the doll to bed and came along sweet as you please."

Week after week, the family watched Mina's body become thick at the waist, then swollen with pregnancy, until she seemed to be bursting with child. Mina was cheerful but blind to her condition.

Anna thought Mina was hopelessly lost, but at least there was one consolation. If this infant was stillborn like all the others, Mina wouldn't suffer as much, believing that she already had a "baby."

But Emma rejected what Anna called the bright side of the tragedy. "I don't see it that way at all. You're talking as if she's lost her mind completely and forever. I don't believe it. I have faith in God's love for those who suffer. God will let this baby live, and the minute Mina feels that warm little bundle at her breast, she'll forget about the doll and become the sweet happy girl she used to be."

Anna looked at her mother in amusement. "You believe God will let this baby live? Why would he help Mina now, instead of last year, or the year before?"

"Maybe her need is greater now."

"I try to have faith, Litt Mor," Anna said quietly, "but sometimes what I really need is proof."

Six weeks later, Tim O'Donnell borrowed Farmer Dahlgren's horse and wagon to go get the midwife. With Emma and Anna in attendance, Mina gave birth to a daughter. It seemed as though Emma had been right. The infant was tiny, but breathed easily and cried lustily for her first meal. Emma waited anxiously to see the miracle she had been praying for—the feel of a live baby driving the demons from Mina's twisted mind.

While Granny Green, the midwife, began the rituals of afterbirth, Anna went downstairs to put on some coffee. The quiet was shattered by a high-pitched scream, so shrill and loud it hardly sounded human. Anna bounded up the stairs. The door to the bedroom was closed. Emma stood in the hall, her face ashen and her dark eyes wide with shock. In her arms was the healthy baby God had finally granted.

"Mina tried to kill her," Emma said shakily. "When Granny laid the baby down beside her, Mina sat straight up and started to scream. She grabbed the little thing with both hands and would have thrown her down on the floor . . ." Her voice broke off.

Anna trembled with apprehension. "Mama! Is the baby all right?"

Emma nodded speechlessly.

They could hear Mina's pleading voice in the bedroom repeating over and over, "Give me my baby! What did you do with my baby?" Suddenly the room was still. Anna went to the door, opened it quietly, and peered inside.

A grim-faced Granny Green was packing up her midwife kit. But Mina's face shone with contentment as she rocked back and forth, singing to the doll she held against her breast.

"I had to give it to her," Granny Green said. "There was nothin' else to do."

For Tim O'Donnell, the incident was doubly tragic. The child he had wanted for so long had to be taken away and put into the arms of a wet nurse. Meanwhile its mother was in the grip of a madness made worse by the birth of a healthy child. Naming the little girl was all that was left to him; he called her Emily. When he told Mina, she looked at him so blankly that Tim didn't refer to their daughter again.

Dr. Jonas was an aging, plump little man. He had a balding pate fringed with pure white hair and bright blue eyes that peered out humorously from beneath bushy coal-black eyebrows. He had known Tim since childhood; he had set the bones when Tim fell off a wagon and a wheel rolled over both his legs. Years later Dr. Jonas had used silver wire to sew up Tim's arm when it got caught in a gear at the sawmill. He had heard the stories about Mina that were circulating in the village. One afternoon he stopped Tim on the main street, steered him into a tavern, and bought two mugs of beer.

"Time for plain talk, Tim. Your wife is very sick. Has been for a long time. If you know how bad off she is, you've been pretending you don't. Now she's sicker'n ever. I'm not the best doctor in the world but I've been watching the changes in her and I say she's getting worse. You probably think you're doing the right thing, keeping her at home instead of sending her away. Thirty years ago that would have been the best thing. What they called the Lunatic Asylum for the Insane and Idiotic, down south in Monticello, was a terrible place. But conditions are better now. I can't promise Mina will respond to treatment, but she's not getting any treatment at all at home. And she's making your life hell. Don't you think you ought to see if the hospital can help her?"

Tim had to agree with the doctor's blunt advice. He let Dr. Jonas make arrangements for Mina's commitment to the state hospital at Steilacoom, a remote settlement ten miles from the town of Tacoma. The site of an old army fort, the hospital buildings had been the barracks for soldiers stationed there to protect settlers from Indians until the fort was abandoned in 1863. Two traveling guards were dispatched to Ballard as Mina's transport. Mina went along willingly, with a happy smile on her face, the doll cradled lovingly in her arms.

At the last minute, Tim could not let her go there alone. While the guards smiled their understanding, he said, "I don't know exactly how to get there. I better go along and learn the way, because after today I'll be making the trip alone."

The route to the hospital began with a forty-minute trolley ride from Ballard to Seattle, then an hour's train ride to Tacoma, and finally a rural trolley from Tacoma to a small waiting station in the village of Steilacoom. Then they proceeded on foot for a mile and a half to the hospital grounds. It was a tedious journey, yet Tim made it every Sunday, leaving on the first trolley in the morning. If, as often happened, he missed the last car at night, he walked six miles to a dark and silent house.

Tim's visits with Mina were pleasant enough. She was a docile patient and had been rewarded with freedom to roam the grounds. When the weather was good, she seemed to enjoy strolling through the orchard and around the barns where the livestock was raised for hospital use. But her serenity was fragile, as Tim discovered when he suggested they leave the "baby" in her room while they walked outside. Mina's response was so hysterical that he never suggested it again. Except for that outburst, she seemed almost too content. She didn't plead with him to take her home, as he had expected, and she never once asked when she might be allowed to leave.

Emma Peersen had been so shocked by Mina's violence toward her newborn infant that she was beginning to accept the reality of Mina's condition. But Tim still clung stubbornly to the belief that seeing and holding her real baby would clear Mina's mind. But Emily was still nursing; it was impossible to take her on a full day's journey unless the wet nurse went along. Anna did not share Tim's hope, but she could never say no to anyone who needed her. On a warm Sunday in August, Anna and Tim and the wet nurse set out together. The delicate baby was securely cradled in a sling resting against her nurse's breasts.

At the hospital Mina hugged her sister affectionately but ignored the wet nurse and Emily. Then Tim asked her to put down the doll and hold her daughter, a shrewd look replaced Mina's welcoming smile. "I know what you're trying to do." Her voice rose a little with each word. "You're trying to take my baby away. But I won't let you! Get away from me, both of you!"

Tim tried to calm her down. She ignored him and stared at Emily with such naked fury that Anna swept the baby into her arms and fled the room.

Though sorely disappointed, Tim refused to believe Mina would continue to reject her own child. On the way home he said, "I think seeing the baby was good for Mina. Sure, she got excited, she was angry, but I wonder if that's so bad.

Maybe it's the way to help her get better. I'll keep bringing Emily. Mina will scream and yell, but someday she'll realize which is the real baby, and after that, she'll be all right.''

Anna smiled sadly. "Tim, I want you to write to the hospital doctor. If he says it's good for Mina to keep on seeing her baby, I'll help you."

Tim hadn't written more than a dozen letters in his life, but the next day he followed Anna's advice. His letter to the doctor went out Monday afternoon. Two days later he received a letter from the hospital, also written and mailed on Monday.

The superintendent sincerely regretted to inform him that his wife, Mina O'Donnell, had run away sometime Sunday evening after their visit. Mina had taken no clothes other than what she was wearing, nor the money Tim had left her to buy extras at the hospital store. Nothing was gone from her room except her doll.

The superintendent assured Tim that a search was being conducted. He emphasized that runaways were usually quite easy to track down and the many of them returned on their own. He admitted that Mrs. O'Donnell's escape had taken the nurses and guards by surprise; until yesterday she had been such a contented patient.

Now Tim was forced to think about his daughter's future. Leaving Emily with a wet nurse had been an emergency measure—a temporary arrangement which would come to an end when Mina recovered and returned home. But six months had passed and Mina hadn't been found, nor had she returned of her own accord. Tim had no choice but to make other plans; he was no different from a man whose wife had died. What sort of life could Emily have while he was at work ten hours a day? What did he know about feeding and caring for a child?

The Peersens hadn't pressed the issue; they were waiting to hear from Tim. After the next Thursday dinner, he laid the problem before the family.

Worry lines were showing between Emma's eyebrows. "If Emily lived here, Tim could stop in to see her every day on his way home from the mill."

Trygve's face shone like a loving uncle's. "I'll move in with Kibun. That way Emily will have a room of her own."

A lively discussion began about the benefits of life in Grandmother's house. Anna did not speak for some time. When she finally spoke, her voice had its old happy ring. "Tim, please listen to me for a moment. I've been working here with mother in the bakery since I left the Whitings. If you'll let Emily live with me, I'll move into 'Anna's *hus*' and stay home instead. The two of us, Emily and I, will become a family. It will make me happy to be her mother. And she'll be near you, so she'll also have a father."

The faces around the table reflected surprise. Suddenly everyone began talking at once about the beauty of Anna's proposal. Emma alone was too moved to speak. Mina had slipped out of their lives, but Anna had begun to find her way back. The windows in Anna's *hus* would open wide, the sun would stream in. The terrible emptiness of the house and Anna's own heart would be filled with the presence of a child.

17

In June 1900 Trygve Peersen stepped into a unique spot in the history of the Ballard educational system. He was the first boy to graduate from its high school. Ordinarily Ballard boys found jobs in shingle or lumber mills, in the shipyards, working for the halibut fishermen, or as purse seiners, hoping one day to buy boats of their own. The girls mostly went to work as housemaids, in the fish cannery, or with their mothers at home.

In Trygve's class only six students were left to receive diplomas by the end of the year—Trygve and five girls. The student speaker at graduation was customarily selected by classmates. Trygve was their unanimous choice.

The six graduates of the Class of 1900 and guest speakers waited in a classroom adjacent to the assembly hall while spectators at Ballard High School's seventh commencement exercises seated themselves. Then, at a nod from the superintendent of schools, they walked into the hall and arranged themselves on the platform in order of importance. The high-school principal was seated directly in front of Trygve, but was too small to block his view of the audience. Trygve could see the expectant faces of his family in the very center of the throng. They were only a small patch in a crazy quilt of familiar faces, but they alone came into focus. His mother was wearing the skirt and shirtwaist Anna had bought at Sears, despite Emma's reluctance to accept them.

"What have you done!" Emma exclaimed. "Spending money on store-bought clothes!" She had sounded even more scandalized when she opened the box and lifted out a rose-colored taffeta shirtwaist trimmed with black-and-white silk braid, and a dark red skirt with a wide velvet band around the bottom. "You know I can sew for myself, and spend not even half as much as this must have cost."

"Of course you can sew," Anna said, "but you haven't had any time since you started baking, and you know it."

"I don't need new clothes. My bombazine will do fine."

"It's black. You haven't worn anything else since Father died. When our brother graduates from high school, his mother should be wearing something cheerful."

In the assembly hall Anna was seated at Emma's right. Looking down into his sister's peaceful face, Trygve thought: What a change Mina's baby has made! After Ivar's death, Anna had also worn nothing but somber mourning tones. When she and little Emily moved into Anna's *hus*, all of that changed. Tonight she wore a frilly shirtwaist as pink as her lips and cheeks. It seemed to Trygve that she was the prettiest— maybe even the happiest—girl in the room.

The chair between his mother and Anna was occupied by a young girl in a crisp white sailor suit with red-and-blue braid along the collar and a burst of red-and-blue ribbons spilling over the brim of a perky sailor hat. A stranger, making herself right at home in the middle of his family!

Trygve recognized her then; although she had grown in the last year and a half, there was no mistaking the red hair that framed her face and settled on her shoulders in rings of soft curls. And there was no way to confuse the spirit in those bold green-blue eyes with the modest expression you saw in other girls' eyes. What was *she* doing here? Anna's doing, of course. It was like Anna to invite Sarah to his graduation without mentioning it to him. Well, he was fifteen now, too old to be flustered by a little girl in a young lady's sailor suit.

After a suitable pause in which chattering voices faded into an expectant silence, the minister of the Ballard Lutheran Church rose and delivered the invocation. Next the superintendent of the district made some general remarks about the state of the district's finances, followed by Principal Storm, who stumbled through a few words of welcome before introducing the main speaker, the chairman of the school board.

Then it was Trygve's turn. He advanced to the podium,

placed his speech on the lectern, and began in measured tones with "Reverend Luchesen, Superintendent Bailey, Principal Storm, Chairman Wright, Miss Thorne, Miss Parker, fellow graduates, parents, and friends.

"First I want to say how glad I am that the girls chose me for class speaker." He turned toward his fellow graduates and said formally, "Thank you, Wilma, Antonia, Sally, Hilda, and Jeanne."

Once more facing the audience, he said, "When Mr. Storm introduced me, he mentioned that I'm the first boy ever to graduate from Ballard High." He paused and let his gaze move slowly across the audience before he continued, lowering his voice as he emphasized each word. "I see at least a dozen boys here tonight who *could* be sitting in the chairs up here, and that's where they *should* be sitting. They aren't up here with the graduating class of 1900 because their parents didn't think a high-school education was important. They didn't get to go to high school themselves, so they think: Why should their children? Why stay in school when you're strong enough to work in the mill? Isn't it better to bring money home than to spend money on books and pencils?"

Trygve paused again. For the first time in his life he felt the excitement of creating a mood with his own voice and his own words. His head had never been clearer. He sought his mother's eyes and spoke directly to her. "At first my mother and father thought this way. *They* never went to high school. My mother didn't get beyond the sixth grade. They never had any more money than any of the other mothers and fathers sitting in this room. They might have been willing to let their daughters stay in school for an extra year or two, if my sisters had really wanted to. But a son? Let a *son* stay in school, especially a big guy like me? Incredible, but they did. That's why I'm thankful I was born to Einar and Emma Peersen. The fact that they didn't get to go to high school themselves didn't make them think it wouldn't be important for me. I hurt my father when I told him I didn't want to be a fisherman all my life, but the last thing he told me before he started off for Alaska was that one way or another, he and my mother were going to make it possible for me to graduate, not only from high school but also from the University of Washington.

"Next week I'm going to take a special exam to see if they'll let me into the university. I have to do that because Ballard High School is only a two-year program. When you graduate from a four-year high school, you can go to the university without taking any examinations.

"Why doesn't the Ballard School Board offer a four-year course? Let me answer that question. . . ."

Trygve took a deep breath. "The only reason the Ballard School Board hasn't tried to offer a four-year high school is that the members don't believe it's important to the community. Parents should begin by telling the school board that a complete high-school education *is* important. Important because a person with an education can *choose* what he wants to do. He has dozens of choices, not just three or four. It's going to be hard on my mother to have me in college instead of working. But when I told her it was foolish to take that entrance exam at the university next week because I'm sure to flunk it, she looked like she was going to bring out the old leather razor strop. She said, 'If you don't pass the first time, you'll study the part you didn't know and you'll take the exam again. There's something a lot worse than failing,' she said, 'and that's never failing because you were afraid to try.'"

He had finished. Now he waited for the audience to react.

There was no question about his own family. His mother's eyes were wet but her smile was one of pride. Anna's arm was around her mother, hugging her in speechless enthusiasm. Sarah was thumping her hands together in thunderous applause, which, after a few strained seconds, was echoed by timid clapping from the general audience. Trygve folded his notes and resumed his seat in the back row.

The chairman of the board rose. After clearing his throat, he said, "I'm sure we're all grateful to Trygve Peersen for giving us so much to think about," and hastily called on the principal to distribute the certificates. The ceremony ended with the minister's prayer. Then Trygve and the five girls were caught up in a cluster of parents, most of whom seemed far more enthusiastic about congratulating the girls than they were when they spoke to Trygve.

Trygve's favorite teacher, Miss Parker, stood apart from the swarm. As soon as he could do so politely, Trygve approached her.

"Well done," she said, offering a firm handshake.

"Some people didn't like what I said."

"Did you expect everyone to approve? If I know you at all, Trygve, the pleasure you got out of your speech was knowing they wouldn't. I hope you'll never become so comfortable or so prosperous that you fail to speak up. But remember this: he who criticizes the old system must be willing to give himself wholeheartedly to the building of a new one. A true leader doesn't just start something, he fights to make it grow."

While the others were congratulating Trygve, Carl Franzen remained in the background, surrounded by his wife and children—he was obviously restraining them from coming forward to shake his hand. Christina's unhappy face apologized for her father and for her own weakness in obeying him, but the full force of Franzen's disapproval didn't hit Trygve until everyone had returned to the Peersen home for the graduation party. Franzen joined in a toast to Trygve's future, but his face remained sullen. When other guests were drawn to Emma's bountiful platters of smoked venison, pickled fish, goat cheese, and rye bread, he drew Trygve aside. "You can wait a little," he muttered, "because I got something to say to you."

Franzen's sour disposition was well-known, but Trygve had not anticipated the anger that was so visible in his pale close-set eyes. "All right, Mr. Franzen. But I think we better go into the parlor." Trygve felt his mother's anxious glance following him as he led Franzen into the next room. As he went inside he gave her a smile that was a lot braver than he felt, and carefully closed the door.

Franzen began without preliminaries. "So you're going to go to college. Exactly how long is *that* going to take?"

"It could be four years. Or three, because then I'll be old enough to go to law school."

"Law school! You never said nothing about that before. Not to Christina, anyways."

"Not to anyone, Mr. Franzen, because right now I don't even know if I can get into the university."

Franzen's pale eyes blinked furiously. "Three or four years for the university," he said. "How many more for law school?"

"Only two."

"Only two, he says!" Franzen retorted, his voice rising. "That makes five, maybe six, in all. What's that going to cost you?"

"Nothing, sir. It's free—at the university, that is, not law school. Residents of the state of Washington don't have to pay tuition."

"You're going to stay in school five or six more years and you call that *free*? What's it going to cost your mother to feed you and keep you in clothes? Figure that, if you can."

Trygve felt his dislike for Franzen grow. "Not very much, because I'm going to work every summer. I'll earn enough to pay her room and board. Mr. Franzen, my mother doesn't feel as you do. She isn't thinking about what it will cost her."

"Well, she can praise your pigheaded foolishness if she wants to, but I won't. What I want to know is this: what happens to my daughter? She thinks you're going to marry her."

"I am," Trygve replied with genuine fervor. "But I'm only fifteen years old. Christina's only fourteen."

"I know how old she is!" Franzen said sarcastically. "Her mother married me when she was sixteen. By the time you finish up with law school, Christina will be nineteen. You want her to wait around while all her friends are getting married and all the young men are scared to get near her because she's spoken for? In the same five or six years, you could be working up to good wages and saving to build her a house. There was a lot of people there tonight that thought you made a fine speech, but to me you're nothin' but a fool and a dreamer. Maybe you'll outgrow it. God help you if you don't. I'll tell you this: if you *don't* come to your senses, I'm going to see to it that my daughter does. I remember your poor uncle, Gunnar Frodesen, your mother's brother. I'll see to it that my daughter doesn't stay true to someone like that.''

The high spirits in the kitchen couldn't muffle Carl Franzen's outraged voice. The way they all continued to laugh and chatter without a second's pause when Franzen stomped out of the parlor told Trygve they had heard everything but wished they hadn't. Christina stood next to her mother, misery and embarrassment showing in her flushed cheeks and trembling mouth. Her arm around her daughter, Mrs. Franzen was watching her husband's approach with such bitterness that Trygve hardly recognized the colorless little woman he had always known.

Emma moved quickly into the narrowing gap between the elder Franzens, an empty plate in each hand. ''Marta, Carl. Here, you must fill your plates before these young people clean the platters. Christina, come with me, dear. I'd like you to pass the *spritsar* your mother made for the party.''

A few minutes later, Marta Franzen was sitting next to her husband with a laden plate on her lap, once more the docile wife. Carl's anger seemed to have settled into fretful displeasure. The storm would not be forgotten by the Franzens, but for now it would be ignored.

18

Trygve's goal for the summer was to earn as much money as he could. Though tuition was free at the University of Washington, he would need over one hundred dollars a year for books and other expenses. He knew one way to earn a man's wages that was open to him. His father's gill-netter, the *Konge*, was his property. If the summer run was as good as fishermen were predicting, he could bring in enough salmon to put him through his first year of college. The only obstacle to the plan was Carl Franzen.

Franzen's agreement with Einar Peersen had been that he would use the *Konge* while Einar was prospecting in the Klondike, in exchange for a share of his catch, to be paid to Emma. The promised time had long since expired. Einar had wanted to give Franzen an opportunity to save for a boat of his own, but Franzen wasn't the fishermen Einar had been. His very disposition seemed to invite bad luck, and although he had enjoyed sole possession of the *Konge* for three years, still he had failed to save for a boat. Emma Peersen could see that Franzen was becoming more and more hostile. "If he could buy his own boat, he would like you better, Trygve. Besides, you have a right to fish the *Konge*, and he knows it. That makes him dislike you even more."

"There's another way, Mama. I could ask him to turn the *Konge* over to me for just the summer. For three months he could go back to selling fish. When I go to the university, the boat would be his again."

Emma sighed. "Whatever you do, the poor man isn't going to be happy. But we needn't decide anything today."

The issue was still unresolved when Trygve took the university entrance examination, and failed.

Not by many points, the registrar told him. He was a gentleman of enormous girth, whose basso profundo filled his modest office. But his smile was friendly. "You did well, considering the preparation you've had. Don't be discouraged. Only fifteen, are you? I advise you to go back to high school and take the examination again next year."

"Sir, I've finished high school. In Ballard it's only two years. There's nothing left for me to study."

"I understand the problem," the registrar said sympathetically. "But we want our university to be on par with the finest institutions in the East. To that purpose we insist that every applicant either have a diploma from an accredited high school or pass our entrance examination."

It was Thursday, and by the time Trygve returned from the university the family had gathered for the weekly dinner. Their outspoken indignation over the university's refusal to enroll him wasn't as soothing as it was meant to be. Trygve knew in his heart that placing blame on someone else was equivalent to saying there were outside forces he was helpless to change. He had to disagree. "The examination was fair," he insisted. "Besides, I knew that only a few students from two-year high schools even ask to take it."

Overhearing Carl Franzen's bitter denunciation on graduation night had united the family solidly behind the cause of sending Trygve to college. Though Trygve had seemed worried about the exam, it hadn't occurred to them that he could fail it. There was disbelief on their faces.

"I don't understand," Emma said, turning to Katamari, for he alone was experienced in the mysterious workings of a university. "Trygve has always earned the highest grades in his class."

"His record in school couldn't be better," Katamari replied. "It's the school that failed, not Trygve. And he knows where the problem lies. He said it all in his speech at graduation."

Anna nodded. "That's right! He did! Too bad the register, or registrar, or whatever you call him, wasn't there to hear it."

"Too bad the president of the university didn't hear it," Katamari said dryly.

His words produced a light in Trygve's eyes which Katamari interpreted correctly as the birth of another of his young friend's bold impulses.

The man Trygve was determined to appeal to was one of the youngest university presidents in the country. During his first two years in office he had been entangled in power struggles between the governor of the state and a divided board of regents; he had come through with his Congregation-alist conscience intact, more determined than ever to fight for academic freedom. He also valued the privacy of his own study, where he often retired after dinner to do some quiet reading. But when his wife came in to tell him that for the third evening in a row there was a young man on the front porch with some kind of a paper in his hand, his curiosity was aroused. "What does he want?"

"The last two nights, he insisted he had to see you person-ally. Tonight he's willing to compromise. He says he won't bother you anymore if you read the speech he wrote for his high-school graduation."

"Well and good. Tell him to deliver the speech to my office. My secretary will put it on my desk."

"I tried that," she replied with an amused smile. "You really must straighten up your office, dear. His answer was that it's piled so high with books and papers that his speech would get lost."

"He's absolutely right. My own do quite frequently. He's been here three nights in a row, eh? Well, we better do something to get him off our front porch. Have him come in."

"If the president read it," Emma said thoughtfully, "he must have been interested. What happened after that?"

"I told him all I'm asking for is a chance. I said, 'Let me take the same courses the students who graduated from four-year high schools take. If I fail, the professors can throw me out. But if I pass, then they'll have to let me stay.' "

"That was very bold, Trygve."

"I know that, Mama."

She laughed softly. "But it worked, didn't it?"

"I don't know yet. He said he'd think it over. Tomorrow afternoon at two o'clock I'm supposed to go to his office and he'll give me his decision."

It was a jubilant Trygve who returned from his appointment with the president and dropped a half-dozen battered books on the kitchen table. "The president talked to the professors. He said they'll give me until the start of the winter term to convince them I can do the work. September 14 to November 28. Two months to prove I can keep up with the others."

"What are those books?"

"They belong to the president. He said they're the ones he bought when he started college. Textbooks, Mama. One is a history, one on rhetoric, and one on psychology. Those are the subjects I'm going to take. And one is a Latin grammar, because he said I've got to learn Latin if I expect to go to law school."

"If only your father were here to enjoy this with me," Emma murmured, shaking her head. "Now, which is more important for the summer—that you learn what's in these books or that you fish the *Konge* to earn money?"

"I need money to go to the university."

"Will money get you into the university if you haven't studied the books? Listen to me, Trygve. With the bakery doing more and more business every week, I can certainly feed both of us. It hurt your pride to fail the entrance examination, but that failure isn't important if you've learned from it. Leave Carl Franzen to do the fishing. You read the books. And be grateful the president gave you a second chance."

Trygve was on a trolley bound for Capitol Hill when he saw the familiar figure of Judge Thomas climb aboard and move unsteadily to a seat across the aisle. The judge sank onto the seat with a deep sigh and fell asleep.

Trygve had visited the Thomas home many times since the day he had delivered samples of his mother's pastry there. As the car approached the house on Capitol Hill, it was obvious that unless someone awakened him, Judge Thomas was going to ride to the end of the line.

Tucking a history book under his arm, Trygve crossed to the judge's side of the aisle, shook him awake, and in spite of his sleepy protests, guided him to the steps and down to the sidewalk.

"Look who's here!" the judge said thickly. "An angel of mercy! A guiding hand! My young friend has come to see me home, safe from the dangers of our sin-ridden city!" Each word was delivered as if Trygve were at the far end of the block rather than right beside him holding him up. On the porch, the judge dipped into his hip pocket and produced a ring of keys. Blinking hard, he examined them studiously, one at a time, without finding a key he deemed worthy of unlocking the front door.

Though most of the house looked dark, a dim light shone from a room in the back. "I'll ring the doorbell," Trygve suggested. "Mrs. Thomas will let you in."

"No, indeed! Don't touch that bell! In the first place, Mrs. Thomas has decided to visit relatives for a few days, or a good deal longer, if I caught the drift of her farewell address. The maid is undoubtedly in the parlor eating bread and honey, but she is a hopeless bluenose and I hesitate to give her further proof of her overpowering rectitude. So we shall just heave away and kick the door in."

The judge lurched forward and lost his balance. Trying to prevent him from falling, Trygve grabbed the doorknob. It offered no resistance. He turned it and the door swung open.

Partly by guiding, partly by lifting, Trygve steered the judge up the wide circular staircase and into a bedroom where lawbooks were stacked beside the bed and stray clothing was draped over the back and arms of a black horsehair settee. For all its clutter, the room seemed forlorn. In fact the whole house felt empty in spite of the faint light from the maid's room. It was clear that Mrs. Thomas had gone away, but not for a "few days visiting relatives."

The judge's eloquence faded with the stealthy approach of sobriety. As Trygve helped him to the bed, the significance of the boy's presence in his bedroom began to penetrate the alcoholic fog. "Demon rum," he said, falling back onto the bed and pulling the quilt up under his chin. "He's destroyed better men than I. If you must develop a vice, Trygve Peersen, I suggest you select loose women. Unlike whiskey, they don't come home with you." He looked up into Trygve's face, bringing it into sharp focus for the first time. "What are you doing with yourself this summer? I haven't seen much of you around the courthouse."

"I'm studying some books . . ." The judge listened as Trygve quickly explained about failing the entrance examination and his subsequent appeal to the president of the university.

The story seemed to clear the judge's head. "You've taken the right course. Stay with it. But don't forget that notebook of yours. The one you used to carry in your pocket to write down words you wanted to look up in the dictionary."

"I still use it," Trygve assured him. "At first I wrote down words I didn't know. Now it's more about the way the courts really work."

"Commendable," the judge said with a wry smile. "When you discover who pulls the strings, what are you going to do about it?"

Trygve hesitated until he saw that the question was meant to be serious. "Sir, I already know there are dishonest people in government. Some of them are in such high places that they can control people lower down, and sell favors, and cover up things they shouldn't be doing. But I know I've got a long way to go before I discover who's honest and who isn't, or what a person can do about it."

"Dishonesty in high places . . . In the Halls of Justice. As a young man, I too thought I could do something about it. It took many years and many losing battles to learn where the source of the rottenness is hidden, and by then I had acquired too much power and too much position to risk it all in crusades. To you that sounds weak. But tell me truthfully, are you as noble as you sound? Nothing personal in that notebook for yours? All for the good of the people? No secret grudges or axes to grind on your own account?"

Trygve hung between a simple answer and the urge to tell the judge the story of his father's death and his own vow to expose the true owner of the *Gypsy Queen*. After a moment of painful indecision, the truth spilled out.

When Trygve finished, the judge's head fell back against the pillow. "What can I tell you, young Trygve Peersen? That revenge is never sweet once you've tasted it? Or that your father would be proud if he knew what you've pledged to do? No, I'll spare you the platitudes and get down to facts. Which are, as I see them, that your father, of his own free will, booked passage on a ship that wasn't seaworthy and paid for the mistake with his life. That the owner of the vessel, a man named Lund, was murdered the day before she sailed. Is that all you know? It's not enough. Besides, why the thirst for revenge? Lund caused your father's death, but Lund himself is dead. You can't improve on that kind of punishment."

"But *why* was he murdered?"

"He was killed in a Japan Town alley," the judge said wearily. "My poor innocent, in that section of our beautiful city a man can get his throat cut for his pocket watch. I see no connection whatever between Lund's death and the fact that he gave the order to launch the *Gypsy Queen*. If there *is* a link, then perhaps you've got a case, but first you've got to know a lot more about the man." The judge paused, studying Trygve's face with sympathetic if somewhat foggy eyes. "I can see by the stubborn set of your chin that my counsel has been lost on you. So be it. You're young and vigorous. The world will be a far better place for your charging in there and straightening things out. Go find some evidence—any evidence—that Lund's murder proves he was *not* the owner of the *Queen* and that another man, identity unknown, is responsible for the drowning of twenty-eight people, your father among them. If you can do that, I'll apologize for my skepticism, and I'll help you any way I can."

You've got to know a lot more about the man. It was a vague exhortation, but one that called for action. It was three years since the *Gypsy Queen* had sunk and Trygve had forgotten the details about Jake Lund that might have come out during the inquest. But he still had many sources of information, having made friends in the lower echelons of both city hall and the courthouse.

A file clerk in the police department gave Trygve his first

clue. "When there's a killing in Japan Town, the police report is usually skimpy. Who cares? But I did find you an address. The place Lund was living at the time of his death."

Lund's home proved to be a shabby two-story building bearing a sign: "Rooms—by Day or Week. Baths: $1 an hour." Trygve's knock was answered by a plump gray-haired woman wearing a faded flannel wrapper and felt carpet slippers. Whether it was his wholesome schoolboy complexion or the time of day—it was just after nine o'clock in the morning—she looked surprised to see him and plainly had no intention of letting him enter the house. "You don't belong here, young man," she said amiably. "All the rooms are taken."

Trygve explained quickly why he had come. She continued to block the door, but became more than willing to talk. "Do I remember Jake Lund? Ha! I'm still holding some of his things. Tried to sell the stuff, but couldn't. You related? No? Too bad. He owed me for six months. For the price of one week's rent you can have what's left. One pair boots, two pairs woolen underpants, three chisels, hundred feet of rope—all that's left of his Yukon supplies. He was figuring on going north. He told me that the day he got himself killed."

Off to a good start, the landlady set aside her disappointment that Trygve wasn't here to pay her deceased boarder's back rent and rattled off numerous complaints. Lund was more often drunk than sober. Not a mean drunk. Even when he was on a three-week toot, he never broke anything and never got into fights. A drunk, but never a thief. A kind man, at heart. He should have been making good money—anyone who owned a shipyard two, three years back got rich overnight—but his pockets were always empty. He dressed like a wharf rat, owned nothing but the miserable contents of his room, and was so poor he often had to borrow money from her even when he owed her his rent. Friends? Only other poor drifters like himself.

When Trygve asked why she thought Lund had been murdered, her response was much like Judge Thomas'. "For whatever was on him. He had a ticket to Wrangell. That would do it. Being a stupid drunk, he probably showed it to somebody, bragging about it, and that somebody was waiting for him when he left the saloon."

As he walked away, Trygve thought about his attempt to pry into the life of Jake Lund. Judge Thomas would ask, "What have you learned?" He had learned that Lund had been planning to go prospecting. Why would the owner of a prosperous shipyard risk death by freezing, scurvy, or starvation on the uncertain chance that he would strike it rich, when adding to his wealth in the booming shipbuilding business was a sure thing? No, someone else must have owned the *Gypsy Queen*, if drunken Jake Lund had spent his last dollar on prospector's supplies and a ticket to Wrangell.

To Wrangell! Trygve checked his memory. Yes, that was what the landlady said, that Lund had bought a ticket to Wrangell and had probably been killed for it. But the *Gypsy Queen* had sailed for Dyea! Why would Lund get into the savage scramble for tickets when he worked for the man who owned the *Queen* and could easily have gotten a berth on her? The answer was simple. Lund knew the *Queen* wasn't safe. He had been connected with the shipyard for a long time. He probably remembered when the *Queen* was wheeled out to a ship's graveyard, and more important, why.

Trygve's imagination raced ahead. Lund was a decent man, the landlady said, never mean or vicious even when he was drunk. Maybe he had argued with the owner, tried to keep him from launching the *Queen*. . . . In that case his sudden decision to take off for the Yukon meant he had got himself into such deep trouble that he was afraid to stay in Seattle. Many a "prospector" had gone north for the same reason—to disappear.

Both Judge Thomas and Lund's landlady believed the murder was just part of another Japan Town robbery, not necessarily connected with the shipyard or the *Gypsy Queen*. Trygve's active imagination was whispering something else. But he knew what the judge would say if he told him the true owner of the *Queen* had killed Lund because Lund was trying to keep the ship from leaving port. "No facts. No proof. So far, Trygve Peersen, you haven't got a case."

Reluctantly Trygve admitted to himself that he didn't. He forced his mind back to the more solid ground of uncovering bits and pieces of information that might eventually tell him who owned the shipyard when his father had boarded the

Queen in July 1897. The next logical place to look for clues was the shipyard office, with its file cabinets and desk drawers and dusty stacks of record books.

When Trygve entered the weather-beaten clapboard building that housed the office of Lund Shipyards, the only occupant was sitting at a large roll-top desk. He was a thin man wearing a soiled white shirt, a vest, steel-rimmed spectacles, and a wide-brimmed fedora. He glanced up from the wire basket of papers he had been sorting, made a quick appraisal of Trygve's size and build, and said, "We ain't hiring."

"I'm not here for a job," Trygve said earnestly. "I'm looking for information. I've tried so many places. You're my last hope."

The man looked puzzled.

"My name is Rickert. I have an older brother. James. He disappeared. Three years ago this coming July 29. The police never found a trace of him. There have been notices in newspapers all over the state and in Oregon. The Canadian Mounted Police have his picture—"

"That's a shame, son. But if he hasn't turned up in three years, I don't see how I can help you."

"Oh, it's too much to hope, I know. My mother said not to bother you, but I couldn't help it. Just yesterday, an old prospector was visiting, and got to talking about the day the *Portland* docked, and the Gold Rush. He's got a good memory for boats and everything to do with them. He could tell you something about practically every shipwreck that ever took place off the coast of Washington. Yesterday he happened to speak of one that was fitted and launched right here at Lund Shipyards. The *Gypsy Queen*."

"I wasn't here then, but I know about the wreck." He looked at Trygve closely and frowned. "If your brother was on the *Queen*, you would of known, wouldn't you?"

"That's just it!" Trygve cried. "James was only seventeen years old. He was wild to go north. My mother was against it. They had a terrible argument. James left the house. We never saw him again."

"Look," the clerk said impatiently, "in those days there were ships leaving for Alaska from every dock on Puget

Sound. Steamers, windjammers, tugs. People was so crazy you could of sold them passage in a canoe. What makes you think he was aboard the *Queen*?''

Trygve paused, steeling himself for the lies yet to come. ''Because the day he disappeared was the day the *Queen* sailed. I know that for sure. And I also know the *Queen* was the only ship to leave port that day. Don't you understand? If he did leave on the *Queen*, he's drowned. If he didn't, there's still hope that someday we'll find him. All I'm asking is that you tell me whether his name is on the passenger list.''

The clerk's expression stiffened. ''Sorry. We don't keep passenger lists that far back. To tell you the truth, even if we did, it wouldn't mean much. Back then people could sell a ticket to someone else in an hour, and at double the price. They was plenty who bought tickets just to do that, and made money without going north at all. So names on a passenger list don't mean nothing. But like I said, we don't keep them three years back.''

''You must have some record of the *Gypsy Queen*.''

''We might,'' the man said evasively, ''but all that's confidential. If I was to find something about the *Queen*, I'd get in trouble showing it to you. Anyway, they had a fire before I come here to work, so a lot of those old papers are gone for good.''

As the clerk spoke to Trygve, he had automatically reached out toward a drawer in the roll-top desk.

Trygve let a look of hopelessness pass over his face. He murmured, ''Thank you,'' and left the office. A plan was forming in his mind and he grinned broadly in anticipation.

To carry out his plan, Trygve needed the help of someone physically strong and not overly opposed to committing burglary. The night after his visit to Lund Shipyards, Trygve and Henrik, equipped with twelve feet of rope, a chisel, and a kerosene lantern, walked along the waterfront. They stayed in the shadows of warehouses and avoided the occasional saloon customer on his way home after a long night at the bar.

That afternoon Trygve had studied the shipyard office building. Breaking in through the front entrance was too risky. There was a hotel right across the street where the night clerk, alone in a deserted lobby, might be alert enough to notice. On the roof was an area about three feet square, covered with something like an old ship's hatch; it might be a trapdoor. But carrying a ladder along city streets at one o'clock in the morning was sure to arouse curiosity. A third possibility was the door at the rear, which Trygve thought was the best choice; Henrik promised he could open it with a chisel.

However, the door defied him. "That's what I get for boasting," Henrik grunted after putting his considerable strength into prying it open. "They got the thing bolted up tight on the inside. But that's all right. Forget the chisel. You and me'll put our shoulders together and rush it. We'll crack it wide open." Though he was trying to keep his voice down, it vibrated with enthusiasm.

"We can't do that," Trygve objected. "We'd never get the door put back together again. They'd know someone broke in, and I don't want that."

"Oh, yeah," Henrik agreed in a hoarse whisper. "I forgot. Okay. That leaves the roof. Except we don't have a ladder."

"We don't need one. That's what the rope's for. You boost me up so I can grab the rain gutter. I'll put myself onto the roof and let down the rope and haul you up after me."

A few minutes later they were crawling up the slanting roof, Trygve carrying the lantern and Henrik the rope and chisel. To their relief, the hatch cover yielded easily. Lifting it off, they peered through a jagged opening into total darkness.

"Let's light the lantern," Trygve said. "This roof slants back so much no one will see it from the street."

The pale kerosene flame cast enough light to show them that the hole was surrounded by badly charred wood. "Must have happened when they had the fire," Henrik said. "They didn't bother to patch the roof. They just covered up the hole. What do you see down there?"

"Boxes. Tools. Nothing much. I guess it's a storeroom. Anyway, the hole's big enough for me to get through. So hold the rope, and I'll go down."

"Hey!" Henrik exclaimed. "I'm coming too!"

"Then how are we going to get back up on the roof?"

"We don't have to. We can walk out the back door."

"If we do that, how will we get the door bolted again from the inside?"

"We can't," Henrik conceded. "Okay, it's through the roof. But you hold the rope and I'll go down."

"Oh, no," Trygve said. "This was my idea. If anybody gets caught, it's going to be me. So if you hear me whistle, jump down from the roof and run down the alley. And take the rope with you or they'll know someone else was in on this and got away."

Trygve slipped down the rope, landing softly on the balls of his feet. Henrik pulled up the rope, passed it through the lantern's wire handle, and lowered it carefully. Trygve moved quietly through the storeroom. Crouching, he crossed the office to the roll-top desk. He opened the drawer he had seen the clerk point to. His heart was pounding as he found a folder marked *Queen*. He leafed through its contents sheet by sheet. Kneeling on the floor, he copied the passenger list and some figures into his courthouse notebook and returned the file to the exact spot where he had found it. He crawled back to the storeroom, where Henrik's anxious face was framed by the hole in the roof. The first to be pulled up was the lantern. Next, Trygve. The hatch was back in place, they were both safely on the ground, and the lantern's flickering light was extinguished before either of them spoke.

"Find what you was looking for?" Henrik asked.

"I found something I *wasn't* looking for, a certificate saying the *Queen* was officially inspected and found in good condition for launching. It was dated the day before the *Queen* left port, and it was signed by a government inspector."

"Then the owner of the ship didn't do nothing wrong!"

"That's the way it looks," Trygve said glumly.

"Well, *I* feel good about it, even if you don't," Henrik said. "Now you can forget about getting even with the owner of the *Queen*. You been hating that person for three years. Hate's bad for you. Now you can forget."

"I was wrong about some things," Trygve said thoughtfully. "The government inspector's report proves that." But what about Jake Lund? Trygve asked himself. At this point, it didn't seem to matter. Lund wasn't to blame for his father's death, and the government inspector's signature proved that the *Queen*'s owner, whoever he was, was also blameless. It looked as though he didn't have a case. The vengeful search had ended, but for some reason Trygve didn't understand, he hated to give it up.

II

19

It was the year the Russian Socialist party split into Menshevik and Bolshevik and the Zionist Congress refused an offer for a Jewish settlement in East Africa. The first automobile to cross the United States made the trip in sixty-five days and Henry Ford founded the Ford Motor Company. President Theodore Roosevelt decided to visit Seattle, causing the biggest stir since 1891, when downtown streets had been choked by the crowds welcoming President Harrison.

By 1903 Seattle had acquired a sophisticated skyline. It had five separate, warring street railway companies; ornate Victorian mansions where thick forests once shut out the sunlight; a plan for a comprehensive system of parks and parkways designed by the sons of the man who had designed Central Park in New York City. Most important of all, Seattle had an air of respectability.

Still baking in her own kitchen, Emma Peersen realized that moving the bakery downtown was as inevitable as the growth and change taking place in Ballard.

Just as inevitable was the transformation taking place within the business, as more and more restaurants and hotels offered her long-term contracts. The bakery had begun as an all-Peersen operation—Emma as chief baker, Trygve her salesman and delivery boy. Anna had become her assistant after Mina disappeared when she and Mina's baby settled in the house Ivar had built. Trygve had forecast the future when he hired a half-dozen grade-school boys to work his delivery route.

For the past three years Trygve had been attending the University of Washington, astonishing his professors, though not himself, by his ability to keep up with the graduates of four-year high schools. He also played right tackle on the Husky football team and rowed first oar on the varsity crew; he had no time for the bakery and had been replaced by hired help.

Aside from Mother Peersen herself, Anna was now the only "family" in the family business, and she was the reason Emma had been putting off the decision to move the bakery to the city. Anna could bring three-year-old Emily to her mother's house, but a downtown location and two long trolley rides a day were out of the question.

Prosperity forced Emma to make a decision. Clearly her business had outgrown her kitchen. There was barely enough room in it for three bakers—herself, Anna, and the hired girl, Martha—and none for a fourth baker or a second stove. Emma would have to limit the number of orders she could accept or move to a place with room for expansion.

It was a natural that the issue be thrown open to family discussion. The traditional Thursday after-dinner conference had been devoted more and more to their business enterprises— Katamari's apartment houses, Emma's bakery. At first they had struggled just to survive in business from one month to the next, Katamari with an abandoned building on a desolate mud flat near Japan Town, Emma with an order for two dozen *Mor Monsen's kaker*. Many moments of decision had arisen since their brave early beginnings, and looking back, Emma realized that merely being content had never appealed to the "family."

Katamari's scheme to renovate a nearly worthless building and to use the rental income to buy and remodel another had made him one of the biggest landlords in South Seattle. Now he was planning to invest a portion of his profits in another kind of business. "Diversification" was the term Katamari used—a little too elegant for Emma, but she understood the principle and had been trying to think of some way to do the same thing. But the first question concerned the immediate future of Mother Peersen's Home Bakery—to stay home, or to venture into the city?

As Emma had foreseen, Katamari didn't hesitate when she brought up the issue Thursday evening. "I have wondered when you would reach this crossroads," he said in his quiet way. "I think I know why you have hesitated. A Seattle store will have to produce more in order to pay your overhead, and as the volume increases, you will have to hire more and more bakers. This will force you to become a manager instead of a baker. But I think you will like that. You are a natural businesswoman. Let others mix the dough and decorate the cakes. You'll be right there to make sure they do exactly what you've been doing in your own kitchen. In fact, that will be the secret of your success—that in the midst of all those ordinary commercial bakeries and their identical and tasteless products, yours will always keep the genuine Old World quality, the taste and smell of a home kitchen."

Anna had been watching her mother's face as Katamari spoke. "There's another reason you've hesitated, isn't there, Mama? You know that with little Emily to take care of, I couldn't work in Seattle."

"True," Emma conceded. "Not only because I would miss you, but because I wonder, what will happen to you? If I open a bakery in Seattle, I'm sure I'll keep the customers we have now, but there will be rent, and in the beginning, so many extra costs that I won't have much income."

Anna smiled. "Mama, I'm your daughter, don't forget. For months I've been watching you worry about moving to Seattle, knowing that eventually you would. Do you think I haven't been planning how I will take care of Emily? I'll keep a small Mother Peersen's Home Bakery open here in Ballard after you move. Ballard isn't a village anymore, you know."

Emma smiled. "That's a wonderful idea. A small bakery in Ballard, the size you can handle alone."

"Wait, Mama!" Anna said. "I have a second plan. What's that big word of yours, Katamari? Diversification. Remember when I was still in school. I used to earn a little extra by making up lunches for fishermen? They weren't fancy, but it was a sort of catering. Mama, a bakery is a natural way to work into a fancy catering service. There are a lot of Scandinavian specialties besides cookies and tarts and sweet bread. Think of putting on a complete *smorgasbord*. For private families that want to have something special for a holiday party. For clubs and hotel banquets—''

Emma raised both hands and bowed her head in a gesture that begged for a halt. "Enough! Yes! I agree to it all. But first we must find the new home for Mother Peersen's Home Bakery, and that won't be easy.''

Katamari said, "I have taken the liberty of finding out what commercial space is available. I knew this day would come for you. Tomorrow I will take you to see the best location.''

"Please," Emma said weakly. "I think I'd like a small glass of wine.''

For Trygve, too, it was a crucial year. He would be eighteen in May, the minimum age for entering the University of Washington's law school. According to the dean, his academic record for the past three years entitled him to enter without taking the preliminary examination given in the fall. But cutting short his undergraduate career would take him away from the university life he had come to love. The law school had its own separate faculty, its own curriculum, and was located miles from the campus in the old Territorial University building in downtown Seattle.

Law school or a fourth year at the university?

It was Christina who influenced his decision. It was during a cold spell so severe that Green Lake, near the northern boundary of the city, was frozen over. Winters in Seattle were usually mild, and the rare opportunity to go ice skating caused a stampede. Skates came out of attics and closets. Local hardware and sporting-goods stores sold out their small stock of skates in an afternoon and everyone who remembered how to do it—emigrés from the Midwest, for the most part—along with hundreds who had never tried, converged on the little lake. On a Sunday afternoon Trygve, Christina, and two of Christina's brothers were in the crowd.

The sun was brilliant, the air crackled with the cold. The sound of laughter mingled with the thumps and groans of the fallen, while along the lakeshore spectators applauded the graceful skaters and cheered the brave ones who fell. Here and there on the lake-banks bonfires glowed, gathering a circle of chilled young people with red noses and watery eyes.

Though neither Trygve nor Christina had ever had the opportunity to learn how to skate, Trygve's natural coordination saved them both. After a few spills they were skimming the ice, arms crisscrossed in traditional skaters' grip, bodies swaying a little as their weight shifted from right to left, caught up in a rhythm as strong as the downbeat of a waltz. With their arms locking them together, body to body, Trygve felt an intimacy more sensual than kissing, and better because it was wonderfully peaceful. Their kisses aroused and tormented him. He desired her, he dreamed of having her. When she pulled away whispering, "No, no!" he felt ashamed of wanting her so fiercely, yet angry with her for exciting him. This was different. Skating, they were in perfect harmony. It was a kind of loving that didn't hurt, and Trygve had never felt happier.

While they warmed themselves at a bonfire, Trygve told Christina about his talk with the dean. Her response was a long silence accompanied by a look of complete bewilderment.

"Chris, what's the matter?"

She replied stiffly, "Nothing's the matter. What you're telling me is that you could go to law school this year, but you're not sure you want to."

To Trygve's dismay, there were tears in her eyes. "This is only February. I have plenty of time to make up my mind." But the half-truth sounded worse than a lie: the whole truth was that Trygve somehow had talked himself into believing Christina would encourage him to spend a fourth year at the university.

At the edge of the lake one of Christina's brothers was calling to her to come and skate. She and Trygve had been holding hands as they stood by the bonfire. Now she pulled her hand free. "All I know is, you told Father we'd get married as soon as you graduated from law school. I suppose it doesn't matter if we have to wait one more year." She picked up her skates and walked to the lake's edge, where her brother helped her attach them to her boots. Then she was gone, circling the lake on her brother's arm.

There was only one answer. Trygve owed it to her to enter law school this year. If he had a chance to be alone with her—that is, if her brothers were cooperative—he would tell her his decision on the way home. This time their marriage would be more than a plan, it would be a pledge. As proof he would give Christina the little gold football he had received for playing on a championship team. In the eyes of the world—and more important in her father's eyes—they would be engaged.

He was so engrossed in his thoughts that he was slow to recognize the girl in the green skating costume who was running toward him. One hand clutched the laces of skates slung over her shoulder. The other was waving at him with the vigor of a stationmaster flagging down a fast train at a whistle stop. Coming to a halt, the girl said breathlessly, "Well for goodness' sake, I haven't changed *that* much!"

Sarah Whiting, of course. Yes, she most certainly had changed. She had grown taller, though the top of her head was only even with his vest pocket. Her face had lost the unformed softness of childhood; the features were distinct now, and finely drawn. Her eyes hadn't changed, except to look larger—they were green as sea water, and as bold as ever. "Hello, Sarah. I haven't seen you in a long time."

"It has been a long time. But I've heard about you from Anna. I still visit her every now and then."

"She told me. You've been away at school. The girls' academy in Tacoma, isn't it?"

"I'm fifteen," she announced, as if that were a fact of tremendous interest to him personally and therefore more to the point than answering his question. "I'll graduate when I'm seventeen, and then father wants me to go to college. To Wellesley, outside of Boston, because that's where my mother went. Father believes I'll get a better education back East than I would at the University of Washington. That's nonsense, because I don't want to go to college at all. I want to study music and dance, especially dance."

"I see," Trygve said lamely. Her frankness had always disconcerted him; though he was an agile thinker under normal conditions, she danced so lightly from sentence to sentence that there didn't seem to be any place for him in the conversation. He decided to make one. "Did you come here alone?"

"I could have!" she replied heatedly. "I'm perfectly capable of getting from Capitol Hill to Green Lake without being attacked by wolves. But Father wouldn't allow it. Proper young ladies do not go unescorted to public places. He insisted that Kurt bring me."

"*Kurt . . .*" The leaden emphasis Trygve gave the name was more expressive than a full description of young Bauermeister's arrogance. "So you and he are friends now."

"I detest him," Sarah said cheerily. "But if I had made a fuss, my stepmother would have been upset, and I don't like to do that if I can avoid it. When I was a little girl, I acted badly. I resented her. But I've outgrown all that."

"What does she think about sending you back East for college?"

"She's always careful not to interfere between Father and me. All she's said is not to worry too much about something that isn't going to happen for two years. But somehow she makes me feel she's on my side."

There was so much affection in Sarah's tone that Trygve spoke impulsively. "You really like her, don't you? Anna said you would, given a little time."

Sarah laughed spontaneously. "Oh, wonderful beautiful Anna! She was right, as usual." With another agile leap from the topic to the next, she said, "Let's skate."

"The lake isn't that big," Trygve said. "We're bound to run into Kurt. What happens then?"

"We ignore him and skate the other way," Sarah replied, grinning broadly.

Because the university campus was so far from the courthouse, Trygve hadn't dropped in to visit Judge Thomas as frequently as he would have liked, but he did look him up whenever he was downtown. After the night Trygve helped the judge get off the streetcar, there had been an element of anxiety in his affection for the older man. Judge Thomas was being talked about. Too many people had seen him doze off while a trial was in progress; too many knew he kept a bottle of whiskey in his desk. Today he hadn't even bothered to close the drawer and his eyes had strayed toward it several times. As Trygve was getting ready to leave, the judge said, "I came across something that will interest you. Remember a long time ago you told me you saw a government inspector's report on the *Gypsy Queen*? I assume that inspection report was signed."

"Yes, it was."

"Do you remember the name?"

"No, but it's in my notebook." The loose-leaf notebook cover had been filled, emptied, and refilled many times since Trygve had begun to write in it as an inquisitive twelve-year-old. He had become an efficient librarian, sorting and cataloging his notes at intervals, filing them in old cigar boxes according to subject matter. A few details were listed on pages that never left the notebook—bits of information he thought of as unfinished business. Among these was the *Gypsy Queen* passenger list, along with the data on the government inspector's authorization for her launching. He opened to those pages. "The inspector's name was Harold Martinsen."

"A middle initial?"

"Yes. T."

"Indeed," the judge said, drawing his bushy black eyebrows together in a frown. "That puts the thing well beyond the long arm of coincidence." He took a file folder from a stack on his desk; Trygve recognized the cover of a prisoner's personal case history. "When a man's released from the federal penitentiary on McNeil Island, it's reported to me. I like to keep track of our graduates, especially those whose cases I've heard. Here we are. Martinsen, Harold T. He started by breaking a few state laws. Nothing spectacular, but enough to get him briefly acquainted with the state penitentiary at Walla Walla. Then he graduated to federal offenses. Became a better class of criminal, you might say. Theft of government property, perjury, contempt of court."

While the judge spoke, everything Trygve had sworn to put out of his mind came flooding back. The old anger returned, and the hunger to find someone to blame for his father's drowning.

The judge looked up and said grimly, "This is what caught my eye. Convicted of soliciting and accepting bribes while an employee of the United States government. Care to hear what his job was? Or have you guessed?"

"Government inspector for the Port of Seattle."

"Exactly."

Barely able to contain himself, Trygve exclaimed, "Then I was right! If I can find Martinsen, and get him to tell me who bribed him—"

The judge lifted a restraining hand. "Slow down, young man. Martinsen was guilty of accepting bribes. He admitted it. But let's get something straight. Your father sailed on the *Gypsy Queen* in July, right? That has to be the sailing because it was the only time she left port after she was hauled out of the junkyard and refitted."

"July 29, 1897—that's the day he left."

"Martinsen was arrested on May 25, convicted in June, and stayed in the county lock-up between his arrest and the day he was transferred to McNeil, which was June 15. He couldn't have inspected the *Queen*."

"But his signature—"

The judge shook his head. "*Someone's* signature. Not his."

Trygve clung to a shred of the elation he'd felt a few minutes before. "I still think if I could find Martinsen, he would know who was in a position to sign his name. There were two other inspectors at the time."

"Think harder. We'll say one of the remaining inspectors was paid to report the ship was in good condition. Why would he sign Martinsen's name? His honest colleague would have caught it immediately and reported it, unless of course he, too, had accepted a bribe. But why would the inspector who had lined up a profitable deal decide to share it with his associate? And how about the owner of the *Queen*? If the inspection certificate he paid money for didn't bear the name of the man he had paid off, what protection did he have? What would he do when the man he bribed got indiscreet and began telling too much about the ship's actual condition?"

"I know you're right," Trygve said reluctantly. "But someone signed that certificate. He's the man I want to look for. Where do I start, if not with Martinsen?"

"Martinsen's a start, if you can locate him. I'll let you have the address he gave the warden when he was released, but I would be truly amazed if he's living there, or for that matter, ever has. He's completed his sentence. He's under no obligation to anyone in the judicial system to account for his movements. Right now he's probably known as Jim Thompson and working in a mine in Montana. A hard man to trace. But it seems fairly apparent that you're going to try."

Trygve grinned self-consciously. "I thought I'd forgotten about the whole thing. But I never really put it out of my mind. I stored it up."

"Do what you have to do. But keep your sense of proportion. You've got three more months at the university. Make the most of them. After that, you're going to read law for me and study actual trials like a chemist in a laboratory. I'm making you a damned generous offer, and you'd be a fool if you didn't make the most of that too. Then it's law school in the fall. Don't disappoint me."

"I won't," Trygve promised without a flicker of self-doubt. "I'm not really crazy."

"Don't brag," Judge Thomas said dryly. "You're just too damned ambitious to let your mind run wild."

20

The summer passed quickly. Trygve let nothing divert him from his course of intensive study. He spent long hours in the law library and as much time as possible observing and analyzing every kind of courtroom procedure. Right from the start he was more interested in the function of the judges than in that of the attorneys. He decided his goal would be to run for election to the Superior Court bench.

Nothing Trygve studied that summer came under such careful scrutiny as the judges Hackett, Browning, and Dorsett because it was through the back door to chambers of those three that he and Katamari had once seen a dangerous Japanese labor agent enter surreptitiously. Their personal habits, as well as their decisions, were described in detail under the heading "Superior Court"—a section of his notebook that fattened rapidly as the summer progressed.

Hackett was a small quiet man. Had he worn elastic armbands and a green eyeshade he could have been mistaken for the bookkeeper in a small department store.

Judge Browning was tall, rawboned, and careless in his dress. He looked judicial only when a black robe concealed his flannel shirt; he kept his mud-caked boots hidden under the bench. He was assigned more civil cases than Dorsett or Hackett, and he was undoubtedly exposed to more ways in which to improve his official salary. Yet his shabby appearance and notorious parsimonious habits had Trygve convinced he must be honest. The notion made Judge Thomas chuckle and say, "Contrary to popular belief, the successful villain does not dress for the part. Being corrupt need not improve one's taste in clothes. Look at me.''

"You shouldn't say things like that," Trygve objected— his friendship with the judge now permitted this level of criticism. "I know you're joking, but I'm not sure everyone else would."

"Well, then, everyone else knows me better than you do, my fine, upstanding, earnest young man."

"It's not just Judge Browning's clothes. He lives in an old farmhouse."

"Mercy Maude!" Judge Thomas exclaimed, pursing his lips. "Making a home in a hovel with a privy in the backyard is proof of one's undefiled rectitude? I live in a mansion on Capitol Hill. What do you make of *that*?"

"Maybe Mrs. Thomas comes from a wealthy family."

For several seconds Judge Thomas stared at Trygve; then he laughed lividly. "Bull's-eye," he sputtered, wiping his eyes with the back of his hand. "As Muggins might have said to the good Dr. Switcher, 'Fools ask for the truth and wise men speak it.' I commend you. But where did you pick up that bit of information?"

"You told me yourself, sir."

"Did I indeed! I must have been drinking. . . . No need to answer *that*," he added, wagging a forefinger at Trygve before he opened the lower drawer of his desk and reached for the ever-present bottle of whiskey.

Judge Dorsett received more of Trygve's attention than the others did because he appealed to his sense of the dramatic. Neither Hackett nor Browning could do what he had seen Judge Dorsett do the morning the "gold ship" *Portland* came into port. Hackett and Browning simply didn't have the commanding presence that would allow them to stride toward an excited mob so that a path opened up, as Einar Peersen had said that morning, "like the waters of the Red Sea." The man who had looked lordly on the pier was no less imperious in the courthouse. His English worsted suits, pinstriped trousers, black bowler, and gold-headed ebony cane were in perfect harmony with his manner of dealing with the public. He terrified young attorneys and silenced witnesses. His instructions to a jury were often lengthy expositions of his personal views on the guilt of the accused. Trygve disliked him instinctively long before he learned enough about courtroom procedure to realize that Dorsett invented new rules whenever established procedures didn't suit his purposes. Dorsett seemed to control the courthouse the way he controlled the space around him. But did that make him necessarily dishonest?

"We don't talk about Judge Dorsett," one of Trygve's courthouse informants told him. "We just try to stay out of his way."

One of Judge Dorsett's habits was to pound his gavel at exactly noon, announce that court would be in recess until two o'clock, and depart for lunch. By talking with the bailiff, Trygve learned that the judge ate with the same friends at least three times a week, and always in the same place. When Trygve asked, "What place is that?" the bailiff winked and said, "If I was to talk about his private affairs, I wouldn't be his bailiff very long, now, would I?"

Where a judge took his noon meal hadn't seemed important until that moment. His curiosity piqued, Trygve waited outside chambers until Judge Dorsett emerged, swinging his cane as he strode down the corridor, oblivious of those who tried to speak as he passed. His pace never altered as he walked downhill from Seventh to Fourth Avenue and then north to Marion Street, advancing along city streets with the same indifference he displayed in courthouse halls. At the corner of Marion, Judge Dorsett proceeded purposefully up the concrete walk to the stately Victorian mansion that had been converted into the private Cascade Club for men.

From the sidewalk Trygve could see the doorman clearly enough to recognize him. Johnny Winters, once a Ballard boy and a classmate of Anna's. As soon as Judge Dorsett was safely inside, Trygve walked boldly across the lawn and up the steps to the entrance.

Johnny Winters grinned with pleasure at seeing him. "You didn't know I work here? Sure! For almost a year now. Inside, until a couple of months ago. I like this better. You have to do a lot of bowing and yes-sirring, but it's better than sweeping the dining room or scrubbing cook pots. And look at this suit," he said proudly, patting the sleeve of his livery.

"I'd wear it to dance if it didn't have these big initials embroidered on the sleeve."

Johnny needed little encouragement to talk about his job and the important people he was meeting in the course of a day's work. Trygve quickly learned that one of the men Judge Dorsett lunched with was Jonathan Wise, owner and publisher of the Seattle *Daily Chronicle*, the *Tribune*'s powerful rival; the other was the Reverend Thomas George, minister of the largest and most prosperous church in the city. "A rich preacher, a rich publisher, and a rich judge. Quite a combination, eh?" the doorman bragged. "I tell you, there isn't a man goes through this door that ain't got all ten fingers into something big."

"Any idea what the judge and his friends talk about?"

Johnny shrugged. "I used to hear a little when I was working in the dining room. Especially the Reverend George. He's so used to standing up there in the pulpit, he's forgotten how to talk except to shout. Maybe being a preacher is the reason he always has a lot to say about what he's against. Like he's dead against drinking. Jesus, is he against drinking!" Johnny tilted his head, twisting his mouth into an expression of furious disapproval as he imitated the righteous Reverend George. "A man who lets liquor pass his lips should be removed from office! A councilman who knows the taste of whiskey cannot be trusted to lead our city into the future!"

"How about a judge who drinks!"

"That's his favorite subject. There's one in particular. I don't know who the poor sot is, but I can tell you this, Tryg. Old Saint George is going to get him someday."

"Does Judge Dorsett talk about that too?"

"Not that I know of. But most of the time I don't get close enough to hear. Anyway, the guy who owns the newspaper and the preacher are the loud ones. The judge lets them talk, but believe me, when *he* has something to say, they both go mum, and they *listen*."

Mother Peersen's Home Bakery opened its new downtown location in June. Anna's Ballard "branch" in Emma's kitchen was also prospering.

The summer was memorable too, for Katamari Tamesa. Jim Hill, president of the Great Northern Railway, had paid him generously—not only for the land he wanted for a future railroad station but also for Katamari's several business trips to the East Coast and Japan. He was looking for new products and new markets that would increase the volume carried by Great Northern freight cars. Katamari now owned so much property that instead of spending his profits on more apartment buildings, he converted a large one-story building into a small department store and stocked it with Oriental merchandise. Silk kimonos, brocaded satin, lacquered dinnerware, bamboo furniture, and carved teakwood screens were on one side of the building. The other was a grocery store that sold fresh octopus, tiny dried shrimp, and wild mushrooms, as well as rice, pickles, and vegetables—the cheapest and the finest side by side.

It had been almost six years since Kurt Bauermeister's mother had married Sarah's father and Trygve had sent Kurt sprawling on the floor of the professor's study. Kurt had made little effort to conceal his hatred since that day. "A mean person has a long memory," Anna had warned her brother at the time. "So stay away from him, Litt Bror. The truth is, he's a very unhappy boy."

Avoiding Kurt hadn't been difficult, even while he and Trygve were attending the university at the same time. Kurt had different interests—he was the leader of a militaristic student club called the Patriots and his friends were the kind of haughty young men Trygve had no desire to mingle with.

During the winter of his last term at the university, Trygve had seen Kurt only twice. The first was the afternoon in February when he and Christina were skating on Green Lake. Trygve had stayed as far away from Kurt as the small lake permitted; the second time, Kurt invited a confrontation.

Trygve adn Katamari were in a popular café near the campus when Kurt and four of his fraternity brothers walked in. Ignoring the vacant tables in other sections of the café, Kurt led the group to a table next to Trygve's. He turned his back and began a steady monologue, raising his voice so that he was sure to be heard not only by Trygve and Katamari but also by a dozen or more students seated nearby. His companions listened with sheepish grins and anxious glances in Trygve's direction.

Trygve was able to ignore the remarks that were obviously aimed at him. "There's the big man on campus. Right at the next table, all muscles and thick skull. But that makes him a good football player. He gets along all right on the crew, too, as long as the rest of the oarsmen pull hard enough. But who writes his term papers for him? *That's* the mystery." Finally, tiring of this approach, Kurt turned around in his chair to address Trygve directly. "Well, it's the big man himself! Hello, Peersen. Who's your little friend?"

Trygve pushed back his chair and stood up. Recognizing the light that came into his friend's dark blue eyes when he was angry, Katamari also got to his feet. "He's not worth it," he said quietly. Reluctantly, Trygve let himself be guided toward the door.

"You don't have to fight for me," Katamari said when they were outside. "At least not with your fists."

Struggling to control his fury, Trygve said, "The last time I saw that bastard, he was with Sarah at Green Lake. I can't understand how she puts up with him."

"He is part of her family whether she likes it or not, and she's learned to be considerate of her stepmother's feelings. And she's away at school most of the time."

Trygve saw Kurt again in the middle of the summer, this time in a neighborhood where he would least expect to find such a caste-conscious young man.

On his way to visit Katamari at his new Oriental department store, Trygve passed the office of the radical labor newspaper, the weekly *Union Record*. A mob of poorly dressed men, all noisy and many drunk, was gathering in the street in front of the building. Trygve pushed his way into the center, asking, "What's happening here?"

The replies were meaningless. Growls, curses, fists shaken at the *Record* building, with the most coherent of the rabble muttering, "We come here to do what we got to do, buddy. Keep asking questions, and you'll get your head broke in."

Trygve had first encountered street brawls when he fought to save his dog Venn. Since then he had learned a lot, including when to back off before he got hurt. This was clearly one of those times. But now that he was close to the *Record*'s big front window, he could see that there were two men inside: one of them was Sarah's brother, Benjamin.

He slipped out of the crowd and hurried around the building to the back door. It was open. He went inside, locked and bolted it. "Ben!" he said urgently. "I don't know what you're doing here, but that's a crazy gang out there. You better leave while you can. Both of you."

Ben looked both frightened and stubborn. The second man, whom Trygve judged to be a few years older, stood at ease, his inner strength as palpable as an electric current. The man's face was peaceful, though the deep-set gray eyes reminded Trygve of storm clouds.

"Trygve, may I introduce Peter Scott," Ben said as ceremoniously as his father might have introduced a distinguished visiting professor. "I'm sure you've read his column in the *Record*, as well as his editorials."

Trygve had been reading the *Union Record* since its inception three years before as the official organ of the Seattle Central Labor Council. He had friends and relatives working in logging camps, so Peter Scott's name was indeed familiar. Scott's column, "The Voice of Radical Labor," was known for its fiery denunciation of lumber barons and the miserable living conditions in Northwest logging camps. Though small, and so poorly funded that it was always on the edge of bankruptcy, the *Union Record* continued to contribute to its self-destruction with slogans such as "The people revolt when justice can be had no other way." In the minds of affluent Seattle businessmen, what began as a pathetic little rag was becoming a menace. Jonathan Wise's Seattle *Daily Chronicle*, speaking for its advertisers, had begun to publish antilabor editorials as furious as Peter Scott's editorials. But here was Scott himself, acting as if the brawling, cursing mob at his doorstep didn't exist. Or he's a fatalist, Trygve decided. It's not that he doesn't recognize danger. He just deals with it as best as he can, and knows he can't do more.

"Mr. Scott, have you called the police?"

Smiling at Trygve's naiveté, Scott replied, "Twenty minutes ago."

Mystified, Trygve blurted out, "But the main police station is only three blocks from here!"

As if his words brought them into existence, four uniformed officers appeared at the far end of the block and began to advance slowly toward the *Record* office. Rather than dispersing at the sight of police, the mob grew more violent. A rock crashed through the front window. Then the door splintered under the weight of several bodies and a dozen brutish figures leapt over the shattered door and began throwing chairs, papers, and books into the street through the window's gaping hole. The shouting and cursing diminished as the intensity of the physical attack increased. Trygve was strong enough to pick up two men at a time and throw them back through the broken window. But he knew that the wise street fighter—unless he is very drunk—fights to win rather than opting for inglorious defeat, and there were at least twenty toughs in this wrecking gang. Through it all, Peter Scott neither moved nor spoke, and Benjamin Whiting stood solidly beside him.

The police officers continued their unhurried pace. If anything, they seemed to slow down as they drew near. Something was wrong; they should have been running. Trygve had been brought up to respect police and see them as protectors. In his confusion, he shouted, "Police! Hurry up! Help us! They're breaking up the place!"

Then Trygve saw for the first time that one of the loudest of the demonstrators was Kurt Bauermeister.

Despite his long-standing disdain for Kurt, Trygve's reaction was simple and direct. In seconds Kurt would be arrested and jailed. He couldn't stand by and let that happen. Trygve raced out the back door and through the crowd, ducking fists and tearing away from hands until he reached Kurt. Grabbing his arm, he shouted, "For God's sake, Kurt! The police are coming. You'll be arrested!"

Kurt jerked his arm free. "Take your hands off me!"

Ignoring the fury in Kurt's face, Trygve tried again, this time using such force that Kurt was helpless. The police officers had reached the outskirts of the mob. They stopped, surveying the destruction like interested spectators. Trygve's naiveté died when he saw the smugness on their faces.

Suddenly the mob began to disperse, but at a leisurely pace, many of them grinning at the officers as they passed. Kurt looked up into Trygve's face and laughed. "If you don't let go of me, *you'll* be arrested."

Trygve released Kurt and slowly went inside. Peter Scott and Benjamin had already begun to sweep up shards of glass and to sort out the papers and books lying in heaps on the floor. In the street, the police officers took a final look at the battered building and then walked away as they had come, like strollers on a Sunday afternoon in Woodland Park.

Trygve exploded. "They didn't even bother to come inside and see if anyone was hurt."

Peter Scott's sensitive face remained composed. Only his stormy gray eyes showed that he wasn't indifferent to what had happened. "They did what they were sent to do. What they were well paid for."

"They must have been sent to do nothing," Trygve said indignantly. "Who would give orders like that?"

"If it was true to form, they got their instructions from their sergeant. The sergeant had his from higher up—his captain. The usual chain of command. But when it comes to the payoff, there are some missing links in the chain. The thugs were paid. I know most of them—they're not antilabor or pro-city hall, just mercenaries who hire on when their pockets are empty. They all know where to go to earn a few dollars. But the police officers didn't get paid, and neither did their sergeant. The captain did, and believe me, he doesn't share bribes with officers of lesser rank because he doesn't have to. Anyone on the force who doesn't follow his orders is investigated by a special review board selected by the captain himself, and the accused is fired immediately thereafter for disobeying the command of his superiors."

"If that happened to me," Trygve said earnestly, "I'd let the public know about it. I'd go to the newspapers, and the city council, and if I had to, to the mayor himself."

Ben Whiting spoke for the first time, turning to Scott for his approval. "Doesn't he sound the way I used to when I first started working here?"

Scott smiled with warmth his lean face hadn't shown before. "Pretty close, Ben, but I have a feeling Trygve is tougher and will learn faster. All right, Trygve, what happens when the officer who was fired for being honest wants to tell the world all about it? If he takes his story to the *Tribune*, a reporter will sympathize and write it all down, but not a word of it will appear in the paper. When he goes to the *Daily Chronicle*, a very critical editor will demand proof of such outrageous charges. Both newspapers will have already received a release from the police department stating that after an impartial hearing before a duly constituted board of review, Officer So-and-so was given a dishonorable discharge. It's this disgraced patrolman's word against the department.''

"It's like a bad dream," Trygve said. "I still don't understand who paid for the gang today."

Scott answered with a shrug. "The money comes from private individuals, goes to powers in city hall, and filters down to men such as you've seen today. Which private individual set up this particular attack, I can't say, but a hundred to one, it was the Reverend Thomas George. That shocks you, doesn't it? But it's true. A man of the cloth, with the biggest church in the city. He's got power, and he likes to use it.''

Trygve's expression of dismay had a different origin than Scott realized. The Reverend George, who ate lunch at least twice a week with Judge Thomas Dorsett. . . . What had his friend the Cascade Club doorman told him? That the preacher talked loudest and longest, mostly about the evils of drink, but that when Judge Dorsett spoke, he and the publisher, Wise, went mum, and listened. "It's rotten," Trygve exclaimed with fervor, sensing his own helplessness. "I'd sure like to do something about it."

Scott replied like a sympathetic older brother. "I hope you will. But you'd better accept the fact that it won't be a fair fight. There are too many of them and not enough of us. They're rich, we're poor. So don't get into it until you're ready. Read the editorials in the *Tribune* and the *Chronicle* and try to analyze what's behind them. And learn to be careful. That young man you tried to drag away from the riot—you thought he would be arrested and you tried to prevent it. He must be a friend of yours."

Trygve glanced automatically at Ben.

"He's my stepmother's son, Peter," Ben said quietly. "Trygve knows him, but they're far from friends."

"Ah." Scott's face was full of concern. "And of course he saw *you* in here, didn't he, Ben?"

"I'm sure of it."

"Which means your father's going to learn you were in the company of a notorious radical, unless your stepbrother's a nicer guy than I think he is."

"He isn't. He'll tell, and he'll make quite a story of it. But it doesn't matter. I've already made up my mind that if I can't do the work I believe in and live in peace with my father at the same time, I'll leave home. If Kurt brings it about sooner than I planned, it's just as well. Maybe he won't. It would be more like him to try to trade off what he knows about me for something he's afraid I might know about him. He only dislikes me. It's Trygve he hates."

"Then I can promise you that right now he's reporting Trygve to the men behind the riot. He'll tell them everything he knows, and a lot of vicious fabrications—anything he can think of that will put Trygve on their black list of dangerous radicals, *someone to be watched.*"

"Let them watch," Trygve said defiantly. "I don't care."

Scott looked at him thoughtfully. "You don't know what it's like to be on that list, or what it's like to be watched. If someone you know got hurt because of it, would you care? If your house burned down because of it, would you care? If you were charged with a crime you didn't commit and the judge's verdict was 'Guilty' . . would you care?"

21

The letter from his father in Yokohama did not surprise Katamari; it did surprise the family gathered in Emma Peersen's kitchen for their traditional Thursday-night dinner. Katamari had told them that his father had discussed his future with their respected friends Mr. and Mrs. Mita and had agreed that Katamari would make a suitable husband for Tomoko Mita, age fifteen. Katamari was to sign an affidavit to the effect that he had proposed marriage to Tomoko Mita and that she had accepted. With that document, Mr. Mita would take the girl to the proper office in Yokohama, where she would be registered by the U.S. Immigration Service for entry into the United States, and would be issued a passport. Mr. Mita would then buy his daughter passage on one of the cargo-passenger vessels that transported picture brides to Canada and the United States.

A "picture bride," or *shakonsai*, Katamari explained, was a girl introduced to a Japanese male by way of a photograph. The Japanese population in Seattle was growing rapidly. One lone male had come up from San Francisco in 1880; now there were some four thousand Japanese in the city. As the Issei community grew, so did the number of young men who were seeking wives.

By choosing to build his future in the Western world rather than returning to his father's business in Japan, Katamari had broken with family tradition. Yet, to the Peerens' amazement, he had accepted the traditional arrangement between his parents and the parents of the bride-to-be. "I am twenty-eight years old," he said calmly. "I do not wish to be an old man with young children. And there is a saying: 'Happiness comes to the man who marries a Japanese girl and lives in a Western house.' Though I sometimes feel as American as any of you, I think it is wise to marry someone who comes from the same background. And there's another reason.'' Katamari took a small photograph from his breast pocket and placed it on the table. ''That is Tomoko, my bride. Beautiful as a flower, pure as a prayer.''

When she boarded ship, Tomoko Mita was wearing a light blue silk kimono with a delicate print of white waves and flying birds, a sash striped with black, blue, and orange, and sandals with white and orange straps. She was nervous about leaving everything familiar behind, but she was also excited. This was the beginning of what the Americans called an ''adventure.'' Besides, she was intrigued by the handsome young man whose photograph she had been studying in private. She waved good-bye to her parents without tears or regrets.

As soon as she went below to her quarters, the pleasant feelings vanished. She had expected a cabin of her own, but she was sent to the hold, along with two hundred Japanese immigrants and twenty Russian men and women. Only a thin board separated the women's section from the men's. There were wooden bunks in two long rows like silkworm racks, each bed covered by a coarse blanket. Wondering how she would keep warm at night, Tomoko peeled back the bedcovers one by one. Under the last was a layer of dried hay. She would be sleeping on top of feed for cattle!

Her small space was in the top tier directly below an air vent. It hadn't been cold on shore, but now the ocean wind blowing down the vent pipe was bitter. Tomoko looked at the faces of the other girls, who, like herself, were dressed in light kimonos. They were whispering together, too shy to complain out loud, but their faces revealed their feelings. They were dismayed, even revolted, but they were pledged to endure. How often had her own mother reminded her, ''Endurance is the way of women.'' In a dirty cold place like this, the maxim didn't comfort her. Discouraged, Tomoko climbed up into her bunk and tied her straw hat over the air vent. Some wind seeped through, but it was a little better.

The first day at sea a Japanese deckhand came below to issue each girl a bowl, a cup, and a dish. These, he said, would be theirs to use and wash for the remainder of the trip. He was a rough-looking man, with coarse features and the speech of an uneducated farmer, but he reminded Tomoko of the gardener who had worked for the Mitas for many years. The resemblance gave her the courage to ask. "Where is the dining room?"

The man grunted. "There isn't any, for you. You all eat down here in the hold."

"Excuse me, sir," Tomoko replied with modesty, "if we must take our meals here, where do we wash and bathe?"

"Bathe? Twice a week, with salt water. One dipper of fresh water to rinse off. Wash for dinner? Before we bring your food, you will be shown."

Tomoko's misery deepened as the distance between herself and home widened. She became exhausted by it and began to live like an animal in hibernation, sleeping as much as she could, trying not to feel. She tried not to listen to the tales the other girls exchanged—mostly about picture brides who had never arrived at their destinations. Instead the brides had been met by a "boss," who sold them for one hundred dollars each to a bigger boss. Some disembarked at ports where there were no immigration officers, so they had to be unloaded at night. Two girls from the Okayama prefecture had been drowned in the process. Several picture brides had been grabbed by crewmen, gagged, and nailed into boxes and unloaded like cargo—they, too, were never heard from again.

Many of the girls reported something Tomoko realized must have happened in her own case. Their fathers had paid for passage in a cabin, but when they showed their tickets to the purser he had laughed, saying there must have been a mistake back in the shipping office and there was nothing he could do about it. Still, Tomoko thought, in comparison with the flood of rumors about picture brides who disappeared, crossing the ocean in the hold was uncomfortable but at least it was relatively safe.

* * *

The day his bride was to arrive began auspiciously for Katamari. He had successfully completed a business arrangement with Jim Hill at the Great Northern office in plenty of time to return to his apartment. It was important that he dress properly for his first meeting with Tomoko Mita.

A block from home, he could see that some kind of disturbance was taking place at the entrance to his apartment building. He hurried toward it. A single Japanese was trapped in the center of a dozen roughly clad whites, who were beating him with fists and clubs. Katamari broke into a run. The victim was Tokio Hanada, his manager, the old friend whose daughter had been raped and beaten to death by a labor agent.

Katamari knew he was being foolish; still he pushed through the gang, shouting, "Do not beat him! He has done nothing!"

The violence stopped abruptly. The man who had been gripping Tokio's arm while the others struck him released his hold. Tokio slumped to the sidewalk, his head bloody and his body limp. He was barely conscious.

"Back off," one man growled at Katamari. "This dirty yellow *sukibai* isn't even a citizen of our United States and he makes more money with all his apartments than us good citizens put together. So stay out of this, Jap!"

To be called a "Jap" was a routine insult, but the word *sukibai*, dirty old man, was foul. But Katamari ignored it, intent on saving Tokio, whose frail body couldn't survive many more blows. "He is a poor man, like yourselves. He is a janitor, nothing more. You don't want to kill a sick old man."

The man who had spoken was obviously the leader. He didn't stop Katamari from picking Tokio up and carrying him into the building, and the other men didn't move. Katamari put Tokio to bed, washed his face and head, and wrapped it in a clean towel to stanch the bleeding. When he left Tokio's room, the surly gang was waiting for him in the hall. The leader snarled, "He's the janitor? I guess that makes you the owner of this building and all those other apartments around here."

A lie would not save him from what he knew was about to happen. At least the truth could be spoken with dignity.

"Yes, I am the owner." That's all Katamari had time to say before someone threw an arm around his neck and jerked him backward as a man in front brought his fist up in a murderous blow to the face.

During Tomoko's last hour aboard ship, she had witnessed a kind of abuse as bad as anything her shipmates had been whispering about. One of the men identified himself as a "public health inspector." He separated a picture bride from the group, accused her of being "diseased," and ordered her to submit to a pelvic examination. She pleaded without effect. When he grabbed her wrists, she struggled, but it was useless.

Signaling one of his colleagues, the inspector threw the girl onto her back on top of a stack of cargo. While the second man held her down, he performed a prolonged pelvic examination in the presence of a half-dozen Japanese crewmen. The humiliation was so horrible that Tomoko wondered why the girl didn't just throw herself into the sea. She only wept bitterly, and was still weeping when she and the other brides were finally released from inspection and herded down the gangplank to meet their husbands waiting on the pier.

Now it was Tomoko whose bitter tears acknowledged her arrival in the strange land that was to be home forever. It had been four hours since the ship docked, two since the last passenger had disembarked and the last picture bride had identified her husband. The handsome prince of her photo still had not come to claim her. She sat on an empty packing box at the end of the pier, prepared to scream and run if anyone tried to drag her back onto the boat, yet terrified to leave the place where Katamari would expect to find her. She knew a dozen words of English—not nearly enough to give her the courage to approach one of the longshoremen in the warehouse and explain her predicament. "Endurance is the way of women." She sat shivering and sobbing, simply enduring until someone arrived to take her away.

Daylight was fading when a man appeared at the far end of the pier. He strode toward her with long purposeful steps and stopped in front of her. She stared up at him, paralyzed by his size and apparent physical strength. He was a huge American, with pale gold hair and clear blue eyes. When he leaned over her, he shut out the sky.

"Tomoko Mita?"

His voice was deep and pleasant. She nodded, using two of the English words she was sure of. "Yes, sir." The result was a baffling string of English. At least he hadn't touched her or tried to kidnap her. Timidly she tried the rest of her vocabulary. "Sorry, sir. Not speak your language."

For some time Tomoko had been aware that one of the crewmen was watching from the deck just above her. She looked up at him, calling in Japanese, "I do not know what this man is saying. Can you talk to him?"

A conversation between the yellow-haired giant and the steward ensued. The steward clearly had trouble following it, but eventually understood enough to translate. "He's a friend of Katamari Tamesa. His name is Peersen. Katamari had an accident and he is in the hospital. It took a long time for this man Peersen to hear about it, but now he's come to get you and your baggage and take you to your man."

"Is it safe to go with him?"

"I think so. He does not seem the type to do you harm."

The Wayside Mission Hospital was on the waterfront at the foot of Jackson Street. It was a derelict side-wheeler, purchased for two hundred and fifty dollars by a steamship captain whose hobby was dealing in junk. With the cooperation of a benevolent society formed for the purpose, the captain had her dry-docked on a grid of beams and fitted her out as an emergency hospital.

The ship's upper deck was the hospital pharmacy. Surgical instruments, fifteen in all, were sterilized in the onetime ship's galley. The hospital rooms had once been passenger cabins. There was no running water, no bathrooms or toilets, and little heat, but for the past five years a doctor had managed to treat the sick and had patched up drunks here.

In one of the converted cabins, Tomoko met the man she had come to marry. At the sight of him, she gasped and covered her mouth with her hand. Both of his eyes were cut and badly discolored. Blood from scalp wounds had soaked through the bandages which concealed most of his face, and there were dark bruises around his neck. Whatever damage had been done to his slender body was hidden under bed-clothes, except for the arm in its plaster cast that was resting on top of the bedspread.

What Tomoko murmured and Katamari replied, Trygve could understand not by language but by instinct. Katamari's good eye seemed to shine on Tomoko as she approached the bed and timidly put her fingers to his cheek. Trygve turned away quickly and left the room.

Trygve attended his graduation from law school with his mind more on Christina Franzen than on himself. In a way it was as important an event for her as it was for him, because now, after years of patient waiting, they were to be married. But Christina wasn't there to see the ceremony. She was in bed at home, suffering from a nameless ailment Mrs. Franzen was treating with herbs to cool her fever and clean her blood.

Judge Thomas was Trygve's most prestigious guest. He joined the family at the entrance to the auditorium after the ceremony and pulled Trygve aside.

At some point during the ceremony Judge Thomas had decided that Trygve's future was in politics. He said now, "You're determined to become a judge, and a seat on the bench is best obtained through politics. You'll have to jump right into the dirty mess of politics with both feet. Are you sure you want to do that? Do you think you *can* do that?"

Trygve had just enough time to nod before the judge continued, "Then focus that fine mind of yours on city hall. Don't miss a meeting of the Seattle City Council, because that's what you're going to run for. In politics, your first try should be for a position so small you're bound to win it. Candidates who lose once have only a fifty-percent chance the next time they try. Candidates who lose twice remain in the public mind as the man who always loses. Candidates who run for office a third time and lose ought to devote their lives to picking hops and canning salmon." He winked at Trygve wisely, patted his shoulder, and departed.

Trygve went to Christina's house as soon as the graduation dinner ended. His head was full of things he could finally say to her for the first time. He could talk about marriage, not as a hope for the future but as a plan for the present. Just this morning the dean of the law school had given him the names of three Seattle firms that wanted him to make an appointment for an interview. In order to be licensed, he still had to pass the state bar examination, but any firm would pay him a small salary in the meantime. Hurry up and get well, Christina. We can get married whenever you say.

Carl Franzen answered his knock on the door. "No use you coming in," he said, his mouth drawn into a thin hard line. "Christina took worse. We got Dr. Jonas to come give her some medicine but he wrapped her up and put her in his buggy and drove her to the hospital with her mother."

"Which hospital?"

"Mercy," Franzen snapped, and slammed the door.

The last trolley to Seattle had left. Trygve walked the eight miles from Ballard to the hospital, arriving at one o'clock in the morning. There was a light in the emergency room, but the nurse who answered Trygve's frantic ring refused to let him enter the hospital. Yes, the log did show that a Christina Franzen had been admitted, but she did not have the authority to give out information about the condition of any patient. Dr. Jonas would be in in the morning. He would be the one to talk to. . . . Finally, seeing how distraught Trygve was, the nurse softened. "Go home," she said gently through the half-open door. "Come back tomorrow. I promise you that everything possible is being done for her."

When the nurse closed and locked the door, Trygve moved away from the entrance and sat down on the ground with his back against the wall. Arms crossed and supported by his knees, he rested his head on his forearms. He slept in that position for brief periods until the hospital doors were unlocked in the morning. It had been a warm night, but his new suit—a graduation gift from his mother—was wrinkled and soaked with night dampness, and his chin was rough with the stubble of his reddish-brown beard. The nun in charge of the wing looked at him curiously, but when she learned that he was engaged to Christina, she led Trygve to the ward. "She's in the last bed. Her mother's with her."

For three days Christina burned with fever and cried out during periods of delirium. Through it all Trygve sat beside her bed. When her parents or sisters and brothers were in the room, he gave up his chair and stood at the window. He relived, one by one, the experiences they had shared over the years. He thought back to September, when he and Christina had joined a group of young people to go to the hop field south of Seattle, where they were paid one dollar for filling a box as big as a coffin. He remembered every detail of this excursion, each memory came back to hurt him. Christina calling "Checker!" when her box was full. Christina trying to talk Chinook jargon with the Indians who came to the fields by the hundreds when the hop harvest was ripe. Christina clapping delightedly when the Indians played the stick game, and looking enviously at the baskets the older squaws had to sell. Christina with her face dusty and bits of pungent hop pods caught in her hair, reaching timidly for his hand when they were riding the streetcar back to the city. Christina whispering, "Don't you wish we could get married?"

She died before dawn on the fourth day. The sympathetic nun who had permitted Trygve's continuous visit had been watching him anxiously. She came up to him and said softly, "It's over. Let her parents be alone with her now."

Trygve obeyed numbly. Walking the dark streets of the sleeping city, he cursed himself for letting the selfish pursuit of a law career postpone their marriage. After a while he began to cry. He cried without shame until he was thoroughly exhausted. When he finally reached home, shimmering pink-gold light was beginning to brighten the eastern sky and the moon had disappeared behind the Olympic Mountains to the west.

Emma was sitting at the kitchen table with an empty coffee cup and her Bible. She was wearing her flannel bathrobe and her hair was in braids. There were dark shadows under her eyes and her skin was pale with strain. She hadn't slept. Somehow she knew what had happened even before she saw it in Trygve's face.

Trygve paused, but he was unable to speak. Respecting his silence, Emma was silent as well. But her eyes followed him as he walked through the kitchen, and when his heavy footfalls sounded on the uncarpeted stairs to the second floor, she dropped her head onto her hands. She remembered how bitterly she had wept some ten years before, and wondered whether Trygve, like herself, would never cry again.

22

By the end of her freshman year at Wellesley, Sarah Whiting had come to the realization that although she still wanted to become a dancer, she was glad her father had forced her to go to college. The private academy where she had attended high school had turned out to be far less puritanical than Professor Whiting himself. Though inclined toward primness, the administration assumed that all its students were good girls—or they wouldn't be there—and therefore wouldn't be corrupted by acting in plays or learning the basics of classical ballet.

Sarah discovered that she was very good at acting. She could become whatever character the drama instructor assigned; she was inside the other person, looking out. But Sarah was not completely fulfilled on the stage. She would have liked acting more if she had written the plays herself—her natural instinct was to create rather than serve as a tool for someone else's creation. She found more freedom in dancing because she could speak through the movements of her own body.

Her drive to express her emotions in her own way did not make her the best pupil of classical ballet. When its formal patterns interfered with her personal reaction to the music, Sarah simply ignored the instructor's dictates and danced to please herself, not minding in the least that she was leaping about the gymnasium doing the *grand jeté* while everyone else was moving to the side, executing the graceful *glissade* in perfect unison.

Her ballet instructor, a realistic Frenchwoman, soon gave up the unequal fight. "My dear Sarah," she said after several weeks, "you move with grace, but no one will ever make you into a ballet dancer. Ballet is a *disciplined* art. You were born to dance barefoot in a Greek tunic like Isadora Duncan. Someday you will see her, and then you will recognize the kind of dancing meant for you. Meanwhile, you must continue with ballet, because your body is still soft and unformed. Ballet can strengthen it and teach you to control it, and until you understand every part of your body and how to call upon it, you will never be a dancer of any kind."

By the time Sarah graduated, her mind was made up. Since she was going to be a dancer, she had neither the need nor the desire to attend college. That had been her response last year when her father announced that she had been accepted at Wellesley College.

"A dancer?" Professor Whiting's face paled. Cold eyes fixed on his wayward daughter, he told her, "If you pursue such a course, I will disinherit you."

The discussion went on from there, with Sarah holding stubbornly to her refusal to attend college and her father repeating his threat. Professor Whiting brought it to an end as he had all discussions since Sarah was a small child. He ordered her to her room; she was to remain there until she was penitent.

Through it all Sarah's stepmother, Angela, had listened in silence, watching with sad eyes. As soon as she could leave the library inconspicuously, Angela followed Sarah upstairs. She sat down on a wing chair in the bedroom and said with a sigh, "This is not as bad a moment as it seems to you now. I advise you, dear Sari, to go to Wellesley as your father has planned. A truly great dancer offers much more than graceful movements and pretty leaps and pirouettes. She expresses *ideas*. A college education will only add depth and scope to your ideas. It will not force you to abandon dance as a way of expressing them. Go to Wellesley for your own sake, not your father's. Believe me, dear, angry as you are right now, you don't really want to lose your father. You love him. You just don't realize it now because you are afraid of him."

Sarah had given in reluctantly. Boarding the train for Boston, she decided she could suffer through one year at Wellesley, but was secretly determined to put an end to her "compromise" after that. Now, homeward bound at the end of one year, her head was humming with all the things she was going to tell her father and Angela about the courses she planned to take in the fall. She was also thinking of all she was going to tell Ben in secret—especially about the solo she had danced in a pageant before a large audience seated on the grassy slope below College Hall.

Sarah and Ben had always confided in each other, particularly ever since their mother's death. Now Sarah was eighteen and Ben was twenty and a senior at the University of Washington. The future had become serious business; they were both intensely concerned about what their roles would be. They hadn't seen each other for ten months, but the bond between them felt stronger than ever. Their first private talk revealed that the courses they were pursuing were completely at odds with the goals their father had set for them.

The direction Ben was taking was as scandalous as Sarah's dedication to professional dance. He was becoming involved with the labor movement. After Sarah entrusted him with the secret of her solo in the dance pageant, he confessed that he had been attending meetings of the Industrial Workers of the World—the infamous "Wobblies." As often as he could steal time from his university classes, he was working at the *Union Record*. "Remember a few years ago I told you I saw Kurt in a gang that attacked a newspaper office? When Trygve Peersen happened to come by and tried to get Kurt away before the police came? That was the *Union Record*."

"Of course I remember," Sarah said fervently. "Trygve should have let the police arrest Kurt."

"They didn't arrest anyone, Sari. They stood and grinned while a bunch of hoodlums wrecked the office. The workingman doesn't have a chance against organized government and organized graft—not unless the workers get organized too. Look at the big timber company that just gave Kurt a job. Do you have any idea what the living conditions are like in the logging camps that company owns? If you did, you'd know why I've got to keep on working in the labor movement. You *should* know about these things, whether I do or not. There's an IWW meeting next week. Come with me."

* * *

The hall was filled with men wearing heavy woolen jackets, workpants coated with the oily grime of the deep woods, and muddy boots. Their voices crowded the room with a blend of rough laughter and angry complaint until an officer of the Industrial Workers of the World called the meeting to order. The roar sank to a murmur as they took their seats. Gavel suspended in the air, the man on the platform called, "Brothers! Let's get on with our meeting."

Curious stares followed Sarah as she and Ben walked along the aisle and sat down at the side of the hall. Not only was she the only woman in the room, she was wearing a tailor-made cheviot serge suit with velvet trim and satin lapels. Her coppery red hair was braided into a single thick plait that hung down her back almost to her waist; a perky narrow-brimmed hat adorned by two brown duck wings perched on top of her head. Her posture was patrician but her step was light. As the meeting got under way and many of the men were called upon to air their grievances, their eyes frequently strayed to see how the young lady was taking it.

The loggers had a lot to say. Bunkhouse vermin, six months without a day off, twelve hours' work for three dollars, atrocious living conditions, inedible food—these were the things Sarah heard about that night at the IWW meeting. The litany of complaint was frequently relieved by the loggers' special brand of humor, and in Sarah they had a perfect audience because she listened with her heart. The term "radical labor movement" had had little meaning for her because it had to be understood rather than felt. Sarah responded instantaneously to the men's personal stories and with such feeling that she was either angry or tearful throughout the meeting.

Tangled up with her reaction to the logger's descriptions of their living conditions was her bitter dislike for Kurt Bauermeister. At home she managed to maintain a superficial politeness toward him, at least in Angela's presence. Here among the loggers her disdain for him grew. Several of the men who described filthy bunkhouses, rotten food, and miserable wages were working in one of the camps operated by Kurt's company. She knew he wasn't directly responsible for their suffering—for all his self-importance, she doubted he was responsible for much of anything except time sheets for office employees—but his smugness made her want to blame him. She imagined herself suggesting to him innocently that since he had never visited a logging camp he ought to try working in one for a month or two, just to get a better understanding of his job.

When the meeting ended, Benjamin led Sarah through the noisy crowd to the platform, where Peter Scott was the center of a group from the Seattle Central Labor Council. As they were introduced, Scott's gray eyes caught and held hers for a long moment. It was a look of intense concentration that separated Sarah from her brother and the men surrounding them. She murmured the proper words, Scott said something about how important Ben was to him, and a few minutes later she was sitting across the table from Scott in a small café. She only half-listened as he told Ben about a problem at the *Union Record*, watching those gray eyes. She had not been so affected by a man's nearness since she had been a young girl with a crush on Trygve Peersen. The quiet voice, the sensitive lips, the hands with long slender fingers, the slight but graceful body—she was aware of all these, not as separate features but as a presence that enveloped her like an invisible cloak.

After a few minutes Scott switched abruptly from his conversation with Ben. Looking directly into Sarah's face, he said, "You heard about things tonight that you never knew existed."

"Yes! And I feel ashamed of my ignorance, or perhaps I should say, humbled by it."

Scott smiled. "Are you always so sincere?"

"She doesn't know how to be anything else," Ben said. "That's what gets her into trouble."

Scott laughed and the conversation returned to the *Union Record*. Sarah was aware of Scott's thoughtful gaze often resting on her face even as he was talking to Ben. She felt a strong attraction for Scott, and she could spend no time defining the nature of the attraction. It confused and frightened her, because whatever Peter Scott was awakening felt like a force she wouldn't know how to control.

Sarah saw Peter Scott many times that summer, at first because she maneuvered Benjamin into bringing about accidental meetings. After a few weeks, Peter put an end to her pretense.

Sarah had dropped in at the *Record* office, ostensibly to meet and go home with Benjamin. She hadn't been there long before Peter said, "Ben, I'd like to talk to your sister. You go on over to Bill's Saloon and I'll join you there."

When they were alone, Peter left his desk and walked across the room to the chair where Sarah was sitting. He held out both hands, she gave him hers, and he pulled her slowly to her feet.

"I'm many years older than you," he said quietly. "And I live in another world, a world that intrigues you because it's different from what you've always known. And much as I hate to say this, you intrigue me for the same reason. But I'm too busy for games. For your sake as well as mine, I don't want to see you again."

"It's not a game." Sarah's voice trembled. "It's more than that."

"You think you've fallen in love with me." It was an honest statement, spoken in a voice filled with pain.

Sarah nodded mutely.

Peter's grip on her hands tightened convulsively as he looked into her face. The tick of the schoolroom clock on the wall behind them seemed to grow louder as the silence lengthened. "Peter," Sarah whispered, "can't we just see each other sometimes?"

Peter released her hands. "Sit down, Sarah." He took another chair a few feet away. "Just see each other sometimes," he repeated softly, as if they were the words of a song he hadn't heard for a long time. "How simple you make it sound. Perhaps, for you, it is. God forgive me, I haven't the strength to say no to you. But if we meet in the future, it isn't going to be in secret, or by chance, or through any subterfuge which, I gather, you and Ben are accustomed to using in order to avoid trouble with your father. We'll see each other according to the rules of the world *you* live in. You'll introduce me to your father, and I'll ask permission to take you to the kind of event that proper young men and women commonly attend together. If your father approves, we'll see each other—but not to the exclusion of the eligible suitors who are undoubtedly ringing your doorbell as often as they dare.''

To Sarah's enormous relief, the meeting between her father and Peter Scott went smoothly. Benjamin had persuaded Peter to relent a little on the subject of subterfuge. Peter finally agreed that if everything Ben and Sarah told their father about him was true, some facts could be omitted. The acceptable facts were that he taught economics in a small college in Wisconsin, where he made a special study of the operation of timber companies in that area. A book on the subject now occupied most of his time, though he also wrote for magazines and newspapers. He had met Ben while attending a lecture on reforestation, a new concept in the United States. No mention would be made of the *Union Record*; since Professor Whiting refused to read anything he suspected might be a ''radical'' publication, it was safe to assume he wouldn't connect Peter's name with the small weekly.

Ben arranged to be at home with Sarah when Scott first called. His abbreviated but accurate introduction satisfied his father that his son's friend was an educated man. Professor Whiting had always had a high regard for anyone whose profession was writing, though his definition of the word ''profession'' was austere. It could only be accorded to writers of what he called serious works—history, biography, and philosophy—with only marginal recognition for those who wrote fiction. Peter Scott was obviously a scholarly author, so he passed the test easily.

The professor invited Scott to join the family for tea. When at last the opportunity came for Peter to ask if Sarah might accompany him to a concert, Professor Whiting turned to his daughter. ''Do you wish to go, Sarah?''

'Yes, Father. Very much.''

''I should think it would be over by ten o'clock,'' the professor commented, sipping his tea with a happy light in his eyes.

*   *   *

For the rest of the summer, Sarah saw Peter once or twice a week—always, at his insistence, within the code for virgin daughters of affluent first citizens. Whether it was a lecture, a walk through the arboretum, or a picnic at Alki beach, Professor Whiting's permission had to be obtained and he always dictated the time Sarah was to return. Often when they returned in the evening, the professor was still in his library and would call Peter into his sanctum to talk for a while. Professor Whiting seemed almost to be waiting up for these conversations with Peter.

"Your father likes your young man, Sari," Angela confided. "And Peter *is* charming. When I first met him, I had the impression I had seen him before. But I can't think where that would have been."

Neither Sarah nor Benjamin had considered the possibility that Angela, through her late husband, might have had some contact with Peter Scott's activities. "It's a common name," Sarah said, striving to sound casual. "Besides, Peter hasn't been in Seattle for long. You must be confusing him with someone else."

"In any case, it doesn't matter." Angela put a forefinger under Sarah's chin and lifted it, looking into her eyes. She said softly, "What does matter is that I've never seen you look so happy and beautiful. Isn't it a wonderful feeling, falling in love?"

The threat of disclosure of Peter's real work vanished from Sarah's mind. Angela knew how she felt! The last barrier between them crumbled as Sarah realized there was actually someone who wasn't ashamed to talk about the emotions everyone else seemed to pretend never to have experienced. "Oh yes, it truly is," Sarah agreed fervently. "A kind of joyful feeling. It's never happened to me before."

"It's called first love. It often comes when you least expect it, and nothing quite like it will ever happen to you again. But that's not to say it isn't serious. Gracious, to me it was not only the most serious event that had ever taken place, it was the *only* one."

Sarah looked curiously at Angela. "How old were you?"

"Fourteen."

"*Fourteen*?" Sarah exclaimed, and from the perspective of her greater age, added, "Isn't that too young?"

Angela smiled. "I'm not sure there is such a thing as too young. Falling in love doesn't follow a schedule, like a train you can expect to arrive at the hour stated in the timetable. I was only fourteen, but I was just as much in love as you are."

"When I was that age I thought I loved Trygve Peersen. But that was a childish wish. I got over it a long time ago." Sarah hesitated a moment and then asked, "Whatever happened to that boy, your first love?"

"I married him."

"That boy was Mr. *Bauermeister*? You mean . . . If you were fourteen . . ."

Her remark brought a delighted laugh. "We did wait awhile, Sari. I was twenty years old and Mr. Bauermeister was twenty-five when we married. So you see, my first love turned out to be my one true love." She paused, reading the unspoken question in Sarah's face. " 'First love, one true love.' Those are merely the words I'm using to describe a particular kind of feeling. Love comes to you differently at different times of life. I do love your father, Sari. I love him sincerely."

The statement was meant to reassure her but it had little effect on Sarah. She had always taken for granted some sort of "love" between her father and stepmother. Angela's first and one true love was too wonderfully romantic to have any connection with it. "I know you do," she said, and quickly went back to the intriguing subject of Angela's late husband. "What was he like?" she asked eagerly. "Mr. Bauermeister, I mean."

"Handsome. Tall, with a military bearing. Wavy dark brown hair, very pale blue eyes. If you like, I'll show you his photograph, and you can judge for yourself. He worked hard, he didn't laugh often, but he was always considerate of my feelings and interested in the welfare of our son. In some ways he was like your father."

The wound of her mother's last illness had healed but Sarah was still sensitive to the touch of another person's loss. "Maybe I shouldn't ask this," she said somberly, "but Father never told me why Mr. Bauermeister died. Was he sick for a long time?''

Angela shook her head. ''No, he wasn't sick at all. He was killed in a logging accident. Even as president of a large corporation, he went into the woods whenever any new methods or new equipment were put into use. He started working in the woods when he was only fifteen. At one time or another he had done all the most dangerous jobs and had never been seriously injured. Ironically, he was killed when he should have been completely safe—observing the operation of a new kind of donkey engine. A cable snapped. It was nobody's fault. A lot of loggers die that way—when something just happens, and it's no one's fault. Logging accidents . . .'' Angela stopped suddenly. ''Of course! It just came to me. I knew I'd heard of Peter Scott, but I made the mistake of assuming it was here in Seattle. It was in Wisconsin, a year or so before I came west, during a conference on safety procedures with the new logging equipment. Peter Scott attended it. There were several items in the newspapers about him because he was there to represent . . .'' Again her voice broke off mid-sentence, but this time her facial expression changed abruptly. Peering anxiously into Sarah's face, she said slowly, ''Peter Scott was there on behalf of the Industrial Workers of the World. The Wobblies. But you already know about that, don't you, Sari?''

''Yes,'' Sarah said unhappily. ''That's where I met him. At an IWW meeting.''

''You're more daring than you should be, but not quite daring enough to venture down alone into the part of town where such meetings are held. Am I correct in thinking that your brother suggested it, and took you with him?''

Sarah's immediate reaction was to protect Benjamin, but at this moment of deep understanding with her stepmother, she knew anything but the truth would stick in her throat. ''I don't want to get Ben into trouble. Yes, he suggested it, but he didn't really urge me to go. You know how Father is. You must understand why we hide things from him. When I came home from college, Ben and I talked a lot about what we had been doing, and what we wanted to do. So naturally I told him about my dancing, and he confided in me. He wants to spend his life working to improve the wages and living conditions of laborers, like the loggers who live in company camps. That's how we got to talking about the IWW. He wanted me to hear the loggers talk for themselves so I'd know the reason for his decision.''

"Please understand me, Sari," Angela said gently. "I sympathize with your interest in dance. As for Ben's determination to help underpaid and misused loggers . . . When Mr. Bauermeister and I were first married, he was working in the woods for eleven hours a day, for which he received three dollars. He was the only married man in camp, the only one who had a home other than the bunkhouse he lived in six out of seven days a week. That surprises you, doesn't it? He's only remembered as a wealthy lumber baron. Your own father is one of the few who know about the hard struggle that eventually put Mr. Bauermeister at the top of the industry. So I can sympathize with Ben, too. It's the deception that bothers me.

"However, I have no intention of revealing his plans, or yours, to your father. I hope to somehow help you get closer to him so that you'll trust him enough to tell him yourselves. Meanwhile, he is getting to know Peter Scott as an individual— not a symbolic figure to be classified as a dangerous radical. And he likes Peter so far. So let's be optimists, Sari dear. Let's hold the good thought that by the time the truth comes out, your father will be so fond of Peter that he'll understand all the reasons why he would make a fine son-in-law.''

Summer moved into fall. Fireweed and goldenrod and Queen Anne's lace bloomed in profusion, as if to soak up the last of the August heat before the September haze settled over the fields. It was time for the harvest of wild fruits. Plump clusters of tiny purple grapes hung between the prickly leaves of the Oregon grape bush. Blue-black berries ripened on the stems of the low-growing salal. Among the formidable spikes of stalks growing taller than the tallest man, masses of Himalaya and Evergreen blackberries were still juicy as ripe peaches, weeks after their tiny cousins had been eaten by the birds.

The quality of the season was in harmony with Sarah's mood. Her time with Peter was running out inexorably, as summer slipped away into fall. In mid-September she would board the train for Boston, but until then she floated in suspended time, through a dreamlike sequence of days when she saw Peter, future days when she expected to see him, and the sweet remembering days in between. For the first time in her life there were no conflicts with her father. Even Kurt Bauermeister had been removed from her sunny world; he had been transferred to his company's office in Tacoma and had taken an apartment in that city. He came to the house infrequently, to visit his mother.

One afternoon in early September Kurt was in the living room with Angela when Peter Scott brought Sarah home. From a far corner of the room, unnoticed by Sarah, Kurt watched Peter go into the library to pay his respects to Professor Whiting, emerging a few minutes later to say goodbye to Sarah at the front door. When Sarah passed the arched entrance to the living room on her way upstairs, Kurt whispered to his mother, "Don't call her. I don't want that dreadful girl around."

Angela waited until Sarah was sure to be in her bedroom. Then she said with unusual sharpness, "I've spoken to you many times about your inexcusable rudeness to Sarah. I will not have it in my house—this is her home as much as mine. I'm embarrassed by the way you act in her presence, and insulted by the way you speak of her. You are my son, my only child. I will always love you, Kurt, but I would like to be able to respect you as well."

In petulant silence Kurt looked around the living room, then turned to Angela. "Sometimes I wonder about your feelings for me, Mother. Whenever something about Sarah Whiting comes up, you take her side rather than mine. All right, you're trying to love your stepdaughter as if she were your own. But I wonder how much *respect* you'd have for her if you knew who that man is who brought her home a little while ago."

Angela replied calmly, "I do know."

"I don't believe it! That's Peter Scott. He's an anarchist, a rabble-rouser! He puts out a dirty little newspaper called the *Union Record*. My God, Mother." Kurt shook his head.

"You allow that girl to be seen in public with such a dangerous and notorious man? Where do they go?"

"This afternoon, to an exhibition of Eskimo scrimshaw. Otherwise, the usual sort of thing young couples enjoy. Concerts, walks, picnics, boat rides."

"You sound so unconcerned. Does your professor husband realize who his daughter's escort is these days?"

"He does not, and I do not intend to tell him. Peter Scott is a good deal more than a radical, Kurt. He is also a writer, a scholar, and a gentleman. That side of him is just as real as his political life and that's the side Professor Whiting knows and likes. As a summer friendship, it can't do Sarah any harm. If it grows into more than that, her father will have to be told the whole truth, but I would prefer that Mr. Scott do that himself."

Kurt muttered, "What's happened to your principles?" A few minutes later he stood up, clicked his heels together sharply, bowed his head in a cold gesture of farewell, and left the house.

Two days later Professor Whiting sent the housemaid to Sarah's room with the message that she was to come to the library immediately. When she walked in, he was waiting impatiently in his desk chair, an open newspaper spread across his knees. He greeted her by holding up the paper and reading from it aloud. "*People revolt when justice can be had no other way.*" He slapped the page with the back of his hand. "The author of that statement, and the rest of this vicious article on the so-called crimes of the wealthy, is your friend Peter Scott. The name of the newspaper is the *Union Record*; he is apparently the publisher, editor, and writer, all combined."

Sarah was too shocked to think past the fact that someone had deliberately let damning evidence against Peter fall into her father's hands. "Where did you get it?"

"It came in today's mail. I do not know the sender, though I am grateful that someone is sufficiently interested in your welfare to take the trouble to inform me. I don't wish to hear your excuses, nor am I interested in learning how much you have known about this raving socialist's duplicity. I prefer to assume that you knew nothing of it. You will, of course, never see Mr. Scott again. You are not to meet him, talk to him, or write to him. Should he come to this house, you will instruct the housemaid to tell him that he is no longer welcome here and that you personally do not wish to have any contact with him in the future." He tore the newspaper in two, dropped it into the wastebasket, and swiveled his chair around to face the roll-top desk. With his back turned, he polished his spectacles, adjusted them carefully on the bridge of his nose, picked up a pen, and resumed his writing.

Sarah left the library without protest, her mind fixed on one terrible truth: Benjamin would never have sent the newspaper to her father; Angela was the only other person who knew Peter's true identity. Angela was resting; under ordinary circumstances, Sarah wouldn't have disturbed her. Today she walked into the master bedroom without waiting for an answer to her knock.

Angela sat in a chair by the window with an embroidery hoop in her lap. She was threading a strand of silk through a needle, her hands poised motionless in midair as she looked up in surprise. In a gray silk peignoir, with her long black hair hanging loosely down her back, she looked young and vulnerable. "Why, Sari," she said with a worried frown, "what's wrong?"

"Someone sent a copy of the *Union Record* to Father."

Sarah didn't need to elaborate. Angela saw enough anger and misery in her face to guess what the result of the anonymous mailing had been. She was touched by the conflicting emotions that shone in Sarah's unhappy green eyes. The look said "I hate you for what you did!" and at the same time cried "I know you couldn't have done it." Dropping her embroidery into a basket beside the chair, Angela stood up and put her hands on Sarah's shoulders. "Sari," she said softly, "I did not send the newspaper."

"No one knows about Peter except you and Ben."

"And you know Ben wouldn't dream of telling your father. So you think . . . Believe me, dear, neither did I. It was a cowardly thing to do." Her voice faltered as the truth came to her. She went back to her chair, sat down, and was silent for a long moment until Sarah asked, "What's the matter?"

"I'm . . ." The serene woman whom Sarah had never seen cry suddenly had tears in her eyes. "I'm heartsick. Kurt was with me in the living room when Peter brought you home after you'd seen the Eskimo carving exhibition. He recognized Peter and he was very upset. I think . . ." She patted her eyes with a small handkerchief and waited to regain a degree of composure before she spoke again. "I'm sure Kurt believed he was protecting you."

Something Benjamin had told her came back to Sarah in a rush. Kurt had been in the angry mob that attacked and wrecked the *Union Record* office. He was the hired thug who laughed in Trygve's face because Trygve was naive enough to believe the police would arrest him. All summer Peter had been coming to the house two or three times a week. Why hadn't she realized that Kurt might be visiting his mother at the same time? Should she tell Angela now that her son belonged to a group of street fighters paid to beat people up, wreck buildings, and set fire to labor-union offices?

The look in Angela's dark eyes gave her the answer. Angela was already in pain because of what Kurt had just done. It would be unthinkable to add another and deeper hurt. It wasn't Angela who deserved to be punished. It was Sarah who had deceived her father, and Sarah who had to be punished. She had always accepted the fact, even as a child.

Sarah put her arms around Angela in an embrace that was both fierce and protective. "It isn't your fault. It's mine, for not realizing Kurt and Peter might meet here. It could have happened at any time."

"That's my only consolation," Angela murmured, letting her head rest against Sarah's shoulder. "That it didn't happen until now. At least you've had a lovely summer, haven't you, dear?"

As Sarah was leaving, Angela became aware of a firmness in her step, a determined set of her chin that was not at all like that of a young girl who has been severely chastised and is heartbroken because she will never again see the man she loves. "Sari?" she called after her. "Don't be rash." But Sarah had already closed the door.

*　　*　　*

235

"Don't tell me I shouldn't have come here."

"It wasn't wise, but for selfish reasons I'm glad you came," Peter said quietly. "I wouldn't have liked having the maid shut the door in my face. Here, let's sit down. This office is a mean little place for our last farewell, but at least we have it to ourselves."

"I don't want to sit down."

"Be reasonable. You look as if you've run all the way from Capitol Hill. You're upset and you're out of breath, and this isn't the way to begin an important conversation." He took her hand and began to lead her toward a chair.

Sarah freed her hand with a rebellious jerk. Flinging both arms around him, she pressed her body against his with a passion their chaste kisses had never satisfied. "I won't sit down and I won't be reasonable. I want to be loved."

"You know I love you." Peter's voice was husky but the tone was reserved.

"That's not what I mean!" Her sentence ended in a little sob.

Peter lifted her chin and kissed her. It was an ardent kiss, lingering on her lips longer than he had ever allowed himself. Eyes closed, Sarah clung to him fiercely. When the kiss ended, she pulled his head down so that he was kissing her again.

Peter's careful detachment dissolved. He was no longer the older man coping wisely with the impulse of a young and inexperienced girl. Touching, fondling, kissing deeply, their bodies met with an awareness that had always been dangerously close to the surface. It was the moment Peter had been afraid of all summer—when the intensity of Sarah's awakening would burn through the control he had sworn to impose on both of them. Yet even as he caressed her with the feeling this couldn't be stopped, the strength to stop it gradually returned. Her innocence inflamed him, but it also made him her seducer.

He pulled away from her and they stood facing each other, both trembling. "Sari, it's not the right time."

Her stubbornness had vanished. Like an obedient child, she took the chair he offered.

He sat next to her, holding her hand. "God knows I want

you, but not now. Not that it would be 'wrong.' The physical act of love is not a sin. But it is a mistake to believe that desire is enough in itself. At least not for me, not with a person like you. I know you're eighteen, but you're very young, Sari. You're passionate and you're curious, but you're also innocent. Be careful. No man is going to desire you more than I do, but some of them aren't going to love you as much, and they will hurt you." He pulled her to her feet and kissed her lightly on the cheek. "I want you go to home now, before you've been gone so long your father will expect you to explain where you've been. And if he does, please resist the impulse to insult his authority by blurting out the truth. I'm glad you came; I had a message for you I was going to send home with Ben, and I'd much rather give it to you myself. I'm going away on a business trip. I'm leaving on the first train in the morning and I won't be back until long after you've left for Wellesley. So your father's orders aren't depriving us of any time together. In fact, I've been with you one more time than I expected. Now I'll take you home. Not to the door, but at least as far as the nearest street corner."

"I'd rather go by myself."

"Then you must stop crying. The wrong kind of people like to help beautiful girls in distress."

"I'm not crying!"

"My mistake." The corner of a lace-edged handkerchief protruded from the beaded reticule she clutched in one hand. Peter pulled it out, carefully dried her cheeks, and stuffed it back into the little bag. "I love you, Sari. Now go, alone if you must, and don't look back."

Sarah wrote her first letter to Peter the night she arrived back at Wellesley. In it she stated that whatever the consequences, she was determined not to give him up. She would marry him with or without her father's consent. She had considered the matter carefully, and that was her final decision.

Waiting expectantly for his response, Sarah continued to write to him every day, pouring out her feelings, opinions, and plans for their future. At night while her roommate was asleep, she wrote poems and sent them along with her letters. Two weeks later, his first letter arrived. It contained a description of a recent union meeting and a humorous incident at the *Union Record* office, both beautifully expressed but as impersonal as any column intended for public display. There was no reference to the most important decision she had ever made.

Sarah continued to write, though less frequently as the weeks went by. Her roommate, a treasury of information on matters of this kind, assured her that men didn't know how to express their emotions the way women did, and Peter was one of those businesslike males who were cautious about what they committed to paper. Sarah accepted the explanation gratefully. Though his occasional letters were disappointing, she told herself it didn't matter. She would be back in Seattle in June. The minute they were together again, nothing would be able to separate them. This would be her last year at Wellesley; she wasn't going to leave Peter again.

Ben could have spared Sarah her frenzied search for Peter when she returned to Seattle in June. But according to Professor Whiting, Ben was up north in Whatcom County, at a conference of "educators." As soon as she could invent a plausible reason for going downtown alone, Sarah hurried to the *Union Record*. The door was locked. Peering through the big front window, she could see that the office was deserted.

Though she had never been to his apartment, Sarah had gotten Peter's address from Ben so she wouldn't have to mail her letters to his office. She walked to the building and entered the foyer, looking for Peter's apartment number on the mailboxes. There was a name on every box, but no Peter Scott.

Sick with the premonition of what she was about to discover, Sarah found the door marked "Manager's Office" and boldly rang the bell. The elderly man who answered had apparently been awakened from his nap. After a sleepy scrutiny of her forest-green shirtwaist and matching skirt, he told Sarah querulously that it wasn't any of his business where a tenant moved when he took off.

"At least you can tell me when he left."

"The first of last month. Five weeks back."

Five weeks . . . In her excitement about their upcoming reunion, she had written Peter at least three letters during that time. "What do you do when mail comes for people who don't live here anymore?"

"Send it to them, if they leave me an address. Mr. Scott didn't. And he ain't come by to pick it up."

"Then you do have letters for him here."

Indifferent as the manager was to the whereabouts of former tenants, he clearly didn't lose interest in their personal mail. "Exactly three, miss. All the same handwriting, all the same postmark. Someplace in Massachusetts, but I ain't going to try to pronounce it."

So she had reached the end of the line, like her letters. No place to look for Peter, no one to ask about him.

By the time Ben came home from Whatcom, the sense of desertion had entered Sarah like a deep chill. "He's someplace in Montana or Nevada," Ben explained. "The dockworkers are getting organized, and so are the loggers. Peter wants to help strengthen the miners. He had to shut down the newspaper temporarily because the man who's going to take over won't get here until next month."

"Do you know when he's coming back to Seattle?"

Ben shook his head. "No, Sari. I wish I could say sometime this summer, but I doubt it."

"Ben!" Sarah exclaimed. "I understand that when he's moving between two states you can't know exactly where he is at a given time. But surely you know how to get in touch with him."

Ben's honest blue eyes were full of sympathy. "Yes, I do. But he asked me not to tell you."

She stared at her brother blankly, stunned by the final devastating proof that she had been abandoned. Not accidentally, but deliberately and forever, by the man who had caressed her in ways that excited her dreams, the man who aroused appetites that for nine months had been stored in a secret corner of her senses. "He wanted me," she said quietly, "but he doesn't want me anymore. Or maybe he never did."

"Sari, listen. Cruel as it seems, Peter is doing the right thing. He would never make you happy. He's a missionary. His crusades will always come first. No woman, no matter how much he loves her, will ever keep him from leaving her when there's a strike in Nevada or a union in Oregon needing help. Besides, his work is dangerous. He's a socialist, and proud to be one. He stands up on open platforms at public meetings and advocates the overthrow of capitalism. He organizes strikes and boycotts and tells the newspapers he's doing it. I'm working in the radical labor movement, so I run risks too. But for Peter the danger is a thousand times greater because he's prominent. And as the opposition to the movement gets stronger it will get more dangerous than ever. Give him up *now*. Forget him. I mean it, Sari. Much as it hurts, forget him."

"I'll try," she said bleakly, "but what if I can't?"

23

"Tweedy and Peersen, Attorneys-at-Law" had been in business for four years.

After graduation, Trygve had met with the senior partners at a number of prestigious firms, but when he learned that most of the firms' regular clients were either companies whose labor practices he abhorred or whose hiring practices were guided by bigotry, he decided that he couldn't represent such interests. Without a twinge of regret, he turned down the most lucrative offers a young man with a pristine license could have hoped to receive.

"High principles don't bring high prices," Judge Thomas remarked when three months had gone by and Trygve, once the envy of his classmates, was still looking for a place to start using his law degree. "And if you won't take clients who discriminate against the Japanese, there isn't a bank, a hotel, a restaurant, a theater, or even a barbershop in the city of Seattle that you'll be willing to represent."

The judge continued, "I suppose I ought to applaud your indifference to receiving a good salary. But think ahead. You've got your eye on the Superior Court bench. Before that, you plan to run for City Council. That means financing at least two political campaigns—more, if you lose one and have to try again. Money can get you what you're going to need—a campaign fund."

Judge Thomas had paused, tipping back his massive swivel chair and meshing his fingers across his chest. In a more conciliatory tone he added, "I don't intend to advise you about your private life, but money has considerable effect on that, too. You're going to want a wife and children—"

"Judge, the truth is, I'm not even thinking of getting married. When Christina died . . . oh, hell, other girls just don't interest me."

"Yes, I know," the judge said quietly. "It's too soon. Nothing wrong with throwing all your energy into your career. It's the right time for making your work more important than anything else. But eventually there will be a 'right time' for a girl. You'll know her when you see her."

The following week Katamari Tamesa gave Trygve a set of lawbooks as a graduation gift. It was so complete it undermined Trygve's most compelling reason for entering an established firm—the firm's law library. Trygve described the set to Tweedy, a law-school classmate he often met for lunch in a café near the courthouse. "Now I can open my own office," he said with a wry grin, "or I could, if I had enough money to rent some space."

Physically, George Tweedy was the least impressive member of their class. He was short, walked with a permanent stoop, wore spectacles with lenses so thick he peered at the world with the eyes of a nervous mouse, and talked with a slight lisp. But he was always bright and often brilliant. Law firms interested in hiring a brand-new graduate were enthusiastic about his academic record and lost interest as soon as he appeared for an interview.

"Well, Tryg," he said with a grin, "you've got the books but no money to rent an office. I've got the office, but I can't afford to buy the books. Do you think we could get along?"

Tweedy and Peersen was built on a firm foundation. The partnership gave both of them full scope to practice what they did best. Trygve came to life in the courtroom, an arena so terrifying to George that his arguments became almost inaudible. George found fulfillment in disentangling knots of contradictory precedents, discovering obscure statutes, and in the sanctum of the office, composing arguments that were as brilliant as Trygve made them sound in court. Trygve was fast developing a reputation, while the only visible proof that

George Tweedy was practicing law was the sign on the office door; but George wasn't worried. George was the scholar and Trygve the actor, a symbiotic relationship that worked so well they were making money, despite Trygve's facility for finding clients who couldn't pay.

His first four years in practice had been a period of intense single-mindedness for Trygve. He moved from Ballard to an apartment downtown, where he usually spent the evening with work he brought home from the office. There was no wife or sweetheart to distract him. The "kindhearted widow" Judge Thomas had introduced him to was a good listener as well as a good lover and that was all he wanted. The social invitations he received came from people he knew professionally, and he accepted them for that reason. He was maturing fast professionally, but socially he hadn't gone much further than the world of family celebrations and Thursday-night dinners. All his excess energy and leisure time went into sharpening his intimate knowledge of the way the City Council, the mayor's office, and the county judicial system actually functioned—and who was pulling the strings.

At the same time, he was developing a courtroom style that won applause in some quarters even when he lost the case, as happened when he defended a logger named Peterson against a charge of disturbing the peace.

Peterson had been crippled in a logging accident. He was on a downtown street corner, letting the public know how little lumber companies cared about safety measures, when a police officer pushed through the audience, locked his wrist into a handcuff, and dragged him to the city jail. Trygve agreed to represent Peterson, though he could foresee the outcome as soon as he learned that Timothy Dorsett would hear the case.

Dorsett's close friend Jonathan Wise frequently used his newspaper's editorial page to broadcast scathing judgments about "Red Flag" socialists, Bolsheviks, Wobblies, and traitors. As far as Wise was concerned, they were all the same. Judge Dorsett didn't own a daily newspaper, but he often voiced his personal opinions as noisily in the courtroom as any soapbox orator. Anyone who dared criticize his courtroom statements was fined for contempt.

The Seattle *Tribune* was the *Chronicle*'s spirited critic and fiercest opponent. Its political reporter, a friend of Trygve's, agreed to observe the Peterson hearing. After a trip to the bank, Trygve went to court with his coat and trouser pockets sagging with the weight of silver dollars. He wasn't going to win the Peterson case, but he intended to use the defeat to his own advantage.

The proceedings were brief. Judge Dorsett's opening remarks condemned the "insane zealots" who abused their rights as citizens, shouted lies on the street corners, and incited rebellion against laws which protected their loyal fellow Americans. Pointing an accusing finger at Peterson, he ordered the accused to repent and to cease fouling the clean fresh air with alien sentiments.

Trygve jumped to his feet, advanced to the bench, and without a word scooped out his pockets and dumped the contents on the bailiff's desk.

"What is this?" Judge Dorsett demanded angrily.

"Your Honor, I have just paid the maximum fine for contempt of court."

The astonished judge stared at Trygve for a second before he roared, "You have not been so fined, Mr. Peersen! Explain your behavior!"

"I can do that by describing yours. Your Honor, my client is entitled to a fair hearing. This is his constitutional right. But before hearing his case, you have condemned him in a way any fair-minded person would recognize as an abuse of your authority."

"Contempt!" the judge screamed, banging his gavel furiously. "I order you to . . ."

Threats to disbar Trygve and strike his name from the roll of attorneys followed Trygve as he and Peterson walked out of the courtroom. Peterson spent six months in a jail cell, and a witty piece entitled "A Fair Trial in Our Fair City" appeared in the *Tribune*. The foundation was laid for Trygve's reputation as a dramatic, if foolhardy, trial lawyer.

Two years after Trygve began to practice, Judge Thomas told him that a member of the City Council was about to resign, and advised Trygve to run for the seat. "Your chance has come," Judge Thomas said. "Talk to the right people. Considering the years you've spent snooping around city hall, you ought to know who they are. Get yourself appointed to fill the vacancy."

"Is that the best strategy?" Trygve asked thoughtfully. "Or should I wait for the election? I'll have to run then, even if I get the appointment."

"Of course. But you'll run as the incumbent, and that gives you an advantage."

"Won't it put me in the debt of the person who appoints me? I would automatically be considered 'on his side,' and I don't want to be on anyone's side before I even address the issues."

"Would that be so painful if the person is a friend?"

"With all due respect, Judge, I don't want to have any tag put on me. The election is coming up in a few months. I'll wait."

So for the first time Trygve Peersen's name appeared on the ballot. Fortunately for him, Ballard had been annexed to the city of Seattle; the results of the election proved that a block of Ballard votes more than outweighed the advantage an incumbent would have enjoyed. Trygve won by a large margin, and took his seat on the City Council.

The Peersen family's traditional Thursday dinner was no longer a weekly affair. Though Emma still lived in Ballard, and Anna and Mina's daughter, Emily, were close by in the house Ivar Hilsen had built, the rest of the family had dispersed into a larger, more complex world. Trygve lived alone in an apartment near the courthouse. Tim O'Donnell was gone. After Mina's escape from the state asylum at Steilacoom the house they had shared for so many years became a haunted and lonely place. But Tim refused to sell it. Instead he nailed boards across the windows, packed his clothes into a wicker suitcase, and left. Everything in the house remained exactly as it was when the asylum guards took Mina away. Her clothing hung in the bedroom closet, her good dishes were neatly arranged in the old mahogany buffet, her pots and pans and copper washtub were in their proper places in the kitchen. As far as the family knew, Tim was somewhere in British Columbia. He wrote often, his longing for Emily evident in his letters. But Tim had accepted the fact that living with Anna was best for Emily. He would remain in the background, resigned to letting Emily live her life as part of the Peersen family, whom he loved and respected.

The Japanese members of Emma's enlarged family had also been carried off by the changing times. Katamari lived with his bride, Tomoko, and their two children on the top floor of his finest acquisition—a hotel with ninety-nine rooms and the only hot water in any Japanese-owned building. Kibun Sakai's departure was inevitable. He made his living growing vegetables and selling them at the Pike Street market, and as the city expanded, he found he could not compete with the prices of farmers who had much larger acreage. Real-estate values were skyrocketing, and he couldn't afford to lease more land in the Ballard area. When an opportunity came to move south, Kibun accepted it.

One of Emma's occasional Thursday dinners became Kibun's farewell party. He had lived in the little bedroom upstairs for almost twelve years. Leaving was a wrenching experience for him, though it hadn't been for Emma's more adventurous children.

Kibun had always been the smiling but silent member at Emma's table, but that evening he fortified himself with several cups of sake and as dinner progressed he became quite eloquent. "I leave this house with great sorrow. But I have known for a long time that this day would come, and I must accept the change. You have allowed me the use of precious ground, too precious now for growing peas and cabbages. It is time to return it to you, and I do that with my heart full of gratitude. Now I will tell you where I am going, and about the generous man who is helping me."

Carefully selecting words he felt would show his profound respect for the man, Kibun told the Peersens about Ezio Rinaldi. Rinaldi had left his father's vineyard in Tuscany with a steerage ticket, seventy-five dollars, and dreams of a farm "out West." He had worked his way from Boston to Seattle as a railroad section hand. He worked as a harvest hand on truck farms owned by other Italians, saving some money even at a dollar a day. Next he leased a tract, and after three years he owned the land outright and was able to send a steamship ticket to his wife.

Ezio was different from most Italian farmers, Kibun explained. He didn't fight Japanese farmers at the Pike Place market or try to get their stall space. Unlike most of his countrymen, who wouldn't hire anyone but Italians when they needed hands for the harvest, Ezio had several Japanese working for him and paid them more than they would receive from other Japanese.

Kibun had arranged to lease fifteen acres from Ezio that were not under cultivation because they were wooded. Ezio was only asking two hundred dollars a year; most leased farmland couldn't be rented for less than a thousand. Once Kibun had cut the trees and pulled the stumps, he could farm some of the richest soil south of the Duwamish River. He would then be able to start saving to buy the land rather than lease it, provided, he added philosophically, he had not improved Ezio's fifteen acres so much that Ezio's price would be beyond his reach. But, so far Ezio had been friendly and Kibun admired and trusted him. And he would get some help with the heaviest part of land clearing, rooting out the stumps. His old friend Henrik, who had shown him how to clear a field of rocks years before, was so excited about Kibun's farm that he had asked to work for him in exchange for meals and a place to sleep.

Thursday dinners had always included reports about the family's various enterprises. Now that the Peersens weren't meeting every week, there was a lot more catching up to do. When Kibun had finished, Anna asked her mother if she had considered renting a stall in the Pike Place market.

"Open another bakery?" Emma asked in surprise.

Katamari said, "People are coming to the market from all over the city because they can buy there for less; the wholesale houses and the middlemen don't get their fingers into the purse. So why not Mother Peersen's homemade bread and pastry? Not another bakery. An outlet for the bakery you already have."

"I'll certainly think about it," Emma promised, and the encouragement she received was so forceful that within the week she and Anna visited the market to talk with its supervisor. Every stall was rented, but more were being added and Mother Peersen put her name on the waiting list.

They also stopped to chat with Kibun, who insisted they meet his benefactor. Ezio Rinaldi was a slender blue-eyed Italian with streaks of silver threaded through his black hair and an engaging smile that helped fill the gaps in his command of English. During the ride back to Ballard, his name scarcely entered the conversation between Emma and Anna. When they reached Emma's house, Anna said abruptly, "Isn't it sad, what happened to Mr. Rinaldi's wife."

"What was that?" Emma asked.

"She died several months ago. She'd been sick for a long time, but in spite of that I'm sure it was a terrible shock. And there are two young children. They're staying with his sister, so they're being cared for, but they must miss their mother, too."

"My goodness, Anna! How did you learn all that?"

"He told me," Anna said simply.

Where were my eyes? Emma asked herself. I didn't think she looked at him twice.

24

Kurt Bauermeister would soon be transferred from his lumber company's Tacoma branch to a mill under construction in a town north of Seattle. In the meantime, he was living in the Whiting household—a temporary arrangement and an awkward one for everyone except Professor Whiting, who seemed insensitive to the undercurrents his wife felt so strongly. Though Sarah made a sincere effort to be pleasant, Kurt was barely civil. Angela felt trapped between a son who was never quite rude enough to be reprimanded and a stepdaughter with little taste for holding her tongue.

The situation was a little easier than it would have been if Ben were home more often; Angela knew that in the past there had been a serious confrontation between Ben and Kurt. It didn't matter now—Ben had a new job with a real-estate company specializing in industrial properties and was so absorbed by it that he might as well have moved to another city. Why his position would require three- and four-day business trips and keep him out late so many nights was puzzling, but Angela didn't probe for fear of finding out something that his father wasn't supposed to know. In any case, her immediate concern was keeping the peace and making Kurt feel welcome. For Kurt's birthday, Angela decided to invite a group of young people to a picnic at Madison Park.

Kurt's reaction was disappointing. "Why Madison Park, Mother? You can get there by cable car, so everybody goes. Fat mamas and papas, noisy children—the kind of people who are attracted to the Pavilion because they can get free beer. I can't name a friend of mine who's ever been there."

"Then it will be a new experience for them." Angela had become so vexed by her son's attitude toward people he considered "common" that she was shorter with him than she meant to be. "There may be free beer, but on summer evenings there is also dancing. Besides, we'll picnic outside on the lakeshore. The gardens are lovely this time of year."

Kurt grudgingly agreed and wrote a guest list. It was some time before Angela realized the true reason for his reluctance. He knew Sarah would be invited. But it would be unthinkable to exclude Sarah, and cowardly to invite her with a hint that since she hardly knew Kurt's friends, she might wish to excuse herself. What a mess Angela had made of it! Her only intention had been to show affection for her son by arranging a party for him, and she had stumbled into a way to make their relationship even worse.

The day before the picnic Sarah brought about a disaster far greater than any Angela could have anticipated. While on a guided tour of the Alaska-Yukon-Pacific Exposition, Sarah saw a familiar figure pass between the pergolas at the entrance to the Agriculture Hall. It had been two years since she had last seen Trygve Peersen. Lifting her full skirt between thumb and forefinger, Sarah broke away from the tour and ran after him.

She caught him just inside the door to the hall. Sarah dropped her skirt and smiled up at him, suddenly unable to think of anything to say.

"Why, Sarah Whiting!"

For several seconds they gazed at each other in silence, measuring the ways in which the other had changed. Trygve was taller and more handsome than Sarah remembered, but the exciting difference was the quality of his greeting. There was none of the old aloofness in his deep blue eyes, none of the younger Trygve's condescension toward the pesty little girl who asked too many questions. He was as surprised and glad as she was that they had met by accident. Sarah had never tried to conceal the spontaneous delight that Trygve brought out in her. Today's Trygve, the "promising young attorney with a natural instinct for the dramatic" whom Sarah had read about in the *Tribune*, was undoubtedly an expert at hiding his feelings. But at the moment he didn't seem to want to.

Sarah and Trygve talked until she was in danger of losing her tour group among the thousands milling around the Exposition grounds. When she came home that evening, everything was forgotten except the terrible thing she had done.

"I just wasn't thinking," she confessed to Angela. "I was so excited about seeing him that I invited him to the picnic. I didn't even mention that it was a party for Kurt or that Kurt would be there. That was stupid, wasn't it?" she said apologetically. "I'll call him and tell him not to come. If he'd known it was a party for Kurt, he wouldn't have accepted anyway."

"I can't allow you to do that. It would be worse than rude, because it would suggest that he isn't acceptable to a group of Kurt's friends. His sister was our housemaid; it would seem as though we were reminding him of that. No, Trygve will remain invited. I'll explain it to Kurt and we'll pray that past differences can be forgotten, at least for one afternoon."

Kurt killed Angela's fading hope that it would work out. Cursing Sarah and Trygve and his mother's incredible stupidity, he refused to take part in the picnic or any kind of birthday celebration. "I also refuse to be placed in the embarrassing position of explaining this mess to my friends. You invited them. You call them."

The heedless blunder that widened the rift between Angela and her only child gave Sarah a sense of unworthiness unlike anything she had ever experienced. She had never been ashamed of disobeying her father; she had angered but never hurt him and her stoic acceptance of the penalty for getting caught expunged the guilt. With Angela no punishment followed to wash away the blame. It wasn't that Angela had excused her; she simply accepted Sarah's tearful apology, adding without rancor that she had acted immaturely for a girl of twenty.

"I'd feel a lot better," Sarah cried, "if you'd lock me up on the sleeping porch with nothing to read but the Bible."

"It isn't so easy now that you're an adult," Angela said quietly. "When you act on impulse without considering the effect on other people, you're bound to share their pain. But let's not dwell on it. I must call Kurt's friends. I'll expect you to telephone Trygve.''

To Sarah's surprise, explaining the situation to Trygve wasn't difficult at all. ''You could have called me and told me straight out that it was Kurt's party. Believe me, I'd have thanked you for it. However, I'm going to ask you to look at this situation from my point of view. I'm one of those struggling young lawyers still worrying about how to pay the rent. The only social events I don't have to be forced to attend are those where I'm likely to pick up a client who can actually pay for my services. I haven't exactly been sleeping with my head on a lawbook, but that's how I feel. Then today, all of a sudden, I bump into a girl I used to know and she gets me thinking about sitting outside in the sunshine, smelling roses, and eating chicken with my fingers. To put it bluntly—if you don't let me take you on a picnic at Madison Park, I'll spend one more beautiful Sunday afternoon alone with a stack of lawbooks. Don't you think you ought to save me from that?''

They went canoeing on the lake and strolled along paths bordered with fragrant flowers. Sitting on the grass under a huge western maple, they laughed heartily because the Whitings' housemaid had put three varieties of Mother Peersen's Home Bakery products into the picnic basket. They had lengthy conversations and comfortable silences. After an hour or two they were ready to swap confessions. Trygve revealed his audacious proposal for reforming City Council procedure and Sarah described the secret trip she had made to New York City to see Isadora Duncan's first performance in the United States.

Trygve's keen eyes watched her, sometimes thoughtfully, sometimes with frank amusement, always assuring Sarah that he was delighted by the ways the duckling he used to know had grown into a swan. As the afternoon progressed, his approval blossomed so rapidly Sarah sensed he was as surprised by it as she was. Was this the first tentative reaching out, the first barely discernible sensation she knew as falling in love? If it was, shouldn't she recognize it? But she didn't. With Peter Scott it hadn't been this way at all. Peter had aroused intense emotions, but he had never made her feel that a completely natural Sarah would hold his attention. His awareness of Sarah had been a current she had to keep generating or it would flicker and go out. But with Trygve . . . Fiddle, she said to herself. Peter is gone and Trygve is here, and whatever this funny lighthearted sensation is, he obviously feels it too. It's going to be a very pleasant summer after all.

There was nothing formal or abrupt about Trygve's departure. He lingered on the Whiting doorstep, telling Sarah over and over how much he had enjoyed the afternoon. She was trying to guess what he would suggest they do the next time they went out, when he said, "Tell your girl she certainly knows what to put into a picnic basket." With a last "Thanks" and a friendly smile, Trygve turned and strode down the walk to the street.

Sarah set out to find Angela, hoping to rid herself of her disappointment by dumping it at her stepmother's feet. She found Angela sitting alone on a marble bench in the walled garden at the back of the house. Her eyes were dry and her voice was steady, but despair was etched clearly on her face. Kurt was gone. He had left sometime early that morning, without saying good-bye. When he didn't appear for breakfast or lunch, Angela had become concerned and had gone to his room. It was bare. His clothing and all his possessions were gone. He must have been planning to leave when they were having dinner together the night before; clearly he *could* have said good-bye. That was what hurt Angela the most. She said it over and over again: "He didn't even say good-bye."

The next afternoon a Western Union boy on a bicycle delivered a telegram from Kurt. It informed his mother that he had closed his bank account and was boarding a train for New York City, where he would book passage on a steamer bound for Germany. Germany was his true home; he had never been happy in the United States. And there the message ended—Kurt still hadn't said good-bye.

Anna refilled Trygve's coffee cup and pushed the platter of almond tarts closer to his spot at the kitchen table. "Listen, Litt Bror. You may be the cleverest attorney in the county, but I can remember when you didn't know how to lace up your boots. I'm glad you came to see me. To tell you the truth, I'm surprised to see you showing up in the middle of the afternoon. You haven't done that for the last three years. So don't expect me to believe there's nothing on your mind. Oh, you've been telling me plenty. You had dinner with the Tamesas and Tomoko is starting sewing classes for Japanese girls. The *Konge* is getting old and needs repairs. Your law partner is honest, but maybe some others in and around the courthouse aren't, and you're worried about your friend Judge Thomas because he's drinking more than ever. You've talked a lot but what sounded loudest to me was the little bit you said about you and Sarah Whiting having a picnic at Madison Park. It's time you began to notice young girls. Oh, yes, I know about your widow friend, and I don't have anything against her. An older woman has been good for you in a couple of ways. She doesn't bring back memories of Christina, and she's 'safe' because she doesn't expect you to marry her. But if you go on protecting yourself from marriageable young girls, you better be sure all you need out of life is a successful career."

Trygve rewarded his sister's lecture with a boyish grin. "I knew I was coming to the right place. Guilty as charged. Except that remembering Christina doesn't hurt the way it used to. I can't forget her, but she doesn't haunt me anymore."

"Good. So where are you and Sarah going the next time you see her?"

Trygve shook his head. "I'm not going to see her." He picked up his coffee cup, drained it, and looked down into the empty cup as if his true feelings were written at its bottom. "I don't know a girl more beautiful," he began, speaking slowly, "or more interesting. But I don't think of her as . . . well, as marriageable, to use your word—at least not for me."

"Then how do you think of her, Litt Bror?"

"As family."

Anna's eyes sparkled and she said solemnly, "Then you'll invite her to our Thursday family dinner."

"I didn't know Mama had one planned."

"She hasn't," Anna said sweetly. "But she will."

*   *   *

The Thursday gathering in Emma Peersen's kitchen was unlike any family dinner Sarah had ever known. In addition to the three Norwegian Peersens, the table included three Japanese and an Italian. Mina Peersen's daughter, Emily, the Tamesas' two children, and farmer Ezio Rinaldi's little black-eyed daughters, Maria and Donna, chattered and giggled at a smaller table in the corner. Compared with the propriety of the family reunions over which Professor Whiting presided, this was a peasant celebration. They laughed without restraint and leapt nimbly from one conversation to another, letting the various topics romp joyfully along separate courses without quite colliding. Yet just beneath the surface there was structure—a ritual with great dignity and a subtler meaning than the sterile formalities Sarah ws accustomed to.

When Emma announced that it was time to take their places, a hush fell over the room and they all moved to the long oak table. With a nod, Trygve signaled that Sarah was to be at his right. Each person apparently knew which chair to take, but no one sat down or spoke as Emma slipped her hand under her son's arm and Trygve escorted her ceremoniously to her position at the head of the table. Except for the scraping of chair legs against the hard oak floor, the silence continued as the family took their seats.

Trygve alone remained standing as the others bowed their heads. Sarah followed suit, noting out of the corner of her eye that even the children at the smaller table knew what to do, though there hadn't been so much as a pointed look from any of the parents.

"Since Sarah hasn't been with us before," Trygve began quietly, "I'll explain our Thursday night grace. On most nights, my father used to say a simple prayer in English. 'We thank thee, O God, for thy bounty and pledge ourselves to thy service.' After Mina married and Anna left home to work, Thursday was the one time we could all get together—Anna's day off—so dinner that night became a family conference as well. Since it was a special occasion, my father always began it in a special way. He recited the Lord's Prayer in Norwegian. He drilled me until I could do it too. So this will be our grace tonight."

The prayer concluded, Trygve sat down and addressed the platters and bowls of food that had been placed in front of him, along with a dozen large dinner plates and ten smaller plates for the children. Here the basic ritual was familiar to Sarah: ladies were served first, then the gentlemen, beginning with the eldest, and finally the children. The mystery was how the exact order of individuals served had been established, for obviously it was as changeless as the position of their chairs at the dinner table. An interesting question, but Sarah couldn't dwell on it; the conversation had come back to life and she was busy with her first impressions of Trygve Peersen's astonishing "family."

"Quite a gang, isn't it?" Trygve commented with a sympathetic grin at Sarah's amazed expression. "You'll learn a lot about them before the evening is over. Since we don't get together as often as once a week anymore, Mother calls on everyone to report what they've been doing since we last sat down together."

Sarah smiled. "I remember meeting Katamari a long time ago. Remember? When he was living here?"

"How could I forget?" Trygve asked. "You're the only person who ever arrived here with an escort from the Seattle Police Department. You were supposed to be locked up in your sleeping porch, reading the Bible. In fact, I saw you there, before you ran away from home. I threw pebbles at the screen and your head popped up and you waved."

Sarah turned to him in surprise. Some of the things he had said to her at Madison Park had given her the same sensation she was feeling now: a curious tightness in the chest, a pulse that seemed to lose its sense of rhythm for a few seconds. "You remember that! I shouldn't think you would. You never liked me much."

Trygve was smiling but his eyes were serious. "I thought you were the most impossible brat I'd ever met, but at that moment I felt sorry for you. You were so little and so alone, but the way you laughed and waved at me, you might have been watching a circus. Suddenly I understand why: you thought I was a clown."

Sarah shook her head. "*I* thought *you* were the most wonderful boy I'd ever seen. Even the first time I saw you—on the pier the day Anna took me to see the *Portland* come in. Don't laugh. I was only nine years old, but I fell in love and my feeling about you was just as intense as it was many years later, when I . . .'' She stopped abruptly, regretting the impulse that had led her to speak so frankly. But something in the way Trygve was looking at her compelled her to finish. ''When I was old enough to really fall in love.''

Trygve's level gaze didn't waver. ''I don't care who it was. But I do want an honest answer to one question. Is it over?''

Sarah was too shaken to do anything but nod.

''You've forgotten him?''

''That's a little different, isn't it?'' Sarah retorted, sounding a little like the feisty redhead Trygve remembered. ''I know about Christina. Have you forgotten her?''

''You're right. Of course I haven't, and I shouldn't expect that you could forget the man you loved. The difference is that Christina is gone. She's a memory, but not the kind that will ever get in the way of falling in love with someone else. Your man may be a memory that can come back into your life.''

''That will never happen.'' Sarah's tone reflected her bitterness about the way Peter Scott had rejected her. ''He hasn't lived in Seattle for the past two years. And since we're being so painfully truthful, I might as well confess that he dropped out of my life deliberately. He didn't want me.''

''I doubt that. Unless the man was a complete fool—and you wouldn't have noticed him in the first place if that had been the case. What if he came back to Seattle? If he showed you he did want you? What then?''

''It wouldn't make a particle of difference.''

For several moments Trygve's gaze searched her face. Sarah's eyes, looking directly into his, were just as questioning, just as hopeful. With the clamor of conversation eddying around them, they were as much alone as if no one else were in the room.

Finally Trygve spoke. ''I'm going to do everything I can to make sure that it doesn't.''

*　　*　　*

Though Trygve became a frequent visitor, Professor Whiting didn't subject him to the interrogation he would have insisted on had he thought of Trygve as a serious suitor. Trygve's outstanding college career and his growing success as an attorney were well-known, but to Professor Whiting Trygve was still housemaid Anna's little brother.

Trygve's status was contradictory. He had all the privileges of a trusted big brother, but he was disqualified as a suitor. Angela was not as class-conscious as her husband, nor was she as blind to what was happening. But she was so relieved that Sarah had chosen the honorable Trygve Peersen that she was reluctant to open the professor's eyes. In any case, Trygve was strong and determined; judging by his professional life, he was also quite skillful at dealing with difficult human beings. If her husband was to be enlightened, Angela wouldn't be the one to do it. Instinctively she knew Trygve would be furious if she tried.

Toward the end of the summer, Trygve made a difficult decision about the *Konge*. She was old and weather-beaten. She had been damaged and badly maintained by Carl Franzen and realistically wasn't worth repairing. Trygve had received more than one offer for her, but it would be unthinkable to sell his father's boat. As he explained to Sarah, there was really only one answer. Trygve would do what Einar would have done; he would beach the *Konge* and set her afire.

"That's going to be an ordeal for you," she said. "I'd like to be with you."

"If you really want to be, I'd like to have you there."

Late one afternoon they sailed the *Konge* to an isolated cove where Trygve and Sarah sat on a drift log for two hours, watching her burn. The flames took a long time getting to the name *Konge*, printed in bold letters on the bow. When they finally did, Trygve clutched Sarah's hand convulsively. His head dropped forward and he began to cry.

Nothing had ever moved Sarah so deeply as the sight of this powerful man sobbing helplessly over the death of his father's exhausted little sailboat. She didn't see it as weakness. Torn apart, Trygve revealed that he loved with great strength—the strength ran so deep that he wasn't embarrassed by his feelings. This was her childhood idol grown up into a man who demanded her admiration as much as her love, and now he was hurting.

When the fire died out, Trygve threw seawater on the ashes. Hand in hand they climbed the slope above the beach and started along the trail to Ballard. It took them through a wood so dense the sunlight penetrated the shadows in brilliant streaks like theater spotlights, and from there into a meadow where the wild grass grew tall enough to brush against their knees.

At the edge of the meadow, Sarah dropped to the ground and pulled Trygve down beside her. He said hoarsely, "You don't know what you're doing."

"I know what I'm feeling." She put her arms around him and drew him into her embrace.

That evening Trygve visited the Whiting home. Angela answered his ring and nodded when he asked to see Sarah's father. "He's in the library. I believe Sarah is in her room. Should I ask her to come down?"

"If you will, please. What I have to say concerns her. I'd like you to be there too."

"I'm glad to hear that," Angela replied with a twinkle in her eye. "That will save me the trouble of eavesdropping outside the library door."

Professor Whiting greeted Trygve cordially, but he failed to conceal his surprise at the intrusion into a sanctuary even members of his immediate family didn't enter for something as trivial as casual conversation. The surprise deepened when Trygve was followed almost immediately by Angela and Sarah, who took chairs side by side and looked like patrons of the opera waiting expectantly for the first thunderous notes of the overture to break the silence. The twin questions "What shall I talk about?" and "How soon can I politely conclude this annoying interruption?" were answered for him almost immediately. Still standing, Trygve said, "Professor Whiting, I've come here this evening to tell you that I intend to ask your daughter to marry me. I hope to obtain your approval."

Professor Whiting had always known that someday a young man would present himself for just this reason, but Trygve's approach was so outrageous that he could only stare. This young man—admittedly acceptable in some respects, an excellent marital prospect for some young lady other than his daughter—this brash young man didn't ask permission to propose marriage to Sarah, he *intended* to do so. He *hoped* to obtain her father's *approval*—not his permission!—which said plainly that if he didn't receive it, he'd proceed without it.

"I've given lengthy and serious consideration to what I can offer Sarah," Trygve continued, ignoring what another young man in his situation would have recognized as disapproving silence. "And I've asked myself whether it's enough. I care for her, but that alone is no guarantee that I can make her happy." He pulled a sheet of notepaper out of his inside coat pocket, approached the nonplussed professor, and presented it to him.

Professor Whiting accepted the paper, adjusted his spectacles, and began to study the page of Trygve's neat script with the frowning concentration of a man trying to decipher a cryptogram.

After several minutes of heavy silence, Angela turned to Sarah. "Your father should have a little time to go over the information Trygve has given him. Why don't you two go out to the kitchen and have a cup of tea or a cool drink." Closing the door after them, she approached her husband and said, "Jerry, dear, that's a fine young man."

Professor Whiting raised the page of notes aloft like a flag. Whipping it back and forth, he exclaimed, "Is this the way young men today ask for a young lady's hand in marriage? Paragraph one, educational background. Paragraph two, professional qualifications. Paragraph three, current financial status." Snapping at the last few lines with thumb and forefinger of his free hand, he exclaimed, "Listen to this! 'Ultimate goal: United States Supreme Court'! A presidential appointment. He's only twenty-four years old!"

"That's not too young to have a strong sense of direction," Angela put in gently. "And he didn't say next year."

Somewhat mollified, the professor nodded his head, then suddenly burst out again, "But there's no *family* here! His people are immigrants."

"My dear husband," Angela said with a smile, "have you forgotten? So are yours. True, the Whitings arrived four hundred years ago. Not to be facetious, but one of Trygve's forebears had explored New England six centuries before that. And after all, family background has little bearing on Trygve's suitability as a husband, as your daughter recognizes." Angela left her chair, crossed the room, and stood in front of her husband. Resting her hands on his shoulders, she said softly, "It takes a little getting used to, doesn't it?"

Professor Whiting looked up into the face of the woman whose warmth and humor could disarm him even in his severest moods. "You think I should give them my approval."

Angela nodded. "You must make a choice. Give them your blessing, or deny it. But be willing to face what will happen if you try to stand in their way. They desire each other. If they're thwarted, they will act rashly."

Indignation and disbelief sharpened Professor Whiting's retort. "Are you suggesting that Sarah and Trygve would not wait to be married?"

Angela bent a little to kiss him gently on the cheek, and whispered, "Did we?"

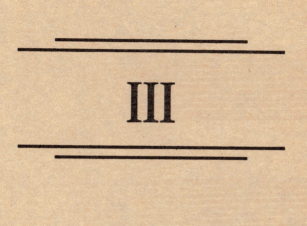

III

25

1915

On the eve of her sixtieth birthday, Emma Peersen took stock of her eighteen years as housewife-turned-businesswoman. Mother Peersen's Home Bakery had grown into a big business. In addition to the large central plant in downtown Seattle, Mother Peersen's now included a stall in the Pike Place market and branches on Queen Anne Hill and Capitol Hill; in Ballard, Washington Park, and the University District. Its first offspring, Mother Peersen's Catering—originally launched with more bravado than good sense—had developed a reputation that was as fashionable as its clients. And Emma's third business venture, a *smorgasbord* restaurant located on Seattle's waterfront, was now two years old, thriving despite what had first appeared to be a stroke of formidable bad luck. Less than a year after Mother Peersen's restaurant opened, statewide prohibition went into effect. Undaunted, Emma detected an alternative route to prosperity. The law prohibited the sale of liquor in saloons or restaurants, but it continued to allow the importation of liquor from outside the state "for private use." Abandoning conventional advertising tactics, Emma promoted Mother Peersen's as an ideal spot for private groups and family parties—occasions when wine and spirits could flow within the law because the general public was excluded.

At sixty, Emma was enjoying prosperity, but she did not allow it to run her life. She could afford a mansion, but was content with the little white house in Ballard where she had lived for forty years. At the insistence of her children she had planning a pilgrimage to her birthplace, the Lofoten Islands in Norway, but the outbreak of war in Europe now made that trip impossible. Secretly, she was more relieved than disappointed. In her absence something bad might happen to her children or grandchildren; besides, she didn't really believe the business could get along without her for three months.

About the time the *smorgasbord* opened, however, Emma's usual thriftiness did yield to one extravagance.

Mother Peersen's headquarters had been enlarged three times since its first home in the small storeroom in back of the downtown bakery. Now Emma was forced to consider the acquisition of still more office space. A few blocks to the south, the most spectacular building Seattle had ever seen had been under construction since 1911 and would be ready for occupancy in another year. Fascinated, Emma had watched the mammoth skeleton slowly rise above its foundation.

The Smith Tower at the corner of Second and Yesler was variously advertised as the tallest building west of New York, the tallest building west of the Mississippi, and the tallest building west of Chicago. It was a twenty-one-story structure topped by a tower of the same height—the first two floors were of granite, the exterior of ornamented terra-cotta. Twenty Oriental craftsmen were hired to carve the teak wall and ceiling panels in an observation post on the thirty-fifth floor. There would soon be six hundred office rooms, eight high-speed elevators—from these exotic details a desire began to sprout in Emma's mind that was as foreign to her frugal nature as the teak wall and ceiling panels on the thirty-fifth floor. She had the money. She could afford it. She needed a larger and better office for her growing business. Wicked as the desire was, she really did want to become one of the Tower's tenants.

The most radical aspect of her lust for a Smith Tower suite was its complete detachment from the bakery. Each time her business office had been enlarged, the remodeling took place within the walls of the building. Her desk was no longer wedged between the flour bins and the ovens as it had been in the early days, but a connecting door between the office area and the bakery plant satisfied Emma's need to see for herself that everything was being done right. If she were enthroned in the Smith Tower, such surveillance wouldn't be possible. Emma's conviction that the bakers would forget how to bake if she weren't in the next room defied her vision of an office with blue walls, a flowery blue carpet, and furniture upholstered in blue velour. Her secret yearning won. This was the one luxury she could allow herself after all her years of hard work. She went to the tower's rental agency and signed a lease for a suite on the fourteenth floor.

She wasn't as brave when it came to telling her children what she had done. They would be startled, probably shocked. This was so unlike the Emma they knew. When she made her confession at a family dinner, she was unprepared for the hearty cheer that went around the table. Her children were happy to see her finally treat herself to something special.

"How will you manage, Mama?" Anna asked in mock dismay. "You won't be able to sneak into the bakery and snoop."

"Don't pay any attention to Anna," Trygve said quickly. "It's wonderful, Mama. Maybe this is a good time to tell you my own good news." He paused, and with a boyish grin announced, "I'll see you in the Smith Tower elevator, Mama. Tweedy and Peersen, Attorneys at Law, will be just two floors down."

When Anna told her mother that she and Trygve planned to take her out to dinner on her birthday, Emma reacted just as her children had expected. "It costs too much to go out to dinner," she said. "We'll have a family dinner at home."

"So you can spend your birthday cooking? It won't do any good to argue, Mama. We've already decided."

"Well, if it must be a restaurant, we can go to our own. We'll know the kitchen is clean and what goes into the food."

"We can't. A private party has already taken over the restaurant for the evening."

"Then we'll celebrate my birthday some other time. For a party that size, I always help in the kitchen."

Anna shook her head. "Not this time. I've already made all the arrangements. You won't be needed, and neither will

I. It's out of your hands, Mama. We're going to take you to a nice little restaurant that's owned by a friend of Ezio's.''

"An Italian restaurant?" Emma exclaimed.

"Come on, Mama! You've been eating Italian food at my house ever since Ezio and I got married."

Emma laughed. "I give up. And I thank you for the invitation."

Though Emma was stubbornly opposed to entrusting her life to an automobile, Anna won that point as well. "No, Mama, you're *not* going to take a streetcar to Seattle, and that's final. Ezio and I will pick you up in our new car."

On the way to the Italian restaurant, Anna remembered some last-minute instructions for the woman she had left in charge of the *smorgasbord*. When Ezio stopped his shiny new Reo at the back of Mother Peersen's, Anna said, "You may as well come in, Mama. I'll be a few minutes. No use waiting outside in the car."

Delighted with this opportunity to make sure everything was being done properly, Emma followed Anna through the back door. The kitchen passed inspection, but not a sound was coming from the dining area. Puzzled, Emma turned to a waitress who seemed to be listening as anxiously as she was for the hum of voices on the other side of the swinging doors. "Haven't our customers arrived yet?"

"Oh, yes," the girl replied. "But it is quiet in there, isn't it? I'd better go check to see if something's wrong."

Emma couldn't leave the checking to anyone else. She followed the waitress around the partial wall that hid the swinging doors to the kitchen and stepped into a dining room, where some forty men, women, and children were waiting expectantly for her entrance. There were Peersens, Rinaldis, Frodesens from Bellingham and Frodesens from Portland, Sakais and Tamesas. Emma's entire family and her almost-family. Standing modestly on the edge of the noisy crowd wishing her "Happy Birthday!" were Angela and Professor Whiting and his son, Benjamin—they weren't shouting like the rest of them, but even the professor was laughing without restraint.

* * *

Late that evening when she was alone in her own kitchen, Emma was able to linger over the birthday gifts that had been piled on a table in the corner of the restaurant. The best was an album of photographs Trygve had made up. It contained pictures of everyone at the party—under each was a caption with the names and ages of the children shown and a description of the occasion when the photograph was taken. In the case of latecomers to the Peersen clan, there was an additional sentence or two about when and how they had joined Emma's family circle. Emma sat down at the long oak table with her usual bedtime cup of coffee and went through the album slowly.

On the first page was a photograph of Einar Peersen. Even after so many years, looking at Einar's likeness brought tears to Emma's eyes.

She turned the pages quickly. Her gaze lingered on a picture of Anna and her husband, Ezio. For a time Emma had lost hope that Anna would ever recover from the tragedy of Ivar's death. But Ezio with his two motherless little girls had reached her as perhaps no other man could have. What a wonderful marriage it was! The Rinaldis had been photographed in front of their big white farmhouse in the Rainier Valley. In the background was the flat expanse of rich farmland that produced vegetables so generously that Ezio was now hauling his produce to market in two Ford trucks. Ezio was a little grayer, but still as handsome as ever. Anna, with a contented smile, was hovering over her growing clutch of chicks—Mina's daughter, Emily O'Donnell, now fourteen, Ezio's daughters Maria and Donna, and the twin boys born four years ago to Anna and Ezio.

Emma focused her attention on pretty dark-haired Emily, who looked so hauntingly like her mother. Poor, lost Mina was one of the irremedial sorrows of Emma's life. For a long time after Mina ran away from the asylum, Emma had been certain that she was alive. Then all hope of seeing her again was shattered by a man who presented indisputable proof that Mina was dead.

He appeared at the door carrying a large cardboard box. He wore a dark suit and black fedora, and his expression was as solemn as his clothing. "Mrs. Emma Peersen?"

"Yes."

"My name is Peters. Marshall Peters."

A sense of foreboding went through Emma like a sudden chill; there was sympathy in his voice, and an apology for the nature of his errand. "Please come in."

"Thank you." He took the chair she indicated and sat up stiffly with the box across his lap.

"A cup of coffee . . ."

"Please don't trouble yourself. I won't be long." He watched Emma intently as she sat down and faced him. He had obviously brought bad news before. "I am an administrator at Newmount state hospital. We have just learned the true name of a patient who passed on this last February. Mina O'Donnell. Your daughter, Mrs. Peersen, I'm sorry to say. I would have preferred to notify her husband, but I understand he no longer lives in Ballard."

Emma's voice was weak but steady. "Yes. He finally sold their home. He's working in a fish plant in Alaska. Mr. Peters, please tell me everything you can about Mina."

Marshall Peters nodded soberly and proceeded, pausing occasionally to be sure he had omitted no detail. He explained that Newmount routinely received reports of runaways from other institutions, but when a county hospital sent them a woman called Mary Benedict, they had no way of connecting her with a Steilacoom escapee by the name of Mina O'Donnell.

"Benedict . . ." Emma murmured. "That's the family Mina worked for before she married Tim." Her voice broke, but in a moment she added, "They had a daughter about Mina's age. Her name was Mary. . . . Excuse me, Mr. Peters. Please go on."

Speaking softly, Marshall Peters continued. He told Emma that very little was known about how Mina had subsisted between the time she ran away from Steilacoom and when she was admitted to a county hospital. She had been found wandering the streets of the town of Bellingham. The local police had been alerted that a woman was behaving strangely— shrieking at children she passed on the street and frightening them. The police picked her up and took her to the county hospital, where she told them her name was Mary Benedict.

The doctors examined her and after a few days transferred her to the state institution at Newmount. Marshall Peters glanced at the box on his knees. "She always carried a doll with her and became hysterical if anyone so much as touched it."

"Her baby . . ." Emma put in brokenly.

Peters nodded. "Yes, that's what she considered it. Her baby. She carried it wherever she went, and when she went for a walk outside, she wrapped it carefully in a blanket. But she was docile and pleasant, seemingly quite content. Over the years we exhausted every means we have to locate her family. And then your daughter tried to run away once more, as she had at Steilacoom. We found her the next day, but she had been exposed to severe cold and heavy rain. She developed pneumonia and lived for only a week, though our doctors did everything they could to save her. As I said, that was in February."

Emma replied, "All these years I've prayed that she was alive and well, and at the same time, that I'd know when she died. I'm grateful to you for bringing me this information. But how did you find me? Did she tell you who she really was? At the end, when she knew she was dying?"

Peters shook his head. "No, she didn't. Probably she only thought of herself as Mary Benedict. We learned her true identity from a man who I believe knows you and your family well, a Dr. Jonas. I understand he treated you and your children for many years, and at one point advised you to have Mina hospitalized at Steilacoom."

"That's true. But Dr. Jonas is retired now. He hasn't lived in Ballard for a few years."

"Yes, I know. He lives in Bellingham now, where he has a number of relatives. One of them was a patient at Newmount in January of this year—a cousin, I believe. Dr. Jonas came to visit her and stopped in my office to discuss a legal matter in connection with her commitment; this was shortly after your daughter Mina's death. Her doll was in a cupboard I had to open in the course of our conversation. Dr. Jonas recognized the doll. Apparently Mina had carried it around so much that it had become a familiar figure in the village. With Dr. Jonas' help, the doll has led me to you."

*　　*　　*

Every page in the album evoked memories, none more vivid than the photograph of the Tamesas and their two children, taken in the lobby of the largest apartment hotel in the Tamesa chain. Trygve had printed under it, "Katamari arrived in Seattle in April 1897, at the age of twenty-two." Was it possible? Could he be forty years old, almost as old as she had been when Trygve led the slender Japanese university student into her kitchen and announced that he was going to live in the extra bedroom upstairs?

On the next page was Kibun Sakai, the second young Japanese to be rescued from a filthy bunk room in a Japan Town slum. In Emma's mind, though not in the album, was a clear picture of Kibun's first vegetable garden—the two acres that simpleminded Henrik had helped him clear by harnessing himself to a homemade sled. Now, some fifteen years later, Henrik was Kibun's partner on a truck farm adjacent to Ezio's. How ironic, Emma mused, that the Alien Land Law should prevent Kibun from owning the ground he had transformed from nearly worthless stump land into a richly productive truck farm, while Henrik, who needed to be cared for like a child, was able to be the legal owner.

The photograph of Professor and Mrs. Whiting was a formal studio portrait. Angela looked gracious and gentle, the professor stern and dignified. She was still beautiful, though in the last few years her dark hair had turned silver-gray. Emma guessed that the sadness in Angela's eyes, even when she was smiling, was in large part due to her son, Kurt. He had hurt her in so many ways—disrupting her relationship with her stepchildren, remaining openly hostile to Trygve, and then rejecting both his mother and his family by returning to Germany.

Kurt was now back in Seattle, still convinced of the superiority of the German race, but not to the extent of taking part in his chosen homeland's war against France and Great Britain. He could now visit his mother without creating the ugly scenes that had erupted when Sarah and Benjamin were still living at home. At least superficially the rift between mother and son had been bridged. Still, Anna had told Emma that Kurt was asked to the party but had ignored the invitation. He was being more discreet about his pro-German sentiments, but whatever that arrogant young man was up to, it wasn't putting a smile in his mother's eyes.

On the last page was a photograph of Trygve and Sarah. Sarah, due to deliver her first child in only a few weeks, looked absolutely triumphant. Yet something in Sarah's expression made Emma uneasy, something that was not quite hidden behind her brilliant smile. A look of discontent, or, if an anxious mother-in-law was reading too much into it, at least a look of restlessness. The same expression had been on Sarah's face at the party tonight, a barely perceptible contradiction to the merry conversation. Anna had said more than once that Sarah and Trygve seemed to be going off in opposite directions, Trygve concentrating too hard on his own political plans to notice that Sarah was throwing all her energy into developing a dancing school. Tonight for the first time Emma admitted that Anna might be right. But soon the baby would come. Surely, Emma prayed, that would bring them together.

Finally she closed the album. But her feeling of uneasiness about Trygve and Sarah would not leave her.

For Sarah, it had been an exhausting celebration. The weight of her body sapped her strength, so that standing made her back ache and sitting was awkward. No one, least of all Emma Peersen, would have been affronted had she remained at home. Women far less advanced in their pregnancies were not expected to go out in the evening. But Sarah was too proud of her pregnancy to play at genteel Victorian modesty, and too fond of Emma to miss her sixtieth birthday party. Still, she had to admit to herself that the entire Peersen clan, along with Sivertsen cousins and Japanese protégés, had generated a degree of noise and exuberance that tired her to the bone.

Yet she wasn't sleepy. On the way home her mind was busily forming a mental image of lying in bed with Trygve, nestled in the cradle of his arm with her head resting against his shoulder, their bodies pressed together in a kind of communication that wasn't dependent on words. It would be comforting to talk as well, but after they left the birthday party Trygve had hardly spoken. She knew that when he was preoccupied, she must repress her own need for conversation. His political career, a difficult case, a speech he hadn't finished writing—whatever the reason for the wall of silence he had erected between them, it was useless to try to break through. Affection, just the warm feel of him as they lay in each other's arms—that, Sarah told herself, was enough, at least for tonight.

Having parked the car, Trygve put his arm around her and helped her up the stairs into the house. Truly solicitous, Sarah thought to herself, albeit a little absentminded. He was equally thoughtful in guiding her up the stairs to their bedroom. With her eyes on that wonderful refuge from politics and the practice of law, Sarah exclaimed, "Think of it, Tryg! We've slept in that bed ever since our honeymoon. I don't care how rich or famous you become. That's going to be our bed for the rest of our lives."

Trygve's smile was pleasant but vague, as if she had been in mid-sentence when he began to listen. "I didn't know you were so frugal."

"Not frugal," Sarah said snappishly. "Sentimental."

"What? Oh, yes. It's a great bed. Happy memories."

"Memories? Only *memories*?" All their nights of passionate comingling, gone forever, as perishable as a bridesmaid's bouquet? Of course, Sarah thought, suddenly seeing her ungainly body as ugly. At one time, making love to me was important. But be honest with yourself, Sarah, it isn't just the pregnancy. Long before that, lovemaking had become a necessary ritual Trygve performed when he wasn't too tired.

For the first time in their married lives Sarah took her nightgown and robe into the bathroom so that Trygve would not see her undress. When she came out, he was gone. She walked down the stairs until she could see into the living room. He was sitting in his armchair with an open briefcase on his lap. He often brought work home, but what could be so important when it was almost midnight?

"Tryg? Aren't you coming to bed?"

"Not right away. You go ahead." Even as he spoke, he was picking up papers and beginning to leaf through them.

Sarah hesitated on the brink of saying more, something like, "But tonight I need you. It's important to me." Instead she turned and laboriously reclimbed the stairs. Somewhere inside, a stubborn little voice insisted she didn't want to go to bed alone, she wanted *him*. She didn't even feel like going back into their bedroom. The freshly painted, fully equipped nursery was just across the hall. She went in, switched on the light, and surveyed what was to be Daniel Einar Peersen's room, or perhaps Amanda's.

Her yearning for the baby grew as she moved slowly from one piece of furniture to the next. The mahogany cradle . . . Her fingers stroked the wood as if in recognition, for it had been hers and Ben's. Next the rocking chair where she would sit when she nursed the baby. On to the chest of drawers . . . She opened a drawer and looked lovingly at the garments, all neatly folded and stacked. Two long dresses lavishly embroidered by Anna. The tiny lace cap she had worn as an infant. Soft flannel wrappers and booties in pink and blue knitted by Emma. . . . As her fingers lingered on each unbelievably small article, the longing swelled for the child who would wear it. Was it wrong to put so much faith into what this baby would do for her marriage?

She glanced at the little enameled clock on top of the baby's bureau. Half-past twelve! She had been in the nursery much longer than it seemed. Yet weary as she was, the thought of getting into a cold and empty bed was strangely frightening.

She went into the hallway and resolutely made her way down the stairs to the living room.

Trygve looked up in surprise. "What are you doing, Sari? You should be asleep by now."

"I haven't gone to bed because I knew I wouldn't be able to sleep."

"But in your condition, you need rest. And you said you were tired."

"Of course I'm tired!" Sarah burst out. "But for some reason I can't even explain to you, I would like you to come to bed with me."

Trygve frowned and said heavily, "Believe it or not, I'm tired too. However, I have a client coming up from Olympia tomorrow afternoon. In the morning I won't have time to study his case because I'll be in court until noon. So tonight, whether I like it or not, I have to stay up late."

"If it wasn't a client from Olympia, it would be something else." Sarah's voice was rising with every word. She heard its shrillness and detested it, but couldn't stop. "Don't you realize that your work is taking over your life? Not just *your* life, either! It's running my life as well."

"You're overlooking something, my dear Sarah," Trygve retorted angrily. "Have you ever considered what the Sarah Peersen School of Dance is doing to mine? I haven't complained when I've come home to rattle around in an empty house because you were staying late at your studio. I've often regretted that you're too involved in your dancing school to accept invitations to events of interest to me, the sort of thing a so-called 'helpmeet' does in order to give a boost to her husband's career. You're so busy dancing that I'm even afraid to ask that you invite some of my business associates to dinner. But I haven't gone around whining. Please remember that marriage is a two-way street, if you'll forgive such a hackneyed expression."

"The school is my *work*!" Sarah cried. "And it's just as important to me as your work is to you. Why are you always so critical? Why do you find fault . . . ?" Her voice broke. Crossing the room so blindly that she nearly stumbled, she tore the papers Trygve had been reading out of his hands, dropped them into the briefcase, closed the case with a snap, and threw it across the room. Angry tears were rolling down her cheeks as she sobbed, "All I wanted was for you to come to bed."

Trygve rose and turned out the lamp. "I will, Sari. Right now. But I think you should keep one thing in mind. A man prefers to go to bed with a woman because he wants to, not because he's forced to."

26

The firm of Tweedy and Peersen had developed a reputation that Trygve knew would not be an asset if he decided to run for the Superior Court in the fall—they were now representing Japanese in their losing battle for recognition as citizens. Trygve had defended Japanese whose citizenship, acquired through legal means, was later ruled invalid.

Kibun Sakai was one of several farmers on whose behalf Trygve had challenged the law prohibiting a Japanese from owning or leasing land. Another case he had very little chance of winning involved a Japanese alien, honorably discharged as a soldier in the United States Army. Trygve had cited the Act of 1862, which provided that any alien who had been honorably discharged was eligible for naturalization, pleading that his client was entitled to apply. The federal judge, his patron, Judge Thomas had heard the case and ruled that although "any alien" was mentioned in the Act of 1862 and again in the Act of 1901, the words meant any alien who was a "free white person." The privilege of citizenship offered to other men who served in our armed forces could not be extended to a member of the Japanese race.

That issue had resulted in the only bitter argument with the judge that Trygve could remember in their long friendship. "I understand your feelings," Judge Thomas said. "But this is a matter of law, not emotion. It's perfectly clear that the intent of Congress was to maintain a line of demarcation between races. Your client is of a different race, therefore the court—my court or anyone else's—is constrained to deny his application."

Trygve had known the judge was right. If he wanted to

change the law, he would have to go howl at the people who had enacted it. Congress was the forum he would have to address, not the local judiciary. In the meantime, Trygve would continue to represent the Japanese.

Now he had taken on a client whose situation was different from that of any Japanese he had represented—a native of Japan who had applied for admission to the Washington State Bar. The same obstacle would be a threat to winning the case—attorneys admitted to the practice of law had to be United States citizens, and Trygve's client was definitely not a citizen. But there was one crucial point in his favor. Years before, this particular Japanese had fulfilled all the requirements for naturalization; the record proved that an order had been entered by the Superior Court admitting him to citizenship.

It was a grueling session in court. The prosecution held that the attorney, being Japanese, was of the Mongolian race. Trygve argued that the recent controversy caused by the exclusion of the Japanese from San Francisco schools had brought out that Japanese are *not* Mongolian. But the judge's decision was that even though the Japanese may not be Mongolian, no one could claim that they *are* Caucasian or African—the only races specifically eligible under the law.

Trygve's trump, the recorded fact that the Superior Court had already admitted his client to citizenship, was also covered by a higher card. Federal law supersedes state law. Being a state court, the Superior Court had not acted within its jurisdiction and therefore its judgment was void and must be disregarded.

The hearing left Trygve frustrated, bitter, and very much in need of a drink. His impulse was to go straight home and no matter how preoccupied Sarah might be, demand that she sit down with him and let him talk about his disappointment. Then he remembered that it was Wednesday. On Mondays, Wednesdays, and Fridays, Sarah's dance classes continued until six and sometimes seven o'clock. She wouldn't be home for several hours.

Trygve decided an empty house wasn't the place for him right now. He wondered if he and Sarah had made a terrible mistake in getting married. His picture of married life had been formed by the warm relationship he had seen between his parents. But Trygve was not even-tempered as Einar had been, and Sarah was not the diplomat that Emma was. If he wanted their marriage to work, Trygve would have to give up the hope that she would one day share in his life and not need to seek her own so desperately.

He shook his head and cursed under his breath. No, Sarah would not give an inch.

On the way out of the courtroom, he saw a woman standing just outside the entrance, watching his approach. She was tall and slender. In her late twenties, he guessed. He knew he'd seen her someplace before, and stopped in front of her. "I'm the last to leave, so you must be waiting for me."

She had an oval face framed in smooth chestnut-brown hair and friendly brown eyes. "Lydia Bishop, Mr. Peersen. I'm with the *Tribune.*"

"That's where I've seen you. I drop into the city room from time to time."

"You've got good friends there," Lydia Bishop said with a warm smile. "One of them is my boss. He sent me here today to observe this naturalization hearing."

"To do a story on it?"

"Probably. But how much of a story, or what kind . . . that's what I'd like to talk to you about, if you have a few minutes."

"I have a lot more than that," Trygve replied, feeling as if he'd been snatched back from the lip of a precipice. "I've just been asking myself how a badly depressed trial lawyer spends an afternoon when there's no one at home and he doesn't want to go back to the office."

They sat at a table in a café near the courthouse and sipped coffee in comfortable silence for several minutes. At the moment Lydia Bishop was the kind of woman Trygve needed—a lively conversationalist on the way to the café, but now perfectly at ease when no one was talking. He realized with a sense of guilt that he was comparing her serenity with Sarah's highly charged personality, and enjoying a distinct feeling of relief.

At length he said, "I've lost cases before, but this one hurts."

"Perhaps because your client is a lawyer like yourself— you're sharing his frustration and helplessness. An intelligent, hardworking young man who has sacrificed years in his struggle to obtain a law degree he'll never be allowed to use."

"Have you been studying the case, Miss Bishop?" Trygve asked in surprise.

Lydia laughed. "No. I'm quoting something you said yourself during the hearing. But I have been collecting material about our Japanese community. I'm acquainted with your friend Katamari Tamesa, by the way. I've done a story on his wife's sewing school for Japanese women, though the paper hasn't used it yet."

Trygve grinned. "Katamari's a Prince Charming who turned his story into such a pretty fairy tale. His is not a typical case, Lydia."

The first name slipped out so naturally Trygve wasn't aware he had used it until Lydia said, "I wondered when you would dispense with the prim 'Miss Bishop.' You don't have a reputation for shyness, Trygve Peersen. And I probably should tell you—it's Mrs. Bishop. My husband was killed three years ago in a mine disaster in Idaho. I'd been a schoolteacher there, but when he died I knew there were two things I never wanted to do again—one was live in Idaho and the other was teach school. So I came to Seattle and began a new career as a newspaperwoman, of sorts. I'm not a salaried reporter. I do special assignments for the *Tribune* and for other publications as well."

"Not for the *Chronicle*, I hope."

"Even an independent self-employed writer doesn't write for two competing dailies, at least not in this city," Lydia replied with spirit. "But I wouldn't take an assignment from Jonathan Wise's newspaper under any conditions. I detest his editorial policies and I don't much like his friend the Reverend George."

Trygve looked at her in admiration. "We think alike."

Lydia paused for a moment, then continued in a thoughtful tone, "Those two men are vicious. They can do a lot of damage to a political candidate they don't like."

"So you know that, too."

"That you may file for election to the Superior Court? That doesn't make me a mind reader. It's the city's most publicized secret."

Trygve said wryly, "I've had something to do with spreading the secret around. It's a way of testing your chances. Your friends always tell you you're the finest candidate. It's the reaction of your enemies that tells you what you need to know."

"Will you run?"

"I'm still trying to make up my mind. My good friend Judge Thomas once warned me against getting into a contest I'm almost sure to lose."

Again they sat enclosed in a comfortable silence. Then Lydia said, "Why are you hesitating to file for election?"

"Basically because I don't want to lose and I can't make up my mind what my chances of losing are."

"What about your chances of *winning*?"

"I'm thirty years old, thirty-one by election time. No one that young has ever been elected to the Superior Court. Judges are usually older men who've had years of experience as attorneys. The bench is more like a second career."

"Why not turn the situation around? Campaign on the grounds that what our judicial system needs is an energetic *young* man who will bring a fresh viewpoint to the bench, along with knowledge of the newest ideas. Judges *are* older men. What we need is *change*."

"Not a bad idea. But it's hard to beat incumbents. If they get a majority of the votes in the September primary, the law provides that they'll run unopposed in the general election in November. One judge has been in office for fifteen years another for thirteen, a third for eleven. They just don't leave unless they resign or voluntarily decide not to run."

"Will that situation be any different four years from now?"

Trygve smiled. "No, of course not."

"Why else are you expecting to lose?"

"My dear lady," Trygve objected, "you're too good a reporter to misquote me. I didn't say 'expect.' You know as well as I do that I've espoused some unpopular causes. I've represented the Japanese, I'm a known associate of labor—

which in any *Chronicle* editorial dumps me in the same bin with radicals and anarchists—I've refused to represent more than one big corporation, and corporations are the fountainhead of campaign funds. I don't know who or where all my enemies are, but believe me, I'll find out when I run for the Superior Court.'' He paused and turned to Lydia in astonishment. ''I believe I just heard myself say 'when.' ''

She laughed, delighted by his expression. ''It's time for me to go home. I don't want to be here when that marvelous look fades from your face. I must go, in any case. I have work to do.''

''Where do you live?''

''In Laurelhurst. A *small* house in Laurelhurst.''

''I live in a middle-size house in Laurelhurst. I'll drop you off on the way home.''

27

Trygve flew into the house on the wings of his final decision to file for the judgeship. He had made up his mind. He was not going to wait for the 1920 election. He wanted so badly to catch Sarah at the right time for a long, relaxed conversation that he was reciting his opening lines when he burst through the front door.

To his dismay, the living and dining rooms were occupied by pupils of her dance school. Barefoot, clad in knee-length Grecian tunics, they were arranged in fours, each girl clutching a corner of an immense silk scarf which her group was energetically raising and lowering in time to a Chopin prelude emanating from the Victrola. Sarah was stretched out on the davenport, issuing instructions. "*Up* two three . . . *One* two three . . . Now, girls, *down* two three, *one* two three . . . *Grace*fully, *grace*fully . . ." The mound of her abdomen looked like an enormous pillow accidentally dropped on top of her. Peering over it, Sarah waved and called out, "We'll stop when the record runs down."

Trygve stood on the periphery of the waltzing dancers, his briefcase in one hand and evening newspaper in the other. He had left his office because there were too many interruptions and he had to finish the Erickson brief today. In black silence he pushed through the dancers to the Victrola, lifted the playing arm off the record, and dropped the lid. One little girl giggled nervously. The rest just stared as he continued up the stairs to the second floor.

For a few seconds Sarah lay motionless, too shocked to register any emotion. The sound of an upstairs door slamming shut brought feeling back in a rush, and it was cold anger. Her pulse beating furiously, she lifted herself up from the davenport, walked across the room, and rewound the Victrola. "I know I promised this would be the last time you'd have to rehearse the waltz, but I think we'll go through it once more, from the very beginning." She opened the lid, put the needle back on the record, and moved the starting lever.

Sarah was hardly aware of her pupils; she neither called directions nor corrected their mistakes. The music played on and on, its merciless notes pelting her like stones thrown in anger. At length the ordeal was over. The girls changed from their costumes into school clothes, and the last mother came to take the last pupil home. Finally the time had come to do what she had resolved to do when Trygve strode out of the room.

She called his name from the foot of the stairs. He didn't respond. She called more loudly, and this time he appeared. "I have something to say to you, Trygve, and I don't want to shout it. Since it's easier for you to come down than it is for me to climb stairs, perhaps you'd be considerate enough to join me here."

Trygve descended the stairs, carrying what was obviously the legal document he had been reading.

Why? Sarah asked herself. Why such a rude reminder that I've interrupted him while he's working? "You needn't have brought that with you," she said bitterly. "I just wanted to point out that I have never stormed into your law office the way you burst into my dancing class this afternoon."

"This is not your place of business," Trygve replied coolly. "It is our home. I have never stormed, as you put it, into your studio downtown. Which, by the way, I believe the doctor advised you to close during this last month. So what were those girls doing in our living room?"

"The school has been closed for two weeks. The girls who were here today have to practice for our dance recital at the end of May."

"May? The baby isn't due until the first of April! Do you plan to go back to teaching dance classes the minute you get out of the hospital?"

Sarah wanted to shriek: Why do you always exaggerate

when the subject of my school comes up? Why can't you believe in something that's important to me? But she had resolved not to lose her temper, not to cry, not to beg. In a voice stiff with self-restraint she said, "Not the minute I get out of the hospital. Understand something, please. I *want* this baby. This baby is going to receive all the love and care I can give it. But I can be a mother without giving up my right to be an individual with my own interests. And you may as well know right now that the performance in May isn't going to be limited to pupils of the Sarah Peersen School of Dance. I'm performing two solos."

Trygve's voice was low but furious. "Seven or eight weeks after our child is born? You're going to romp around the stage in a skimpy little Greek costume? I never expected to use this word in our marriage, but this situation calls for it. I *forbid* it."

"Whom will I be hurting?" Sarah cried. "Not the child. Not myself. When I saw Isadora Duncan's concert in New York, she was still nursing her baby. I was in the front row, so I could see that breast milk had soaked through her tunic."

"My God . . ." Trygve glanced at the legal papers in his hand and tossed them into his armchair. "I'm going for a walk."

Sarah approached him awkwardly, both hands extended, wanting nothing more than to be held. "Please don't leave now. We can talk about it. If you'd only stay, and talk . . ."

Trygve shook his head. "You're upset. I'm angry. It's not the time for a discussion." He turned, took a jacket from the hall tree at the door, and was gone.

Trygve set out aimlessly, with no particular destination in mind. An hour later he found himself in front of Lydia Bishop's house. When she opened the door, he said, "I went for a walk. I didn't mean to come here, but here I am."

Hours later, walking home along the dark streets of Laurelhurst, the euphoric suspension of anxiety that he had enjoyed in Lydia's company came abruptly to an end. How would he explain his absence to Sarah? He couldn't have been walking for two hours. But why was he searching for a believable lie? Because he knew the truth wasn't believable.

Sarah's reactions to social conventions might be unpredictable, but to most people, spending more than an hour in the home of an attractive young woman was proof of infidelity.

Even his partner, George Tweedy, as nonjudgmental a friend as he'd ever had, would give him a knowing look if Trygve told him that he and Lydia had never left the living room. They had talked about Pershing's pursuit of Pancho Villa and a fourteen-year-old golf champion from Georgia named Bobby Jones and the future impact on the country of the fact that twenty-four out of forty-eight states had gone dry. All that, and never once touched each other? It had been as innocent a meeting as he might have had with another man.

Innocent? Completely, Trygve reflected, if one deals with surfaces. But he had no taste for self-deception. He had been drawn to Lydia's house by a need for her attentiveness as strong as the feeling of a man who has just discovered the lover he thought he'd never find. Now he was coming away fulfilled, released from tension, as if he'd come from his mistress's bed. No, they hadn't embraced. They had been absorbed in the exhilarating process of getting to know each other. But every minute they were in the room together, he had been physically aware of her.

When he returned home, Trygve was prepared to apologize and suggest that they try to talk things over calmly. But the house was deserted. A note from Sarah explained: Labor pains had begun shortly after he left the house. A neighbor had driven her to the hospital.

Trygve had received a cryptic message from Judge Thomas. "Meet me at the Dockside," the message ordered authoritatively. "Twelve o'clock. I've got something for you."

As Trygve anticipated, the bottle Judge Thomas kept "hidden" in his chambers had defeated the purpose of the new dry law. Eyes just slightly out of focus, Judge Thomas was smiling benignly, free from care and sorrow and happy to see Trygve. The middle-aged dignitary of 1897 was now an aging widower who shook his fist at the scandalmongers bent on disgracing him. Still he didn't, or couldn't, remove the cause of the scandal.

The judge signaled the waiter and ordered lunch for both of them. "Now then," he said as soon as the waiter was on his way back to the kitchen, "I understand you have just added a new role to your awesome repertoire. I refer to fatherhood. Boy or girl?"

"A girl. Amanda."

"Good. There's nothing in the rules of admission that says a female may not matriculate in the university's School of Law. Nothing to keep a girl from being admitted to the Washington State Bar, either. And you've only recently passed another of life's landmarks—moving to a better neighborhood. Ballard did a lot for you when you ran for the City Council; luckily the place was annexed by Seattle in time to get you all those newly enfranchised voters. But when you run for a position on the Superior Court, Laurelhurst is a better address." The judge paused as the waiter returned and set a platter of raw oysters before him. "I said I have something for you. I do; three items. But let us not mix business— monkey business, I can assure you—with our appreciation of such succulent beauties as have just been laid before us."

They had finished rare roast beef as well as the oysters before Judge Thomas was willing to reveal the reason behind his invitation to lunch. Taking several folded sheets of paper from his inside coat pocket, he said, "I have here three documents. A deposition, a passenger list, and a government inspector's report. We shall begin with the last." He selected a single sheet, unfolded it, and handed it across the table. "You've seen this before."

"Years ago," Trygve said grimly. "The night I broke into the Lund Shipyard office. The official clearance for the *Gypsy Queen*, signed by a government inspector. The report that made it legal for the ship's owner to send her off for Alaska."

"Legal, except that the inspector's signature was a forgery."

"I know. You discovered that about the time I went into law school." Tapping the name with his forefinger, Trygve read, "Harold Martinsen. But at the time, the real Harold Martinsen was locked up in the federal penitentiary on McNeil Island. If I had realized it was a phony signature, I would have taken the report with me. I left it behind because I'd already made such a nuisance of myself around the shipyard.

I was afraid that someone would notice that a document in the *Gypsy Queen* file was missing, and then the burglary would be traced to me.''

"You were thinking like a scared kid. Lund Shipyard would never have filed charges against you or anyone else. That would have meant putting the whole *Gypsy Queen* mess on exhibition in open court.''

"Nevertheless,'' Trygve continued, "what was the point of taking it? It proved my suspicions were wrong. It proved that the damned boat *had* been officially inspected, it *was* seaworthy. So I gave up. Until you ran into proof that the report was false. But it was too late by then. Martinsen was long gone. No way to trace him so I could ask questions. And the forger was just as far out of reach; God knows how I would have found him even if I had stolen the report that night.''

"You can't trace a signature. Only stumble across it, and of course you couldn't do that without the forgery to compare it with. Well, now you have it, courtesy of your friend Judge Patrick Thomas. Take a close look at that handwriting. Notice the way the letter T is crossed, and the boxy-looking R.''

"Nothing unique about either letter, is there?''

"The capital M isn't unique, either, nor the way the letters are spaced, nor the way the handwriting slants to the right. But a combination of all five characteristics—maybe that is somewhat distinctive.''

"But good Lord, how can I trace this handwriting?''

"Memorize that forgery. Get a picture of it so well fixed in your mind that you won't have to take that report out of your pocket to recognize handwriting similar to it. If you're lucky, and you keep your eyes open, you may run across it someday.''

Unfolding a second sheet of paper, the judge continued his presentation. "Next, the deposition. This could be called a stroke of incredible luck. Or proof that the Supreme Being doesn't want your thirst for revenge to slack off. Harold Martinsen, the *real* Harold Martinsen, bless his felonious heart, came to see me last week. For some obscure reason, he's convinced that his so-called reform or rehabilitation isn't complete as long as he claims he's Jim Smith or Walter Brian or George Mars, his most recent alias. So he tried honesty, and as any well-informed convict could have told him, he's experienced difficulty finding employment under his own name. He appealed to me because he thought a letter from me attesting to the fact that he hasn't committed another crime since his release from McNeil— and he hasn't, at least not as Harold Martinsen—might help him get a job.''

"Did you write the letter?"

With pursed lips and a judicial frown, Judge Thomas replied, "Not immediately. I wanted to do a little trading first. I showed him that document you have in your hand. He said, 'What bastard signed my name to that!' or something to that effect. I replied that I agreed heartily, and would he care to put it in writing, though not necessarily in that language." The judge handed the sheet to Trygve. "There it is. A written record of Harold Martinsen's testimony, made before a public officer for purposes of court action, to the effect that he did not sign that inspection report and that the handwriting is not his. His signature on the deposition makes it obvious that he's telling the truth."

Trygve sighed. "I thank you sincerely, Judge Thomas. Now I've got evidence of a forgery, but I still need someone to accuse of doing it."

"As I said, you can't do any more than keep your eyes open. I'll do the same. Now, let's proceed to the third and final document I have for you today. This one is also from the *Gypsy Queen* file." He opened the sheet and flipped it across the table. "The passenger list. You look puzzled, Counselor. I'm just thinking ahead. I'm betting that at some time in the future, you're going to put all these bits and pieces of information together. Finally you're going to know the identity of the man who sent that rotting hulk out to sea."

"I'm going to keep on looking until I do."

"Ha!" Judge Thomas chuckled. "The first time I heard you say that, you were delivering coffee cake and walking from Ballard to save a nickel carfare. Of course you won't quit. You're like the cat who starved to death waiting for one particular mouse to come out of the hole. All right, let's assume that you eventually discover who the true owner of Lund Shipyard is. What are you going to do about it?"

"Expose him. Let the public know that he caused the death of twenty-eight people. That he falsified an official document. With evidence like this," Trygve added, pointing to the deposition and the false inspection report, "he'll be convicted."

"That isn't evidence of anything except that a forgery was committed. Which gets us back to the way that T is crossed, and the square-shaped R. Whose handwriting is it? Did the anonymous owner of the *Queen* sign Martinsen's name, or did he get someone to do it for him?"

Trygve said thoughtfully, "I'm inclined to think he got someone else to do it. He used Jake Lund to cover up his ownership of the shipyard. My guess is that he used some hireling, only it couldn't have been Lund because he was murdered before that certificate was issued."

"Ah!" the judge breathed as if he were savoring a sip of good whiskey. "You just explained why I'm giving you the *Queen*'s passenger list. Our villain, who thrives by getting others to do his dirty work, paid someone to murder Lund because Lund was going to call the cops. Your investigation is going to churn up some muddy waters. The man you're after has ways of knowing what's going on or he wouldn't be able to protect himself. He won't know *who's* muddying up the water, but he'll know someone is altogether too interested in Lund Shipyard and the history of the *Gypsy Queen*.

"Now, it won't take him long to figure out that person's motive. You've used the word yourself, many times: revenge. His pursuer blames him for the death of someone who died as a passenger or crewman on his rotten little steamer. So he gets hold of the passenger list in a hurry, runs through the names, and comes to one that sounds familiar—Einar Peersen! Who else but the father of that attorney who does unprecedented things in court? The man who got himself elected to the Seattle City Council and has been fighting half his fellow councilmen ever since. You get talked about and written about, Tryg. From the point of view of the man responsible for launching the *Queen*, that makes you too dangerous to be ignored. Shutting up poor drunken Jake Lund was relatively easy. Getting you killed would be more complicated, but he could probably manage to do it."

Trygve's gaze rested on the list as if he'd never really seen it before. "So by confiscating the names of the passengers, you've hidden the connection between me and the *Queen*."

"That's my intention."

"I'm amazed," Trygve murmured, "and grateful. Wait a minute. I haven't even asked how you obtained these records."

"In a way that will never be traced to you. Of course our man will get wind of the fact that the *Gypsy*'s file has been raided, if he hasn't already through the shipyard clerk who surrendered the stuff. But he won't find anything about my interest in the documents. I issued a writ in my official capacity as a federal judge. If Mr. Anonymous were to come to me, demanding to know why I needed the documents— don't we wish he would!—I'll tell him the truth. In connection with a case involving falsification of an official government order." The judge paused and added ruefully, "I should mention why I went through this procedure at this particular time. I had to do it while I still retain the authority to issue such a writ."

"What are you talking about?" Trygve exclaimed. "What's happened?"

Judge Thomas' expression changed abruptly. The merriment left his eyes, and his mouth and jaw hardened. He looked bitter and defeated, suddenly overtaken by a cruel sobriety. "I'm surprised the news hasn't reached you. A congressional subcommittee is coming to Seattle next week to open impeachment hearings against me. It seems my drinking has become a serious threat to the federal judicial system. Ordering the shipyard clerk to turn over those papers was my last official act."

"There's no reason to say that!" Trygve replied with a good deal more conviction than he felt. He was not the only lawyer who had seen the judge fall asleep while a trial was in progress. Trygve had grown increasingly concerned because when his drinking began to undermine his reputation, Judge Thomas reacted by drinking more, and more openly—courting disaster rather than avoiding it. Nevertheless Trygve protested, "You don't know what the outcome of the subcommittee's hearing will be."

"Why don't I? You do, though you're trying to pretend you don't. You and a parcel of other lawyers will be asked to testify, and you know what those congressmen will ask you about. If you didn't answer truthfully, I'd regret every minute I ever spent teaching you the best of what I know. You were a big awkward kid when you told me proudly that you were going to be an honest judge. Well, you're on your way. You're an honest attorney. But don't worry, you're not going to have to tattle. I've resigned."

"No, dammit! Don't!"

"I said, I have resigned." The judge gave Trygve a wan smile. "I've dedicated twenty years to the bench. It will be a delight to dedicate the next twenty years to loose women and the breeding of fluffy ruffle petunias. And now, Counselor, I'm going to ride the Broadway streetcar to my lonely mansion on Capitol Hill, where I intend to get drunk, for which I have a certain flair." He rested a paternalistic hand on Trygve's shoulder. "Don't look so stricken, Trygve. 'Weeping may endure for a night, but joy cometh in the morning.' Psalm thirty, verse five. You see, I did go to Sunday school."

Sarah was concerned about her marriage. There were moments when she and Trygve laughed together, nights when they made love, but both the laughter and the loving were riddled with tension. She knew Trygve was aware of it, and once he had been as anxious as she was to untangle the knots. But in recent weeks he had shown no interest in discussing what was happening. He was pleasant enough. Since Amanda's birth he had been coming home earlier; Sarah the mother had his complete attention when what she had to say concerned the baby. Toward Sarah the wife he was friendly but withdrawn. She felt as if he were waving at her from a distance.

Sarah could still confide in Ben as freely as she had when they were children. "What's wrong between us is under the surface," she told him over lunch in a cafeteria near her dancing school. "Either we're too proud or too disappointed in each other to bring it out in the open. Or perhaps we don't know how. I certainly don't."

"No serious talks?" Ben asked. "Why not?"

Sarah shook her head. "It's probably my fault. Whenever everything is going wrong between us, I feel too miserable and depressed to talk about it. All I want is to hug Mandy and dance more and harder. During the rare moments when we're both relaxed and Tryg seems to feel a little closer to me, I don't want to do anything to spoil his mood.''

Ben sighed. "I've seen this coming, Sari."

Sarah looked at him curiously. "You and I have always been able to talk. Why haven't you said anything?"

"I'm not sure. Maybe because I couldn't comment without sounding critical, and I hate to hurt you."

"Fiddle!" Sarah exclaimed. "Go ahead. Tell me what you've been thinking."

"Actually my criticism applies as much to Trygve as it does to you. He's too tied up in his law practice and his political aspirations. You're concentrating too intensely on your dancing school. Mandy is the only real bond between you; Tryg's a great father and you're a marvelous mother. But as adult man and wife . . ." Ben shook his head sadly. "This may sting, but I've got to say it. What I see is a couple of self-centered people, both with a lot of talent and a lot of ambition, going off in different directions."

"What should I do?" Sarah asked tearfully. "Give me some advice, Ben. You're the only person in the world who can without making me mad."

"Trygve is a warm and loving man. Learn to communicate with him."

For Sarah, most abstractions were meaningless. "Learn to communicate" sounded like wise counsel, but what she needed was a course of action. Groping for an answer, she decided to accompany Trygve to some of the meetings that were taking up more and more of his time. A Socialist rally that Ben was also attending seemed a good place to start, particularly since it involved a man who would be one of Trygve's opponents in the upcoming election, Judge Dorsett.

Jonathan Wise had never ceased his editorial battle to keep "radicals" off the streets. His friend the judge had a legal weapon against "radicals;" to the consternation of his more prudent colleagues on the bench, he used it, issuing a court order enjoining soapbox orators from speaking on their favorite street corners.

For the past six or seven years, individuals had often been arrested and sentenced to short jail terms, but Judge Dorsett's measure elevated a petty misdemeanor to the level of a constitutional issue—violation of the right of free speech. Having resolved to continue speaking despite the injunction, prominent Socialists had now drawn up a petition against Dorsett and had organized a protest rally.

"Are you sure you want to come with me?" Trygve asked Sarah incredulously. "It's bound to be noisy, and if the police get involved, it could turn into a fight."

"No one hits a woman," Sarah replied. "It's too risky."

"How about Amanda? It's one thing to take her to dancing school, but she's a little young for a Socialist mass meeting."

"I've got a woman coming in. I really do want to go with you, Tryg. Ben will be there too, and I don't know much more about what he's involved in these days than I do about you."

The hall was so crowded that dozens of protesters were standing at the back and along the aisles. The clamor died down when the main speaker mounted the podium and raised both hands for silence. He had the crowd's respect; he was one of several Socialist leaders who regularly courted arrest. He had been speaking for less than ten minutes when three uniformed police officers burst into the hall, marched to the speaker's stand, and produced a bench warrant for his arrest.

Shouts and curses thundered through the hall as the police put the speaker in handcuffs and led him away. The noise ceased abruptly when a gray-haired man in business suit and bowler hat strode down the center aisle and took the place of the speaker who had just been taken away.

"My name is Luther Grant," he announced. "I come to you this evening as the personal representative of the Honorable Judge Timothy Dorsett. I am here to explain the action one of our most distinguished citizens deemed necessary, and to denounce the radicals who have prepared a petition against him in defiance of his order. Free speech is not an issue here!"

An angry murmur had been building up from the moment the man stepped up to the podium. It exploded into a roar when he added, "Judge Dorsett himself is a sincere advocate of free speech."

Standing at the back of the hall between Sarah and Ben, Trygve said, 'Luther Grant, whoever he is, must be crazy to come here alone."

"He probably didn't," Ben responded with feeling. "He does this kind of thing for Dorsett because he's well paid, not because he wants to be a martyr. Believe me, arrangements have been made."

The angry sounds from the protesters suddenly switched to shouts of applause as a slender man emerged from the mob, leapt up to the platform, and faced Judge Dorsett's lonely advocate. "You may speak for the judge," he said in a voice that was low-pitched but carried to every corner of the hall. "I will speak for the people."

The appearance of Peter Scott completely stunned Sarah, so that she was only partially aware of what followed. Scott was nine years older than when she had last seen him. His hair was almost pure white, his body thin to the point of emaciation. But the voice carried its familiar quality of deep, though repressed, emotion.

Scott challenged Grant to debate, and Grant refused angrily as applause for Scott rose in a deafening crescendo. As if on cue, the "arrangements" Ben had anticipated came into view. Fifty or sixty men scattered throughout the crowd opened a barrage of catcalls and abuse, shouting down Scott along with "all the other red-flag Socialists!"

The protesters answered in kind, though they were disorganized and confused by turncoats who had come to the meeting dressed in workclothes like their own, and who had sounded just as infuriated by Judge Dorsett's enjoining order until now.

Trygve shouted to Ben, "Get Sarah out of here! The police are probably outside waiting for the signal to raid the hall. I don't want her here when they start making arrests, and you shouldn't be caught here either—unless you want your father to read about you in the *Chronicle*."

"What are you going to do, Tryg?" Ben asked.

Trygve grinned. "Six months, probably. Now go!"

Ben steered Sarah out of the hall and past the police

officers outside. Safely in his car, he said, "I had no idea you were coming to this rally, Sari, or I would have warned you."

"How long has he been in Seattle?"

"A week."

"Is he back here to stay?"

"Yes. Dammit all, Sari, you're not going to open that up again, are you?"

Sarah shrugged. "I'd just like to talk to him."

'Listen to me," Ben pleaded. "With so much tension between you and Tryg, it's a bad time to try talking to a man like Peter Scott."

"A man like Peter Scott?" Sarah repeated resentfully. "He's an understanding man."

"Oh, yes. And also completely self-centered and completely dedicated to his work, to the exclusion of everything else. You should remember that. You were in love with him once."

"That was a long time ago. It doesn't matter anymore."

"I don't believe you, Sari," Ben said sadly. "I think it does."

An hour after Ben left Sarah at her door, Trygve arrived. "No, I wasn't arrested," he said with a grim smile. "In fact, no one was. The police were apparently sent to break up the rally, but not to fill the jail. However, my presence was noted by Judge Dorsett's man Luther Grant, which isn't going to do a lot for my political career." He put his arm around Sarah and drew her close. "Thank you for coming with me. You've never done it before."

Sarah was still badly shaken by the surprise reappearance of Peter Scott, and was much too tense to respond. She quickly discarded Trygve's thanks, hearing only the implied criticism in "You've never done it before." She pulled away from him, and before she could stop herself, her retort was out. "Then perhaps you can take the time to go to a dance concert with me. Ruth St. Denis and Ted Shawn are coming up from Los Angeles with a small group of their pupils."

Trygve walked away from her with his hands in his pockets. Finally he said quietly, "When is it?"

Though she was already feeling miserable for destroying the affectionate moment, Sarah was swept along by the impulse to justify herself. *I went to the rally because it interested him*, she thought. *Don't I have a right to expect him to attend an event that interests me?* In a brittle voice she replied, "On the twenty-fifth."

"Mmm . . ." Trygve pulled a small notebook from his pocket and opened it. "Sorry. I've invited a half-dozen friends to come here that night to talk about my campaign fund. I should have mentioned it earlier. I'd like you to serve something—coffee, sandwiches, cookies—whatever you choose."

"I don't choose," Sarah snapped. "I won't be home that evening." Trygve looked genuinely surprised, which was even more infuriating to Sarah than his assumption that the dance concert was a dead issue. "I'll be in the theater watching Ruth St. Denis."

"You can go to the concert another night. In fact, I'll go with you any night but the twenty-fifth."

"There's only one performance. Ask your friends to come another time."

"I can't do that! I've got a tight schedule between now and the primary. My friends are busy men too, and since they've set the date—not to mention that they're contributing generously to my campaign—it's hardly politic to put them off to another time just because I prefer to watch a couple of dancers from California!"

"Suit yourself," Sarah retorted. "I'll go alone."

"But I'll need you here! You're my wife. You're the hostess. A woman who is sincerely interested in her husband's career . . . That is, I'll bet another woman . . ."

The emotional crisis that had been building up in Sarah suddenly reached its climax. "Then get another woman!"

For several seconds Trygve stared at her in silence. Gradually his expression softened. "Isn't this ridiculous, the way we're shouting at each other? Because you won't do what I want and I won't do what you want? Come here, Sari." He walked toward her and reached out to pull her into his arms.

He expected her to give in! To forget his indifference, to overlook his arrogant assumption that she would play the good wife and bake cookies. He really thought she would melt and be grateful! Sarah's hands clenched into fists. She struck at him blindly, with all her strength. She hit him again and again, maddened by the fact that he neither moved nor spoke. Exhausted, she let her arms drop to her sides. Still saying nothing, Trygve turned and walked out of the room.

The next day Trygve telephoned Lydia Bishop. "Now that I've decided to run, I need a campaign adviser. Are you coming into the city today?"

Lydia laughed. "Campaign adviser? You've called the wrong number, Mr. Candidate."

"No, I haven't. Four years ago our state legislature gave women the vote. That means there's a whole new bloc of voters out there—you understand them better than I do. So you've got to have lunch with me and help me map out my strategy."

"Not today, Tryg, much as I'd like to. I'm working on an article about the Watanabe case. Remember, I mentioned it to you."

"Watanabe? Proxy wife detained for deportation? That settles it. We've got to talk. I've studied the case. I'll help you with your article and you can help me figure out how to appeal to the female electorate. How about the Dockside at one o'clock?"

Trygve chose the Dockside for the same reason it had been Judge Thomas' favorite—it was seldom patronized by the gossipy community of lawyers and judges. That lunch was to be followed by another at the end of the week, when he suggested that since Lydia came downtown every Thursday for an editorial conference with the editor of the *Tribune*, they should plan to meet regularly on that day. She agreed, but with a somewhat troubled expression in her usually serene brown eyes. He didn't prod; he was too intent on securing her promise to meet him every week.

But that moment of doubt registered, and for the next three days his anxiety grew as he anticipated a call from Lydia, telling him that she had changed her mind, that she felt they shouldn't meet. No such dreaded refusal came, and on Thursday at one o'clock he was waiting for her at a table at the Dockside.

Lydia was always punctual, a quality he particularly appreciated, since it was so lacking in Sarah. So at the end of half an hour Trygve knew it was useless to wait. Unlike Sarah, Lydia would not come bursting into the restaurant with hair flying and hat askew, bubbling with explanations about a dance rehearsal that had lasted too long or a clock that was running slow. But Trygve stayed, forcing himself to concentrate on the book he had bought for Lydia, to keep himself from watching the door.

At two o'clock he telephoned his office to ask if he had received any calls. He had, but none from Lydia. "Tell Mr. Tweedy I won't be in the office this afternoon," he instructed his secretary. Then, in feverish haste, he paid for his coffee, left the restaurant, and drove to Laurelhurst.

Lydia's face was ashen when she answered his furious knocking. He strode in, slammed the door, gripped her shoulders with his hands. "Why didn't you come?"

"I panicked," she said simply. "Suddenly I couldn't pretend that I don't know what's happening. I was unforgivably rude. But I was terrified."

"So you ran away."

She nodded. "It was like that."

"But you didn't run very far. Not really away, as you could have. You knew I would come looking for you."

She shook her head, and with uncharacteristic vehemence replied, "No, I did not think that! I thought you would be angry. Perhaps angry enough to call and demand an explanation."

"And then without facing me you would say it is not your custom to become involved with a married man, and I would accept your explanation, and it would all be over."

"Yes," she said unhappily. "You say it too bluntly, but that is what I imagined."

Trygve swept her into his arms. Holding her tightly, he said, "This is not a Victorian melodrama. The heroine has recited the proper lines, but the hero is not going to play his assigned role and say good-bye bravely and sorrowfully. We are real, you and I, and we have to live each experience without any guarantee of a happy ending. I need you. I desire you. God, how I desire you! There is an important place for you in my life, if you will accept it. And if you honestly feel that I can add something important to your life, too.''

She pulled away from him and looked into his face for a long moment. Neither spoke when she took his hands, and with tears streaming down her cheeks, led him up the stairs to her bedroom.

28

From the moment Trygve announced his candidacy, the *Daily Chronicle* mounted a campaign to defeat him. Whether incumbent Judge Dorsett was behind his friend's editorials was not a question worth debating. They were both the enemy, and in the events of that summer, they found ample ammunition.

One was Trygve's "unfortunate" involvement in the Socialist rally, where, the newspaper conceded, he had been present only as a spectator and had not been arrested. Nevertheless he had revealed himself as a friend to radicals and anarchists.

Trygve made himself an even better target when Judge Dorsett ordered seventy-five protesters to appear in court to show cause why he should not hold them in contempt for writing a petition against his injunction. Trygve offered to represent the protesters. On the first day, he watched hopelessly as one by one, his clients were ordered to stand at attention and Judge Dorsett sentenced each to the maximum fine or a term in jail. At the end of the session, two dozen men had been found guilty and were returned to their cells. Fifty still had to be tried, and at that point Trygve advised them to petition for an unprejudiced judge. Another man might free them on a writ of habeas corpus.

Trygve wasn't certain who among the eight other Superior Court judges were under Dorsett's control, but luck smiled on him. A presiding-judge system had been adopted two years earlier, and only a few days ago the position had rotated from Judge Dorsett to Judge Crowell. Crowell's favorite subject, *mirabile dictu*, was constitutional law, and the issue here was the right of free speech. His dream was that one day a president would consider him qualified for the federal bench. Over the next two days, twenty-five of the defendants sent to jail by Judge Dorsett were released by Judge Crowell.

It was a triumph for Trygve, but a Pyrrhic victory from a political point of view. News reports in the *Chronicle* were routinely laced with editorial comment. Publisher Wise, the fervent critic of street-corner oratory, used his entire newspaper as a soapbox. Immediately following the release of the protesters, Trygve's name began to appear in stories with which he had only the remotest connection.

A *Chronicle* photograph showed him leaving the Japanese labor union's office. The two Japanese with him were identified in the caption as "organizers for an underground movement against the government." A libel suit on behalf of the Japanese would be ludicrous, Trygve decided, and there was no other way to attack the newspaper's technique of guilt by association. Even the *Chronicle* obituary following the death of Judge Thomas included a gratuitous reference to Trygve as the late judge's intimate friend. An editorial in the same edition drove the point home. Referring obliquely to Judge Thomas' "misfortune," the article hinted that after Thomas resigned to avoid the disgrace of impeachment, Trygve dropped him as a friend.

The severest blow came from an influential businessman, Harvey Judson, the chief organizer of a group of wealthy "Citizens for Peersen." He came to Trygve's office unannounced and obviously troubled.

"I've got a problem I'd like you to handle for me, Tryg. I know I can count on your discretion. I came here because I didn't want to discuss it in my office."

"I'll certainly help you if I can."

"You can," Judson said curtly, dismissing Trygve's proviso. "I need a lawyer."

That was a puzzling statement, for Judson's construction firm had two company attorneys on its payroll. But Trygve said with a grin, "I can pass for one. I gather it's not a company matter."

"Strictly personal. My son Jimmy is about to graduate

from the university. He's a fine boy with a good future. There's a girl trying to ruin his reputation."

"You'd better give me the whole story."

"Her name is Christy Johnson."

"Daughter of Matt Johnson, the boatbuilder in Ballard?"

"That's the one."

"I know the family. The girl is a close friend of my niece, Emily. Christy's at the university too."

Judson shrugged. "In a manner of speaking. She lives at home. I guess they can't afford to pay for a sorority."

"True. But she's a good student."

"Is she? Well, that's beside the point. Jimmy took her out once, to a fraternity dance. Of course it was against house rules but he asked her anyway. I think he felt sorry for her because she wasn't in a sorority."

"I know about that house rule," Trygve said, trying to muffle the harshness in his tone. "I dropped out of my fraternity because of it."

Trygve's point was lost on Jimmy's distraught father. "I tell you, my son hardly knew the girl! And now she's accusing him of rape!"

"Christy Johnson?" Trygve exclaimed. "Harvey, do you mean your son is innocent and she's setting a trap for him? She's not that kind of girl."

"You only think you know what kind of a girl she is," Judson said shrewdly. "She fooled Jimmy, too. Now she's showing her true colors. But she's not going to get away with it. I want you to take Jimmy's case."

Restraining himself with difficulty, Trygve replied, 'I'm willing to help if I can, but I don't take a client until he asks me to represent him."

"*I'm* asking you."

Trygve shook his head. "Sorry, Harvey. You're not the accused. I've got to talk to Jim."

Plainly annoyed, Judson agreed to bring his son into the office in the morning.

It was a stormy interview. Jimmy was calm and self-assured, seemingly amused by the excitement over something he viewed as a prank. Ignoring his father's furious attempts to prevent Trygve's questioning, he recited the facts as if they would exonerate him. After the dance he drove Christy home by way of Volunteer Park. He stopped there in a secluded spot and after an argument, they had sexual intercourse. He added that Christy had already done the same thing with a friend of his.

Turning to the boy's father, Tryge said, "When we talked on the telephone, you said you wanted me to take Jimmy's case. That sounded as if Christy had actually brought suit, which startled me because it's so completely out of character. Christy is the kind who would rather die than have to appear in a public courtroom and swear she had been raped."

Harvey Judson said shrewdly, "Well, no, she hasn't done anything *legal*; that is, not yet. But when Jimmy tried to talk to her a couple of days ago, just in a friendly way, she gave him this story of hers about being forced and said she wished there was some way she could show him what a bad thing he did. Now that's a threat if I ever heard one. She's one more lower class girl trying to take advantage of a boy who's got money behind him."

Restraining himself with difficulty, Trygve replied, "Until your son has been formally charged, you don't need a lawyer."

"But I *do* need you. Maybe not as a lawyer, but as the man to keep this thing from getting into court. It would be embarrassing to me and it would hurt Jimmy's reputation at the university. I want you to take care of it quietly. Go to the girl's father. *He's* the one who's going to try and make a good paying thing out of this. You're clever, Tryg. It'll be a cinch to prove that the girl is promiscuous. Just you show that to that father of hers, and he'll leave us alone."

"Just a minute!" Trygve's tone startled Harvey Judson into silence. "I'd like to clear up a few points. And it's high time you let your son speak for himself. Jim, you used the words 'after an argument.' After an argument, you and Christy had sexual intercourse. What sort of argument? What did Christy say?"

Jimmy shrugged. "Mostly 'No, no. I never did that . . .' That kind of stuff."

"What did you say?"

"I said I'd heard differently. If she'd do it with another guy, why not with me?"

"What was her answer?"

"She claimed it wasn't true, that she was a virgin."

"*Was* she?"

"Maybe. I don't know for sure. By that time, I was too far gone to stop. She fought for a while, but that's part of the act. Then she cried, but a lot of them do that too."

"I see. One more question. You said a friend of yours had sexual intercourse with Christy. I'd like to talk to him. What's his name?"

For the first time there was a visible crack in Jimmy Judson's arrogance. "Did I say that? Well, actually, he wasn't a friend of mine. My friend told me about what happened between Christy and a friend of his. I don't know the guy's name."

"But you can get it. Ask your friend."

"I wouldn't want to do that!" Jimmy said indignantly. "He probably wouldn't remember who it was, anyway. I think it happened quite a while back. Besides, I wouldn't want to drag a pal of mine into a mess like this."

"*Your* mess, Jim. And you and your father will have to clean it up without my help."

A few seconds later, Trygve watched his wealthiest supporter walk out the door.

Trygve didn't know Matt Johnson well, but until Anna married Ezio Rinaldi and moved with Emily to Ezio's farm south of Seattle, Emily and Christy Johnson had been inseparable. The Peersens considered Christy to be "family" —something like a distant cousin.

Emma Peersen's affection for the girl was intensified by her concern for someone who wanted more than what her parents believed was good for her—an education past the eighth grade. Matt Johnson, far more than Christy's mother, had the old-fashioned attitude toward high school and college that Emma understood all too well. Before Trygve had come along to agitate the calm waters of tradition, Emma herself had held the same view. Christy's father had never actually interfered with his daughter's efforts to prepare for the university; he simply refused to help her. Christy could continue to live at home and put her feet under his dinner table, but beyond that she would have to manage for herself.

After her father's ultimatum, Christy's struggle became a Peersen family struggle. She had done odd jobs in Katamari Tamesa's apartment buildings, and after Emma opened Mother Peersen's *smorgasbord* restaurant, she had been alternately a waitress and vegetable cook during summer vacations. It was in the restaurant's dry food storeroom that Emma found Christy weeping silently in the dark. Reluctantly Christy told her what had happened the night of the fraternity dance.

The next morning Emma called Trygve to come to her office. "Christy Johnson is in serious trouble."

"The dance? Jimmy Judson?"

Emma nodded vigorously. "That's his name. You've heard about it? I'm surprised. The poor child is sick with fear that someone will find out."

"I didn't hear it from Christy, Mama. From the boy's father. He asked me to help his worthless son, which meant haggling with Matt Johnson over the amount of money it would take to prevent him from reporting his daughter's rape to the police, or threatening him so he wouldn't ask for anything."

"Christy would be mortified if she learned that you know. She's always looked up to you. She was raped, yes. I doubt she'll ever recover completely from the shock. But that's only part of the damage—she's pregnant."

"My God, by young Judson?"

"Do you doubt her?" Emma retorted sharply. "Have you swallowed the Judson story that he wasn't the only man?"

"Peace, Mama. I can't believe Christy would lie to you, and I know Jimmy lied to me at least twice."

"Forgive me, Tryg. I'm upset and that sharpens my tongue. Imagine—assaulted, pregnant by a young man who won't marry her . . ."

"If he begged her," Trygve put in, "I'd advise her to refuse him."

"So would I," Emma agreed fervently. "And as if Christy hasn't been hurt enough, her father is going to make her suffer still more. He's thrown her out of the house!"

Trygve stared at his mother in disbelief. "Does he blame her for being raped?"

Emma said wearily, "In a way, I think he does. He takes the view that she should never have gone out with a rich university student."

"Sure," Trygve said angrily. 'I know Matt Johnson. What he really means is that she wouldn't be in trouble if she'd listened to him. She insisted on going to the university, so she brought it all on herself."

Trygve left his chair, paced restlessly across the room and back to his mother's desk. Still standing, he said, "All right, Mama. What are we going to do?"

"I'd be glad to have her come live with me, but Ballard is still a small town. People have known each other much too long to mind their own business. Christy would hear them whisper and see them staring. I think we should spare her that."

Grinning, Trygve shook his finger at his mother. "I thought I'd learned to read the signs, but you can still lead me by the nose all the way to the trough before I catch on to where we're headed. Christy should live someplace where no one knows her. Someplace where she could even use another name. That's not Ballard. That's Laurelhurst."

"You can pick her up at my house. Her sisters packed up all her things and she's expecting you."

"It does seem to me," Trygve said slowly, "that I should at least extend Sarah the courtesy of a telephone call before I waltz through the front door with a pregnant girl and three or four suitcases."

"She doesn't have that many clothes." Emma Peersen's voice was serene and her smile radiated satisfaction. "Besides, I've already spoken to Sarah."

"Have you now, Mama. What did she say?"

"Not much. She was in a hurry. She said to tell you that if you can bring Christy home by three o'clock, she won't have to take Amanda to dancing class."

The morning after Trygve lost the September primary, he met Lydia Bishop in what had become their favorite spot for a quiet hour together—a small Japanese café whose customers were almost exclusively Oriental. "My defeat was predictable," Trygve told her. "Just as you said—success in politics is a matter of timing. I did too many of the right things at the wrong time."

"My advice wasn't much good to you."

"The mistakes were mine, Lydia."

"Nevertheless, I think from now on I'd better confine myself to encouraging you. Can you come to my house for a while this evening?"

"Yes. Sarah will be late coming home from her studio."

"I think you need to talk."

"I need *you*," Trygve said with feeling. "I'll be there at seven."

29

The distance between people, Sarah decided, was more emotional than physical. She and Trygve could have been living a continent apart for all the closeness of their relationship. Since the night of the Socialist rally she had not seen her husband alone for more than a few minutes each day. He used the excuse of work or political obligations to stay away, but Sarah knew he was avoiding her. The few times she had tried to approach him with the intention of apologizing, he had been standoffish and her peace offerings had only led to more bickering between them.

One night, after a particularly bitter fight, Trygve stormed out of the house. Sarah lay alone in bed for hours, waiting for him to return so they could make up. She fell asleep finally, and when she awoke early in the morning she saw that he had never come to bed. She assumed he had slept in his office.

Sarah began spending more time at her dance studio. She had been too busy even to think about Peter Scott. Then one day she saw him walking out of the union office, which was located only a few blocks from the studio. He turned the corner before she could reach him and she told herself she was glad he had not seen her. Still, every time she passed the union office she half-hoped he would be there.

After the first shock of seeing Peter at the rally, Sarah thought it made no difference to her whether he was in Seattle or still in Montana or Idaho. But she found herself wondering how he had changed in the past nine years. She decided she had to talk with him, just once, to satisfy her curiosity.

If Sarah had been more introspective she might have realized that her interest in Peter Scott was growing in direct proportion to her feelings of being rejected by Trygve. The more Trygve ignored her, the more she wanted to see Peter.

Sarah didn't know where he was living, but the men in the union office might; Ben had pointed out that Peter stubbornly courted danger by refusing to conceal either his political views or his whereabouts. He wouldn't be in hiding.

When she walked into the office, the only occupant was a big man with graying hair, a ruddy complexion, and the rough dress of a logger straight from the deep woods. He sat at a desk with a pad of paper in front of him and a pencil in his hand.

Sarah was no longer the meticulously groomed young lady she had been when, as a college sophomore, her appearance had startled the loggers at an IWW meeting she attended with Ben. With her life centering more and more around dancing, she tended to think of clothing as theater costume and often looked as if she had dressed only seconds before the curtain went up. But she was still a striking figure, even with strands of long red hair coming loose from their mooring under her green velvet hat.

The weather-beaten face of the man who greeted her was suffused with curiosity. He dropped his pencil, stood up, and asked politely, "What can I do for you, miss?"

Sarah never planned her strategies; they just came to her. "I'm Ben Whiting's sister."

"Well! Ben and me've done a lot together. He's a fine young man."

"I understand Peter Scott is back in Seattle."

The big man thumped his palms together as if to celebrate that fact. "You bet he is, and he couldn't be with us at a better time, what with the shingle weavers on strike in Everett."

"I'd like to get in touch with him. Would you give me his address, please?"

"Sure! But if you hang around a few minutes, you'll see him. He's due to come in almost anytime now. Have a chair right over there."

"It's such a lovely day," Sarah said quickly. "I'll wait outside."

When he saw her, Peter approached wordlessly, without

smiling. But his gray eyes, so often bitter or remote, were soft with recognition.

Though her pulse was racing, she met his sad remembering look with a prim announcement. "I realize you had no intention of seeing or talking with me again, but I do think you owe me one conversation, and I'm here to claim it."

Peter replied quietly, "Where is that conversation to take place?"

"Not in there," Sarah said, glancing toward the union office. She was discovering that meeting Peter face to face was entirely different from thinking about him. Being near him was strangely disturbing. If she'd had any plan for how this meeting was to proceed, it was lost now. Peter waited, still unsmiling, refusing to put her at ease. "My car is just a few blocks away. We'll drive to . . ." She paused, then added impulsively, "We'll go to Woodland Park."

"Oh to be a child again." His tone was amused, but not sarcastic. "Agreed, provided we avoid the zoo. I don't like to see wild animals in cages. However, I'll have to explain to the man in the office that I'll be in a little later."

"My car is four blocks north of here. I'll wait for you there."

She had barely reached the roadster when Peter caught up with her. "I'm sorry, but I can't go with you." The remembering look in his eyes had vanished. "I have business in the office that can't wait."

"Not even for an hour or two? I wouldn't have asked to talk to you if it weren't important." Her manner was defiant as she added, "At least, important to me."

"What I have to deal with is urgent. We can have our conversation another time. Here . . ." He pulled a small notebook out of his pocket, tore out a sheet, and wrote something hastily. "This is my telephone number. If you really want to meet me, you can reach me there. Or through the union local down the street. Good-bye, Sarah."

Her car was parked outside the entrance to the dancing school. As Peter turned to leave, his eye caught the sign, "Sarah Peersen School of Dance," painted on the second-floor window. "Your school," he said thoughtfully. "So this is where it is." And he was gone.

Ben's warning ran sharply through Sarah's mind. Totally self-centered and totally dedicated to his work, to the exclusion of everything else. Like Trygve, she thought.

But the sense of Peter's nearness grew more acute. Like the *scene à faire* her college English professor had analyzed—the confrontation needed in a work of fiction to resolve the plot, she had to have her "one conversation." The rejection she had felt when Peter deliberately cut himself off from her had been lying dormant all these years. What did she want from him now? What could he say or do that could purge the long-ago hurt? She didn't know, didn't really want to know. But the scene had to be played out. She phoned him, reaching him the third time she tried. At his suggestion, they met one afternoon in the lobby of a small hotel where it was highly unlikely she would be seen by anyone who knew her.

In the hotel coffee shop, Sarah was overcome by a primitive animal awareness of the male sitting across from her. She stumbled through questions about his work, his health, his travels in Montana and Idaho. Scarcely waiting for his answers, she rushed on to vital statistics about herself.

At length Peter raised a hand. "I know all about you. Your marriage, your daughter, your dancing school."

"You do?" Sarah's frantic recitation came to a halt. She saw an understanding in Peter's penetrating eyes that made everything but honesty unnecessary. Her head cleared, her nervous pulse subsided. "Then you must have asked Ben about me."

"Whenever I saw him. I've kept up with everything you've done since the last day we were together. In the *Union Record* office, September 1907."

"Why?"

"Because I love you."

Anguish, or remembrance of anguish, made Sarah's voice turn harsh. "Then how could you abandon me so completely?"

Peter said gently, "My dear, beautiful Sarah. You know the answer. Why must you hear it from me? You were what—eighteen, nineteen years old? I'm almost fifteen years older. You were innocent, untouched—you kissed like a child. My world was—and still is—a place where you don't belong. That summer I wanted you so much I convinced myself you could live in it and that somehow I could live in yours. It was an inexcusable self-deception, a cruel mistake. I don't expect you to forgive me, but I do insist that you are wise enough now to admit that breaking it off abruptly, before you were truly committed to me, was the right decision.''

"Ben thinks it was."

"Ben knows me better than you do. Whatever his judgment may have been, whatever he said, was completely fair."

"But you deserted me! I wrote you saying I would marry you even though it would mean being disowned by my father! You didn't even acknowledge the letter."

"Because in my mind, discussing what I knew was inevitable would only have prolonged the pain. All right, I deserted you, but I did it before it was too late. It hurt, but made you angry, too, and that helped, didn't it? There's still a little anger left—I can hear it in your voice. As for the hurt—a girl of eighteen heals very quickly."

"I could have fitted into your world," Sarah insisted.

Peter's mouth set in a grim line as he studied her face. Instinctively she lifted her chin and met his cool, appraising gaze. "Yes, I could have," she repeated.

"Sarah, do you want to go back? Let's look at *your* world as it is *now*. Let's make this a real conversation, not a capricious romp through the past which you can indulge in with complete safety because when you tire of it, your home in Laurelhurst, your admirable husband—I say this in all sincerity—and your child are all there to welcome you back. You don't appreciate the fact that in your world, you are free to develop yourself as an individual; unlike the average American wife, that's necessary for you. With me, you wouldn't have that freedom. The labor movement is not the Salvation Army, but one aspect of it is the same, at least when you're involved in it as deeply as I am. In the Salvation Army, a man and his wife cannot have separate careers. They are both soldiers, with equal status, and marriage between a soldier and someone outside the Army is not permitted. This makes sense to me. The job of 'saving' is so difficult it requires the wife's total dedication, just as much as the husband's. My wife would have to be a soldier too. In a different sort of army, but she would be equally deprived of any interests separate from her husband's. I've never wanted to ask any woman to enter such a relationship—least of all you, Sarah. Your dancing school is important to you, isn't it? In *my* world, it would be impossible."

Looking at him across the table, Sarah felt as though Peter were already receding into the distance. As if his voice were becoming fainter, the slender figure smaller and mistily outlined. She wanted to cry: Don't go away! But in a husky voice she murmured, "There's nothing more to be said, is there, Peter?"

"No," he said quietly. "Although I love you."

Looking down at her hands, Sarah whispered, "I think you'd better go now." She heard him move, heard his footsteps retreating across the bare coffee-shop floor. When she looked up, he was gone.

It was late afternoon and her pianist and the last of her pupils had gone home. Sarah heard a knock on the studio door. Then it opened, and Peter Scott stepped in.

For a few seconds she stood as if paralyzed, and he made no move to come farther into the room. She walked toward him slowly, her eyes fixed on his face, searching it for a sign of the same foreknowledge that was flooding through her. It was there, around his mouth and in the intense awareness that shone in his gray eyes. She met him, body pressed against body, her mouth finding his with a hunger so fierce she began to tremble. When she was a young girl, Peter's kisses had aroused sensations so new to her that she was absorbed by them, remaining innocent of where they might lead. Now she knew her body and had experienced the headlong rush to fulfill it. This was the long-ago first birth of passion, but without the innocence. She would find the fulfillment here that she and her husband no longer gave to each other.

Neither of them spoke as Sarah closed and locked the door, grasped Peter's hand, and led him to a daybed in the studio dressing room.

"Is this what you truly want?" Peter asked.

"Don't talk," Sarah murmured against his mouth. "Lie with me."

*   *   *

Two emotions swept over Sarah in the days that followed: guilt and longing. She had glimpsed guilt briefly that afternoon in the studio, sensing its whispering presence while she was dressing. But what a trick her Puritan inheritance played on her! She might have thought guilt would triumph over longing, thus bringing atonement. But it wasn't true at all. The joy she had felt at being with Peter armed her against the guilt, almost obliterating it.

She thought the nights would be hardest—that in daylight the pain would be bearable, confined by the necessities of housework and caring for the baby, and that when dark fell, the torment of guilt would be at its worst.

But that wasn't true! At night she was exhausted from the long day of fighting off thoughts she didn't want to entertain and feelings that hurt too much. Her senses were dulled.

She knew she wouldn't see Peter again. They had discussed it; realizing it would be senseless to continue something that could lead nowhere. She was married to Trygve, Peter to his work.

As the days and then weeks went by, her sense of longing retreated and guilt took over full force. She welcomed it. The afternoon of lovemaking had caught her looking the other way. She had known what the ending would be all along. She and Peter would not meet again, and in time she would learn to care less.

30

Sarah had always been uneasy about her brother's involvement with the labor movement; her anxiety had grown during the summer because for the first time Ben seemed to be avoiding her questions. She could guess why. In Everett, some thirty miles north of Seattle, the shingle weavers were fighting a desperate battle for better wages. After a failed strike protesting a pay cut, they had gone out again on May Day. By the middle of August the picket line had dwindled to fifteen or twenty men. The Everett police rounded them up easily, bringing the strike to an end.

All this had been reported in both the *Tribune* and the *Chronicle*: of course, the *Chronicle* embellished its accounts with savage editorials about the "Wobblies," described as "Bolsheviks hiding behind the title of Industrial Workers of the World."

Ben did admit that he was spending more and more time in Everett, under cover of his real-estate job. "There are no city limits in a fight like this. A union is a brotherhood." But he kept the details of the fight to himself, and that frightened Sarah. Secrecy had been necessary to living in peace with their stern and domineering father, but it had never come between the two of them until now.

She sensed a crisis when Ben asked to borrow her roadster for a few days, explaining that his own car was under repair. "Ordinarily I could manage. But I have a special assignment and there are other people depending on me for transportation."

"Of course you can have the car," Sarah replied. "Now that we've got Christy living with us, I don't have to use it to take Mandy to the studio. But you sound so vague. Special assignment? In other words, nothing to do with the real-estate firm.''

''No. It's union business.''

Fear for her brother erupted in an angry rush. ''And no doubt that's all you intend to tell me. Don't you trust me anymore, Ben?''

''Calm down, Sari. Of course I do. But there've been some ugly incidents and there may be more. No use worrying you, since you can't do anything to help me.''

''Or to stop you. But I *am* helping you, by letting you use my car so that you can get mixed up in what you call an ugly incident. I've got a sick feeling that I'm going to regret it, too. It has to do with the shingle weavers, doesn't it?''

Ben nodded. ''That's the immediate issue, yes, but it's part of a much bigger picture. Freedom to meet, the right to free speech, the crime of management using the police to keep loggers and lumber workers from organizing—that's what we're up against. Believe me, what's really happening doesn't get into the newspapers—not the ones you see, at any rate.''

Sarah said, ''What I want to know is, what's happening *now*?''

Ben sighed. ''God, Sari, if you really have to know, all right. IWW lumberjacks have voted to fight for free speech, which means fighting to reopen the union hall in Everett. We've just organized a defense committee and we're getting together to make plans for a street demonstration. But the committee's not going to meet in any regular union hall. The police have been keeping such a close watch on those places they might as well put an armed cordon around them. That's why we need your car. And that's why I've been keeping everything a secret, even from you. There's always the risk that some disgruntled or greedy union member can be bribed and the police will find out about our plans before we can carry them out.'' Ben paused and added with a wry smile, ''Pity the company stiff who tries to bribe you, Sari. You'd claw his eyes out. But I still won't tell you where we're meeting, because there's no need for you to know. It's going to be relatively dull stuff, anyway. Just arrangements—like how to call for volunteers. And it won't be a big meeting, either. Two, three dozen loggers, myself, and the chairman . . .''

His voice broke off abruptly and Sarah knew he'd stopped short of finishing the sentence. "Who is the chairman, Ben?''

"Peter Scott, of course.''

It was about eight o'clock at night. Amanda was asleep in the nursery, Christy Johnson had gone to bed, and Sarah and Trygve were reading in the living room. Sarah's attention was drawn from her book by the glare of headlights shining against the front windows as a car turned into their driveway.

It had been two days since Ben had borrowed her roadster. "It must be Ben, returning my car.'' She jumped up, dropping her book onto her chair. A premonitory chill went through her as she ran across the room to welcome her brother. She opened the door without waiting for his knock. The pale glow of the overhead porch light revealed what she had feared instinctively. It wasn't Ben. A stranger in muddied workclothes was slowly mounting the steps, clutching the railing for support, and pulling himself up with obvious difficulty.

Trygve had followed her out to the porch. He stepped forward quickly to put a supporting arm around the man's back. "Easy,'' he said, guiding him to a chair in the living room.

The man dorpped into it but his back remained ramrod straight, as if the chair were to good to touch.

"Relax, man,'' Trygve urged. "Lean back.''

The stranger's voice was hoarse. "I don't want to dirty up your nice furniture.''

An anguished exclamation burst from Sarah's mouth. "Tryg! Look at your sleeve!''

From wrist to armpit, the arm Trygve had used to help the man inside was wet with blood. "Get a bath towel,'' he said to Sarah. He turned to the man: "How badly are you hurt?''

"I took a beating, but no bones broke.''

The sickening evidence was soon visible. Sarah returned with towels and a basin of warm soapy water and Trygve stripped the man to the waist. Blood oozed from long jagged tears across both his back and chest.

"They hit you with something sharp.''

"They was using a lot of different things. What I saw was a table leg, with those long screws at the top sticking out of it—the ones you use to attach the leg to the tabletop."

"While my wife is washing these cuts, I'll go call our doctor. He lives right down the street."

"No, sir. Don't waste time doing that. That's not what I'm here for."

Sarah already knew why he'd come. Her eyes fixed on the man's wounds, she whispered, "What happened to Ben?"

"We was having our meeting. A gang broke in, shouting they were deputies of the law. They pulled guns on us, loaded us into trucks, and took us into the woods near some railroad tracks. Kind of a little park, near Monson Lake. That's where they dragged us out of the trucks, and then them so-called deputies lined up along both sides of the tracks—except for one, I guess he was their leader. He kept a gun on us and forced us, one at a time, to take off our shirts and run down the middle of the track. We was getting hit and kicked and cursed at from both sides, and everybody got cut up pretty bad by the time we run the whole way. Then the rest of the loggers, they began running for their lives and the deputies didn't try to stop them. But I seen that two of us never got to the end of the lineup so I circled back. One of the men who fell and couldn't get up was your brother, Ben, Mrs. Peersen. They kicked his body off the tracks and rolled it down through the cinders into the woods. They was all laughing and sounding mighty pleased with themselves when they got into the trucks and drove off.

'When I got to Ben, he was still conscious, but so broke up I was afraid I'd kill him if I tried to drag him away. He told me to get back to the place we was meeting and take his car to his sister's and tell her what happened. Then he halfway passed out. So I run through the woods, cross-country—a shortcut to the car and a good way not to get spotted. Your name and address was inside the car. That's how I knew where to come."

"A wood near a railroad track," Trygve said, "near Monson Lake."

The man nodded. "Right below a real high trestle."

Trygve nodded. "I know the spot. I'll go get him."

"I'm going with you." Sarah's voice was low and steady and left no room for argument.

"Someone should stay and take care of this man. I suppose we don't really need a doctor, but he ought to be put to bed."

"Christy can do that." Sarah turned back to the logger. "You said there were two men who failed to run the gauntlet, two who dropped before they made it to the far end. Who was the other man, besides my brother?"

"The chairman of our committee, ma'am. Peter Scott. I don't think you should go with your husband, Mrs. Peersen. You shouldn't see what they done to him."

Sarah's answer was to run to the hall closet and take out her coat.

Benjamin was dead. Peter Scott was still alive, though it was some time before Sarah and Trygve realized that the shadowy form suspended from the side of the trestle was the body of a man. After carrying Ben's body to the car, Trygve climbed the trestle. In the flickering beam of the flashlight Sarah was holding thirty feet below, he untied the ropes that held Peter Scott.

Trygve's descent in semidarkness with the unconscious man over his shoulder was painfully slow, but the burden was slight. Scott was so thin he felt no heavier than a child. Like the others, he had been forced to strip before he ran the gauntlet, and his back and chest bore such dreadful lacerations that in some places it looked as if a sharp metal instrument had almost run through his body. When Trygve lowered him to the ground, Sarah's flashlight fell on the true horror of what had been done to him. Before the "deputies" had strung him from the side of the trestle, they had ripped apart his trousers. He had been crudely emasculated.

Trygve and Sarah did not try to talk on their way to the hospital, nor when they drove home after the doctor in the emergency room said, "I'm sorry, Mrs. Peersen. Of course you know your brother was dead on arrival. But for the older man, it's also too late."

Inside the silent house, Trygve went straight to the guestroom. The logger whose name he still didn't know was asleep, his chest and back carefully wrapped in layers of gauze bandage. Satisfied that Christy had done a thorough job and that Amanda was also sound asleep, he returned to the living room.

Sarah stood just inside the front door, where she had been when he left her to go upstairs. He went to her, gently removed her coat, and hung it up in the hall closet. Then he picked her up in his arms and carried her up the stairs to their bedroom.

Her eyes were wide open, but curiously blank and tearless. He set her down on the edge of the bed, as stiff and lifeless as a doll on a shelf. He wanted to tell her: I understand, Sari. Your loss is so much heavier than you dare to let me know. But I already know, Sari. It isn't just losing Ben. Scott was your lover, wasn't he? That first romantic love before we married, and then, not long ago, a complete lover. I think I know when that happened. I saw the beginning, the shock of recognition at the Socialist rally. So you see, Sari, I do understand. . . .

Understand! What right have I to be so noble! What cheap magnanimity—forgiveness from the person whose secret is that he needs to be forgiven. Cheaper still—the impulse to tell you all about Lydia, purifying myself at your expense, adding the meanest kind of hurt to the grief you feel for both Scott and your brother. If there's a time for confession, it isn't now.

So all he said was, "I hate to see you suffer, Sari. Sleeping will help a little. I'll bring your nightgown and get you ready for bed."

They lay side by side in the darkness, neither sleeping, Sarah grieving for her brother and for Peter Scott, Trygve anticipating the pain of giving up Lydia Bishop. Though his resolve was born in part from remorse, it was also the product of a new self-realization. His marriage had been deteriorating badly. Trygve knew he could not salvage it without breaking the bond to Lydia. And salvage it he must. After seeing tonight's brutality, he felt an overwhelming desire to keep Sarah and Amanda safe. Sarah was like a high-spirited thoroughbred who must be restrained from racing too hard or too long. Though she would never admit it, she yearned for applause, for the security of a comforting partner. As for

Amanda, Trygve was more than a father. He was her play-mate, her friend. She was at an age when "Daddy" was, and should be, the only man in her life. Sarah needed him, Amanda needed him . . . and as the sleepless night wore on, Trygve knew just how desperately he needed and wanted them, too.

31

In a peaceful harbor across Puget Sound from Seattle, Kurt Bauermeister was playing chess with the master of the German steamship *Saxonia*. The *Saxonia* and the three-masted windjammer *Steinbek* had taken refuge in American waters when Canadian cruisers patrolling out of Vancouver made it too dangerous to go to sea. Kurt had met their captains through friends in Seattle's German-American community, and had been coming on board once or twice a week.

Today he and Captain Franz Helfer were bent over the chessboard. Captain Johannes Wohlers, master of the *Steinbek*, looked on, the ship's blue-gray Maltese cat asleep in his lap. The three men had emptied several steins of beer; all their toasts were to the Fatherland.

Captain Wohlers addressed Kurt in a sleepy voice. "You are acquainted with the airplane plant on Lake Union?"

"I know where it is. A pilot named Boeing built it about a year ago. You have some information about it?"

"I am a sea captain, not a spy," Wohlers replied, stroking the cat. "What I know, I read in the Seattle newspapers."

"Then you're aware that Boeing is building training planes for the navy."

"*Ja.* I read that, too. Also about the new ships being built in Seattle. Three freighters were started last February. Now a cruiser, for a half-million dollars. I would conclude, Mr. Bauermeister, that your country is getting ready to go to war."

"Our young friend is here to play chess, Johannes," Captain Helfer said curtly. "Please allow our game to continue."

They played in silence until a ship's officer strode across the deck, saluted smartly, and handed Captain Helfer a note. "From the radio room, sir."

"So it has happened finally," the captain remarked as he scanned the message. "President Wilson has asked Congress for a formal declaration of war against the empire. You know what that means for us, Johannes. Get back to your ship quickly. We'll meet again soon, I can promise you, but it won't be on the deck of the *Saxonia*. Kurt, you must go ashore." He turned to the grim-faced officer standing at attention. "We will be boarded as soon as the Americans get their orders at the navy yard. You know what our procedure is. Begin immediately."

As he shook hands with the captain, Kurt promised fervently that he would do everything he could for the Fatherland.

"If you mean that," the German said impatiently, "you won't make a fool of yourself. I have come to know a good deal about the German-speaking people in this city and I am convinced that most of them will remain loyal American citizens. But war breeds hysteria. Everyone with a German name will be suspected, even those of the second or third generation. If you rush into some scheme to come to our aid, you'll accomplish nothing for us and you'll stir up hatred for people who don't deserve it."

"I consider Germany to be my true homeland," Kurt replied stiffly. "I love the Fatherland."

"Do you love your mother?" the captain asked softly, and walked away.

Two tugboats manned by fifteen marines were dispatched from the Puget Sound navy yard under command of navy pilot Captain Joseph Reardon. The *Saxonia* and the *Steinbek* were boarded and the flags of imperial Germany hauled down. The crew of the *Saxonia* had followed their captain's orders to the letter. The ship's engines had been wrecked, fires had been set under dry boilers, copper piping was removed, castings had been destroyed and cylinders drilled. Aboard the *Steinbek*, all the main rigging had been sliced. The American navy officers also discovered that many of the crews had deserted well before the declaration of war. Only thirteen men remained aboard the vessels—Captain Helfer, Captain Wohlers, and eleven sailors. They were placed under arrest, brought to Seattle, and interned in the immigration station.

That night Kurt Bauermeister packed a wicker picnic basket with dry rags, matches, a can of gasoline, and, almost as an afterthought, a short but sturdy chisel. Hiding in the shadows thirty feet from the airplane plant on Lake Union, he watched the factory windows for any sign of light or movement. Satisfied at last that the building was completely dark and unguarded, he crept forward and along the wall to what was apparently the entrance to an office. He tried the door. It was locked, but it didn't matter. He had come prepared.

Moving to the nearest window, he opened the picnic basket, took out the chisel, and jammed the blade between the frame and the windowpane. He tried to force the semicircular lock to slide open. The lock held firm, so he put more weight behind the chisel. The window frame creaked loudly, and the sound was instantly followed by another—the deep growl of a dog.

Startled, Kurt leapt back so quickly that he lost his balance. The chisel soared out of his hand and crashed through the window.

As the shattered pane fell into the building, the growling became murderous and the wolfish head of a dog with teeth bared appeared in the opening only inches from Kurt's face. Kurt ran.

Back in his apartment, he began to worry that there might be something in the basket that could be traced to him. He concluded that there was not. Clumsy as he'd been, he'd thought of that, at least. His chief mistake had been haste. Whether it was this plane factory or some other target, the next time he would make more careful plans.

In the midst of seventy thousand acres of prairie land south of Seattle, an army post named after Captain Meriwether Lewis of the Lewis and Clark expedition was under construction. The Ninety-first Division—dubbed the "Wild West Division"—was activated in July, and Trygve Peersen made the decision to enlist.

"You realize you won't be drafted," Sarah pointed out. "Not a married man with a child."

"It's unlikely. That's why I'm going to enlist."

"I'm not objecting, Tryg. I hate it, but I do understand how you feel."

"I'm not trying to be noble, and I'm not necessarily very brave. I'm only doing what has to be done."

With a sad smile, Sarah nodded. "I know. It's the only decision you can make. It just makes me sad that we have to be separated, now that we've found each other again."

The erection of a "city" of almost eighteen hundred buildings was completed in ninety days. Early in September recruits began moving into Camp Lewis. Reserve and regular army officers already settled into barracks were on hand to greet the first draft train when it disgorged the disparate collection of sailors, ranchers, schoolteachers, businessmen, longshoremen, and factory workers about to be transformed into soldiers. Among them was Trygve Peersen. The spirit of the men was evidenced by the slogans they had chalked on the sides of the cars: "Hell, High Water, or Huns Can't Stop We'uns!" "Keelhaul 'im, Kerosene 'im!"

Though the Ninety-first was made up of men from eight states and the Territory of Alaska, an effort was made to group recruits according to the state and city from which they came. However, when Lieutenant Peersen emerged from the organization process, he was in the 364th Infantry, most of whose men were drawn from the southern half of California. There were so many first-generation Italians among them that one squad needed a corporal who could translate drill orders rapidly.

Trygve's first conversations with the other members of his platoon were about the weather. The complaints were understandable; though designated as "complete," the camp was as unfinished as the Ninety-first. With no paved roads or sidewalks, the men marched in either a desert of dust or a sea of mud. Even on a hard dry field, their drill wouldn't have been stylish. Aside from khaki leggings, their military uniforms were a comical combination of government issue and the clothes they had brought with them.

There were no sheets on the beds and the mattresses were stuffed with straw. But after seven hours on the drill field, relieved only by picking up stones to build walks, no one complained that he couldn't sleep. Few messes were lucky enough to have a cook who had worked in the restaurant business in any capacity. The general feeling about the watery beef stew was: You don't have to like it, you just have to eat it.

The Reverend Thomas George had found fresh material for the most vituperative sermons of his career. The presence of more than a hundred thousand soldiers just outside the city of Seattle was initiating a widespread campaign to impeach the mayor because of his tolerant attitude toward sin. But the Reverend George didn't confine himself to vice. At a mass meeting of enraged righteous citizens, he added the crime of sedition. "There are twenty-three hundred hardened prostitutes in our city," he told an audience made up primarily of women. "Our young soldiers at Camp Lewis are being corrupted. The commanding general *must* act. We have spies in our midst, for it was here in Seattle that Kerensky's overthrow was hatched."

Eccentric as it might seem to claim that the Bolshevik revolution in Russia was planned on Puget Sound, the message was carried even further. The minister's friend Jonathan Wise published supporting editorials in the *Chronicle* and eventually impressed the general in command of Camp Lewis. Seattle was officially declared off-limits to all military personnel.

As a result of the ban, Trygve could no longer obtain a pass to visit home. This was a cruel twist of fate to Sarah; since the murders of her brother and Peter Scott, a bond had begun to form between herself and Trygve. She had no desire to define it. Holding it up to analysis was too much like experimenting to see if a beautiful icicle would melt when suspended over a hot stove. Affection, mutual acceptance, and a gradually emerging sense of family—these were the threads Sarah could identify. But they needed the strengthening that Trygve's home visits supplied.

Sarah had never discussed her marriage with anyone but Ben,

but she had often thought that Emma Peersen was the person she could turn to most easily if she were ever in trouble. On impulse, Sarah bundled two-year-old Amanda into her leggings and quilted jacket and drove to Ballard.

Before Sarah could explain her presence, Emma's good china came out of the parlor cupboard. Two or three varieties of Norwegian pastry were set on the table and rich dark coffee was poured into Grandmother Frodesen's delicate china cups. Settled comfortably with Amanda in her lap, Emma signaled the beginning of conversation with "How hard for you, Sarah, that Trygve can't come home."

"You've already guessed what I came to talk about," Sarah said with a smile. "I should have known."

Emma laughed softly. "My dear girl, it doesn't take a mind reader to know how you must be feeling. The minute I read that Seattle had been declared off limits for soldiers at Camp Lewis, I began to ask myself: What would I do if I were Sarah?"

Surprised, Sarah asked, "You think there's something I *can* do?"

"Isn't there always?"

"But there's an official order from the commanding officer. Of course it's ridiculous. Twenty-three hundred fallen women! This may be a wicked city, but I doubt that it can support that many ladies of the night, even with the help of an army camp. And that crazy Reverend Thomas George says the city isn't safe for our soldiers because it's full of German spies and Russians with bombs."

"That's what the Reverend George believes," Emma said soothingly, "but I doubt it's the general's reason for the ban. He's listening to the wrong people, of course, but he's probably more concerned about protecting his men from disease than from Bolsheviks."

"I'm sure you're right," Sarah conceded. "In fact, that's just what Trygve says. But as far as I'm concerned, the effect is the same for me and Mandy. I don't know how long it will be before Trygve's regiment is sent to France, but whatever it is, I hate having to spend the remaining time away from him."

"Then, Sarah," Emma said serenely, "since he can't come to you, why don't you go to him?"

"Move to Camp Lewis?" Sarah laughed. "I'm not fallen, but I'm afraid the general might object."

"Come, dear. I'm not advising you to move into army barracks. Camp Lewis is just south of Tacoma. There must be places to rent."

"Yes, I suppose there are. I could leave Amanda with Christy Johnson. Christy's a wonderful little mother and Amanda adores Christy's boy. She won't miss me."

Emma's dark eyebrows raised with her quizzical smile. "Do you suppose Trygve will miss Amanda?"

Sarah looked at Emma with frank admiration. "Oh, Mother Peersen," she breathed, "if only I had half your wisdom."

She could go by rail, but traveling alone with her luggage and household supplies, as well as with a little child, made a train out of the question. She would have to take the car.

Sarah was the only woman in her immediate neighborhood who had learned to drive, and she had never ventured alone beyond the city limits. She tried to think of the trip to Camp Lewis as nothing more than an extension of her regular route from Laurelhurst to downtown Seattle. It was five times as long, but that was the only difference. Her father denounced her plan, Angela was sympathetic but skeptical, her friends were frank in telling her she'd lost her mind. Coming up against a solid wall of negative public opinion—with only Emma remaining steadfastly on her side—Sarah made her plans to leave.

Having secured the family's reluctant promise not to alert Trygve, she packed the roadster with everything it would hold. With Amanda tucked securely between two pillows, Sarah set out to drive to an area as alien as an African jungle. She arrived triumphant, having driven the entire forty-five miles in less than two hours.

As Emma Peersen had guessed, there were plenty of places to live. Just off the highway north of Camp Lewis she found a boardinghouse and an apartment building. The owner of the small grocery offered to rent one of the cabins at the rear of his store. She inspected all three locations and after observing the other tenants, concluded that some of the "fallen women" had already found a way to subvert the general's stern order. "This is no place for us," she told Amanda, who had slept through most of the drive. "And it's miles from the camp anyway."

The next three days were busy. Using a room in the boardinghouse as her temporary headquarters, Sarah laid the groundwork for a home directly across from the camp. Two trips back to Tacoma were necessary, as well as some energetic searching for the owner of the land where her home site would be. On the fourth day, she and Amanda were in the office of the colonel in command of Trygve's regiment.

When Trygve received a summons to report to his colonel, his immediate thought was that one of his men had gone AWOL. They had been restless since the ban had barred them from going to Seattle; the colonel might have learned about the times when Lieutenant Peersen had known what his men were up to and looked the other way. But when he entered the office, Sarah was sitting in a chair beside the colonel's desk. Amanda was on her mother's lap, teething on one of the large mother-of-pearl buttons that adorned the front of Sarah's shirtwaist.

"You have visitors, Lieutenant," the colonel said genially. "Lucky fellow."

The only greeting Trygve could manage was "How did you get here?"

"I drove," Sarah said casually, as if reaching the headquarters of the 364th Infantry had been no more than a leisurely Sunday-afternoon excursion to see the bears at Woodland Park. "We're living just across the tracks."

"Living?"

"Yes. And Colonel Harrison has been kind enough to give you permission to see us home."

Trygve turned toward the colonel, whose face quickly resumed an expression of authority as he agreed that indeed he had done just that.

Sarah's unheralded appearance at camp was no match for Trygve's amazement when he saw the "home" Sarah announced would be hers and Amanda's while he was in training. The small clearing across the railroad tracks was studded with fourteen-foot stumps of virgin timber cut fifty years before. In the middle of the open space was a large tent. A black stovepipe rose like a steeple from its sloping canvas roof.

"I thought there would be apartments for rent close to camp," Sarah explained, "or at least some sort of boarding-house. Well, there are, but I wasn't fond of the kind of people who were going in and out of them. Besides, this is much closer, so you can come here more often."

"Where did you get this? Who put it up for you?"

"I bought the tent, and no one put it up for me. My father believed in fresh air. He took Ben and me camping at least once a year. He had a lot of theories about survival in the wilderness so he taught us how to put up a shelter, how to hunt wild foods, how to make fires without matches—all that sort of thing. Ben and I put up a tent like this together when he was ten and I was eight. I hired a carpenter to build this wood floor, but I did the rest myself. Except for putting up the chimney. The carpenters did that too."

"I'm speechless, but not surprised." Trygve lowered Amanda to the ground and put both arms around Sarah. "What else do I have to learn about you that I never knew before?"

"That I really love you."

"Do you? I haven't always been sure."

"Nor I."

It was an honest response. More honest, Trygve thought guiltily, than he had always been with her. There was a sting in her confessing that she had entertained doubts about loving him. But it was also a healing thing to say, and for the first time he was sure he had been right in saying good-bye to Lydia. His arms tightened around Sarah. He kissed her hungrily, and felt desire for her mounting as it hadn't for a long time.

At length Sarah murmured, "It's time for Mandy's nap. I'll put her to bed."

The tent was furnished with a table, three chairs, a small oak icebox, a black cookstove, a crib, and a wide bunk bed, all purchased and transported from Tacoma in the four days since Sarah had left Seattle and had appeared in the colonel's office. After a dish of applesauce and a cookie, Amanda fell asleep quickly.

Trygve drew Sarah toward the bed.

"Not here," she whispered. "Out in the field."

They walked across the clearing to a lonely spot surrounded by tall bracken fern, and there, on meadow grass warmed by the sun, they undressed and lay down together.

German immigrants had always blended into the general population. Unlike the unfortunate Orientals, they didn't look "different." Now they suddenly found themselves the targets of insults and petty vandalism. President Wilson himself questioned the loyalty of "hyphenated" Americans, while former President Teddy Roosevelt accused German-Americans of being traitors. In the town of Aberdeen, Washington, just west of Seattle, a local German artist put figures of "Prussian" eagles into a frieze he designed for the public library. The library's board of trustees ordered that the eagles be obliterated so that "the patrons of the library would be made to feel more satisfied." The state board of education formally banned the teaching of the German language and called upon private schools to do the same. Hamburgers became liberty-burgers. A German shoemaker in the town of Yakima, Washington, was arrested on a charge of espionage because he allegedly expressed pro-German sentiments and was reported to be "spending much time hunting and killing rattlesnakes for some mysterious purpose."

Kurt Bauermeister suffered more prejudice than many persons with obvious Teutonic surnames because it had taken him so long to recognize the Kaiser's unpopularity. Even after the sinking of the *Lusitania*, he had remained outspoken in his praise of all things German. Angry as he was at being ignored, snubbed, and sometimes cursed, abuse only served to increase his pride.

Still, he did acknowledge that in order to be of service to the Fatherland, he would have to become more discreet. Seattle's Germanic people were busy reiterating their loyalty in every way they could, and pleading, through a publication called the *German Press*, that their neighbors recognize that

"This great nation is not at war with the millions of its citizens of German descent, nor with the German language, literature, art, or science." Kurt considered various ways to disarm the enemy and hit upon a scheme of his own. He would join the Minute Men.

The Minute Men was a branch of the American Protective League dedicated to rooting out sedition and exposing German spies. Though the name Bauermeister was hardly the best reference, Kurt was accepted because of his proposal: he would report on his many German friends, although, as he pointed out, he would be risking his own life.

He was fanatically proud of the double role he had created. On the one hand, he established himself with the Minute Men as a zealous patriot on the hunt for enemy spies. On the other, he was in a position to spy on the spy hunters, and before long, his cleverness bore fruit. During a patriotic rally, he discovered that an unmarked and apparently harmless barge in Elliott Bay was actually loaded with fifteen tons of dynamite.

He had no intention of repeating his mistake at the airplane plant on Lake Union. This time he would plan carefully and scientifically. After spending a week watching the barge from various locations around the bay, he was satisfied that it was unattended. The surest way to blow up the dynamite was both safe and simple. He wouldn't have to row out into the bay and detonate it with a mixture of chemicals. That was risky and unnecessary.

His gun collection, acquired during his many years in military schools, included a 30.06, a rifle with a range up to twenty-six hundred yards. The barge was less than a mile offshore, only 1,760 yards from where he could safely take aim. He would blast fifteen tons of dynamite with a couple of rifle shells and sacrifice the gun by dropping it into the bay. He would be blocks away by the time anyone arrived to see what had happened.

He chose a rainy night so it would be natural to wear a long raincoat. With his rifle tied securely to his side, concealed by the coat, he strolled along the pier. A stack of crates offered shelter. He stepped behind it so that he could not be seen from the street. His excitement mounted as he unstrapped his gun, loaded it, and carefully took aim.

"What the hell are you doing, Kurt?" a rough male voice said behind him. Startled, he jerked his finger, pulling the trigger. In the few seconds before an explosion shook the pier and sent the barge skyward with a thunderous roar, Kurt turned and recognized the man who had spoken. It was a fellow member of the Minute Men—one of his colleagues, dedicated, like himself, to searching out German spies. Forgetting the Minute Men also had to stand guard over barges loaded with explosives was Kurt's second mistake.

Both men were knocked off their feet. In an effort to destroy the evidence, Kurt groped for his rifle. The other man was quicker and stronger. When the police arrived, he was holding the gun to Kurt's head, and Kurt, leaning against a crate, was sobbing like a frightened child.

"I was going to give you five more minutes," the man told the police officers, "and then I was going to take care of this dirty bastard in my own way."

Seattle was no longer off-limits to soldiers at Camp Lewis. The ban had been lifted, in part because the commanding general had begun to make an objective appraisal of Reverend George's statements and decided he shouldn't rely on a Christian clergyman who preached that the country should be put under a dictatorship. Furthermore the Ninety-first Division would soon be deployed to Europe, where the general's men were to be rushed to the western front to battle over crucial German territory. Seen in that light, Seattle's fallen women were a minor threat.

Sarah and Amanda moved back to Laurelhurst, where Sarah immediately reorganized her dance school and began practice for a patriotic pageant. The day before the performance, Trygve came home on leave and was on hand to help set the scene on a grassy slope above Lake Washington. There were folding chairs from a Sunday school for the musicians. A huge billboard, painted to represent the Declaration of Independence, served as a backdrop and was flanked by a dozen American flags. A section of the field was set aside as a stage, with red-white-and-blue crepe-paper streamers twisted into a spiral rope to separate the dancers from the audience.

At two o'clock on a sunny afternoon in June, the skies smiled on a throng of spectators. At the far end of the field opposite the Declaration of Independence backdrop, two dozen nervous pupils awaited their cue to march up the slope, pass through the divided audience, and proceed to the circular area, where they would execute dance routines symbolizing Freedom and Democracy and Love of Country. At that critical moment, waiting tensely for the first notes of "Pomp and Circumstance," each girl knew she was certain to forget her part. Only two-year-old Amanda, who didn't have a part, was enjoying herself.

She had been dressed for the occasion in a white tunic and a red-and-white-and-blue sash, but was expected to remain on the sidelines with her father. The overture excited her, the bright flags and streamers enthralled her. Everything was wonderful, even the great crowd of murmuring strangers whose expectant gazes seemed to be infecting the older girls with a compelling desire to run and hide. The overture ended, and after a brief silence the first notes of "Pomp and Circumstance" rang out.

That was the cue to march, but the lead couple seemed not to have heard it. "Mary! Agatha! Girls, start!" Sarah called out from her position at the rear of the procession.

The dancers hesitated. Amanda didn't. She had heard her mother's command, and before Trygve could stop her, she slipped throught the cordon of spectators and ran to the head of the procession.

The burst of surprised applause didn't frighten her, nor did the laughter deter her from leaping and waltzing the length of the field. She improvised dance steps as she went and showed an unerring instinct for keeping her spot at the head of the line. Not until the processional ended and the performers were grouped for the first dance was Sarah able to catch up with her daughter. She didn't tell Amanda to return to her father. All she said as the orchestra began to play was, "Dance, Mandy! Listen to the music, and dance!"

* * *

That evening Trygve broke the news. "You had so much on your mind, I didn't want to tell you before, Sarah. We're shipping out in a few days."

"I knew you were holding something back. You had that too-cheerful look on your face."

"I'll leave in the morning, but it will have to be very early. I'll say good-bye to Mandy tonight, though I don't really know what to tell her."

"She knows you're a soldier, Tryg. She's seen you in uniform and obviously thinks it's much finer than the clothes other girls' fathers are wearing. Don't worry about what to say. She'll think it's exciting just because you said it."

When Trygve went upstairs, Sarah sat in the living room with the lights turned off, listening to records of songs from *Maytime*. She had purchased a record of the popular tune "Roses Are Blooming in Picardy," but tonight was the wrong time to listen to it. The wrong time for everything—except, if she could, making love with Trygve in a way they would both remember. At length she closed the Victrola and climbed the stairs.

The door to Amanda's room was open. She paused to listen. Trygve did not seem to be having difficulty saying good-bye. He was reaching into his proven repertoire of stories:

> It was a dark and stormy night. The family was gathered around the fireplace. "Tell us a story, Grandfather," the children said, and the old man thus began: 'Twas a dark and stormy night. The family was gathered around the fireplace. 'Tell us a story, Grandfather,' the children said . . ."

Smiling, but almost crying, Sarah went into her own bedroom to undress for her last night with her husband.

32

Camp Merritt, New Jersey
July 10, 1918

My very dear wife:

I was right to discourage you from coming to Camp Lewis to see us off. Breaking up housekeeping caused a special kind of havoc only twenty-seven thousand men could create and when our train began to roll, it would have been difficult to pick your beautiful face out of the throng that waved good-bye. Of course I would have known you because you would have been smiling and crying at the same time. Most women aren't that versatile.

There were eight trains in all, taking three different routes. The train is first-class, with sleeping cars for everyone and a baggage car refitted as a kitchen.

We were cheered all along the way. As we crossed a Montana prairie, a little old woman was standing near the tracks waving a flag and calling, "Go get 'im, Wild West!"

Five days after we left Camp Lewis, we came to the end of the line—the banks of the Hudson, where we left the train and hiked to this embarkation camp. Uppermost in the minds of most soldiers is that great big exciting city on the east side of the river, and how to get there (and what they'll do when they get there, provided they have any money!), but the order is that no one gets permission to go to New York until he's been completely outfitted. Even those who have been issued uniforms, steel helmets, spiraled puttees, and two pairs of hobnailed trench shoes have no guarantee that they'll be in that small percentage of the company to be granted a pass.

Those puttees, by the way, are the valiant 364th Infantry's first battle against superior forces. The canvas leggings we wore at Camp Lewis could be put on so quickly we could snatch a few extra minutes in the bunk between first call and breakfast and still get to the mess hall in fairly presentable condition. But spiral puttees refuse to spiral, and those who give up the unequal fight have to stand reveille in the rear rank (provided they can find a space in the line of the un-putteed) or explain to some heartless officer like myself why they were missing at morning formation.

This is the last letter I will be able to send you for some time. The ship that will transport us to Southampton is waiting in New York harbor. The little I know for a fact is that she's a camouflaged White Star liner fitted with enough hammocks for the whole regiment of thirty-six hundred men. Here in camp rumor is more popular than known fact. Someone heard that someone who heard from someone else that a whole convoy of nurses will be on board—*female* nurses, if you please, and there's a corporal in my platoon who swears there will be two hundred of them. However I don't know whether to believe a man who still hasn't learned to wrap a neat spiral puttee.

Hug Mandy for me.

I love you, Sari.

T.

On the first day of the Meuse-Argonne offensive, American artillery opened up full force at half-past two in the morning. Three hours later, under protection of a rolling barrage, the Wild West Division charged toward the Germans entrenched about a mile ahead.

Cheppy Woods bristled with machine guns. Land mines buried along the trails could be exploded by a soldier's boot. But the Germans had, indeed, been caught by surprise. All morning, long lines of prisoners, in some cases guarded by only one American soldier, slogged back, across no-man's-land to be locked up in the prisoners' cage.

Trygve's men advanced steadily but cautiously, on the watch for land mines, and when they reached buildings from which the Germans had fled, for hidden grenades that could be detonated by the opening of a door. In a main trench near the town of Cheppy, Trygve called a halt.

Their tanks had cleared out machine guns and snipers. Germans attempting to hide in dugouts had been discovered and rounded up. But his company was abreast of the tanks and in the forefront of the attack. Could this whole area, so recently occupied by a German garrison, be as deserted as it looked? The silence was as thick as mist. It wasn't natural.

"Sergeant," Trygve called to the man at his side, "take Corporals Stewart and Dodge, Privates Smith, Caprini, Patricelli, Colello, Sturno, and Marino. Go back the way we've come, then go above ground and crawl forward to the first intersection you see. Drop down into the trench and station yourselves there. Maybe we can bag a few prisoners."

Trygve's instinct was proved right. When he led one section of the platoon along the trench, German officers and soldiers poured out of their hiding places, racing away from him and straight into the sergeant's barricade of men and rifles.

As Trygve approached the captives, a German lieutenant stepped forward. He saluted briskly and stood at attention while his American counterpart gave orders to the second lieutenant to escort the prisoners back to American lines. He made his departure in style. As he was leaving, he turned back, removed the field glasses hanging on a leather strap around his neck, and with great dignity handed them to Trygve.

"I see that you Americans do not have such a thing as these," the *Leutnant* said, his English clumsy and mispronounced but perfectly understandable. "They will be taken from me later in any case. I prefer to give them as a gift. It is a Zeiss lens, the finest in the world."

"I have been looking at them enviously," Trygve replied with equal ceremony. "Thank you, Lieutenant. I will take them home with me and when my daughter is old enough to understand, I will tell her the story about the German officer who gave them to me."

On the third day of the offensive they attacked in a dense fog. Trygve and his men groped their way uncertainly across a pitted field and into a wood where visibility was so poor he could not be sure how near he was to the next man. Now the figures to his right and left were gray shadows. In spite of the fog, they were advancing. They must be getting close to the German line.

Trygve increased his pace; working his way doggedly through a blinding mist and stumbling through underbrush. Gradually the sound of artillery faded. As they had done the first day of the drive, he and his men had outrun the protection of their own big guns. He plunged on, puzzled because he couldn't hear German artillery up ahead.

The fog was lifting. To his left was a field, still misty but clear enough to reveal that soldiers were there. That's where his men were, he had become separated from them in the woods. He moved toward them quickly. He was out of the woods and in plain sight of the German soldiers in the clearing before the truth hit him. These troops were facing in the wrong direction. In the fog and darkness of the forest, he had passed right through the German lines.

He turned and ran for the woods, but it was too late. Something thudded on the ground beside him. Everything around and under him exploded. He yelled, "Run back!" and fell forward on his face.

In October, news from the front where the Wild West Division was fighting told of fierce American assaults and strong German counterattacks. Sarah had received a few letters from Trygve, but so much time passed before they reached her that she could never be certain that he was not hurt. She knew it was a desperate battle on which the final outcome of the war depended. That was plain, despite the general and suspiciously optimistic language of the communiqués. The German Third and Fifth armies had been driven back by the three-day offensive in September, but their trenches, barbed wire, and other field fortifications extended for ten miles behind the front. The Argonne Forest and the Heights of the Meuse had not been taken, nor had the enemy's crucial railway supply line been severed. That much was known. But exact numbers of men killed and wounded, tanks destroyed, and Allied planes downed were still not known.

Meanwhile, another sort of enemy had infiltrated Seattle. It was a silent and indiscriminate killer called "Spanish" influenza because in May an outbreak had taken place in Madrid. The first cases were not properly diagnosed, for symptoms were like those of common respiratory ailments, and the disease traveled with such speed that it had already gained a foothold before doctors began to isolate its victims. Gradually reports from health authorities all over the country revealed the true nature of the plague that had been masquerading as "the grippe." The number of deaths confirmed that the city was host to a murderous epidemic.

In October, newspapers began to carry the warning: "Influenza cannot travel more than people can travel," and the Seattle police department was ordered to enforce stringent public-health restrictions. All places of public assembly were closed, including schools, churches, theaters, and dance halls. Business establishments were put on shorter hours, from ten in the morning until three in the afternoon. No one was allowed to board a streetcar without wearing a face mask made of at least six layers of gauze.

The daily newspapers became a morbid scoreboard on which death vied for space with evidence of life-as-usual. Cartoons such as *Polly and Her Pals, Bringing Up Father,* and *Hawkshaw the Detective* were as cheery as ever. But when a department store advertised bargain-basement winter coats for $6.95 and fur-trimmed coats for $35, the wording implied that keeping warm could be a matter of life and death. "Old Egypt" cork-tipped cigarettes were sold with the suggestion that filling one's respiratory system with tobacco smoke was an important preventive measure.

Funeral directors were more candid. One ran a half-page advertisement in every issue of the Tribune: "Cremation, complete with casket, services, and urn—only $47.50. Earth burial (caskets, hearse, embalming, two cars, and perpetual care in a cemetery lot) $85.00."

By November the public concept of good news was so warped that when the emergency hospital in the old country courthouse reported that no deaths had occurred between midnight Saturday and seven A.M. Sunday, the news was welcomed as a good omen. The day before, six persons had died of the flu in that same hospital, but no one wanted to dwell on that.

The effect on Emma Peersen's commercial enterprises would have been drastic had her business not been so well established. Though regulations didn't require it, Emma closed her restaurant and catering service. The bakeries continued as usual, but under Emma's strict rule that every worker wear a thick gauze mask.

Sarah Peersen's fear of the flu was intensified by the ever-present danger of Amanda's exposure to it. Sarah saw herself and Christy Johnson as the potential carriers, and not only closed her dance school but insisted that Christy and her little boy not leave the house or allow friends to visit. She imposed the same rule on herself, with the exception of necessary trips to the grocery store.

She did make regular visits to her father's house, more for Angela Whiting's sake than the professor's. Kurt Bauermeister's arrest and conviction had been a heartbreak nothing could heal. Only George Tweedy's handling of the case had saved him from hanging. Through years of disappointment in Kurt and their gradual estrangement, Angela had remained a warmly social person, serene as a Madonna but full of delight and laughter. But the day a police officer came to the house to tell her that her son had destroyed ammunition stored on a barge in Elliott Bay, she began to change. She neither gave parties nor accepted invitations. She was as loving as ever toward Sarah, but only Amanda could make her smile. She seldom left the house; now the epidemic gave her reason not to leave at all.

Occasionally, at Professor Whiting's urging, Angela would allow Sarah to take her out for a drive. Sarah always brought Amanda along, because the little girl insisted on sitting in her grandmother's lap. With that self-confident little presence against her breast, some light and color returned to Angela's pale face. Her son was a prisoner in a federal penitentiary. Sarah's husband was somewhere in France—perhaps wounded, or a prisoner, or even dead. For both of them, Amanda was more than a comfort. Her bright blue eyes, her endless repertoire of questions, and her innocence of sorrow represented life itself.

On November 11, a red banner headline dominated the *Tribune*'s front page: "HUNS GIVE UP FIGHT—WORLD WAR ENDED" Below were the details. The State Department announced that at three A.M. Seattle time, Germany had signed the terms of an armistice. Practically all of Germany had fallen into the hands of revolutionists. The King of Prussia had abdicated, a republic had been proclaimed in Bavaria, and the kings of Saxony and Württemberg were in hiding. Schleswig and Silesia had proclaimed their independence from Prussia, and the Kaiser and his eldest son had fled to Holland. With no central authority, no cohesion between parts of the empire, the Huns were in chaos.

The news was spread by newsboys running along Seattle streets shouting the headlines and by the siren atop the *Tribune*'s buildings. Telephones circulated the message to the far corners. As had happened when the steamship *Portland* came into port with news that launched the Klondike gold rush, people from all over the city and adjoining communities began to converge on the downtown area.

In a city flooded by a seething mass of humanity, the lights in hotel rooms flashed on as their occupants dressed hastily and poured into the streets. When a soldier in khaki uniform appeared, he was picked up bodily and carried through the streets. By noon the widest avenues were jammed with automobiles, each car loaded with as many as a dozen cheering riders. Streetcars rolled sluggishly through the mob, losing most of their passengers at any street corner where a newsboy was shouting "Extra!" Newspapers were shredded to make confetti. Strangers hugged each other. To cheers from the spectators, the Kaiser was burned in effigy. At one intersection an enterprising young man set up a stand where he offered paper streamers inscribed "THE YANKS DID IT!" and was quickly sold out. Actors and actresses on vaudeville tour for the Pantages circuit formed a parade and danced along the business streets doing a comic imitation of the goose step. In fifteen minutes, four thousand Seattleites had joined the march.

Those who couldn't dance the goose step or play in the band expressed themselves by making noise. Tin cans tied to automobiles clanked and rattled as they bounced off the concrete. Cars with horns honking drove out through the residential districts; church bells pealed incessantly, and every whistle valve in the city was tied open. It was Saturday night gone crazy with joy.

Seattle health-department restrictions were lifted except for the wearing of masks, so theater managers prepared for audiences thirsty for entertainment after a drought of almost six weeks. Annette Kellerman in *Queen of the Sea* was at the Clemmer: "See her 85-foot dive from a cable into the sea." There were two shows at the Rex, Douglas Fairbanks in *The Half Breed* and Fatty Arbuckle in *Bright Lights*. Admission: twenty-five cents for adults and a dime for children.

Sarah's first thought when news of the armistice reached her was that the celebration and the parades would be a healthy distraction for Angela. Though reluctant at first, Angela agreed to an hour or two downtown.

They were jostled by people who didn't say "Excuse me" and deafened by a medley of discordant sounds, but as Sarah had hoped, Angela was caught up in the excitement. "All hostilities ceased at eleven A.M., Paris time," they read on the bulletin board outside the *Tribune*. Trygve would be coming home, and neither of them said out loud, ". . . if he is still alive." Where was Company L, 364th Infantry, Ninety-first Division, today at eleven A.M., Paris time? How many had been killed thirty minutes earlier? Sarah tried valiantly to put such questions out of her mind; Angela was actually laughing at the clowns that were dancing down the street in the wake of the Pantages parade.

Not until she was home telling Christy Johnson about the antics of the crowds did Sarah realize that in the mob of delirious human beings who had pushed and shoved and embraced them, she and Angela hadn't seen anyone wearing a mask.

"And neither did we!" Sarah exclaimed. "We took them. They were between us on the front seat of the car. But by the time I found a place to park, we'd seen so much excitement that we just got out and began to move with the crowd. If I'd seen anyone wearing a mask, I would have remembered and would have gone back to get them, but I didn't."

"Weren't any policemen on duty?" Christy asked.

"Oh, yes. I saw a lot of them. They were celebrating, like the rest of us. They certainly weren't enforcing the rule."

"Don't worry, Mrs. Peersen. All the other restrictions were lifted. That must mean the epidemic is over."

"Not so suddenly," Sarah said, fear sweeping through her. "Not overnight. And I've been holding Mandy, and kissing her."

"You'll be all right," Christy said bravely. "I know you will. A lot of people are immune to the flu, and you weren't downtown for very long."

"I'm going to stay away from Mandy." Sarah's voice trembled. "Explain it to her, will you, Christy, but try not to frighten her." Suddenly the full extent of the terror struck her. "Angela! She's been exposed."

Sarah rushed to the telephone. "We weren't wearing masks, Father," she said thickly. "No one was."

"So I just learned." Professor Whiting's voice was hardly recognizable. "In the evening papers, I read that the police had been criticized for failing to enforce the rule."

"What can we do?"

"Pray to God," Professor Whiting replied. "And be grateful that the disease strikes quickly. The incubation period is from one to four days. We won't have to wait long to know."

Recognition of early influenza symptoms had become widespread as the epidemic soared. For three days after the armistice celebration, Professor Whiting watched Angela as closely as he could without frightening her, stoically keeping his fears to himself. Then the disease struck. He went directly to the telephone and called his doctor.

"Mrs. Whiting is ill, Dr. Talbot," he said crisply. "A sudden fever, muscular aches and pains, inflammation of the respiratory mucous membrances. But I will not have her taken to the hospital. I can give her better care at home and can promise she will be completely isolated. No one will be allowed to enter the house and our maid will not go into the bedroom. I will expect you to come as quickly as you can."

His next call was to Sarah, and began with the same disciplined tone of voice. But when she broke down, he softened. "Don't cry, Sarah. I will see to it that everything possible is done for her."

"It's my fault!" Sarah wept. "If I hadn't forgotten about our masks . . ."

"She forgot too. Everyone forgot," her father replied sternly. "But you're not to blame. I will not have you torturing yourself with that thought. *I* do not blame you, and I am not angry because you took her downtown. I urged you to take her into the city. We must put our trust in a merciful God."

"Angela is older than I am, and not nearly as strong," Sarah said bitterly. "Why did God let the flu strike her instead of me? Is that what you call merciful?"

"My dear Sarah," Professor Whiting said with a gentleness so unlike him that Sarah began to cry again, "now you sound more like the rebellious little girl you used to be than the mature woman you are now. You have been spared. Is it wrong to thank God for that? Angela may recover. Isn't it better to be hopeful that she will, rather than angry because she is ill?"

"I'm angry because I'm scared," Sarah sobbed.

"So am I," Professor Whiting said quietly. "Through and through."

* * *

Several days had passed, with Angela Whiting losing her battle a little more every day. At the end of the week pneumonia, the dreaded complication, took hold of a body already weakened by fever and infection.

The doctor visited her both in early morning and in midafternoon. On the tenth day, he said, "Professor Whiting, we've done all we can, and it isn't enough. I'm amazed that she's survived as long as she has. She's put up a valiant fight."

"I understand, Dr. Talbot." Professor Whiting spoke calmly, though his hands were trembling. "Will you come back later today?"

"I'll come whenever you call me," the doctor replied, and both men understood.

Professor Whiting was sitting at his desk in the library when the telephone rang and a male voice he didn't recognize asked to speak to Mrs. Whiting.

"Mrs. Whiting is too ill to come to the telephone," he replied.

"Am I speaking to her husband?"

"You are. Your name, sir?"

"This is Warden Thompson at NcNeil. The penitentiary. I'm calling in regard to her son, Kurt Bauermeister."

"If you have news of Kurt, please give it to me, Mr. Thompson. I will convey the message."

"To be honest, I'd rather tell you than his mother. Kurt died this morning in the prison infirmary."

"Of influenza?" Professor Whiting asked. Now that the epidemic was killing thousands of people every day, any other cause of death seemed remote.

"No. Let me explain something, Professor Whiting. Prisoners have a pretty stiff code of their own. They admire inmates who have committed certain crimes—bank robbery, for instance—but they can be hard on men who commit crimes they don't approve of. Kurt Bauermeister would have been in danger from the minute he stepped off the launch and walked through the gates. We knew that, so I saw to it that no one except myself and my assistant warden knew what he had done, and that included the guards. But we couldn't keep

Kurt from bragging. In the tool shop where he worked, there must have been a dozen prisoners who heard from Kurt himself that he blew up ammunition so it wouldn't be used against the Germans. Inside the walls, that kind of information gets around fast. This morning one of the men stabbed him to death."

"I appreciate your explaining this," Professor Whiting said, "but how could you allow the men in your charge to have access to tools that could be used as deadly weapons?"

Rather than resenting the professor's criticism, the warden was amused and didn't bother to conceal it. "Bauermeister wasn't stabbed with a screwdriver or any other tool. And it didn't happen in the tool room, because the men are too wise to pull something like that in a situation where we'd know it had to be one of only a dozen or so who did it. What killed Kurt was a pork-chop bone. Someone sharpened the end of the long thin bone and rammed it through Kurt's jugular when they were out in the prison yard during exercise period. There were two hundred inmates in the yard at the time. Any one of them could have done it."

"Didn't anyone see it?" Professor Whiting asked indignantly. "Surely, in the presence of two hundred men . . . ?"

"Plus prison guards. Oh, there had to be plenty of witnesses, no question about that, probably at least one prison guard among them. If one of them had signaled the tower or yelled for help, our doctor could have patched Kurt up before he bled to death. But no one did. They just kept on doing whatever they'd been doing. Some walking, some throwing baseballs, some just standing around talking, until they were sure it was too late to save him."

"Not one prisoner or one guard with the decency to try to save a man's life?"

"I've tried to explain, sir," the warden said patiently. "This is not polite society. Any prisoner who tried to save Kurt Bauermeister's life would have had to be locked up in solitary for the protection of his own life. Even in the hole, someone could have gotten to him."

The conversation ended after Professor Whiting answered the warden's questions about funeral arrangements. Wearily the professor mounted the stairs to continue his vigil in the chair beside Angela's bed. Though he was shocked by the brutality of it, the killing of his stepson did not move him deeply. He had already recognized what Angela could not see—that Kurt was a dislocated, deeply unhappy, vindictive person. Beside Angela's unconscious form, he bowed his head and murmured thanks for this one small blessing he could attach to her death. She would never have to know what had happened to her son.

33

Shortly after the armistice, Sarah received notice that Trygve had been wounded in combat. A letter from one of Trygve's men, mailed in October from a hospital in the Bordeaux area, gave a complete story of the last battle Trygve had fought and explained that due to the seriousness of his wounds, Trygve would not be sent home until January.

When Trygve returned from France, he had not fully recovered from his wounds, but he was alive, and he was home. Emma Peerson felt his returned demanded a traditional Thursday-night family dinner. Eleven adults and nine children would make her house in Ballard seem even smaller than it was; since the state department of health had ordered an end to Seattle's flu-epidemic restrictions, Emma could have held the party in Mother Peersen's. But to her, using a commercial location would be just short of blasphemy.

This time Professor Whiting was invited to dinner, along with his sister Prudence from Boston, his companion and housekeeper since Angela's death. Anna and Ezio and their children came from their farm in the Rainier Valley, bringing with them Kibun Sakai and his partner, Henrik. Katamari Tamesa and his wife were there with their son and two daughters.

The complexion of the family had changed as well as the size, but some Peersen traditions prevailed. On Trygve's arm, Emma was escorted ceremoniously to her chair at the head of the table. The children were lined up against the wall, where with bowed heads they listened to Trygve recite the Lord's

Prayer in Norwegian before they were allowed to take their places at the table set up for them in the parlor.

After the special grace, Emma asked that the decanter of plum wine be passed around the table, for they would toast to the safe return of their soldiers. Knowing Professor Whiting's abhorrence of all alcoholic beverages, she had set a pitcher of apple cider in front of him and his sister.

The decanter came to "Auntie Prue" first. The small gray-haired woman in somber navy blue glanced at her brother with a mischievous smile and poured her wineglass almost to the brim. As he accepted the bottle, Professor Whiting hesitated, his eyes darting from the decanter to the cider pitcher and back again. Finally, with great dignity, he filled his own glass with wine.

Like the family itself, the ethnic purity of Emma's meal was now graced with exotic infusions foreign to the rugged coast of Norway. To the main course of roast venison with goat-cheese sauce, Katamari's wife, Tomoko, added *sumashi wan*, a clear soup with soybean curd, dried kelp, and shrimp, and Anna brought Ezio's favorite pasta. Aunt Prue's contribution was a thoroughly blueblood crock of baked beans. Sarah, whose cooking could only be called imaginative, brought a large fruit salad.

For the most part, the dinner conversation was cheerful. The war was over. The influenza epidemic was finally on the wane. Thanks to Aunt Prue, Sarah's father was beginning to cast off the despair that had so numbed him when Angela died.

Trygve looked around the table. He said a silent prayer of his own in thanks for being returned to these people he loved. He caught Sarah's eye and they smiled across the table, a private smile filled with trust in their future together.

Anna was in the farmhouse kitchen several days later when she saw smoke. Through the window above the sink she had a clear view of Kibun Sakai's house and barn, built on property that had originally been part of Ezio's acreage. A thick column of smoke was swirling upward, creamy-white against the slate-colored winter sky. She knew instantly that it was the barn, and that the fire had been set deliberately.

Several barns in the area had burned to the ground, all of them leased and operated by Japanese. Kibun's draft horses, his winter supply of hay and oats, his tools, and Henrik's beloved milk cow—they would all be lost, along with the building Kibun and Henrik had labored so hard to erect.

Who could save them? Ezio had left early in the morning for the Pike Place market, taking Kibun with him. Slow-witted Henrik was at home, and brave and strong as he was, he was easily confused by anything outside the familiar routine of the day-to-day existence. He would be helpless in the face of this disaster.

The old sweater Anna wore when she went to the henhouse to collect eggs was hanging on a wooden peg beside the kitchen door. She pulled it on, picked up two buckets as she crossed the barnyard, and raced across the strawberry fields that stretched for ten acres to the boundary of Kibun's farm.

She ran with the memory of the fire at her sister Mina's as vivid as the flames she could see at the far side of the field. She had never recovered from the terror of the day, when Mina had appeared at an upstairs window already framed by spitting tongues of fire, smiling triumphantly because she had "saved" the china baby doll she was holding in her arms.

In her panic, Anna forgot the drainage ditch that dissected the strawberry field. She stumbled on the edge of it and fell forward into two feet of muddy rainwater. The buckets flew out of her hands, hit the side of the ditch, and rolled back on top of her. She pulled herself up, grasped the bails and slung the buckets to dry ground. Digging the toes of her shoes into the dirt, she climbed out of the ditch, recovered the buckets, and ran on, scarcely aware that her wet housedress and sweater were clinging to her body and that with every running step, tiny jets of muddy water were squirting over the toes of her shoes.

The barnyard was deserted. Flames encircled the barn like the petals of an evil flower that had trapped and was now devouring its victim. Screaming "Henrik!" Anna ran around to the side where wide doors opened onto the pasture.

Kibun's massive workhorses were in that pasture and seemed bewildered by the roaring heat. Both were wearing halters. True to their training, they stood still, having been taught not to move when their halter ropes dropped along the ground. Evidently they had been in their stalls, and someone had rescued them. "Henrik!" Anna shouted again, for suddenly she understood. Having saved the horses, Henrik had gone back for his cow.

Through the angry cackle of the fire Anna heard something that confirmed her thought—the bawling of a panic-stricken animal. With that sound she lost the fear that had always sickened her at the sight of a burning building. Henrik's cow, Henrik's own life, depended on her. With fervent thanks to God for the drainage ditch she had fallen into, she took off her dripping sweater and wrapped it around her head, leaving the smallest possible opening through which to see. Smoke was billowing out through the open doors, and the walls on all sides were on fire, but as far as she could see through the pall of smoke, the interior of the barn was not.

Taking a deep breath, Anna advanced, guided by the cow's terrified cries. She didn't call again. Whevever he was, Henrik could not answer and her own breath was precious to them both.

Just beyond the horse stalls she saw him, facedown on the barn's dirt floor. He had managed to untie the cow, for the end of the rope was clutched in his hand. She was within a few feet of him when a flaming roof timber collapsed and fell across his body.

Frantically Anna gathered her dripping skirt and whipped it against the wood. The flames died down somewhat, and she grasped the charred timber in both hands and with strength born of desperation rolled it off Henrik's unconscious form. Her eyes were burning and her lungs were bursting with acrid heat. She groped blindly for Henrik, finally lifting him high enough to hold him firmly under one arm. She used her free hand to pick up the end of the cow's tether. With the helpless man dragging along the ground and the bawling cow following at her heel, Anna stumbled out of the barn and into the open air.

Only after she was sure that Henrik was still alive, that he and the animals were at a safe distance from the burning building, did she begin to face what must be done next. The barn was gone, but the house could still be saved. It was separated from the barn by a wide expanse of bare ground now providentially soaked to a depth of several inches by recent rain. With her buckets and water from the horse trough, Anna might be able to keep the fire from spreading even after the walls of the barn collapsed, as they were sure to do within minutes.

An hour later, a farmer and his wife were driving along the isolated country road. Seeing the smoke rubble of the barn, they climbed down from their wagon and hurried around to the back of the house, where they found Anna sitting on the steps with the buckets beside her. Under sooty smudges, her face was pale and her eyes were glazed, but she was alert and spoke sensibly. "Henrik is all right," she told them. "When he woke up he was sick for a while, and I put him to bed. There's no danger now that the house will catch fire, so I'll go home."

She would have walked back across the strawberry fields if the farmer and his wife had not insisted on taking her there in the wagon. When the woman exclaimed, "Mrs. Rinaldi! Look at your poor hands!" Anna lifted her hands and noticed for the first time that big water blisters had formed on the backs of them and that her palms were so badly scorched the skin had split, the raw flesh showing through the cracks. She knew it would take days for them to heal, but that was a small price to pay for saving Henrik's life and her friend's home.

34

When Sarah and Trygve had brought Christy Johnson into their home, it was to provide refuge for a terrified girl of seventeen. Living with the Peersens, the injured adolescent healed gradually and dared to believe in a happy future. Sarah and Trygve had restored her faith in herself, but both conceded that the real miracle worker was a logger by the name of Joe Turner.

Turner had been a victim of the same attack that had caused the death of Peter Scott and Sarah's brother, Ben. Beaten raw, his clothes sicky with blood, he had found his way to the house in Laurelhurst and, at Sarah's insistence, had stayed until his wounds were healed.

During that time, Christy Johnson nursed him. After he went back to his logging camp in the foothills of the Cascades, he wrote to her. She replied, and a long courtship-by-letter began, quickened by Turner's occasional trips to the city. Now they were to be married. Christy and her three-year-old son would leave right after the wedding.

As her dance school grew, Sarah had become more and more dependent on Christy. "What will I do without her?" she asked Trygve. "I really can't get along without help."

For several weeks after Christy's departure, Sarah's half-hearted attempts to find a housemaid produced nothing but descriptions of the applicants she had turned down. "I'd rather do the work myself than bring in the wrong person," she explained so cheerfully that Trygve suspected she was actually relieved every time someone didn't suit her.

Aiding and abetting Sarah's dilatory tactics, Amanda was

delighted by the unique experience of seeing her mother in the kitchen. Like a joyful fairy godmother who dropped in for the fun of it, Sarah concocted things to eat that Amanda had never tasted before. The big mahogany Victrola, wheeled to a new position right outside the kitchen door, issued bursts of classical music punctuated by the hiss and burble of pots boiling over and the tapping of Sarah's toe while she washed vegetables at the sink.

With no one in the house to care for Amanda, Sarah had to take her to dance school. But spending four or five hours a day in dance classes was perfectly agreeable to Amanda. She explained solemnly when Trygve asked about it, "It's fine, Daddy, because that's what I did when I was little."

But it was apparent to Trygve that the house suffered from the lack of a dedicated housekeeper. While he accepted the situation philosophically, Amanda's reaction to the untidiness was a relevation. She swept, dusted, and arranged everything she could reach into neat piles, doing it all with such single-minded purpose that when Trygve came home in the evening, he got a hasty hug and kiss from her and then she returned to work.

"Did you tell her to do that?" he asked Sarah the first time he saw Amanda pushing the carpet sweeper. "She's so small she has to grab the handle in the middle."

"It's entirely her own idea," Sarah replied. "You can tell her she doesn't have to, but it won't stop her. I did, and she ignored me."

It had been a particularly difficult day. By the time Trygve drove home, he was yearning for his big leather armchair, a glass of his mother's homemade plum wine, and his daughter sitting in his lap.

The thunder of an exultant male voice greeted him before he opened the front door. Inside, he dropped his briefcase, leaned against the wall, and stared.

There were two persons in the living room, Amanda and a barrel-chested, heavily bearded man wearing a visored leather cap, high cavalry boots, and worn workclothes with the trousers tucked inside the boots. Chaliapin's booming rendition of "The Song of the Volga Boatmen" was pouring out of the hand-cranked Victrola. The stranger was competing in the great basso's native tongue, with Chaliapin the obvious loser, while Amanda, an enthralled audience of one, listened from the depths of Trygve's armchair.

The little girl waved gaily. Seeing Trygve in the doorway, the singer lifted the playing arm off the record, set it down tenderly, and removing his leather cap, said something Trygve assumed to be a greeting. He had a wide, ebulliently friendly smile. When Trygve extended his hand, it was taken by a massive grip and shaken vigorously, not once but five times.

Amanda ran to her father to be picked up and hugged. "This is Dedushka. Babushka is in the kitchen with Mama."

Trygve recognized "Babushka" as the Russian word for grandmother. "Dedushka," then, must mean grandfather. "I see." Meeting the older man's lively dark eyes, he said, "How do you do?"

Dedushka nodded ecstatically and replied with a stream of words unintelligible to Trygve but, on some mystical level, apparently clear to Amanda. "He means he's glad to meet you too. He talks Russian."

Trygve put Amanda down and advanced to the kitchen. There Sarah and a short plump woman in a black cotton skirt and blue shirtwaist were standing in front of the electric stove.

"Oh, Trygve!" Sarah exclaimed. "Wonderful news! At last I've found someone. This is Babushka. I'm trying to teach her how to use an electric stove. She doesn't seem to have seen one before and she doesn't speak English. But she's so friendly and cheerful!"

As if to confirm this statement, Babushka bathed Trygve in a friendly and cheerful smile. Small, slightly slanted eyes twinkled at him from a face as round as a full moon. Her thin straight hair was pulled back tightly and coiled into a little knot pinned to the top of her head. From the tips of boots that peeked out under the hem of her full skirt to the little round bun of hair, she reminded Trygve of a tea cozy.

So this was to be their live-in housemaid! "Sari, what about the booted and bearded gentleman in the next room?"

"That's *Mr*. Agafadaroff. Doesn't he have a marvelous voice!"

"Yes, but what does he do? Where does he work?"

"That's just it, Tryg. He can't find a job. The language barrier, mostly, but on top of that, he's not familiar with American equipment."

"What kind of equipment? What's his trade?"

"He's an auto mechanic. He used to own a garage and he had three men working for him. That's why he had to leave Russia. That little business made him a capitalist. He and Babushka escaped by hiding in a freight car all the way across Siberia to Vladivostok, but they had to leave their six children, and they don't dare write to the friends who are taking care of them because they would put them in danger, and the children as well. Babushka and Dedushka were destitute by the time the White Russian Relief Group heard about them. They were living on a miserable little houseboat on Lake Union, eating carp they caught through a hole in the floor, and not much else." She paused and looked at Trygve with a rueful smile. "You understand why I couldn't say no when the agency called me. Frankly, I didn't realize Dedushka would be part of the bargain. But he'll find a job eventually. Meanwhile, he can fix things around the house."

Scouring his imagination for something around the house that an auto mechanic might repair, Trygve asked uneasily, "Things?"

For a moment Sarah seemed to be at a loss, but she recovered and answered brightly, "The washing machine."

"Is it broken?"

"Well, no. But you know how machines are."

Within a few days, Babushka had proved her worth. She cleaned with the relentless thoroughness Trygve associated with his mother's housekeeping. She washed, ironed, and mended clothes. This done, she rescued and darned socks Sarah had put into the rag bag, having considered them beyond redemption. Cabbage soup began to appear on the dinner table with more frequency than Trygve would have liked, and some familiar food substances took on unfamiliar flavors, but Sarah could once again devote herself to her dance school. Most important, Amanda was in the care of a loving grandma. That the rotund little Russian woman couldn't speak English was a barrier Amanda didn't recognize. Babushka spoke Russian, Amanda responded in English, and if Trygve and Sarah didn't know what they were talking about, Amanda explained it.

"It's as if they had some secret language," Sarah confided to Trygve. "Not Russian, not English."

"The things they have to communicate about are simple, Sari. Besides, Babushka is fairly childlike, and Mandy has a broad streak of adult intuition. They don't need a lot of words."

Sarah laughed. "Mandy is going to change that. When I came home this afternoon, she had Babushka firmly by the hand and was tugging her along from one piece of furniture to the next, teaching her the English terms. 'Chair,' she'd say. 'Chair, chair, *chair*.' Then 'Table, Babushka. Table, table . . .' She made that poor soul repeat every word several times before she relented and went on to something else. You never saw such a solemn schoolmarm."

"What was Babushka's reaction?"

"She giggled, and did as she was told."

Even with Christy Johnson in charge of the house, Sarah had never enjoyed such freedom. Babushska did everything, and though she continued to rely on gestures rather than speech, she seldom needed instruction. Sarah could leave for her studio as early as she liked, and come home late, knowing that if Trygve arrived before she did, the evening newspaper would be there beside his armchair, Dedushka would be confined to the kitchen at a safe distance from the Victrola and Chaliapin, and a hearty meal would be ready whenever Trygve wanted it.

The Russian couple, having been forced to abandon their own children, now had an alert and inquisitive little girl who gave hug for hug. They loved and protected Amanda, neither expecting nor trying to enter the sanctum of her own family. But they supplied a kind of security for all three Peersens, especially for Amanda, whose need for continuous activity was finally being met. Between projects like helping Dedushka take the washing machine apart ("He had to," she explained to Trygve, "so that he could find out how to fix it if it ever gets broken.") and her responsibility as Babushka's English teacher, the child was learning more than she would when she was old enough to attend kindergarten. For Trygve, the Agafadaroffs provided assurance that his daughter was not suffering from her mother's frequent absences. During the coming year, when he would be rebuilding his law practice, such peace of mind would be all-important.

Like Trygve, Sarah felt freer than ever to pursue her career. While Trygve was contemplating redirecting his professional life into a new channel—politics—she too was beginning to feel that her future in dance need not, *should* not, be limited to teaching.

She had opened the Sarah Peersen School of Dance five years before. Its growth had satisfied her until recently, when one of her pupils joined a professional dance troupe that toured the country on a vaudeville circuit. For the first time Sarah saw her school as a dead end. True, more and more students were being enrolled, but she was teaching them the same techniques. Even composing new dances for a concert, the only creative aspect of her work, was so limited by the age and skill of her pupils that it was beginning to pall. The old restlessness was seeping back. If one of her pupils could meet the standards of a professional troupe, why couldn't she?

Such fitful daydreaming continued for weeks, encouraged by daily evidence that if she ever decided to go on tour, Babushka would take care of everything. But she couldn't gather the courage to reveal her thoughts to Trygve. Their marriage had survived after her affair with Peter Scott and had been growing steadily stronger during the three years since his death. Like scar tissue, their bond was tougher than it had been before the wound. They now laughed together, made love with new tenderness, accepted each other as they truly were. What would such a radical proposal as her leaving home do to them?

Sarah had no talent for dissembling, and Trygve, though preoccupied with his separate concerns, was sensitive to signs of her various moods. Their most intimate talks took place when they had just gone to bed, with the lights out and the house quiet. Trygve took such a moment to ask, "What's bothering you, Sari?"

"Nothing, really."

He put an arm around her and drew her closer. "Come on. Let's have it."

There was a long pause. He waited patiently, until at last she said, "Mandy's four now."

"Four going on ten."

"That's about it. She's old for her age. And well adjusted to Babushka."

"She loves Babushka," Trygve agreed. "She's a little worried about Dedushka, though. He isn't learning English as fast as she thinks he should. She wants me to teach her to read so that *she* can teach *him.*"

"Do you have time to do that?"

"I'll find it."

"Mandy will love it. She'll learn faster from you than she would at school."

Trygve let another silence continue for a minute or two and then said, "Try again, Sari."

"Try what?"

"Talking. Telling me why you've been so restless these past few weeks."

He felt her body tense, then suddenly relax. "You remember when Marta Skinner, one of my pupils, left Seattle to go on tour with a professional dance troupe? I love you, I love Mandy, I love my home, and everything is going well with my school, but I can't get it out of my head that I would like to do the same thing."

"Tell me more about it." His tone was deliberately calm.

"I wouldn't consider the idea if we didn't have Babushka. I know she gives Mandy green tea and I don't really approve of that, and she insists on closing Mandy's bedroom windows at night because she believes night air is poisonous, but otherwise she takes wonderful care of her."

"Mandy wouldn't grow pale and wan if you were gone for a while, but I might. How long does a dance company stay on the road? At one stretch, that is."

"I honestly don't know. I haven't talked about this with anyone but you."

"Then you haven't had an offer?"

"Heavens, no!" Sarah exclaimed. "I'm probably foolish to think anyone would hire me."

The ache in the pit of Trygve's stomach began to ease. Taking a deep breath, he said, "In that case, we don't have to settle anything tonight. Think about it carefully, Sari. It would be a big step."

"I realize that. The neighbors would be shocked. My father . . . I don't dare think of what his reaction would be."

"Never make an important decision on the basis of what the neighbors will say. Nor on the basis of whether your father approves or disapproves. We're talking about *your* life. . . . Just remember it's also *my* life, and Mandy's."

President Wilson was on a speaking tour in an effort to gain support for ratification of the League of Nations, and Seattle was to be one of his stops. On arrival, his motorcade would proceed from the railroad station north along Second Avenue.

"Would you like to see the President of the United States?" Trygve asked Amanda.

Amanda had seen and coveted the legendary penny in Grandfather Whiting's desk drawer, the family talisman flattened by the wheels of the hearse that carried Abraham Lincoln's body through the streets of Albany. "Grandpa saw a president when he was a little boy. Can I throw a penny and get it squashed?"

"It wouldn't work, Mandy. This president will be riding in an automobile. Autos have rubber tires. They're too soft to squash a penny."

Crowds began gathering along Second Avenue hours before the President was scheduled to appear. Trygve and Amanda stationed themselves near the intersection with Virginia Street, where Trygve found a gap wide enough to allow them a spot on the curb. There for the first time he discovered how determined his daughter was to create a talisman penny of her own.

"What have you got there?" he asked, pointing to her tightly clenched fist.

"A penny." There was a defiant lift to her chin. "Mama gave it to me."

Trygve smiled. "Well, if the President doesn't squash it, at least he'll run over it. Shall I throw it for you?"

"No, thank you," Amanda said primly. "I'll throw it myself. Otherwise it wouldn't count."

After a few minutes, Trygve noticed that some sort of organized activity was going on to the north of them. Several men were moving through the throng that packed the sidewalks on both sides of the street. They stopped every few feet to talk, apparently giving instructions. Trygve recognized several of the organizers. They were Socialists, Wobblies, and pacifists, all bitterly opposed to Wilson because he had broken his promise to keep the country out of war.

Eventually a murmur rippled through the crowd to Trygve's right. He stepped out into the street. Due to his height, he had a clear view of the motorcade's approach.

In the downtown area below Virginia Street, well-dressed spectators were giving the President a hero's welcome. Cheers, shouts, and wild applause greeted the procession as it moved slowly uptown. The excited mob was pressing so hard against the police cordon that in one place it burst, spilling a dozen of Wilson's admirers into the street. They ran along shouting beside the limousine until officers caught up with and hauled them back. A block away, the President and Mrs. Wilson were clearly visible. Mrs. Wilson was nodding graciously. The President, smiling, was waving his top hat.

The scene changed abruptly when the motorcade crossed Virginia Street. On both sides of Second Avenue men stood shoulder to shoulder, arms folded across their chests, rigid, silent lines several men deep, lining the street along the curb. Not a voice was raised either in derision or in approval. No hurrahs, no hisses, hardly a movement in the solid ranks of the angry.

The President gave a tentative wave, doffed his hat, hesitated with it in midair, and then quickly set it back on his head. Badly shaken, he slumped forward, while Mrs. Wilson's icy stare was directed straight ahead. The procession rolled on through walls of dead silence that extended for several blocks. As soon as it was out of sight, the crowd began to disperse, as silently as fog creeping across the water.

Trygve looked down at Amanda. Her face had been radiant as the presidential procession approached. Now it was solemn, with tears of disappointment threatening to spill over and run down her cheeks. Feeling his gaze, she brushed her coat sleeve across her eyes and looked at the penny, lying so new and shiny in her open palm. "I forgot to throw it," she said in a small voice. "Now there's still only one squashed penny, and it belongs to Grandpa."

It had been several months since Sarah confided that she wanted to travel with a professional dance troupe. Trygve knew her too well to conclude that the issue was closed. If Sarah were unhappy, she might well have thought of going on tour as a temporary escape from the burden of her life with him. But without deceiving himself, he knew their marriage had never been better. Sarah was genuinely happy, though she would probably always be too restless to be completely content. Her desire to be a dancer rather than a dancing teacher was a serious and compelling need and deserved respect. Trygve prepared himself for the inevitable as best he could.

He saw its approach when he learned that the Porter-Manners Dancers were beginning an engagement at the Pantages Theater. That was the troupe Sarah's pupil Marta had joined. Then Marta sent two tickets to Sarah, with a note asking her to come backstage after the performance. A few days later the manager telephoned to offer Sarah a place in the company.

"Mandy isn't the issue," Trygve insisted. "I've asked her how she would feel if you were gone for a while. I didn't say for how long, because in her young mind 'months' is a vague and meaningless term. She thought it was wonderful and exciting. So if you refuse the offer, it will not be because of Mandy, but because of me. And because you think you *ought* to refuse. I don't want that to be the basis of your decision. You would never forget the opportunity you'd forfeited, and I would be uncomfortable knowing that you hadn't forgotten."

"I'm past thirty, Tryg. This is my last chance."

"How old is Pavlova? Or your favorite, Isadora Duncan? How old is she?"

Sarah smiled. "Isadora Duncan must be past forty. Pavlova's a few years younger. I shouldn't have said 'last chance.' Of course I'll keep on dancing. What I meant was that I only want this one chance. I want to do this once, maybe just to do it, later to know that I've *done* it. Just once, and never again.''

''You've got to accept the offer, Sari.'' He almost said ''for my sake,'' but she was in his arms, hugging him fiercely, and that seemed more important.

The next day, Sarah reported to the theater for rehearsal. At the end of the week, she was gone.

35

1920

Though he played the political game of waiting to be asked, there had never been any doubt in Trygve's mind that he would try for a King Country judgeship again. Four months in a hospital in France had given him ample time to reflect on the reasons why he had lost in 1916 and to analyze his prospects for a second campaign. Back in Seattle, he discovered that his law partner had been harboring the same thoughts.

"Your chances have improved," George Tweedy said. "In the first place, you're a little older. Not that thirty-five still isn't young in the minds of a lot of people."

Recalling Lydia Bishop's advice four years earlier, Trygve said, "Why can't we turn a weak point into a strong one? My youth and vigor against men who are growing old on the bench. Too bad our system doesn't have numbered positions so that a new candidate would run against a specific incumbent. I'd file for Dorsett's seat. He's seventy-three years old."

"No, you can't run against Dorsett. It's a wide-open race between nine incumbents and Lord knows how many hopefuls. But there are several judges not much younger than Dorsett. Bronson, for example. He's been on the bench for nineteen years. All right—campaign slogan number one! Let's put new life into our judicial system. Second: your war record. 'Wounded in combat in the battle of Argonne. Captured a whole slew of Germans.' How many was it?"

"Ninety-eight, but stop right there, George. I don't want to capitalize on my army service. There weren't any heroics. It was a miserable dirty business."

"Don't be so damned pure, Tryg. In an election, people out there are trying to get you. If you had been a pacifist, *they'd* capitalize on *that*. We won't brag, but the facts are that you volunteered, that you were shot to pieces in the battle that broke the back of the German army, that you were decorated. We won't put it on your posters, but if I work on your campaign, people are damn well going to hear about it. You'll need every bit of ammunition you have to counteract all the negative factors working against you."

Trygve nodded grimly. "I guess you're probably right."

"One more question," Tweedy, always outspoken, seemed hesitant.

Trygve asked, "What is it, George?"

"It's personal."

"So's everything we've been talking about. Let's have it."

"About women voters. It would be a help if you had the advice and cooperation of a woman. Especially a prominent personality whom women's clubs would invite to speak at their meetings."

Trygve was startled. He hadn't made a secret of his lunches with Lydia Bishop, but Tweedy had never indicated that he knew how far their relationship had gone. "I haven't seen Lydia Bishop for a long time, except to nod and smile when we happened to be in the same place at the same time."

"She's a well-known local writer. Women's groups love to hear about writers. I'm not suggesting out-and-out campaign speeches, of course, but something like a nonpartisan woman's analysis of candidates in the coming election. Would she be willing to make a few speeches of that kind? My wife and I could round up some invitations."

"She probably would, but I wouldn't ask her. That was all over four years ago, and it wasn't an easy break. We'll have to find someone else."

"I'll bet Sarah could make a speech that would keep them on the edge of their seats."

"She could, and I'm sure she would if she were in Seattle. But the tour she signed up for doesn't end until the first of December. She's arranged to leave the troupes for a few days next month to be home for Amanda's fifth birthday, but then she'll be gone again.''

"How's that working out, Tryg?''

Trygve shook his head. "Beautifully, except for me. Sarah's ecstatic about the tour. Mandy's happy with her Russian grandma. I've been teaching Mandy to read, so every evening there's a story hour. That is, Mandy reads stories to Babushka and Dedushka. She's never been better cared for, and hell, neither have I. But Sarah isn't here. Something all-important to me is missing.''

During July and August, Trygve's campaign accelerated so rapidly that it even affected his relationship with his daughter. Despite his late hours at the office and frequent public appearances in the evening, he had tried to preserve at least two hours with her every day, but more and more often some of that time had to be spent rehearsing a speech. To Amanda's delight, Trygve practiced out loud. Whenever she saw him open his briefcase and take out sheets of paper with writing on them, she bounced into his armchair and waited expectantly for him to begin. Trygve had the habit of pacing as he practiced. Like a spectator at a tennis match, Amanda turned her head as her bright eyes followed his progress across the living room, then a pause, a gesture, turn around, and back to the other side.

"I'm sure she doesn't know what I'm talking about any more than she understands Dedushka when he sings 'The Song of the Volga Boatmen,' '' Trygve said when he told George Tweedy about these rehearsals. "But she loves the way I shout and wave my hands.''

Though George Tweedy was allowing himself a degree of optimism, there was one aspect of the election that troubled him. The law permitted "plunking,'' the practice of voting for only one or two candidates rather than nine, the number of seats on the Superior Court. The law also provided that any candidates who received more than one-half of the judicial vote in the September primary would be unopposed in November. Thus a voter who chose to mark his ballot for only two judicial candidates was depriving another seven of his support. This strategy lowered the number of candidates who reached a majority, and if the effort was well-organized, its beneficiaries could eliminate all the opposition in the primary.

"The mathematics are unpredictable," Tweedy said. "All nine incumbents are running again. Ten new candidates have filed. Out of nineteen, only nine can make it to the finals. I'd say plunking is usually organized in behalf of incumbents, so it's likely that only one or two newcomers like yourself will be among the lucky ones who get more than half the vote in the primary."

"With or without plunking," Trygve retorted, "I could get dumped in the primary."

"Hell no, Tryg. You're going to do better than that."

On the morning after the primary election, Trygve was awakened by Amanda's shrill voice calling from downstairs. "Mr. Tweedy wants to talk to you on the telephone! I asked him what happened in the election and he said you won!"

Trygve bounded down the stairs to the landing where the big black telephone box hung in the hall. Pressing the cone of the receiver against his ear, he asked, "What's this? I *won*?"

"Not exactly. Or maybe I should say 'Yes and no.' " For all the negativism that garbled answer expressed, Tweedy's voice was distinctly excited. "In this election, plunking had a funny twist to it. You weren't eliminated. Eight candidates did receive majorities, but you weren't one of them. You're one of the top two candidates for the ninth spot who will run against each other in the finals."

"What's wrong with that?"

"Not wrong, Tryg, just damned ironic. Your opponent in November is going to be the Honorable Judge Timothy Dorsett. One against one. Man to man. I think you've been waiting for this one for a long, long time."

With only two weeks remaining before the election, Trygve's evenings at home were now almost completely devoted to rehearsing campaign speeches. Tonight it was a talk for a service-club luncheon, and Amanda, his loyal audience, wasn't reacting with her usual spirit. His habit of pacing as he talked always delighted her. If he added a few melodramatic gestures, she would laugh and clap. Now she was watching him listlessly, scarcely turning her head to follow his progress from one end of the living room to the other. He tried a snappy heel-clicking turn and a comical salute. She looked at him blankly. His exciting and funny act had suddenly become strange and confusing.

He dropped his speech notes beside the big leather chair where she sat and knelt to look at her closely. "Do you feel sick, Mandy?"

"My throat hurts."

"Well, we'll take care of that with Grandma Peersen's remedy." Relief swept over Trygve with the discovery that Amanda was suffering from nothing worse than a sore throat, routinely treated in the Peersen household by gargling salt and baking soda dissolved in hot water. He patted her hand, meaning to reassure her, and was startled by her reaction. She winced and quickly withdrew her hand.

"What's the matter, Mandy? Did it hurt when I touched you?"

She nodded.

"Where?"

"Here," she said, pointing to her wrist. "And here," she added, touching her elbow.

As his mother had done whenever one of her children became unnaturally quiet, Trygve gently placed his fingers on Amanda's forehead. It felt hot and dry. Fever, tenderness in the wrist and elbow joints, sore throat—the combination didn't fit any of the old familiar childhood ailments that Trygve remembered. "You stay right here," he said as he got to his feet. "I'm going to phone Dr. Bergen and find out what we can do to make you feel better."

In the corridor outside Amanda's room in Mercy Hospital, Dr. Max Bergen spoke in muted tones. It was the first quiet moment since Trygve called him to the house, for he had been dealing with a child who was feverish and in pain, and a man who, under his rigid calm, was a terrified father. Matters were not made easier by the fact that there was a shortage of private rooms in the hospital the Peersens had always used.

"I know you're not Catholics," Dr. Bergen said, "but

Mercy is an excellent hospital. Amanda will be cared for as well as she would be anyplace else."

"I'm sure that's true. In any case, what's religion got to do with it? What worries me is Mandy's reaction to nurses in black habits—I doubt that she's ever seen a nun before—and the picture on the walls in her room. She seems frightened."

"I understand your concern. But, Tryg, the glazed look you see in her eyes is primarily the result of the very high temperature."

"Caused by? You haven't been specific, Max."

"I always avoid a hasty diagnosis. However, at this point there's no question in my mind. Amanda has rheumatic fever. The pain in her wrists and elbows and in her knees and shoulders is due to inflammation of the joints, a characteristic symptom."

"But the attack was so sudden. Yesterday she was fine." Trygve paused, suddenly questioning his own statement. The truth was that for the last few days he had been so involved in meetings and public appearances that he had not seen Amanda, except briefly when he put her to bed at night.

Recognizing the guilt in Trygve's eyes, Dr. Bergen said reassuringly, "A child often appears perfectly normal, even when symptoms are developing. Nothing more than a sore throat—a *mild* sore throat which the most attentive parent in the world wouldn't take more seriously than a runny nose. You couldn't have known something was wrong."

"Thank you, Max." Too distraught to say more, Trygve extended his hand.

As they shook hands, the doctor said, "I'll be back in the morning. Now I'm going home. My advice to you is to do the same."

Trygve shook his head. "I'm going to stay with Mandy."

"So much for medical opinion." The doctor smiled gravely. "I was pretty sure you'd ignore it. But let me caution you, Tryg. We're doing all we can to bring down the fever, but that little girl is only half-aware of what's going on and she could slip into unconsciousness. You've got to be prepared for that. I'll be in touch with the hospital at intervals throughout the night, but phone me anytime if you want to talk."

* * *

After sending a telegram to Sarah, whose dance company was performing in Denver, Trygve went back to Amanda's room and moved a chair so that he could sit beside her. She seemed to be asleep, but when he spoke to her she opened her eyes and turned her head in his direction. She wasn't looking at him. Her eyes, brimming with terror, were fixed on the pictures that adorned the starkly white wall at his back.

Her hands clutched his convulsively as she whispered, "Why is that man bleeding?"

There were three graphic paintings, one of the Crucifixion, another of Christ's head with blood dripping below a crown of thorns, and the third brilliantly red depiction of the tortured Sacred Heart. Gently withdrawing his hand, Trygve said, "I'm going to get something in the car. Don't be scared, Mandy. I'll be right back."

He returned carrying a half-dozen campaign posters and a magnetic tack hammer. Campaign workers had been nailing these posters to railroad trestles, stumps, farm fences, and the outside walls of commercial buildings, placing them in spots whenever possible that could only be reached by using a long extension of the hammer's handle. At Amanda's insistence, they had tacked one poster onto the wall of her bedroom.

Attaching the extension to the tack hammer's handle, Trygve nailed posters to the wall so that all three sacred pictures were completely hidden by a bigger-than-life photograph of Trygve's smiling face. Above, in sturdy block letters, was the legend: "VOTE FOR TRYVGE PEERSEN."

He had barely finished when a movement at the door caught his eye. He looked up. A nun had come into the room. She stared at the posters, then at the tack hammer, silently wheeled around, and went out.

Still holding the hammer, Trygve followed her into the hall. "Wait, Sister," he said as he caught up with her. "Please let me explain."

There was sympathy in the eyes that peered up from beneath the white band of her coif. "You don't need to, Mr. Peersen. I do understand."

"My daughter is only five years old. She's never seen pictures like that. If she were well, I'd be able to tell her what they mean, because she's curious about everything. But she's too sick to understand or even to hear an explanation. It's all strange to her, and she's very frightened.''

"You did the right thing. And though you haven't mentioned it, I suspect that your daughter might also be confused and frightened by nuns with our strange black clothes and funny hats. But Dr. Bergen has already arranged for a special nurse. She'll be here shortly and she'll be wearing the standard white nurse's uniform.''

"Is that why the doctor called for a private nurse? Because she wears white?''

"No, of course not,'' the nun said gently. "Because the regular nurses, like myself, have an entire floor to take care of. Your daughter's condition is too critical to rely on us alone. She needs nursing around the clock, and that's what Dr. Bergen has arranged.''

Sarah went from the railroad station directly to Mercy Hospital. She had been on the train for two agonizing days and sleepless nights, knowing little about the disease Amanda had contracted and nothing about how she might be responding to treatment. When she burst into Amanda's room, her eyes were red-rimmed, her face streaked with soot, and her hair carelessly pinned in a loose bun at the nape of her neck. What she saw brought a wrenching sob from deep in her throat.

Amanda was struggling to lift her head off the pillow, Trygve's arms were around her, holding her down as he pleaded, "It's all right, Mandy. The closet can't hurt you.''

Sarah rushed to the bed. "Mandy! Don't look over there. Look at me! It's Mama! Mandy, look at Mama!''

Amanda fell back and lay limp and still, staring up into her mother's face. "The closet keeps moving.''

"What does it do, darling?''

"It comes at me, and then it goes back again.''

Sarah pressed her face against Amanda's cheek. The heat shocked her so much that tears came to her eyes. "The closet isn't going to move anymore,'' she said brokenly. "Daddy's right here and he won't let it.'' Her arms went around the little girl and pulled her into a desperate embrace. "Mandy? Listen to Mama . . .'' There was no response. Amanda's head fell to one side and hung lifelessly over Sarah's arm. Sarah screamed, "Tryg! Oh, my God! Tryg!"

Tryvge stepped forward. "Put her down, Sari," he said quietly. "She's alive. It's been this way all afternoon. She's floating on the edge of consciousness, in and out of delirium. She's asleep now. Let her rest."

Sarah obeyed mechanically. Turning toward Trygve, she looked up into a face that was haggard with fatigue. "It's all my fault," she whispered. "This shouldn't have happened. If I had been home . . ."

Trygve took her into his arms. In a hoarse voice he said, "Sari, listen to me. I thought the same thing, because I've been so wrapped up in my campaign that I haven't been home very much. But Dr. Bergen set me straight. He explained that no one knows what causes rheumatic fever, so of course no one knows what might be done to prevent it. In Mandy's case the first symptoms were so mild even a doctor would have thought she had nothing more serious than an ordinary sore throat. Don't torture yourself. Babushka has been a wonderful mother. Mandy has been well cared for. You are *not* to blame, and I want to believe that I'm not either."

Clinging to him, Sarah wept helplessly. "I want to believe you. But I can't help it, I still feel so terribly guilty."

"I know," Trygve murmured, desperately needing to hold her as much as she needed to be held and comforted. "I know, Sari, because I feel the same way."

36

Sarah and Trygve moved through the last days of the campaign like marionettes whose strings were being pulled and whose lines were being spoken by frantic puppeteers. Trygve referred his clients to his partner, George Tweedy, and if Sarah had left him, would have canceled all his public appearances.

"If it would do anything to help Mandy, I'd say by all means excuse yourself," Sarah said. "But one or the other of us has been beside her all day and well into the night. She knows we're there. I don't have any other commitments. You do. To your supporters, to yourself, and to me."

George Tweedy was optimistic about the outcome of the election, but pessimistic about the effect of dropping out of the public eye when the momentum of the race against Dorsett was reaching a climax. "We've got them, at least so far. Youth versus age. Friend of the common man versus the powerful rich. In their zeal to keep their man Dorsett in the courthouse, the Reverend George and publisher Wise are using unscupulous tactics they could get by with before the war. They don't seem to realize that unsubstantiated vituperation has gone out of style. However, tides can turn. If you back down suddenly—and that's what canceling well-publicized speeches and meetings will mean to the average voter—only your friends will understand that it's because your daughter is critically ill. A lot of people, and I mean a *lot*, will conclude you've either been scared off or bought off. My God, Tryg! You're being supported by both the Wobblies and the American Legion! You're going to walk away from that?"

Already deeply moved by Sarah's plea, Trygve accepted his partner's advice and kept every appointment on his schedule. As if she were encouraging him, Amanda began to show signs of improvement. "She's getting better," Dr. Bergen assured him. "The fever is down. Not gone, you understand. Attacks of fever can last anywhere from several weeks to several months. But she's out of danger."

Amanda's wide blue eyes were no longer fixed in a vacant and frightened stare. There were no more fits of delirium. Though she admitted that her joints still hurt, the pain had lessened. On election day, with both her mother and father in the room, she was almost the normal Mandy—full of spirit and impossible questions.

For several days Sarah had been carrying a present for Amanda, not wanting to give it to her until she was alert enough to enjoy it. At last that day had come. "I have something for you, Mandy," she said, opening her pocketbook. "Something that will make sure Daddy wins the election, because it's magic."

Amanda sat up and watched eagerly as her mother removed a tiny parcel from her purse. "You open it," Sarah said, "but first, hold it in your hand. Very tightly, so that you can feel the magic."

Amanda looked down at the gift box resting in her open palm and touched it with a reverent forefinger. She was as silent as if the magic object had cast a spell, until all at once her eyes opened wide and she exclaimed, "I'll bet it's Grandpa's penny!"

On any given Christmas morning, Amanda could demolish the most artistic gift wrapping in a matter of seconds. Today she opened the gift gently, folding back the layers of tissue paper one at a time until the coin flattened by Lincoln's hearse lay on her lap in all its talismanic splendor. Sarah fought back a rush of childlike tears as Amanda whispered, "Is it really *mine*?"

"It really is," Sarah replied unsteadily. "All yours, for keeps. Grandpa gave it to me, and I am giving it to you. Someday you'll pass it along to someone else, someone else who understands that its magic is real."

* * *

That night, Sarah and Trygve had a serious talk. They had just gone to bed, the room was in darkness, their bodies were touching inside a warm cocoon of bedclothes.

"I've come home to stay, Tryg."

Suppressing his eager response, Trygve said, "You can't do that, Sari. You signed a contract." But his voice trembled with his desire to believe her.

"Bother the contract! I told the manager why I was leaving the troupe and he was very polite about it. He was too kind to say I wouldn't be hard to replace."

"He couldn't say that. It's not true."

"Tryg, my protector, my champion. Don't look for a dragon to slaughter in my defense. I was adequate, and that was enough for the group parts I was given. But I never would have been given a solo. Soloists, dear heart, are persons who have concentrated their entire beings on dance ever since they were little children. As adults they haven't time for commitments to anything but dance. It's a self-centered life. It has to be. But I'm not that kind of person. I want to do many things. Dance will always be one of them, but primarily as a teacher. I can do that without giving up everything else."

"I'm happy," Trygve said quietly as he took her into his arms. "Hell, I'm overjoyed."

Happiness from another quarter came to him in the morning. By a wide margin, he had defeated Judge Dorsett and won a seat on the Superior Court.

In defeat, his first in twenty-eight years, Judge Dorsett became more arrogant than ever. He would continue as presiding judge until the new term commenced in January. He could have used his authority to assign cases Trygve was involved in to another courtroom, but instead he seemed determined to arrange as many confrontations as possible. His open disdain was flagrant. The authority he had used to curtail hearings he now used to prolong them, as if every second he could use to insult or embarrass Trygve were precious. Quite by chance, he was given an opportunity to embarrass Emma Peersen as well.

Among the judge's influential friends was the owner of a

real-estate firm whose wife had earned a reputation for throwing unique parties. One of her triumphs had been a luncheon in the Japanese style. Prominent Seattle women wearing kimonos and holding fans were seated at traditional low tables and were served from lacquered trays, while a young Issei musician knelt to play the *koto*. Thinking that something authentically Scandinavian might also make for an interesting social event, the woman decided to call on the Peersen catering service to provide a complete *smorgasbord* dinner in her own home.

By this time Emma had turned the management of her catering service over to a younger woman. But the day before the party, the manager became ill. There were at least two workers at the restaurant who could have assumed her responsibilities, but Emma's preference for doing everything herself prevailed. She was dressed in her usual attire: long dark blue skirt, blue shirtwaist, and over all a large ruffled white apron so heavily starched that it crackled when she walked. She was conducting a critical appraisal of the arrangement of dishes when a man appeared in the archway between dining and living rooms.

"Mrs. Emma Peersen, I believe?"

Emma had never seen Judge Timothy Dorsett, but recognized him instantly. "Yes, Judge Dorsett?"

The face was lean, the mouth thin-lipped, the expression at once haughty and amused. Judge Dorsett's pale eyes moved deliberately from her simple shirtwaist to her apron to the pointed tips of high button shoes that were peeking out from under her cotton skirt. "Is it possible that you are the mother of Trygve Peersen?"

The emphasis on "possible" was faint but distinctly insulting—whether to her or to her son, Emma wasn't sure and didn't care. "You know I am."

"Well, yes, I had heard that Mr. Peersen's mother was a baker and that both his sisters had been housemaids. But it was one of the ladies here this evening who established that you are *that* Mrs. Peersen."

"This Mrs. Peersen has work to do," Emma said quietly. "So I will not keep you from your friends."

"How considerate. However, I assume that you can allow

me time enough to offer you a job?'' The judge's tone was sarcastic, but the eyes told Emma he was enjoying himself. "You come so highly recommended that I have decided to employ you to cater a similar party for Mrs. Dorsett and myself.''

Emma looked at him squarely. "I would not even consider it.''

The amusement in the judge's face flickered and died. "I believe you are in business," he said angrily. "It strikes me that you have an extraordinary way of conducting it.''

"Perhaps so. Yes, I am in business, or you might say, in trade. But with me, it is a very personal operation. I do not prepare dinner for people I wouldn't invite to sit down at my own table. I have every reason to respect your hostess here tonight, Judge Dorsett, and so I have gladly cooked for her. I cannot do the same for you.''

The judge said furiously, "I am not accustomed to hearing such impertinent talk from persons of your . . . your class!''

"If you remain in this dining room, you'll hear more of it.'' Smiling sweetly, Emma added, "On second thought, please do stay for a moment, because I have a question. Speaking of being in business, how did you manage to own and operate a shipbuilding firm while serving as Superior Court judge at the same time?''

After a moment of shocked silence, Judge Dorsett sputtered, "Well, I never . . .'' and strode out of the dining room. Emma smiled, thinking: That was a pointless, perhaps a childish thing to say. But oh how good it felt to say it!

The man who had been Judge Dorsett's bailiff for more than twenty years did not react to his employer's defeat as the judge himself did. Walter Smith was a graying, unimaginative little man in his fifties. Selected by Judge Dorsett, Smith had been turned over the years into a resentful but obedient lackey. He had minimal education for the job and little experience at anything else. Though judges did not hire their bailiffs in the sense that they paid their salaries, a new judge frequently preferred to name his own. Smith was facing an uncertain future in which more than twenty years of abject loyalty to Dorsett might be more of a hindrance than a help.

Trygve sensed Smith's anxiety and felt sorry for him. At the close of a hearing, he approached the bailiff. "What are your plans, Walt? You going to retire?"

"I couldn't do that, Mr. Peersen. I have to keep working."

"I haven't made any definite plans in regard to my bailiff. You might give me some information. Make a list of your qualifications. Your schooling, years of service, any other jobs you may have had before you became bailiff."

Smith's mournful expression brightened. "Thanks a lot, Mr. Peersen. Shall I bring it to your office?"

"Why not do it now? Nothing fancy. Just the facts. I'll wait."

When Smith handed Trygve the single sheet of paper on which he had written a résumé of his career, Trygve's first thought was that it was pathetically short. As he had anticipated, education was a weak point, as revealed by two grammatical errors. If he had excelled in any subject, it would appear to be penmanship, for Smith's handwriting was neat and precise.

And distinctive. With a shock of recognition, Trygve realized he had seen it before. Studied it, analyzed it, and as Judge Thomas had advised, memorized it. The boxy R, the unusual capital M, the way the letter T was crossed, the spacing of the letters, and the way the writing slanted to the right. Not one of the five characteristics was unique, but as his old friend had remarked, a combination of all five was definitely distinctive. Judge Dorsett's serf was undoubtedly the man who had forged government inspector Harold Martinsen's signature on the certificate that cleared the *Gypsy Queen* for launching.

Trygve stared at the graying little man who was waiting so expectantly for his comment. Everything suspected, everything known, was falling into place. He thought of his gruff, warmhearted friend Judge Thomas. "You can't search for a signature, you just stumble over it. So keep your eyes open. Miracle of miracles, it could happen, and then you'll have a case."

Trygve's first impulse was to burst into Judge Dorsett's chambers and confront him with proof of the forgery, but he discarded the thought immediately. It was inoffensive Walter

Smith who had committed forgery, not Judge Dorsett, so the case was against the bailiff, though in a very real sense he wasn't the guilty man. Trygve could invade the sanctity of Dorsett's chambers and accuse him of causing his hireling to commit a crime, but was that all he wanted as retribution for the drowning of his father, to hear a corrupt judge deny any responsibility and order him out of the room? No. The angry resentment Tryg had been sheltering for so many years demanded more than alleging that a government document had been forged. Now in possession of facts about a lesser offense that might allow him to unearth facts about a greater one, Tryg knew he must keep his head and plan his strategy. As his father had counseled when teaching him to hunt deer, "Son, when you spot your prey, don't get excited, because if you do, you'll step on a twig for sure."

"This is just what I need, Walt," Trygve told the bailiff. "I have an appointment now, but I'll see you sometime soon. I may have some questions."

Trygve hurried home to check on Amanda for the second time that day. He knew she was fine now but he had to keep reassuring himself.

Katamari's "flower wife," Tomoko, was expecting visitors, and since they had never called before, she was particularly anxious that everything be properly arranged. The Tamesas' house was on the fringe of what had once been called Nihon Machi, or Japan Town, now somewhat changed with the gradual return of the Chinese and the steady influx of Filipinos. Public officials had been proclaiming for twenty years that they would clean up the slums and rid the city of its "bad elements," but in fact gambling clubs, houses of prostitution, and cheap speakeasies were thriving only a few blocks away. It was not a neighborhood either Tomoko or Katamari considered a safe place in which to bring up their daughters, especially now that they were twelve and fourteen years old. Katamari and Tomoko both had ugly memories of the days when Japanese girls were kidnapped and sold into prostitution. Yet all Katamari's efforts to move his family into another part of town had failed. Real-estate salesmen were surprised and impressed by his finely tailored suits and his fluency in English but, as one man who said, not without sympathy, "I wouldn't mind *myself*, but the neighbors would kill me if I sold to a Jap," no one would sell or even rent to him.

"What good is my wealth?" Katamari had asked many times, "if it cannot provide beauty and comfort for my wife and daughters?" Taught from childhood that it is woman's lot to endure, Tomoko did not allow herself to share her husband's resentment. Outside, it was a desolate world, but inside there was beauty, and as she inspected the living room, with its ornate teakwood shrine, elegant tapestries, and carved screens, she was satisfied that her visitors would not find fault.

A knock on the front door surprised her, for she hadn't expected her friends to arrive so early in the afternoon. However, the tea service was already arranged—the *furo*, or brazier, surrounded by a tea bowl, a lacquered tea caddy, the bamboo dipper, the blue-and-white chinaware jar of cold water, the silk and linen cloths she would use to cleanse the utensils before she brewed the tea. With a last quick survey of the room, she hurried to the door, eager to admit her guests.

At Katamari's insistence, the door was always double-locked and bolted. She slid back the bolt, turned the locks, and opened the door, but instead of the ceremonial welcome that was on her lips, she let out a frightened cry. Not the women she had invited, but a man was standing on the threshold, a Japanese with coarse features and a wrestler's broad shoulders and heavy body. She stared at him for two or three seconds, immobilized by recognition of the cruelty in his face. He pushed her back into the room and slammed the door.

"If you don't want to get hurt, do what I say." His Japanese was as coarse as his broad nose and thick lips. "You're coming with me. Quietly. No fuss or yelling for help."

Tomoko threw a panic-stricken look over her shoulder. He grasped her wrist, laughing at her helplessness. "You're coming with me, missus. If your rich husband wants you back, he'll pay plenty to get you. Now, keep you mouth shut and act nice. Don't think you can run faster than I can, because you can't, and I'll kill you if you try."

"Some people are coming." Her voice was a desperate whisper. "They will stop you from taking me away."

Her threat seemed to amuse him. "Then we'd better leave fast," he said, his mouth twisting into an ugly grin.

Nothing mattered but escape. Heedless of his strength and threat to kill her, Tomoko broke away and ran toward the hall that led to the back door. The man pursued her, cursing. He caught her in a few easy strides. Throwing her to the floor, he said hoarsely, "Bitch! Wildcat! But that's the way I like them. So we won't leave fast. Not till I'm done with you."

He straddled her, and while one hand gripped her throat, the other tore at her kimono. When she screamed, he slapped her across the face, once, twice, three times, so viciously that the back of her head slammed against the hardwood floor.

She tasted blood, felt the shock of cold air on her body as his fingers clawed at her clothing. Even while he was beating her, she struggled. She kept fighting until he had succeeded in using her shredded kimono to tie her hands behind her back. "Pretty lady . . . pretty lady . . ." He knelt above her, his knees forcing her legs apart as he murmured, "Pretty lady . . . pretty lady . . ."

Tomoko sobbed, "No! I beg of you, no!"

He laughed and opened his trousers. For a moment, only one of his hands was pressing her to the floor. She wrenched free of it and lifted her head. Blind with terror, she caught his hand between her teeth and bit down hard.

After that she was almost insensible to what was being done to her. A filthy curse, an exultant laugh as he entered her. "I'm hurting you," he crooned. "Tell me how bad I hurt you." With every brutal thrust he begged her to cry to him. And then suddenly, "Aahh! Aahhh!" A shriek, as if the ultimate burst of his body brought exquisite pain. He pulled back, panting, and with a slow and deliberate sweep of his arm, hit first one side of her head, then the other. As consciousness began to slip away, Tomoko was dimly aware of the sound of a door opening, of sudden release from the weight of his body, and of Katamari's voice, farther and farther away as the dark silence swept over her.

* * *

Katamari's apartment manager, Tokio Hanada, was with him. Both of them saw the man who fled along the hallway to the back door. Both recognized him—the labor agent whom Katamari and Trygve had seen enter judges' chambers in the courthouse, the man Tokio had identified earlier as the rapist who beat his daughter to death.

"Stay with my wife!" Katamari called as he reached for the back door.

Tokio's pleading voice followed him. "No, Katamari! Don't try to catch him. He'll kill you!"

"Call a doctor!" Katamari shouted as he disappeared into the alley behind the house. But the agent was fast, and knew the dark corners of the district better than Katamari. In a narrow passageway between a café and a Chinese gambling den, Katamari lost the trail. He knew it would be futile to look for a policeman, since the traditional attitude at headquarters was that protection for "Japs," "Flips," and "Chinks" was a waste of time.

Returning home, Katamari found that Tokio had put Tomoko to bed and that a doctor was on the way. Tokio had also telephoned the police. "The officer I talked with didn't sound interested, but I insisted, and he finally agreed to send someone."

"We both know who the man was. But will it matter? I don't even know his name."

"I have learned it recently. He is called Toby. Just Toby. Nothing more."

The police officers who came to the house had only recently been assigned to what they both called "Jap Town," and neither had heard of a man called Toby. As they were leaving, one explained, "Just part of a name, and you don't know where he works or where he lives. That don't give us much of anything to go on."

The other was somewhat more conscious of his duty as an officer of the law. "Of course we'll report all this to headquarters."

After they had gone, Katamari said bitterly, "The victim is Japanese. We know what to expect."

Tokio nodded. "We do. However, I have heard that there are ways to buy their cooperation."

"I am willing to do that. But not until I've talked to Trygve Peersen."

Trygve's earnest advice was to give the police time to act, and not, under any circumstances, to resort to bribery. He checked with the police every day, and each time was told that officers had been dispatched to bring in "Toby" for questioning, but so far hadn't found him. As a curious twelve-year-old, haunting the courthouse with a schoolboy's notebook in his pocket, Trygve had come to know the officer who was now captain of the precinct. At the end of the week, he went directly to him. "What are your men doing?" he demanded. "You're dealing with rape and attempted kidnapping. Why hasn't the man been arrested?"

"You can't arrest someone you can't find. I've had officers combing the place, north, south, east, and west. They can't even locate anyone who knows this Toby person."

"In the district, *everyone* knows him! Over the past twenty years, hundreds, maybe thousands, have paid him a big price to smuggle them across the Canadian border. A whole lot of them are still paying to keep him from turning them in. And that isn't the man's only business venture. Ask anyone who runs a brothel. He'll know Toby, because chances are Toby was the one who rounded up his girls."

The captain shrugged. "I don't doubt what you're saying, Tryg. But that doesn't get us Toby. If they all know him down there, then they aren't talking because they're afraid of him."

"I'm not!" Trygve said angrily. "If I bring him in, will you book him?"

The captain snorted. "Sure. But you're crazy."

Trygve wouldn't allow Katamari or Tokio to take part in his search for Toby. "My chances of finding him are slim. I'm counting on two things. One is that he hasn't left town. Why would he? He's safer where he knows the territory. The other is that he must have friends, well-paid friends, in the courthouse and police department. He wouldn't be in business if he didn't. So he undoubtedly knows that the police have given up the search, and that adds to his feeling of safety. I don't want him to lose that feeling, because if he skips, we're out of luck. Listen, Kat. He knows you and Tokio. He'd see you coming. He's far less likely to suspect me. Over the years I've had a good many clients in the district. Nothing unusual about my being around on business.''

"He's a dangerous man," Katamari said. "He killed Tokio's daughter because she resisted him. If Tokio and I hadn't arrived when we did, I think he would have killed Tomoko. I have tried to persuade you not to look for him, but if you are determined, you must allow me to help.''

"You can, Kat, and so can Tokio. The two of you know the area almost as well as Toby does. That's what I need from you. A detailed drawing of the business streets. Buildings, alleys, warehouses. And tell me as much as you know about what goes on in them, especially the activity that isn't visible from the street. Who owns the buildings, who frequents them? And above all, who are Toby's friends? They're the people I've got to avoid. Put that information together for me, and then, please, Katamari, leave the rest to me. Toby's strong, and he's vicious. Somebody's got to stop him. The captain says I'm crazy, but I'm going to try.''

Hunting for someone without appearing to do so was a slow and maddening process for a man of Trygve's impatient temperament. After many frustrating days and nights, he was saved by a telephone call from a man who refused to identify himself.

"My name is not important." The caller's speech had the formality and the rhythm of an Oriental who speaks his own language more frequently than English. "The person you want can be found in this way. Go to the building where the Togosaki Tea and Rice Company is located: There is a gambling club on the second floor. It has no windows and can only be entered by a ladder in the corner of the warehouse. In the clubroom there is a large Buddhist shrine. It appears to be flat against the wall, but a section on the right side is hinged and can be swung open. Behind it there is a door into a small apartment. The apartment is not always in use. It is occupied now.''

"Thank you sincerely. One question, please. Is there a way to leave that apartment except through the door behind the shrine?'' There was no reply. All Trygve heard was a faint click as the caller hung up the receiver.

Was the information genuine? Was it a snare rigged by Toby's friends, or help from one of his enemies? In any case, breaking into an illegal gambling operation alone would be suicidal. After a few minutes of reflection, Trygve decided his only recourse was to go back to the police.

The captain was skeptical. ''It sounds to me like somebody's got a real lively imagination. But what the hell. We've got a warrant. I'll send some men, if only to keep you from busting in there yourself.''

Trygve was across the street from the Togosaki company when six police officers arrived. Two remained on the sidewalk, four entered the business office. More by intuition than rational thought, Trygve strolled to the corner, crossed the street, and turned into the alley that ran behind the half-dozen buildings on the Togosaki block.

The tea company's warehouse opened onto the alley. If I were giving the orders, Trygve thought, at least one of those six cops would be stationed right here, in the shadow between the Togosaki company and the next building, with a good view of those wide loading doors. Assuming that every detail given by the mysterious voice on the telephone was accurate, it didn't make sense that a man like Toby would trust a hiding place with only one escape route—through the door behind the shrine and straight into a room that anytime of day or night might be buzzing with lottery drawings, blackjack tables, and the three-dice game called chuck-a-luck.

Trygve glanced at his watch, estimating how long it would take the police to show the warrant for Toby's arrest and demand entrance to the warehouse. Allowing five minutes for them to discover and climb the ladder to the gambling den and one or two more to swing aside the movable section of the shrine and break into the apartment, in less than ten minutes Toby would be handcuffed and on his way to jail in custody of six police officers. Unless, of course, Trygve's hunch was right and there was more than one way to leave the secret room.

Eight minutes passed, nine . . . Suddenly the sound of running footsteps came from directly over Trygve's head. As he peered up through the narrow chasm between buildings, a man jumped across the gap and landed on the next roof.

Trygve leapt into the alley and raced after the figure that continued down the block from rooftop to rooftop. Trygve was waiting when Toby swung himself over the edge and dropped catlike to the soft mud below.

With Trygve almost on top of him, Toby wheeled around. He was crouched to fight, not to run, and his lips were drawn back in a grin so broad his teeth shone.

"You filthy bastard," Trygve snarled, and slammed his right fist into that brutal smile.

Toby staggered, but caught himself and slowly advanced. The grin hadn't faded. The eyes, glinting murderously, were fixed on Trygve's face. He held his arms away from his body, the hands reaching out with fingers working nervously, as if each were eager to bruise and tear. Two or three feet from Trygve, Toby lunged. Trygve leapt to the side, but not far enough. One massive arm went around him, then another. With a throaty laugh, Toby lifted Trygve off the ground and threw him against the building.

Though down in the mud and partially winded, Trygve moved quickly enough to avoid the blow that was meant to knock him out. He rolled onto his knees, and with an inch to spare, ducked away from the heavy boot Toby aimed at the side of his head. Toby grunted as his foot crashed into the wall. In the fraction of a second before he could get back into his fighting stance, Trygve was on his feet, ready to attack.

He had begun the fight in the heat of anger so intense that he couldn't think beyond pounding Toby's face and body with his fists. Memory of his first fight flashed crazily through Trygve's mind. His dog, Venn, roped and muzzled, dragged through the mud by a Gold Rush street bum who was stealing dogs and selling them as sled dogs to gullible prospectors. Anger had given him strength. Though badly beaten, he had rescued Venn and left his kidnapper too groggy to pursue him. Afterward his mother had reminded him of his father's saying—"Cold blood wins against angry heart." Toby was no beery-eyed dog thief, as that other man had been. Now everything, even his own life, depended on keeping his head.

Suddenly calm and clearsighted, Trygve caught the movement of Toby's right hand as it darted into his hip pocket. A knife. A slender blade six or eight inches long, tapering to a stiletto point like a boning knife. With the handle gripped in the palm of his hand, Toby was in position to stab with a fierce downswing, or with a twist of the wrist to swing the blade up in a curve that could rip a belly open. The knife was meant to intimidate, and the triumphant smirk on the labor agent's face showed that Toby was confident it had.

Trygve backed away, keeping his eyes on the knife. He was wearing a heavy tweed jacket. If he was fast enough, he could slip it off while still seeming to retreat. Sure of his victory, Toby was slow to realize that the man he thought he had frightened into running away was in fact getting ready to attack.

Trygve's right hand jerked the coat off his shoulders and wrapped it around his left wrist. With the end of the sleeve held securely by the fingers of his left hand, the thick woolen shield would stay in place. Trygve charged at Toby, bringing his right fist up under Toby's chin. The knife blade flashed down, striking for the heart. Trygve fended it off with his left arm, feeling the impact as it pierced the layers of his coat and its tip bit into his flesh. But the blow to Toby's chin had been too hasty. It threw him off balance, but only for a second. He was advancing. The knife, with blood glistening on its tip, was ready to strike again.

Trygve realized that this time his move must be even faster, but coolheaded, deliberate. Ignoring the knife, Trygve aimed his right hand not for Toby's face but for the hand holding the knife. He grasped the wrist, twisting with such force that Toby cried "Aahh!" His fingers went limp and the knife dropped to the ground.

As Trygve had anticipated, Toby's streetwise reaction was not to swing with his fists but to bend over and retrieve the knife. That gave Trygve the split second he needed. He brought up his knee as Toby leaned forward, the full force of the blow striking him under the chin. With blood oozing out of the corner of his mouth, he gaped at Trygve. Before he came to his senses, one of Trygve's hands grabbed him by the hair, the other slammed him against the building, and then both were pounding him systematically, right, left, and right. When he fell, Trygve's foot was poised to kick him if he moved, but Toby was not faking. He was unconscious.

Down the block in the Togosaki building, Trygve's timetable for the police had proved to be accurate, but only up to a point. It had taken two minutes to show their warrant and gain entrance to the warehouse, five to discover the ladder to the gambling den, another three to move the shrine and burst into the apartment where they expected Toby to be hiding. They found a room that was bare except for the litter of unwashed bowls and dishes, soiled garments, a cot, and a crude ladder below the trapdoor in the roof through which Toby had escaped.

One officer climbed the ladder, surveyed the block of rooftops, and reported that the suspect wasn't hiding anyplace he could see. When all four officers ran through the warehouse and into the alley, they saw Trygve approaching with the limp form of a massive Japanese slung over his shoulder. There was a blood-tipped knife in his hand and a heavy jacket draped over his left arm, its sleeve dragged in the mud as he slowly made his way along the alley.

The police hurried to meet him. A middle-aged officer barked, "Smith, Crowder, you two relieve Mr. Peersen. It'll take both of you to handle what he's doing alone. Mr. Peersen, just dump the bastard."

Trygve let his burden slide to the ground. Handing the knife to the officer who was obviously in charge, he said, "Assault with a deadly weapon. His, not mine."

"Hell, we got him on plenty of counts. Resisting arrest, flight to avoid prosecution, and that's on top of the rape-and-assault charges that have already been filed."

"Sergeant, what about that illegal gambling operation?" The question came from a young officer eager to prove that he, too, had read the criminal code. "Maybe nothing to do with this man here, but we've sure got a case against the Togosaki company."

The older officer winked at Trygve. "He's got a little something to learn, wouldn't you say, Mr. Peersen? We wasn't in that lottery for more than a few seconds, but that was enough for me to spot the son of a city councilman and the wife of a certain police lieutenant, both of them with a fistful of tickets. So I think we'll just concentrate on this fellow here, this Toby What's-his-name. Three, four felonies . . . that'll do me for today.'' He stopped abruptly and gestured toward the jacket Trygve had just removed from his arm. ''Jesus! That coat of yours is pretty well slashed up, Mr. Peersen.'' He glanced at the knife Trygve had turned over to him. ''I see why you had it wound around your arm. Damn good that you did, or you'd be stuck in so many places you'd be leaking blood all over the place. As it is . . . Christ, look at your shirt! He got you, all right. Look here. The wagon's out front. One of my men will drive you to the hospital, and I mean right now.''

''Only a fool would be so lucky,'' George Tweedy said acidly after hearing Trygve's account of the capture. ''A knife wound, twelve or fifteen stitches. Hardly worth mentioning them when the man you deliberately tangled with is a professional killer and unquestionably the most experienced and vicious street killer in the city.''

''At least he's in jail now.''

''Yes, and that's a triumph for our side. So why do you look so glum?''

Trygve shrugged, and with a worried frown replied, ''Because I wonder—what happens next?''

''What do you mean? Arraignment, probable cause, pleading, setting bail. The usual procedure.'' Tweedy paused for a second and added thoughtfully, ''I get it. You're wondering if the case against Toby is going to proceed that way—all nice, clean, and usual. This is not the *usual* run of district criminal. He's got connections, and for years you've suspected that one of them is the man you recently defeated for the Superior Court. If you're right, Judge Timothy Dorsett could be disgraced if the man he's been paying to do his dirty work should decide to talk to save his own skin.''

''Dorsett's term doesn't end until inauguration in January,'' Trygve said. ''He's in a position to release Toby on his own recognizance. No bail, no bondsman, nothing but honest Toby's sincere promise to appear in court on the date of trial.''

"And of course that's the last Seattle will see of Toby. The bird you finally caught will fly away."

Trygve nodded. "Exactly. He'll be over the state line and far away before I get my stitches out."

"Hold on, Tryg. There are nine judges. One for juvenile, two for equity—that still leaves six. You don't know which one of them will conduct Toby's arraignment."

Trygve grinned. "Don't I?"

"Hey," Tweedy said uneasily. "You make me nervous when you get that scheming look on your face. Tell me—do I want to know what you're thinking?"

"You do not. Because I have a plan, or at least the beginning of one, and you're better off not knowing about it, unless I need you. If our man with the tattoo on his chest happens—*happens*—to end up in Dorsett's court, I'll be ready. Not for Toby. For Dorsett."

37

A special bond existed between Trygve and Dick Thornton, the U.S. district attorney. Ten years Trygve's senior, Thornton had also been befriended by Judge Thomas and had often remarked that without the judge's financial help he could not have finished law school. Though they had never became close friends, Trygve liked and trusted him.

In the prosecutor's office, Trygve took several papers out of his pocket. "I've got a federal case pretty well documented, Dick, but there's a catch. I want to talk about it—informally, you might say. It has to do with a Lund Shipyard vessel that broke up on its way to Alaska in 1897. *The Gypsy Queen.*"

"I remember," Thornton said. "A tragedy. A lot of prospectors lost their lives."

"My father among them. So you can understand why I've always had a personal interest in the history of the ship. She was overage and far from seaworthy when she sailed. Lund Shipyard took her out of the junk heap, set up some crude bunks everywhere but in the boiler room, sold passage at exorbitant prices, and put her out to sea. She broke up on a calm day in a spot where there are no reefs or uncharted rocks. Her owner had spent almost nothing to fit her out, and made thousands of dollars' profit in less than two weeks."

Thornton frowned. "At that time the whole shipping business had gone crazy, but there were government inspectors. *The Gypsy Queen* must have had clearance."

"She did, and she didn't." Trygve's voice was grim. He offered Thornton the first of the three documents he had taken from his pocket. "The certificate. Signed by a government inspector named Harold Martinsen." He placed the second paper in front of Thornton. "And here's Martinsen's testimony to the effect that he did not sign the report and the handwriting is not his. Taken before a public officer for purposes of court action."

The district attorney compared the handwriting on the certificate with Martinsen's signature on the deposition. "I'm not a graphologist, but you don't have to be to recognize that these weren't written by the same man. So we've got forgery of a government document. But who's the missing link? Whom do we charge? Come on, Tryg. You've got something more. Let's have it."

Trygve handed Thornton the career résumé Judge Dorsett's bailiff had written. The attorney made a quick check against the inspection certificate and exclaimed, "Walt Smith! My God, *why*?"

"I've got a theory about that. Walt's honest, but not very smart. He didn't get through high school and must have felt that the most wonderful thing that ever happened to him was getting a job in the courthouse. Who could entice him into committing forgery other than the person who gave him that job and had the power to take it away from him?"

The district attorney's face was a battleground of conflicting emotions. Shock, disbelief, disapproval. Finally he asked, "Can you tell me why a judge of the Superior Court would go to such lengths—why he would do anything at all—to ensure that a certain ship would carry passengers to Alaska?"

"I'd better tell you the whole story."

Thornton listened attentively as Trygve described all the links he believed existed between Judge Dorsett and Lund Shipyard. He finished by saying, "I concede that the only criminal act for which there's evidence is the case against Dorsett's bailiff. And I assume that it can't be prosecuted because the forgery took place so long ago. To be honest, I'm glad. I've always felt sorry for Dorsett's bailiff."

Thornton nodded. "I understand. As for the judge, if we could prove that Jake Lund was nothing but a front and Dorsett was the true owner of the vessel, we'd have a case of criminal negligence. However, you and I know you don't go to the grand jury with a pocketful of suspicions. Getting back to forgery . . . if Walt Smith could be persuaded to implicate the judge, his statement might stand up as proof that Dorsett was guilty of misuse of office. But that's not a federal case. If you wanted to pursue it, you'd have to go to the county prosecutor."

Trygve said ruefully, "Which gets back to the issue of whether I want to confront Walt Smith with a mistake he made more than twenty years ago." He picked up the documents he had presented to the district attorney and returned them to his pocket. "Thanks, Dick. You've helped me make up my mind."

Lydia Biship sounded surprised at Trygve's invitation to lunch. "I don't know, Tryg. We agreed . . ." The sentence faded away, but Trygve recognized the indecision in her voice.

"Yes, we did, and I've honored the agreement. But one lunch at the Dockside? One hour together in a very public place? Don't you think that after four years, we can risk it?"

Lydia laughed softly. "Four years? It seems much longer. All right. I'll be the woman in the blue coat."

They had seen each other many times, always a chance meeting in the courthouse or on the street, acknowledged but quickly terminated. Sitting across from her in a restaurant booth, Trygve refreshed his memory. The large thoughtful brown eyes, the shiny chestnut-brown hair still brushed away from her face, emphasizing the high cheekbones and patrician profile—these features, as unchanged as her quiet smile, filled him with nostalgia. "You're looking well," he said, though he meant "beautiful." "Prosperity suits you. Oh, yes, I keep up on what you're doing. Your *Tribune* features hae been getting longer, more frequent, and even *more* perceptive."

"Thank you, Trygve. I value your opinion." Lydia's voice trembled. She recovered quickly and added, "I have an appointment in an hour, so perhaps you'd better start explaining why you want to talk to me. My guess is that it's important, or you wouldn't have called."

As soon as the waiter had taken their orders, Trygve asked, "Would you be willing to attend a probable-cause hearing scheduled for the day after tomorrow?"

"I have other plans, but I can change them."

"Great. Ten o'clock Wednesday, Judge Dorsett's courtroom."

Lydia's eyes showed her surprise. "I haven't been in his courtroom since he lost the election, but the *Tribune* court reporter has told me about his insulting manner whenever you appear. The hearing will be an ordeal, won't it?"

"For someone," Trygve replied dryly.

"At least arraignments don't last long."

"That, too, is yet to be seen."

Lydia looked at him thoughtfully. "I don't mind the air of mystery, Tryg, but on the other hand, if I'm to be something more than a casual observer, it would help to be prepared. Tell me a little about the case and a *lot* about what you expect from me."

"You know almost as much about the issue as I do. You've devoted hours and hours to listening to me when I rave on about the sinking of the *Gypsy Queen*, the murder of Jake Lund, and a Japanese labor agent who appeared to be collecting bribes or wages from someone in the courthouse."

Lydia nodded. "I remember. But you never had a case."

"We do now. The labor agent is in jail. He tried to kidnap Tomoko, the wife of my friend Katamari. When she fought him, he raped her and nearly beat her to death."

"Oh, Tryg!" Lydia exclaimed in an anguished tone. "Surely you don't want me to tell the public what happened to her?"

"No. But I do want you to bring your notebook. And a *Tribune* photographer, if you can sneak him out of the city room."

"I won't have to. A word to the city desk . . . You've got friends over there, Tryg. All I need do is hint that you're up to something and there will be both a photographer and a reporter in the courtroom. The city editor, too, if he can think up an acceptable excuse."

"So I'm good copy," Trygve said dryly. "Well, I've worked hard to achieve my bad reputation. Please forgive the insult—but do you have friends at the *Chronicle*?"

"They're not *all* mirror images of the publisher," Lydia answered, laughing. "Some reporters write whatever they must to curry favor with Jonathan Wise, and of course they get the special assignments. Others are just earning a living, happy that they're *not* the publisher's favorites. Are you asking if I can get a *Chronicle* reporter to attend the hearing?"

Trygve nodded. "Can you?"

"Not openly. But with the help of a friend who is *not* a Jonathan Wise puppet, a true-blue puppet will pick up the rumor that he's sure will lead him straight to an exclusive story, and from there into the heart of the great man upstairs."

Trygve grinned. "The mysterious tipster, who threatens to let the *Tribune* in on his secret if the *Chronicle* reporter doesn't act."

"Something like that," Lydia replied. "Just so the *Chronicle* editor believes that sending a reporter is his own idea."

"I'm grateful to you."

The purpose of their being together had been fulfilled, and suddenly conversation came haltingly.

As they were drinking coffee, Lydia said, "I do have something personal to report. You'll probably hear about it eventually, but I'd rather tell you myself. For the past few months, I've been seeing a man, a doctor in Tacoma. He's congenial and intelligent—one of the most considerate persons I've ever met. Sometime within the next month, we'll be married."

For a moment Trygve couldn't speak. What had he expected? he asked himself. That she would commit a kind of emotional *suttee*, the faithful Hindu wife burned to death on her husband's funeral pyre? That she would dedicate the rest of her life to commemoration of a part of her life that had ended? Trygve was happy for her. "If he's good enough for you, you've made the right decision, and I wish you happiness."

Lydia's hand reached across the table and for a moment rested on top of his. She rose and picked up her handbag, then hurried toward the door and was gone, without once looking back.

*   *   *

There had never been such an audience for the routine procedure of an arraignment. The contingent from the *Tribune* included a reporter, a photographer, and the paper's chief editorial writer, as well as Lydia Bishop. They were installed in front benches when three men from the *Chronicle* entered the courtroom. Two cast haughty glances at the opposition they hadn't expected to see there. The third gave Lydia a secret wink as he and his colleagues secured front-row positions on the opposite side of the aisle. Lydia had not stopped with the two largest Seattle dailies. Through the brotherhood of weekly newspapermen, she had recruited owners of a half-dozen different weeklies inside the county.

Trygve had done his part to pack the courtroom. Two of his former colleagues on Seattle's City Council were present. Harry Ault, editor of the *Union Record*, the only labor daily in the country, appeared with several of Seattle's prominent labor leaders—men who had fought and lost many a battle against Judge Dorsett's rulings on issues such as free speech and the right of assembly. But Trygve's greatest triumph was achieved through a long-time friend in the Seattle Ministerial Federation; Trygve had hinted that the real issues at this hearing were vice and corruption, the Reverend Thomas George's favorite subjects.

When Judge Dorsett strode into the courtroom and assumed his position on the bench, he looked down at an assembly of people whose reasons for being there were, at the very least, obscure. Some faces were openly hostile, others only attentive; all were curious. Some eyes moved away when the prisoner was brought in, but quickly returned to focus on the judge with the lively interest normally shown for the accused. At the last minute, after the opening formalities and just before he asked the prisoner, "How do you plead?" the courtroom doors opened to admit an observer more disconcerting than all the others—Dorsett's good friend, the publisher Jonathan Wise.

The judge's severe expression remained firmly in place as he gave himself a moment to ponder the astonishing scene. The accused, who had given his name as Toby Tobias, looked altogether too confident, while the attorney Judge Dorsett had appointed to represent him was obviously bewildered by the crowd. Rather than focusing on his client, his eyes began roving nervously around the courtroom. His anxiety deepened as he identified the city councilmen, the bloc of labor leaders, and the uniquely large gathering of newspaper reporters and photographers. There were three witnesses. The arresting officer, Sergeant Leon Krause, the wealthy Japanese, Katamari Tamesa, husband of the alleged victim, and finally, the man he despised more than anyone else he had ever known—Trygve Peersen. Casting aside all pretense to judicial calm, the judge bathed Trygve in a look of hatred as raw as an open wound. The meaning and purpose of this disquieting group of observers was still unclear, but somehow the brash young upstart from Ballard was behind it. It was an affront to his absolute power that this man Peersen was so poised, so dignified, even so respectful. If you're up to some trick, the Judge swore silently, you won't get away with it. I have friends more powerful than yours. You defeated me in an election, Trygve Peersen, but I am still the judge here. I have control over what happens to Toby Tobias. And over you. You may have a plan, but I have one too, and the authority to order your arrest if you attempt to disrupt it.

Toby's self-assurance took the form of a twisted grin as he answered the judge's question. "Not guilty, your honor."

Trygve tensed, suddenly striken with uncertainty as to what the judge's next pronouncement would be. He had spent many years studying Timothy Dorsett's tactics, both on and off the bench. There were numerous references to the judge in the notebook he had kept since the age of twelve, a record that was resting today in the inner pocket of his suit coat. Could he have been mistaken? Judge Dorsett's selection of Peter Hudson as the attorney to represent Toby suggested that he wasn't. Hudson had a reputation as a lawyer who did unpublicized favors in return for equally "discreet" cooperation. If not actually corrupt, he was weak, pliable in the hands of a powerful dictator such as Dorsett. Toby's confident leer and frequent glances in the direction of the judge also seemed to indicate that the arraignment had been well rehearsed. Though the audience was behind him, Trygve could feel the tension growing as people who didn't know why they had been urged to attend the hearing waited restlessly to discover what it was they had come to see, to write about, and to photograph.

After a prolonged silence, Judge Dorsett put an end to the suspense by doing exactly what Trygve had anticipated. "I order that this case be adjourned to a later date, Mr. Hudson. I will release your client on the basis of your promise that he will appear on the date of trial." With a hasty blow of the gavel, the judge rose to leave the courtroom.

"Your honor!" Trygve's voice stopped the judge and brought everyone in the courtroom to attention. The *Tribune* photographer jumped to his feet, camera poised for action. The *Chronicle* man, after a startled glance at the opposition, climbed over his reporters in order to take better pictures from the aisle.

Judge Dorsett resumed his seat and said icily, "You obviously have not given my order serious consideration, Counselor, so I'll repeat it. This case is adjourned. The hearing has come to an end."

Though Trygve's voice was low, it was pitched to carry to the farthest observer. "There are two of us here, myself and Mr. Tamesa, who have come as witnesses in what was supposed to be a probable-cause hearing. We have been ignored. The question of probable cause had never been raised. I submit that in the case of Toby Tobias, you are prejudiced, and I intend to file an affidavit of prejudice requesting that this matter be turned over to another judge."

Cameras clicked almost simultaneously, one in the middle of the aisle and the other from the delegation from the *Tribune*. Every reporter in the room had pencil and paper in hand. The labor leaders were taking no pains to hid their amusement.

"How dare you suggest that I . . . that this man . . . ?" The sputtered denial ended in a shout of "Contempt!"

Trygve treated the word as if it were an order to remove his notebook from his pocket. Opening it, he replied, "I dare because it is my duty, as attorney for a man whose helpless wife was attacked and nearly killed, to ensure that the trial is conducted by a judge who is not biased in favor of her attacker.''

''And what,'' the judge roared, ''do you intend to claim in your affidavit?''

A distinct change had taken place in the attitude and facial expression of Toby, the accused man. In seconds, self-assurance melted away and the gaze that had rested so confidently on the judge's face was now fixed on Trygve. His look was both murderous and fearful.

Trygve pointed directly at Toby. ''That man has worked for you in more than one capacity.'' He turned a page in the notebook. As if he were reading from it, he recited, ''Three P.M., July 10, 1899. Japanese labor agent known in the local prostitution racket enters judge's chambers by private entrance usually kept locked. Your chambers, your honor.''

''An absurd allegation!''

Trygve tapped his notebook. ''I have here a number of details about the defendant's visits to your office. I will not read more here today, but I will make them available to the proper authorities.''

''I have ordered that you are in contempt! You are to leave my courtroom immediately or I will have you ejected!''

''Your Honor, you asked me what the affidavit of prejudice is to contain. I interpret that question as permission to speak, and I have only begun to do so.''

A murmur swept through the courtroom while both photographers leapt into position for closer views of the fist Judge Dorsett was shaking at Trygve.

Trygve continued smoothly, ''I will also claim that you are prejudiced because you have directed the accused to go free until a trial at some indefinite time in the future. He is a dangerous man. A separate charge has been filed against him for assault with a deadly weapon. If you would care to look, I will show you physical evidence of that attack.''

Reporters crowded to the front of the room as Trygve removed his suit coat, unbuttoned his shirt cuff, and pulled back his shirt sleeve, revealing the blood-spotted bandages with which his left arm was wrapped from wrist to elbow.

"Sixteen stitches, the result of knife wounds. This is the kind of criminal you believe can be safely returned to the street. I say that if you were not trying to protect him, you would keep him in jail. Furthermore, I charge that an understanding exists between you and Toby Tobias and the attorney you appointed to defend him. Despite evidence of guilt so overwhelming that a plea of not guilty is absurd, you encouraged the attorney to direct his client to so plead. The attorney's transparent promise that the accused would appear in court on the date of trial was also prearranged. I prefer to believe that Mr. Hudson was not told why you intended to release a man accused of attempted kidnapping, rape, and assault with intent to kill, so I will explain it to him now. You knew that the moment Toby Tobias was free, he would disappear. He *promised* that he would, did he not?"

Temporarily shocked into silence, Judge Dorsett again found his voice, but it was weaker and his lips were twitching as he stammered, "The accusations against this man have not been proved. There is no reason that he be held in custody."

A hush fell over the audience. The whispered comments, the rustling of notebooks, stopped abruptly. Trygve turned far enough to scan the people behind him and saw that most of them were staring at Judge Dorsett as if hypnotizied. A few were looking down at the floor, embarrassed to find themselves in the presence of something they didn't want to watch. He wheeled back to address the bench. "Your Honor, any other judge in this country would make that statement honestly, because none of them know, as you do, that there *is* a reason why Tobias must remain in jail. *You* know he should not be releasd because bail is not allowed when the defendent is charged with a capital offense. *You* know Tobias is a murderer. Among the other jobs he has done for you in the past was to stab to death a man named Jake Lund." He opened his notebook and flipped through the pages. Seeming to find what he wanted, he said, "Here it is. Jake Lund, whom you paid to act as the owner of Lund Shipyard because you had good reason to conceal the fact that you were the actual owner. July 1897. You ordered Lund to launch a ship he knew was dangerously unseaworthy. He refused and threatened to expose you." Trygve paused and again pointed an accusing finger at Toby. "That man stabbed Jake Lund to death. And you, Judge Dorsett, know who paid him to do it."

The judge screamed, "Contempt! Mr. Peersen, you are in contempt!" He picked up his gavel and began pounding the bench as he repeated again and again, "Contempt . . . contempt . . ." Finally the hysterical cry, "Officer! I order you to place this man under arrest!"

After a moment's hesitation, the guard who had conducted Toby from his cell to the courtroom left Toby's side and walked across the room toward Trygve. Toby seized the opportunity and bolted down the aisle.

A woman shrieked. A man shouted, "Stop him." The police officer looked from Trygve to the man who was escaping, made a quick decision, and ran after Toby, catching him as he was going through the door. Though Toby struggled, in seconds he was handcuffed and the guard was dragging him back to the front of the courtroom.

A string of oaths poured from Toby's mouth as he cursed the judge, Trygve, and his jailhouse keeper. Through the jumble of filthy words, a single coherent statement was audible to everyone. "The judge paid me to do it! He said if I didn't I wouldn't get no more protection for my houses and he'd make sure me and my girls was put out of business!"

Both photographers rushed in as Toby was forcibly removed from the courtroom. Both then aimed their cameras at the judge. His whole body had crumpled so that the judicial throne looked far too big for him. His face was gray, the lips slack. The eyes stared blindly as Trygve turned another page in his notebook and once more began to read.

"The *Gypsy Queen*. Put out to sea by a man who knew what a terrible risk he was visiting on her passengers, a man so greedy to collect their fares that he cared nothing for their safety. Forty human beings entrusted their lives to his rusted and rotting vessel. Only twelve survived. I will now read the names of those who died."

"Douglas Morton . . . Robert Quinn . . . Harold Swenson . . ."

Trygve called the names slowly, pausing for an instant

before going on to the next. The list became a requiem, spoken in a strong, steady voice, each syllable pronounced with the solemn rhythm of a funeral march.

"Joseph Friedheim . . . Olaf Anderson . . . Bernard Rhodes . . . Howard Jackson . . . Al Albrechtson . . ."

By the time he had read a dozen names, every head in the room was bowed. A few were grieving for the relatives they had lost when the *Queen* went down.

"Philip Bergstrom . . . John Porter . . . Tony Marcinelli . . . Dave Ward . . . Christian Paul . . ."

Finally, the last name, the one that made Trygve's psalm for the dead end with a sob. "Einar Peersen." He closed his notebook. In a broken whisper he cried, "Judge Dorsett, *you* killed my father!"

That evening the *Chronicle* carried a restrained report of the hearing and an editorial blaming Trygve for "an ugly spectacle of unethical courtroom tactics." In the morning, the *Tribune* devoted two pages to vivid photographs, a detailed description of Trygve's accusations and the judge's furious denials, a feature story by Lydia Bishop, and an audacious editorial to the effect that the publisher of the *Chronicle* was a fool and a coward.

In the office of Tweedy and Peersen, George Tweedy reviewed the documented downfall of a judge and asked, "What do you think, Tryg? Will he retire?"

"Why should he? As Judge Thomas liked to remind me, I really don't have a case. Misuse of office, maybe, when Dorsett forced his bailiff to falsify the certificate. But that offense is a dead issue. As for the matter of hiring Toby to kill Lund—that might be worth pursuing. Toby has already blurted out a confession in the presence of thirty or forty witnesses, and since Judge Dorsett can't do anything for him anymore, Toby won't hesitate to implicate him even more than he already has. We'll see. Meanwhile . . ." A wicked light appeared in Trygve's blue eyes. "It just occurred to me that this is the day the awesome threesome of Timothy Dorsett, Jonathan Wise, and the Reverend George never fail to meet for lunch at the Cascade Club. We're members. Shall we eat there today and see how chums hang together during adversity?"

"And watch a clergyman who preaches against vice greet a dear friend who takes money for protecting brothels? Why not?"

When Trygve and his partner entered the Cascade Club dining room, the *Chronicle*'s publisher and the minister were already seated at their usual table.

"The judge is late," Trygve said *sotto voce* as he and Tweedy followed the headwaiter to one of the few tables that had not been reserved. "That's unusual for a man who is punctual to a fault."

"Not very late," Tweedy replied. "Here he comes now, arrogant as ever."

"Too bad we're too far away to eavesdrop. We're going to miss the show."

"Maybe not," Tweedy said. "It looks as if we won't need to hear the dialogue."

Judge Dorsett had arrived at the table. Even from across the dining room it was plain that neither of his friends spoke as the waiter pulled back a chair and the judge sat down. The silence continued. The minister and the publisher were giving full attention to their menus while the judge held his out stiffly, forgetting to open it.

Other diners gradually became aware of the judge's presence and of the strange tableau at this table. Conversation died away until the hush was complete. Every head was turned to watch. A couple of minutes passed, and then, in unison, the minister and the publisher pushed back their chairs, rose, and turning their backs on their friend, slowly walked out of the dining room.

The judge remained motionless, as if transfixed by the unopened menu in his hands. Five minutes went by, ten . . . Like a sleepwalker, Judge Dorsett put down the menu, pushed back his chair, and stood up. His face froze into a sickish smile as he searched the room for an invitation to sit down. No one spoke and no one smiled in return. One by one they all looked away. Bank president, department-store owner, former governor of the state, the city's most respected surgeon, member of the University of Washington board of regents, benefactor of orchestras and art museums, tugboat captain turned millionaire . . . the *crème de la crème* of Seattle's prominent citizens whose friendship was the life-blood of Judge Dorsett's self-esteem, and not one of them knew him now. He stood alone, rigid in his isolation before he broke and hurried toward the door, stumbling against chairs and tables he did not appear to see.

George Tweedy said grimly, "He deserved that."

"I've wanted nothing so much as to see him tried for his crimes and found guilty." Trygve shook his head. "But that wouldn't be anything like the retribution we've just seen. For that man, humiliation is more terrible than a conviction."

Trygve fell silent. His partner did not attempt to continue the conversation, recognizing that in a different way, the drama they had just witnessed was as painful to Trygve as it was to the man whose disgrace he had engineered.

In Trygve's mind, the central figure was not Judge Dorsett, but a man long dead—Einar Peersen, invisible but forever present and suddenly so alive Trygve could almost hear his voice and see the wisdom in his deep blue eyes. Einar Peersen, the best gill-netter in the village, teaching him to fish the *Konge*. Drilling him until he could recite the Lord's Prayer in flawless Norwegian. Stomping into the Ballard Lutheran Church to rescue his son from organ practice and take him to see the steamship *Portland* come in from Alaska with a boatload of Klondike gold.

Father, I've destroyed him, Trygve said silently to that cherished image. *Twenty-three years ago I swore to avenge your death, and now that grief-stricken twelve-year-old boy can rest. It's finished at last.*

Sighing deeply, Trygve said aloud, "I won't stop hating Dorsett, but I'm going to try to put all this behind me."

George Tweedy said with unusual gentleness, "You'll be sworn in next month, and when you put on that long black robe, you'll start a new career. A good time to get rid of the albatross."

Trygve nodded in agreement. "Look ahead, not back. That's what everyone else at my house is doing. Mandy's getting stronger every day. She's already nagging me to bring her books home from the library. Sarah had refused to even discuss her dance school, but now she's starting to make plans to reopen it.'' He grinned and reached over to shake his partner's hand. "You've got my word, George. I'll let the law take care of the evil judge. I'll concentrate on being a good one."

About the Author

Charlotte Paul, a veteran writer of fiction and nonfiction, lives with her husband on Lopez, one of the San Juan archipelago islands off the northwest coast of Washington. She is also the author of *Phoenix Island*, also available in Signet.

TIMELESS ROMANCE

☐ **THE CONSTANT STAR by Patricia Strother.** She was a product of the New York WASP aristocracy, and he had risen from the poverty and pride of the Jewish Lower East Side. This is the bittersweet story of their marriage—in a sweeping saga of a family's dreams and desires, conflicts and changes over two continents and five dramatic decades....
(146042—$3.95)

☐ **SONG OF THE WIND by Madge Swindells.** Marika Magos. Beautiful and brilliant, had come out of the ravages of war-torn Europe to climb to the top of the fashion world. In London, Paris, and New York her name was legend, but none knew of her secret past and her shameful passion for the powerful Nazi who had helped to destroy her family—and had now returned to awaken the fire that raged within her.... (142489—$3.95)†

☐ **SUMMER HARVEST by Madge Swindells.** It was 1938. Her name was Anna van Achtenberg, and she was the beautiful headstrong daughter of Cape Town's richest landowner. In a harsh new land of dreams and desires, she risked all to gain everything. Power, respect, fabulous wealth—and a proud dynasty to inherit it. Everything... except what she wanted most... (135555—$3.95)†

☐ **RIVER OF DREAMS by Gay Courter.** As sensual and haunting as the glittering life of Rio de Janeiro it evokes, this is the intensely emotional story of a woman's romantic quest for fulfillment... and of the two strong men who each possessed part of her, as she burned for the love of one, and was swept up in a fury of passion for the other...
(135105—$4.50)*

☐ **SUSQUEHANNA by Harriet Segal.** Along the banks of the mighty Susquehanna River, they lived a dream called America. From Czarist Russia to America to World War II India, theirs was a story of ambition and heart-breaking struggle, of wildfire passion and love as strong and deep as the river itself... (137973—$3.95)*

*Prices slightly higher in Canada
†Not available in Canada

Buy them at your local bookstore or use this convenient coupon for ordering.
NEW AMERICAN LIBRARY,
P.O. Box 999, Bergenfield, New Jersey 07621

Please send me the books I have checked above. I am enclosing $_____
(please add $1.00 to this order to cover postage and handling). Send check
or money order—no cash or C.O.D.'s. Prices and numbers subject to change
without notice.

Name_____

Address_____

City_____Zip Code_____

Allow 4-6 weeks for delivery.
This offer is subject to withdrawal without notice.

BOLD NEW FRONTIERS

☐ **TEXAS ANTHEM by James Reno.** Johnny Anthem was a man of bold dreams—in a sprawling savage land as big and boundless as America in the making. There he discovered his "Yellow Rose of Texas" in the shining eyes of beautiful Rose McCain. Together they journeyed the blood-soaked trails of the brutal Texas wilderness burning with a dream they would fight for—live for—die for . . . staking their claims in the golden heart of the American dream. (143779—$3.50)

☐ **TEXAS BORN by James Reno.** A soaring American sage of courage and adventure. Johnny Anthem and his beautiful wife carved out a huge Texas ranch as a legacy for their twin sons. Their dreams are shattered when a son is abducted by a Mexican bandit and a daring rescue must be staged. Johnny was ready to defy every danger of nature and man to save his son and forge his family's destiny in a piece of America . . . For driving Johnny was a courage and strength that made him—and his country—great. (145607—$3.50)

☐ **A LAND REMEMBERED by Patrick D. Smith.** Tobias MacIvey started with a gun, a whip, a horse and a dream of taming a wilderness that gave no quarter to the weak. He was the first of an unforgettable family who rose to fortune from the blazing guns of the Civil War, to the glitter and greed of the Florida Gold Coast today. (140370—$3.95)

☐ **THE BRANNOCKS by Matt Braun.** They are three brothers and their women—in a passionate, action-filled saga that sweeps over the vastness of the American West and shines with the spirit of the men and women who had the daring and heart to risk all to conquer a wild frontier land. (143442—$3.50)

☐ **DREAM WEST by David Nevin.** The story of a heroic man and a magnificent woman, whose passion was as boundless as America in the making. . . . "A rich, romantic saga . . . authentic, rousing."—*The New York Times.* A Book-of-the-Month Club Main Selection. (145380—$4.50)

Prices slightly higher in Canada
